Lauren Henderson was born in London, where she worked as a journalist before moving to Tuscany to start writing books. She now lives in Manhattan. She has written seven books in her Sam Jones mystery series: *Dead White Female, Too Many Blondes, Black Rubber Dress, Freeze My Margarita, Strawberry Tattoo, Chained!* and *Pretty Boy*. The Sam novels have been optioned for a movie deal and translated into fifteen languages. She has also written two romantic comedies, *My Lurid Past* and *Don't Even Think About It*, both published by Time Warner, and a non-fiction book, *Jane Austen's Guide to Dating*, which will come out in the US in 2005. Together with Stella Duffy, she has also edited an anthology of girls-behaving-badly crime stories, *Tart Noir*, and their website is www.tartcity.com.

exes
anonymous

lauren
henderson

TIME WARNER
BOOKS

TIME WARNER BOOKS

First published in Great Britain as a paperback original
in April 2005 by Time Warner Books

A CIP catalogue record for this book
is available from the British Library.

ISBN 0 7515 3567 2

Typeset in AGaramond by Palimpsest Book Production Limited,
Polmont, Stirlingshire
Printed and bound in Great Britain by Clays Ltd, St Ives plc

Time Warner Books
An imprint of
Time Warner Book Group UK
Brettenham House
Lancaster Place
London WC2E 7EN

www.twbg.co.uk

exes anonymous

Prologue

A few weeks ago, I saw Patrick's ghost for the first time. Maybe I should call it his doppelgänger. But ghost seems more appropriate, though it's not exactly the right word to use, since Patrick's still alive. Though not for me. Patrick's dead to me. I don't want that to sound melodramatic, but it's true: to me, for me, he's dead. And I'm grieving for him. So, in a way, it was his ghost. And it felt like a haunting.

I was at an Italian restaurant in Soho, with Davey, and he sat down at the next table. In that first split-second I saw Patrick, his image, and I felt suddenly light-headed. It was the exact sensation I imagine that characters feel in the movies when a ghost walks through them. Everything in your body must shift, like a strong wind blowing through your bones and blood and organs, a shudder of spectral energy. But then I realised that he wasn't Patrick. Patrick was thousands of miles away in New York. This man had much darker hair than Patrick's, and it was curlier. But tied back in a ponytail, check. Goatee, check. Though, looking at him more closely, it was more like a beard, growing down over his chin. He had big dark gentle eyes, just like Patrick's, but his were rounder and darker, and he looked scruffy. Patrick almost always dressed down, but he was never scruffy. This man looked as if he hadn't washed in days. A student, I assumed. He was with a girl, and her presence was an extra shock. Lesser, but still horribly unpleasant. I can't think how I would feel if I saw Patrick with a woman. Suicidal. People always throw that word around too lightly. But I would want to blow my brains out over him and his new girl. Have them showering for days to get rid of me. Chips of my blood and bone caught in their hair.

Davey didn't even notice my reaction. I drank my wine and made conversation with him while I watched the man hungrily, projecting Patrick on to him with all the force I could muster. I squeezed my memory as if it were a muscle, wringing out every last drop of Patrick's face and hair and body, trying to raise the dead. It was an awful, guilty pleasure. I made excuses to stay in the restaurant – another coffee, another cigarette – long past the time that poor Davey wanted to be gone, just to be close to that image of Patrick.

Nobody knows. How could they? I look as good as ever. I've even lost some weight from all the grieving, despite the fact that I stopped running after the breakup. All that guff about diet and exercise in women's magazines: just once, I'd love to see an article headlined: STILL STRUGGLING WITH THOSE LAST FIVE POUNDS? LOSE THE LOVE OF YOUR LIFE AND WATCH THEM MELT AWAY! I fit into all my trousers, even the ones I bought on sale that were too tight and I never thought I'd be able to wear without a big sweater covering my bum. I joke and laugh in the office as much as ever. Men whistle at me as I walk down the street and chat me up in bars. I think they can tell I'm unavailable; men love that, it's like catnip to them. I've never had this much attention. Human beings are perverse. There's nothing they want as much as what they can't have. I'm no better. Look at Patrick, how much I wanted him – still want him – because I knew, in the end, he was unattainable.

I'm what the shrinks would call 'fully functioning'. I go to work every day; I hang out with my friends; I go shopping for shoes. And yet I'm not really there. I'm detached from it all. I get myself out of bed every morning, feed myself and send my body and my brain off to the office, while the real me, my soul, is curled up in bed in a tight foetal knot, crying my heart out. If I'd broken my leg months ago and it hadn't even started

2

healing yet, I'd be a medical freak. Doctors would be flocking to my bedside to work out why the hell the bones refused to knit together.

But that's not a great analogy, because I would want my leg to heal; and I'm not sure that I feel the same about my heart. All I have left are my memories of Patrick. If those fade, I'll have nothing left; I'll be completely alone. Because seeing Patrick in the street, in a restaurant, whenever I close my eyes, in every damn sex scene on TV or at the cinema, any time any man in my vicinity pulls off a sweater and for a brief moment, as his T-shirt rides up, shows that strip of skin above the belt on his jeans . . . oh . . . where was I . . . ? Oh yes, every time any of those things happens, Patrick is so close to me in that moment that I cannot truly feel alone.

Which, of course, would be the worst thing of all.

Chapter One

'Lunch! I'm starving!' Davey says imperiously.

'Five minutes,' I say. 'In spreadsheet hell. Hang on.'

Out of the corner of my eye I see Davey sit down on the edge of the pool table. I'm always nervous about pool tables, ever since I saw *A Shot In The Dark* when I was little and Peter Sellers, playing Inspector Clouseau, aims for the ball and rips right through the baize with his pool cue instead. It's become a lifetime inhibition. I wanted Finn and Barney to get a ping-pong table instead, but they wouldn't hear of it.

My fingers are flying over the computer keys. I should hate this part of the job but, perversely, I rather enjoy it. It makes me feel as if I have everything in order, pinned down neatly, under control. The office operates in an atmosphere of barely controlled chaos most of the time and although I know how lucky I am to work somewhere like this, somewhere so resolutely dedicated to being anti-corporate hell, I need to feel that underneath it all I am anchored in something solid and unyielding. I find spreadsheets weirdly satisfying.

'Noodles,' Davey's chanting. 'Noodles in broth, lovely filling soup noodles with coconut milk, big fat squirmy noodles with lots of lovely— Ow!'

Finn's thrown an Action Man at his head. I knew that someone would take care of Davey. That's boys for you – any excuse to show off their aim.

'Watch it!' Davey says indignantly. He picks up the Action Man and gestures with it. 'You could put someone's—'

'Eye out with that,' choruses the entire office. It's a running joke.

'You used the "N" word,' Finn moans. 'You *know* not to use the "N" word, man. It's the only fucking rule in this entire fucking office. It's the only thing I tell people in interviews. You can come into work wearing waders and a thong for all I care, you can screw transvestite tarts on the pool table after hours, just don't use the fucking "N" word, OK?'

Finn has a fixation with noodles looking like worms. This is due to some early childhood trauma whose genesis he's never described in any detail. It makes going out for meals with him very difficult. Office legend has it that Barney once insisted on ordering spaghetti for lunch, and Finn made him eat with the large laminated menu propped up in front of his plate so that he didn't have to watch the strands of spaghetti going into Barney's mouth. Barney tortured Finn by making slurpy sucking noises. Finn wouldn't talk to him for two days. That's nothing unusual. Finn and Barney are constantly fighting.

'I jolly well think Rebecca should *have* to come into work wearing waders and a thong,' Barney calls from across the room. 'It should be in her job description.'

'You wouldn't say that if you'd seen my cellulite,' I yell back, saving my spreadsheet.

'All cottage cheesy, are you?' Barney asks.

'Like two wobbly flesh-coloured oranges covered in hair,' I say.

I'm the only full-time woman in the office and I get this kind of thing constantly. The way to deal with guys is to be more disgusting than they are, which is never difficult. Men are so easily freaked out by women. As I knew he would, Barney makes a retching sound and drops the subject completely.

'Right,' I say, standing up. 'Time to feed the cellulite.'

'We're off to the, um, "N" bar,' Davey says. 'Anyone want to come?'

There's a small chorus of 'no's. I take my coat and we head out to the noodle bar we usually frequent. It has nice big bowls of broth noodles for Davey, and Tom Yum Goong soup plus grilled beef salad for me.

'Are you still on the low-carb thing?' Davey asks as we sit down.

'Doing my best.'

Ever since I got back from New York I've been trying to cut down on carbs. I might as well try to keep off the weight I've lost because of the breakup, and I don't have that much appetite anyway. Never in my life did I think that I would be capable of picking listlessly at a pizza and then throwing it away the next day, hardly touched. I've wanted to be this kind of eater all my life. I just didn't anticipate paying such a high price for it.

'Have you lost any weight?'

'Six pounds!' I say indignantly. 'Can't you tell?'

'I see you every day,' Davey apologises. 'You never notice stuff like that if you see people every day.'

'You just wait. Come summer I'll be wearing my little frocks and you'll suddenly notice that my lumps and bumps are significantly less lumpy and bumpy.'

'I'm doing sit-ups every morning now,' Davey sighs, patting his stomach. 'Fifty crunches before breakfast.'

That's the thing with men when they hit thirty; they start to realise that they can't just keep scoffing fast food and curries and expect to keep their boyish figures. It doesn't hit girls that badly, of course. We've already spent our entire lives dieting. My sympathy for Davey is heavily tinged with *schadenfreude*. In the fourteen years that we've been friends I've watched him eat whatever he wanted without gaining a pound, and I've always resented it. Now, finally, he's paying for his pleasures, and I get to feel smug.

'But I can't give up my coconut broth noodles,' he adds.

'Those are *so* fattening, Davey. Do you know how many calories there are in a bowl of those?'

'I play footie every Sunday,' Davey says defensively, as if

charging around a muddy football pitch with Finn and Barney and the rest of the lads for a couple of hours will magically burn off all the bowls of coconut noodles and breakfast fry-ups.

'And then you go out for a massive fry-up afterwards and eat it all back on again,' I point out.

The chef is sliding our lunch on to the glass shelf which divides the restaurant from the open-plan kitchen. We always sit at the bar. Davey and I know each other so well that we don't have to sit opposite each other at a table and make proper conversation, thank God. Often we'll eat lunch in a companionable silence, when one or both of us is absorbed with work and not in the mood for being chatty.

I look for the soy sauce, but there's none in front of us. There's a guy sitting next to me and I turn to ask him if he has some. It's Patrick. I don't even realise that I've reacted, but his water glass goes flying. It smashes on to the concrete floor. Water's pouring over his lap and on to his shoes. I jump back in my chair, which makes a terrible, nails-down-a-blackboard grating sound across the floor. My whole body is shaking.

'Rebecca! Are you OK?'

I can't talk. I fumble for our napkins and hand them to the guy. Of course he isn't Patrick. But for a moment the resemblance was so acute. The ponytail, the goatee, the dark slanting eyes ... Davey's down on his knees helping the waitress pick bits of glass off the floor. The man next to me is mopping his lap. Thank God he was wearing leather trousers. Patrick would have died rather than wear leather trousers, though I always wanted him to.

'I'm so sorry,' I finally manage to say. My mouth feels half-paralysed, as if I've just come from the dentist. My body is barely under control and will only obey me jerkily, my nerve connections numbed by the shock.

'Did you get cut?' Davey's asking me, aware that something is wrong.

'No, I'm OK – I'm so sorry . . .'

'It's OK,' the guy says, though it clearly isn't. The waitress has produced more napkins, and he's drying off his shoes.

'I was looking for the soy sauce . . .'

'Well, here you go.' He puts it down right in front of me, pointedly, so that I don't have to reach for it and risk knocking anything else over. 'If you need anything else, just ask, OK?' he says sarcastically. 'No sudden movements.'

'Sorry . . . thanks . . .'

The storm of activity subsides. Davey is drawing up his chair next to me again and laying more napkins on the counter-top to soak up the water.

'What *happened*?' he asks in an undertone.

'I was just reaching for the soy sauce . . .'

'But you were in complete shock! I thought you'd been cut! You didn't even help clear up the mess!'

'I'm sorry, I was just a bit . . .'

Davey is looking at me narrowly. 'This isn't just knocking over a water glass,' he says. Davey knows me too well. 'I've seen you spill pints in people's laps before and not react like this.'

'I was just a bit . . .'

I can't get many words out. If I'd seen the guy come in, I would have been fine. Well, not fine, but I wouldn't have knocked over his glass and made such an idiot of myself. I would have been able to sit there, making conversation and stealing glances at him every now and then, relishing the twisted, painful pleasure of his proximity. I would have pretended to myself that he really was Patrick, and that any moment he would turn to me and smile and say something dry and Patrick-like. Then I would look into his eyes and know that however much he controlled himself in public, he loved me and wanted me and that when we took our clothes off and climbed into bed together he would be completely and utterly mine. It was the shock of seeing him like that, when I was unprepared. I couldn't breathe or speak.

8

'What the hell is going on?' Davey's still muttering, so that the guy next to me doesn't hear. 'You look like you've seen a ghost!'

Oh no, I think, please don't let him realise, please don't—

'*Ohmigod!* Rebecca, tell me I'm wrong. Tell me I'm not thinking what I'm thinking.'

I can't look at him. I'm staring at my soup. I know he's looking beyond me, at the guy who looks so like Patrick, and I know he can't fail now to see why I behaved like such an idiot. He puts his hand over mine. 'Rebecca?' he says very gently. 'Is that it?'

'He just looked so like Patrick for a moment . . .' I'm on the verge of tears. 'I thought it might be him . . . not really, not when I really looked at him, but just when I turned round like that I thought it was him and I was so happy . . .'

Oh God, here they come. My eyes well up and any moment now the tears will start pouring down my face. Davey takes charge. He hands me a napkin and says briskly, 'Go outside. I'll settle up here. Go and sit on that bench in Clerkenwell Green. I'll see you there in five minutes.'

I stumble out of the noodle bar and down the street, my face buried in the napkin. People move aside for me; I can see some of them, curious and concerned, turn their heads to look more closely as they pass. I've seen people crying in the street before and I've always been glad that it wasn't me. Now I'm the mad sobbing person, and there's an awful, strange relief in it. This is how I feel. I am the one in more pain than anyone else, the one who's grieving. I don't have to pretend and put on a brave face any more.

I don't completely let go when I reach the bench. I want to sob and howl as if the tears are blood, as if I'm not just crying but bleeding out my pain. When I'm alone at home I cry like that. Not every night now, thank God. Not like it was the first few weeks, but more often than I care to think about. By the time Davey sits down next to me, the napkin is completely drenched. He hands me a new one and pulls me close to him, his arm around me. I resist; not so much physically, though my whole body is clenched stiff, as if all my ligaments have been wound so tight that they'll snap if I make the slightest movement. I'm holding back emotionally, scared of letting go into Davey's warm comforting hug. If I do, there will be nothing left. So I take a deep breath, and mop at my ruined face with the new napkin, and pat at the hand Davey is resting on my shoulder, before I finally get some sort of grip on myself.

'I didn't know it was still this bad,' Davey says.

'Oh, it isn't really,' I say, sitting up straighter and patting my face dry. How many napkins have I soaked through today? The water spill in the noodle bar seems very symbolic suddenly – displaced tears. But I ended up crying anyway.

'It seems pretty bad,' Davey says, not letting me off the hook.

'It was just the shock,' I say, trying to deflect him. 'I mean, how would you feel if you turned your head and saw Jenna sitting next to you?'

'But it wasn't Jenna,' Davey points out.

'OK, someone who looked like her double. You'd probably knock something over too.'

'Yeah, maybe . . .' Davey sounds unconvinced. 'But I wouldn't burst into tears like that.'

'Well of course you wouldn't. You're a guy. We girls have the luxury of bursting into tears because we've got make-up to cover up the ravages afterwards.'

Thank God I have my make-up bag with me. I fish it out of my handbag and take a look at myself in the mirror of my compact. Jesus. The one mercy is that I was wearing water-proof mascara. I have a patent remedy to take down the swelling, but I don't have time for it, and even if I did, I would look even more stupid than I do already lying on a bench in Clerkenwell Green with cold camomile tea bags over my eyes. I extract my secret weapon, Boots' Banana Split, on which I have been relying heavily these last few months. It's almost finished. I make a mental note to get a new one. It's the best thing I've found for red swollen eyelids. Pale lemon powder on the eyelids, and a cream in the same shade for the bags underneath. I breathe on the cream to warm it up, dip in my little finger and pat it delicately into the hollow under my eyes.

'I'll never understand women,' Davey comments. 'Sobbing one minute and entirely focused on doing their make-up the next.'

'All part of those wonderful contradictions that make you love us so much,' I say, trying for winsome.

Davey produces a plastic bag that he had stowed under the bench. 'Well, I'm going to have my lunch,' he says. 'I'm starving.'

Davey tucks daintily into his noodle broth, managing not to spill any on his black designer shirt, while I work on my face, painting it like a canvas. Eyeliner, blusher, powder, more mascara. By the time I've finished I look halfway decent and Davey's stomach acids are hard at work breaking down the noodles and coconut cream.

'Right!' I say brightly. 'Back to work!'

'Eat,' Davey says, handing me a plastic container of beef salad. 'You need calories after that sob-fest.'

I'm not hungry, but I force a few bites down to keep Davey happy. I promise to finish the rest at my desk.

'What are you doing tonight?' he asks.

'Yoga class.'

'When does it finish?'

'Eight. Why?'

'I think I should come round.'

'No, really, I'm fine. But thanks.'

'I don't like the idea of you being by yourself this evening.'

'I'll be fine, Davey. Really.' I squeeze his hand. 'Top friend,' I say. 'Honestly, I'll get back after yoga and have a nice bath and crash out. It's what I need.'

'Really?' Davey says doubtfully.

'Really.'

I know he's keeping an eye on me for the rest of the afternoon but I manage to laugh and joke with the boys and I think by the time I leave he's convinced that I'm OK. I'm pretty good by now at masking how I really feel. Ever since I got back from New York, I've felt as if I have a great empty space under my ribcage. I can only manage by pretending to everyone else that it isn't there. I feel that if someone touched me in the right place everything would cave into the hole and I would bleed to death. I can't let Davey try to prod around for damage.

Yoga was brutal. I'll be sore tomorrow. But I take a perverse pleasure in the pain. It's the one thing that connects me to my body right now. And it stops me thinking. Before Patrick and I broke up, I used to jog, but I found I couldn't run after the split. My body would settle into the repetitive movements and my brain would spin away, finding all the most painful memories and playing them back one after another, telling me that no matter how fit I was, no matter how much I put myself through pounding the pavements of northwest London, it was all for nothing. Patrick had still rejected me. It mocked all my efforts to keep myself fit: why are you bothering? What's the point of toning up your thighs and staying slim when he still doesn't love you enough? And then I'd think of Patrick when he came back from a run and did press-ups on the living room floor and how I wanted him so badly that I wanted to make love then and there on the floor, without my even waiting for him to get into the shower, not caring about the sticky drying sweat on his body, the damp, almost spongy texture of his skin, something that would have revolted me on any other man. I would stop running and lean against a tree and manage to get my tears under control before I walked home again, as desperate to get inside my flat as a wounded animal crawling back to its burrow. I know that sounds ridiculously dramatic, but it's how I felt. When you're in love your brain is full of over-romantic clichés, and it's even more true when you've loved and lost. There is no originality. You feel things you would never tell to another living soul, because you would be humiliated by the sheer banality of your own words.

Yoga saved me. I started doing it more and more often, because I found that I couldn't think about anything but the demands of the class. It was a merciful one and a half hours during which my brain was flooded with a much-needed release. And afterwards I'd invariably feel better. It might not last that long, but there was always another class to look forward to.

I've just got out of the bath when the doorbell rings. Shit. It must be a mistake. I haven't ordered pizza tonight; cutting down on the carbs. Besides, I'm too embarrassed. In the early days after the breakup I could barely face going out the door, except when I had to. I couldn't even manage to go to the supermarket after work; I shot straight home and lived off takeaway food. The delivery guys got to know me so well that they knew what I was going to order before I opened my mouth, just from seeing my phone number flash up on their screen. After a couple of months, the Chinese food guy and the pizza guy both asked me if I was all right. The Chinese guy said, 'Was I ill?' Because he knew a great Chinese doctor who could prescribe me a tonic. And the pizza guy actually told me that he hoped I was eating some fresh vegetables. I was so ashamed that I made a massive effort to go to Sainsbury's and stock up the fridge with oven-ready meals instead.

I towel myself off and I'm putting on my pyjamas as the doorbell rings again. I sneak over to the window and look out. My flat's on the first floor and I get a quick flash of the top of Davey's head before I duck back in again. Shit. I curse myself for breaking down in front of him today. And the lights are on; he'll know I'm home. He'll give me hell at work tomorrow for not letting him in. But I can't. I haven't had anyone round since the breakup and I'm not starting now. Not with the flat the way it is.

Five minutes pass and the doorbell hasn't rung again. I chance another squint through the curtains. No Davey. He must have given up. I relax with relief and go into the kitchen to pour myself a medicinal glass of red wine. Then I hear it: a key in the front door. Davey has my spare set of keys, in case I lock myself out, but it would never have occurred to me that he'd actually use them. I look round the flat wildly, wondering how I can hide the incriminating evidence, but it's much too late. Davey's already on the Yale. I consider throwing myself against the door, but he's stronger than me. Patrick always told me that I should get a chain on the door. Why didn't I listen to him? I just thought he was being his usual manly, protective self – I didn't realise that his advice might have come in handy when my best friend was effectively breaking and entering my flat.

'Rebecca?' Davey calls from the hallway. 'Rebecca, I know you're home. It's me. Are you decent?'

I decide that attack is the best form of defence. Shooting out from the kitchen I shout indignantly, 'I could have been naked! I could have had someone round! How dare you just walk in here like that! I want my keys back right now!'

But Davey's barely listening. He's looking around the living room with an appalled expression.

'*Rebecca*,' he breathes in horror.

'It's not that bad . . .' I mutter. 'It looks worse than it is . . .'

'*Worse than it is?* I don't think that's possible!'

'I was going to take them down . . . well, some of them . . . I just haven't got round to it yet . . .'

Davey's walking around the living room, pacing slowly, taking it all in. I go into the kitchen and grab my wine glass. It's OK to drink in front of Davey now, and I really need some sustenance. I can't do this on my own.

'Twenty,' he says finally. 'More or less. I may have missed some.'

'I needed to feel I wasn't alone . . . well, no, that doesn't sound right. But they cheered me up, they really did . . . *Do*—'

'This is a shrine,' Davey says. 'It's a *mausoleum*. No wonder you haven't had me round since the breakup.' He looks me straight in the eye. 'It's even worse than I thought,' he pronounces. 'What about the rest of the place?'

'No, it's just in here . . . really . . .'

Davey makes for the bedroom. I throw myself in his path. I've drunk half the glass of wine by now, so it doesn't splash. I've spilt enough drinks for one day. 'Don't go in there!' I plead. '*Please*, Davey. I'll take all the photos down, I promise. I was going to, honestly . . .'

'Rebecca. Let me into the bedroom.'

'No. I won't. It's my bedroom. You can't go in there unless I say so.' I sound like a four-year-old. All that's missing is the petulant stamp of my foot.

'Rebecca. Let me past you.'

'No! I won't!'

'OK,' Davey says.

I sag with relief.

'Why don't we sit down and talk about these?' he says, gesturing to the photographs with which every spare inch of table, bookshelf and desk is covered.

I bought a batch-load of frames for them. Patrick and me on holiday in Portugal, our arms round each other, smiling shyly at the camera. Patrick in a wetsuit, looking like James Bond. Patrick lying on his sofa, talking on the phone, wearing his tracksuit bottoms, his bare chest smooth and muscular. Patrick coming back from a jog, hair tied back in a bandanna, shorts sticking to him, his entire body oiled with sweat. He's glowering at me in all those photographs, the Jogging Series: he said I was treating him like a sex object. But how could I not? He was the most beautiful thing I had ever seen, and he was mine. Patrick dressed so badly – big baggy shirts, sweaters

15

that did nothing for him – that nobody knew how handsome he was underneath all the camouflage but me. Every time he undressed I wanted to help. He was like a present that I was constantly unwrapping. The first time we made love I couldn't believe how beautiful he was, his arms thick twists of rope under white velvet skin, his stomach hard and rippled, his hair like a waterfall down his back. I had to bite my tongue not to tell him how gorgeous he was. He got embarrassed so easily.

I sink into the armchair, staring at the closest picture – Patrick playing football in Regent's Park, a really good view of his thigh muscles flexing – and I am distracted by it for a few seconds, enough for Davey, the sneaky bastard, to make a dash for the bedroom.

'No!' I yell, but it's too late.

Silence. I wait for Davey to come back, but he doesn't. Finally the tension is too much for me. I get up and follow him slowly into my bedroom. He's sitting on the end of the bed, staring at the big photograph on the wall opposite. Below it is my chest of drawers, a line of candles flickering on top of it in a long silver holder beneath the photograph. It looks bad; I know it looks bad. There were candles in the living room too, but this really is what Davey called it – a shrine.

I sit down on the bed next to Davey and look at Patrick. The photo didn't enlarge perfectly, but it's good enough for me. It never fails to trigger a rush of happy memories. Patrick's in his swimsuit, launching the kayak off the pier in Portugal. A lock of hair is falling into his eyes. He's waving to me, telling me to come on, to put the stupid camera down, we've been talking about paddling out to that little island all holiday and now we should bloody well get on with it or we'll never do it. He's twisted around, his body in profile, and you can see the smooth curve of his back, the way it tilts down to the swell of his buttocks . . .

'*Right*,' Davey says eventually. 'I had no idea things were this bad. Although I did know you weren't telling me the truth today about that being the first time you'd seen someone who looked like Patrick.'

'I didn't actually *say* that,' I demur. 'I just let you think that.'

'I remembered that time two weeks ago when we were out for dinner in Soho and you kept making excuses to stay on at the table even though we were really tired, and I remembered that I'd thought to myself at the time that the guy sitting next to us looked a bit like Patrick, and I hoped you hadn't noticed . . . That's why I came round. I got all suspicious. And clearly I was right.'

I cringe guiltily.

'This has been going on for ages, hasn't it? The Patrick sightings?'

'A month.'

'Well, no wonder you keep seeing him everywhere! You're surrounded by pictures of him! It's unbelievably morbid!'

'It's not *morbid*. He's not *dead*,' I mutter.

'You are completely out of control.'

'It's just the grieving process. I need to feel that Patrick's close to me still. I can't quite give him up right now.'

'All right then, when?' Davey asks. 'When were you planning to take them down?'

'I don't know. Soon. When it felt right . . .'

My voice tails off. I am lying through my teeth. The thought of having to take down the photographs and lose that link with Patrick makes me as panicky as a drug user told they have to go cold turkey. Davey reads my mind. We've known each other for so long that it's not that difficult for him.

'You are *addicted* to this,' he says very firmly. 'I know better than anyone what that's like. You're addicted, and it has to stop.' He takes my hand gently. 'Rebecca. I'm staging an intervention.'

Chapter Two

My bedroom is painted dark red, and my bed is all white. On top of my bed are white lace pillows, a white coverlet and a couple of big, soft, white velvet throw pillows. I have a beautiful crimson and black Rothko print on the side wall. It used to be where Patrick's picture is now hanging, but I had to move it. I love my bedroom. It's my refuge from the world. And now Davey is trampling through it, metaphorically at least, and telling me that I'm not safe here any more. He's still staring at that big photograph of Patrick hanging on the wall, placed so that I see it every morning when I open my eyes. I know what Davey's thinking. But what he doesn't realise is that every morning when I wake up, I remember that Patrick isn't with me any more. It's the first thing that comes into my head. I don't need a photograph for that.

'I want you to come to an AA meeting with me,' Davey says.

'You think I'm an alcoholic?' I say, panicking. I notice that I have finished my wine, and put the glass down surreptitiously, trying to conceal it under the folds of the bedskirt. I'm self-medicating with wine at the moment: a couple of glasses most nights to help me sleep. I can't give that up as well. He should be bloody pleased I'm not on anti-depressants.

'No, of course not,' Davey says impatiently.

I breathe an enormous sigh of relief.

'But I think, seriously, that you're addicted to this relationship. Ex-relationship. You broke up with Patrick what, five months ago?'

'Nearly five months,' I correct him. 'It was the twenty-third of August.'

Davey sighs. 'OK, nearly five months, and you're still completely unable to let him go.'

'What about you?' I say defensively. 'You haven't looked at another woman since you broke up with Jenna, and that's been much longer!'

'That's because I was coping with AA,' Davey says. 'I told you what they say about not having a relationship in the first year.'

'Yeah, yeah, get a house plant and look after it and if it's still alive after a year then you can start to date . . .' I've heard this hundreds of times now.

'It makes complete sense!' Davey's on the defensive now.

'Davey, you got a *spider plant*. They barely even need watering.'

'I'm not good with growing things,' Davey mutters. 'I have black fingers. Or whatever's the opposite of green.'

'Red.'

'What?'

'Red's the opposite of green. We did that in school art class. Anyway, I know it's not just about AA. You're still keen on Jenna. You'd have her back in a minute if she'd let you.'

'This isn't about me,' Davey points out firmly. 'It's about you.'

'Well, I think you're projecting,' I say sneakily.

It doesn't work. Ever since Davey's been in AA, he's been much more able to deflect me when I try to distract him. He never used to be like that. Before, when he was trying to point out some aspect of my behaviour that he didn't think was a hundred per cent healthy, I could always draw him away from incipient criticism and on to some harmless side issue instead. AA has taken away my happy-go-lucky friend and given me an amateur therapist in exchange. I call that a very bad trade-off.

19

'Maybe I *am* projecting,' Davey admits, 'but that doesn't change anything about your behaviour. Look at this.' He gestures to the picture. 'If I had a picture of Jenna at the end of my bed, what would you tell me?'

I bite back the comment that Jenna wouldn't look half as good in a swimsuit as Patrick does, and say instead, 'I'd think that you were still grieving and needed more time to recover.'

'It's been five months! How long were you going out with him for?'

'Two and a half years.'

'Well, you can still be grieving – that's natural – but these pictures are just feeding that! It's festering inside you! You're obsessed!'

I feel a tide of fury rise up in me and burst out of my mouth. 'No, I *can't* grieve!' I say. I'm not shouting: my voice is low, but it's so hard-edged that Davey sits up straighter in shock.

'I can't grieve, because nobody will let me! Only two weeks after the breakup, every time I tried to talk about Patrick, everyone cut me off. It wasn't healthy, I needed to move on, blah blah blah. If he'd died, you'd all have let me talk about him, and I needed to. It was like a death. Everyone just expected me to forget about him, as if I could erase nearly three years from my memory just by clicking my fingers and going out for a few drinks! Well, I can't! I cried every night for a whole month. Every single night. The first week after we broke up, I slept for fifteen hours a day. I felt as if someone had knocked me on the head. And no one wanted to listen, because they thought that if I talked about him I'd keep remembering him.' I grab a throw pillow and clutch it protectively to my stomach, cuddling it for comfort. Davey's eyes are so full of pity that I can't meet them; if I did, I would burst into tears.

'But of course I remember him,' I continue. 'How could I help it? I love him! I *still* love him! That's the thing nobody wants to hear, that Patrick and I broke up still loving each other! If he'd told me that he didn't love me any more, or dumped me for some skinny New York banker tart because it was easier to go out with her than a girl living in London, it would have been awful, but I would have got over it a lot faster. But I still love him and I know that he still loves me and we can't be together because he's shit-scared of a relationship and it's *tearing my fucking heart out*! How do you *expect* me to feel?'

There's a long silence. I am almost panting with excess emotion. I wish I could get up and refill my glass, but I am held here by the strength of the moment. It's palpable. I am reminded of those terrible discussions Patrick and I used to have, trying to find a way through the mess of our conflicting desires so that we could manage to stay together. Once we had started a conversation about the subject that terrified both of us, it couldn't be stopped until we had reached some decision, even if only a temporary one. I once said to Patrick that it was like wading through water: that hard, that slow.

Finally Davey says, 'I'm sorry.'

'It's OK.'

'No, I'm really sorry. I've been a crap friend, haven't I?' He puts his arm round my shoulder. 'I should have tried harder. You're right about the not talking about Patrick thing. I think I felt it was like probing a wound, you know? That it would be better for you just to let it heal, quietly. But I was wrong. We all were. You did need to grieve.'

Huge relief. I feel a weight falling off my shoulders, and I manage to loosen slightly my white-knuckled grip on the pillow. Davey's going to get off my case about the photographs.

'But just because I was wror
right now,' he continues. 'You
sitting here all alone with it bec
But now I'm here and these ph
for a start.'

'NO.'

I'm feeling that panic all ove
and get up, shrugging off Dav

kitchen. I need some more wine. Also, I want Davey out of my bedroom. It's my private place, I have it exactly how I want it, and he's ruining it for me by telling me I need to change it.

To my relief, Davey follows me. He props his elbows on the ledge that divides the kitchen from the living room; the former is so small that I can practically feel him breathing down my neck as I pull the cork out of the wine bottle and pour myself another healthy dose of oblivion.

'Look, let's try this another way, OK?' he says. 'I just think AA might help you. I mean, addictions are all the same when you come down to it, no matter what the symptoms are . . . Would you come to a meeting with me tomorrow?'

I glare at him. I am extremely resentful of this elision of my totally natural and understandable mourning for the love of my life with the problems of a bunch of sad drunks crawling out of empty vodka bottles.

'Just to make me feel better?' Davey adds coaxingly. 'If you hate it, you never have to come again.'

'I didn't know non-alcoholics could come,' I say, slugging down some wine defiantly.

'It's technically an open meeting. That means outsiders are welcome. Please, Rebecca. Think of it as supporting me, if you don't want to do it for yourself. It would mean a lot to me. I've been meaning to ask you along for ages.'

That was very clever of him. Points to Davey for that manoeuvre. 'All right,' I say, grudgingly, 'but don't expect it to change my mind about anything, OK? I'm doing this for you, not me.'

'Whatever it takes,' Davey says, smiling beatifically.

She thinks one AA meeting is going to make me come rip down all my photos of Patrick and ring up all my see if they know any eligible bachelors they can fix he's putting *much* too much faith in his stupid gramme.

I dreamt about Patrick last night. We were lying next to each other, embracing, his hair falling over our faces like a silk curtain, and we were kissing. No, not exactly kissing; our tongues were in each other's mouths, which is barely possible. I didn't realise its unlikelihood in the dream, but when I woke up and remembered what I had dreamt, I knew that no two people could do that. It was a symbol of how entwined we were: breathing each other's breath, our hearts beating against each other's ribcage, filling each other's mouths. Inseparable.

You never dream about someone when you're sleeping in the same bed as them. Or at least, I never did. I dreamt about Patrick when he wasn't there, as if my subconscious were trying to fill the space between us. As I dream about him now.

The Alcoholics Anonymous meeting is like that film by Ingmar Bergman where Liv Ullmann mutilates her private parts with broken glass: by turns boring, gripping, and horrible. A man with a face utterly destroyed by alcohol recounts how after forty years of drinking (he must have started very early) AA has finally allowed him to confront his demons and give up the booze for ever. I stare at his caved-in cheeks, his swollen reddish nose, his thick veined skin whose pores are so deeply pitted that he looks like a smallpox victim, and wonder how much help AA has really been. Maybe it would have been better for him just to go on drinking. His description of his life now – he has no job or prospects, he's alienated everyone who once cared about him, he's staying in a halfway house waiting to get a council flat, which might take years and will doubtless be revolting when it finally becomes available – is so depressing that I can't help thinking that maybe he should just have gone on killing himself. Perhaps I'm taking that point of view because I'm so depressed myself at the moment. But he doesn't seem to feel a great deal of jubilation at having saved himself from the demon drink. He tells his sad story in an affectless voice, clearly having recounted it many, many times before, and his attitude seems to be that AA is only a better option for him because dying in a gutter would have been worse. He doesn't talk about anything he has to live for; he has no optimism, no hopes for the future. Instead he focuses on the hell he's pulled himself out of, without seeming to wonder where he is escaping to. It's a philosophy constructed purely around the negative.

When he finally sits down, everyone claps. I glance over at Davey, raising my eyebrows in an effort to convey my scepticism; how can he imagine I'm going to get insights into my condition from a story like that? But Davey's too busy applauding to notice me trying to catch his attention, and now the moderator who started the meeting by testifying himself (secret drinker for years, wife never guessed until he got sacked from work for being drunk on the job) asks if anyone else wants to speak.

A very smart businesswoman stands up. There are all types here. We're in a church basement in Farringdon, so it's close to the City, but also convenient for the alternative business types like us, working in trendy lofts along the Clerkenwell Road. And of course there are the people who lived in Clerkenwell long before the dot.com offices, happening bars and expensive restaurants moved in, people who can't afford anything that the new money has brought to the area, people, I have to say, who, here at least, seem remarkably accepting of the richer AA members who are 'fessing up to very expensive drinking habits indeed. Cocktails and Dom Perignon mix here with giant cans of Tennants Extra without any class consciousness. I have been putting out feelers, testing the atmosphere as one person after another gets up to talk, and I sense no resentment at all. An addiction's an addiction, no matter how it's expressed. Still, there's a painful contrast between the poor ruined shell of a man who just spoke, and Smart

Businesswoman, who is talking in a cut-glass accent about her sherry habit.

I sip my coffee. It's six-thirty, a post-work meeting, which I assume replaces the traditional everyone-down-the-pub visit for all the office drones here. The basement is well stocked with a giant coffee urn, cheap polystyrene cups and a huge plate of nasty shiny pastries, the ones with the white lines of piped icing on the top, for those who have replaced their alcohol addictions with an eating disorder. A couple of sad women with rolls of fat like tyres under their loose-fitting crêpe dresses are working their way through them. Lots of people are smoking, despite the no smoking signs which are pasted along the walls between the evangelical posters. I assume AA members get special dispensation from the vicar. Smoking may kill you just as surely as alcohol will, but at least it doesn't cause anti-social behaviour along the lines already described by some of the participants.

'And that was exactly the trouble,' Smart Businesswoman is saying. 'I could talk my way out of anything. It's the classic addict's behaviour, isn't it? We get terribly good at covering up.' Lots of nods from the audience. 'I was driving home after a dinner party one night; I'd had God knows how much to drink, and I had my bottle of sherry on the seat next to me so that I could pull over and have a nip whenever I needed it. I got stopped by the police because I was on the wrong side of the road. Apparently I'd been on the wrong side of the road for ages, they'd been following me, but of course I hadn't realised. I managed to knock my bottle on to the car floor when they pulled me over, but I must have reeked of alcohol. And somehow I still talked my way out of it. I don't even remember what I said – I barely remember the entire incident. They didn't even give me a ticket.'

Bloody hell. Obviously her accent couldn't hurt, but still – *bloody hell*! I can't help but be perversely impressed by this, even though I know I shouldn't be.

Someone comes into the room. The door's behind us, so I can't see who it is, and I don't turn around to look. People have been entering throughout the meeting; because it's an open one there isn't the same privacy there would be if this were AA members only. I hear them making their way along the row behind us and sitting down. A hand reaches forward and taps Davey lightly on the shoulder. He swivels his head round to see who it is, and a lovely smile breaks across his face.

A girl, I think! Davey, that sneaky fox! He's got a girl in AA and he didn't mention it to me. Maybe he thought it would depress me. I have to admit that it would. Practically every single one of my friends is paired up apart from Davey. If Davey fell in love as well, I really would want to kill myself. I remind myself that Daisy, my best girlfriend, is single too. But she's so beautiful that I can't take that as consolation; after all, if Daisy, blonde and drop-dead gorgeous can't find a man, what hope is there for me?

So as I look round, I'm bracing myself for the sight of a girl staring adoringly at Davey. Instead I see a man our age, maybe a few years older. Or perhaps he just looks older because he radiates self-possession and calm. He has thick fair hair shoved back from his face, green-grey eyes and a strong jawline. He's very handsome. There's a bit too much stubble along that jaw-line for me, but I'm prejudiced: Patrick was so smooth-shaven that I wince at stubble now, remembering how it burnt.

He's still got his hand on Davey's shoulder, and Davey's patting it. Energy is passing between them in an almost tangible exchange. If I saw two men in any other set of circumstances looking at each other like that I would assume they were gay. The fair-haired guy is smiling at Davey. He has a very nice smile; his mouth is wide and curls up in a way that makes you want to smile back at him.

I feel as if I'm intruding by watching them, so I turn round again, facing forward, and tug discreetly at the neckline of my sweater so that it hangs as it's supposed to do, in an instinctive response to there being a good-looking man in the vicinity. Heartbreak, I have discovered, doesn't preclude vanity. I'm wearing a black sweater with a slightly off-the-shoulder cowl neck, with my hair up in a high ponytail to make the aforementioned neck look longer, and tight-fitting grey twill trousers. It's boring office wear, but I dressed down this morning, knowing I was coming to AA after work. Somehow I got it into my head that one needed to dress discreetly for a meeting of this sort. It felt a little like going to church – well, it is in a church basement, after all. At least I'm wearing high heels. I contemplate these – black leather ruched boots, bought on sale last week – with considerable satisfaction. Nice footwear can almost always cheer me up.

Meanwhile, Smart Businesswoman is wiping away tears and finishing up her speech, or testimony, or whatever they call it.

'Thanks to Phillipa for sharing that with us,' says the moderator, as we all clap and Smart Businesswoman smooths her skirt beneath her and sits back down again in the first row. 'Who wants to speak next?'

Davey raises his hand. The moderator points to him. Davey turns to exchange another look with the man behind him and then stands up.

I suddenly realise that I have been dreading Davey speaking at this meeting. I don't want him to bare his soul in front of all these people. There is something horribly personal about my witnessing Davey opening up like this before everyone. I feel violently uncomfortable and shift around in the cheap plastic folding chair, crossing and recrossing my legs. Even that – and the consequent view of my nice new boots – doesn't help to relieve the tension that's flooding through me. Maybe it's because the rest of the people here don't have to go out with Davey afterwards like I do; they're all here to give each other support at the meetings and then go their separate ways.

Analysing my feelings, I realise that, while we are hugely flattered when our friends confide their secrets to us, it happens naturally, organically, in the course of a long heart felt conversation, not because it's Wednesday night and it's time to stand up and tell everyone you're an alcoholic. What if I'm not up to the task of comforting Davey afterwards? Will he even need comfort? I realise I don't have the faintest idea how to behave, and it's scaring me. What if I turn out to be a bad friend? Will we be able to snap back into friendship afterwards, or will Davey's revelations just make us awkward and self-conscious? I remind myself that Davey wouldn't have asked me along if he didn't think I could handle it, and anyway, this isn't all about me.

It doesn't help much. Guiltily I realise that I really crave a glass of red wine.

Davey has walked to the front of the room and is standing at the lectern. I assume they put that there so that people don't feel too physically exposed by standing up in front of a group of near-strangers; they have something to shield them, if only symbolically. And they can lean on it instead of worrying about what to do with their hands. It's good psychology.

'Hi, my name's Davey and I'm an alcoholic,' Davey starts.

'Hi, Davey,' we all chorus. The guy behind me says it pretty loudly; he has a pleasantly deep voice, I notice, but he doesn't have to shout.

'I don't have many lurid stories to tell you,' Davey starts. He seems – not at ease, no one could be at ease in a situation like this, but as if he's done this many times before, and is reasonably comfortable with it. This relaxes me slightly. If Davey were obviously nervous, I would be gnawing my nails in anxiety for him.

'When I first came to AA, I felt embarrassed that I didn't have much in the way of dramatic stuff to tell, not like some people here. I felt a bit of a sham. But I quickly realised that being an alcoholic isn't about crashing your car or having blackouts or passing out in the gutter every night. It's about dependence. Dependence on alcohol to cover your real feelings. And by that definition, I absolutely was – *am* – an alcoholic.'

Everyone's nodding supportively. I, meanwhile, am hugely glad that Davey isn't going to shock me with stories about terrible drunken binges. I don't know if I could have coped with that. It's selfish of me, because I'm happier for myself than for Davey. I *am* very selfish right now, I know. Patrick is absorbing me to the point that I don't have much room left for other people.

'I'd always drunk socially,' Davey is saying. 'And that was fine for a long time. Obviously I got pretty drunk at college –' he smiles at me, remembering happy pissed-as-a-fart nights in the student bar together '– and after that it was a couple of pints after work or the footie game on Sunday. I had a bottle of whisky in the house for years and never touched it. And then I met this girl. Jenna.'

He has a hard time pronouncing her name, I notice. He hesitates visibly before saying it. This must be the tough part.

'Jenna was amazing,' he says. 'She was the most beautiful, clever, funny girl I'd ever met, and I couldn't believe she'd fallen for me. But she had. We were insanely happy together. And I probably said "insanely" for a reason. We got together very fast – in retrospect, it was much too fast. We barely had a night apart for six months.'

All too true. It drove his friends crazy; suddenly we couldn't see Davey without Jenna being dragged along too. She was OK – we had no particular objection to her – but we wanted to meet up on our own occasionally, and besides, Jenna was scarcely the picture of perfection that Davey's painting. Still, that's love for you.

'And then we sort of came out of our bubble,' Davey continues, 'and realised that there was a world outside which we'd been neglecting because we were so absorbed in each other. We decided that we ought to go out on our own a bit more. It was the right thing to do, but to my surprise I found I was getting very jealous. Jenna had become my life, and when she wasn't with me, I missed her really badly. The suggestion that we should go out on our own had come from me, more than her, and I think she threw herself into it because she was a bit hurt. Maybe she was trying to teach me a lesson. I don't know. Anyway, I really regretted it, but by then it was too late. I rang her all the time, I wanted to know what she was doing every minute of the day, and it put her off. She still loved me, but now she felt that she needed some space. It drove me crazy. Then suddenly I found myself getting out that bottle of whisky from the back of the kitchen cupboard.'

More nods from the audience. The nods in AA are truly heartfelt. I've never seen agreement so simply but eloquently expressed.

'None of my friends knew about it,' Davey's saying. 'Nor did Jenna, at first. I'd go out as usual, drink a few beers, and then go home to the Bell's. It became my way of cheating on Jenna, within this sort of lunatic fantasy I had that she was cheating on me. As if I was getting back at her somehow for having a life of her own that she didn't tell me every last thing about. Well, I had things I wasn't telling her too. One thing, at least. The whisky became my crutch. It didn't make me feel less insecure, but it was something of my own.'

He pauses. I am incredibly proud of him. Davey's like my brother. We met at college and pretty much adopted each other. Before this I would have said that I knew him as well as I know myself, but here he is baring his soul and I'm learning things about him that he'd only hinted at previously. I realise that no matter how strong I used to think he was, I had no idea of how much strength he truly has. It shames me.

'Of course, the drinking started to affect me,' he continues. 'Not at work, but with Jenna. I started drinking whisky when I was with her, not just at home alone. I was terrified of losing her by cross-questioning her all the time about where she was, and the whisky seemed to help with that. It blunted the edge of my panic. I became more distant with her. I was thinking about when I could have another drink, and another, and another – how long should I leave it? Could I just pop into the kitchen and sneak a quick shot so that she wouldn't realise how much I was drinking . . . ? etc., etc. You all know what that's like. She had no idea what was going on at first, but she could tell that there was something different about me, and she didn't like it. She accused me of being withholding, but I told her she was being ridiculous. And of course, sex isn't that easy when you're drinking a lot. Often I'd just want to go to sleep, or I couldn't do it at all, at least not properly, which made her incredibly insecure. She thought I was having an affair, which was ironic, because that was exactly what I was scared of *her* doing. She kept trying to talk to me about what was wrong, but I was dismissive. And finally she said I was drinking too much, and I blew up at her. I told her I was only drinking because she made me feel so damn insecure. What did she need space for? We were so happy together! She said that we weren't happy any more, that we hadn't been happy for a long, long time, and that she thought it was because I was drinking too much. Of course I completely denied it. I wouldn't admit I had a problem. She told me that it was me being unfaithful, not her – I was cheating on her with a whisky bottle. Then she stormed out.'

Davey runs a hand through his hair. He's always hated his hair, which is a mass of tight, springy, dark brown curls, and he keeps it pretty short. I taught him about hair mousse at college, which helped him considerably. I think his curls are sweet. I'd never say that word to him, naturally: men hate being called 'sweet' – it's pretty much the worst word you can say to them; they shrug off insults much more easily than 'sweet' or 'cute'.

But Davey *is* sweet. I look at him standing up there, his eyes owlish behind his round, dark-framed glasses, his trendy grey shirt buttoned up to the neck, those slightly pudgy cheeks that I sometimes pinch, like an Italian mama, to annoy him, and I want to give him a hug. I realise that I'm on the verge of tears.

31

I love Davey so much and I want him to be happy, and I hate seeing him put himself through this, because I think it's totally unnecessary.

You see, I've never thought that Davey was an alcoholic. I still don't. I think he drank a bit too much and needed to cut down, but that's it. He could just have talked about it with us, his close friends, and he would have sorted himself out with our help. This whole AA business has always seemed to me – and everyone else who knows him – as being a step too far. Way too far. I think he over-reacted to all that business with Jenna, and found AA as a form of consolation, a support group, rather than because he actually *needed* to stop drinking. I'm hoping that in a couple of years he'll settle down, realise that he isn't actually an alcoholic, and be able to come back to happy evenings in the pub where we all get a little bit tipsy. I mean, look at all the other people here! They're clearly alkies! Davey's story is scarcely on a par with theirs! I'm surprised he hasn't drawn the logical inference from that already.

'I should have gone after Jenna and made it up with her and admitted that I had been drinking too much; talked everything through. But I didn't. I buried myself in the bottle instead. I couldn't face opening up to her that much, admitting that she had so much power to hurt me. It made me feel too vulnerable. So I drank instead. And I wouldn't answer her phone calls or her emails. I couldn't risk opening up to her completely and maybe losing her when she realised how weak I was, how much I needed her.'

Exactly, I think. This isn't about drinking, it's about being in love. Davey just needs to go and find Jenna and talk to her, then everything will be all right.

'I didn't have some big cosmic revelation about being an alcoholic,' Davey says. 'There wasn't some blinding moment of truth. I just went to my off-licence to get another bottle of Bell's, and the man behind the counter said: "Getting through these pretty fast, aren't you?" and I went home and looked at all the empties stacked up in the kitchen that I'd been meaning to take to the recycling bin, but hadn't got round to yet. I realised that I hadn't taken them out because I was embarrassed to have everyone see how many there were. And this excuse popped into my head, that if anyone I knew saw me I'd say that it was because Jenna and I had broken up that I was hitting the whisky a bit too hard, and they'd understand. But it wasn't because Jenna and I had broken up. I'd been drinking well before then. Jenna and I had split up *because* I was drinking so much. I'd never quite admitted that to myself before. So I opened the bottle of Bell's and poured myself a drink, then I looked up AA in the phone book and rang the number before I could lose my nerve. And here I am.'

He stops. 'That's it, really,' he adds, to let everyone know he's done.

'Thank you so much, Davey, for sharing that with us,' the moderator says, standing up and going over to Davey as we clap. He puts an arm round Davey's shoulder in that awkward way that men have of showing support. 'Davey's story makes a really important point. Alcoholism is about *dependence*, in whatever form that comes. Recognising your dependence and managing to give it up, by working the Twelve Steps, is what AA is all about.'

More clapping as Davey walks back to sit next to me. We hug, as best we can sitting next to each other. I'm choking back the tears, because Davey was so honest and it was so moving. The man behind us clasps Davey on the shoulder again as we pull apart. This is beginning to get a bit creepy. Who is this guy?

'Rebecca,' Davey hisses, as if he's read my mind, 'this is Jake, my sponsor. The reason I'm here, really.'

I take an instant dislike to Jake. This is the person who's convinced Davey he's an alcoholic, when he's nothing of the kind. This is the person who's preyed on Davey's vulnerability to get him into this sort of cult from which no one is ever

33

allowed to emerge. I nod politely at Jake and then turn back to watch the next actor in the freak show. I reach for Davey's hand and hold it tightly. I want to make a point to Jake. He isn't the only person who's here for Davey, I am too. And just because Jake thinks that this is right for Davey, it doesn't mean that I have to agree.

We were in the pub with Davey and Jenna, Will and Lucy. It's a boring way to spend New Year's Eve, if you're single; if I hadn't been in a couple I would have been trawling round for parties, trying to find the most exciting one, the one that promised, maybe, someone I could flirt with and kiss at midnight, someone who would make me feel that the New Year was a door thrown open on to new possibilities, rather than yet another one slamming shut on my fingers.

But I was coupled up, the ideal state to be in at New Year's Eve, head-over-heels in love with Patrick. I was Ingrid Bergman in Spellbound, *kissing Gregory Peck for the first time and seeing the doors bursting open one by one on to the sky. I was so in love with Patrick, so sexually bound to him, that if the young Gregory Peck had turned up on my doorstep and begged me for a date I would have turned him away regretfully. I would have taken his phone number, of course, but I would have turned him away. I had never felt before with a man that our future was like a wide flowing river. No rapids in the way, no waterfalls. I looked back on my past relationships and they were all narrow little streams with shallow muddy bottoms by comparison. I was flying. I was high on love.*

So there was a charm to being in the pub with my friends and his, to spending a simple evening within walking distance of all of our homes. It was the charm of domesticity: here we were, all so content in our relationships that we could turn down invitations to wild parties and ensconce ourselves happily in the pub like old married couples. I couldn't think of anything that I wanted more than to be an old married person whose friends reproached her for being boring, not coming out to party like she used to do. I wanted to be old and boring with Patrick.

Will, Patrick's friend, was getting very drunk indeed. Will was a large guy with a gigantic capacity for alcohol, and we weren't ordering by rounds, simply going up to the bar whenever anyone wanted fresh drinks, so Will wasn't being held back by our slower pace. He was drinking beer with shots of whisky, and by eleven he was already wasted. The pub was running a private party and could stay open as late as the landlord wanted, which was as long as he was making money. Since it was packed, one could assume it would be open at least till two, but Will was drinking as if he was expecting last orders to come at any moment. Lucy, his girlfriend, usually tried to keep an eye on him, inasmuch as anyone could control Will's appetites. Lucy was a tiny little slip of a thing, as slender as Will was large, but she could drink like a stevedore and tonight she was too busy sinking rum and cokes and telling increasingly filthy jokes to dedicate any spare time to worrying about her boyfriend's descent into utter insobriety.

Meanwhile, Jenna and Davey were in the first flush of their happiness: loved-up, constantly touching each other as if to prove to themselves that they could, that the person next to them was real and not just some wished-for hallucination, that their touch was not only licit but positively welcome. Patrick was less demonstrative. I would have liked him to be more physically affectionate with me when we were out in public, but he made up for it so well when we were alone that I didn't feel I had any right to complain. I couldn't believe there were any two people on the face of the earth who were having better sex than we were.

My heart had been in my mouth the entire evening. Tonight, I had determined, I was going to tell Patrick I loved him. I had been wanting to do this for so long that it felt *as if I would explode if I didn't. On holiday in Portugal I had had to walk away from him several times because I knew that I was on the verge of blurting it out and I was afraid it was too early, that he wouldn't be ready to hear it. I had felt the shape of the words in my mouth, already formed, just about to tumble from my lips, and I had caught them just in time, wrestling with myself to get my impulses under control. Tonight it was do or die. We had been going out for eight months and I knew he loved me, but I knew, too, that he hadn't said the words to anyone yet, and that they scared him. Patrick had never had a serious girlfriend before me. In one way it was wonderful: no competition, no jealousy, no fears about not coming up to the standard set by past beauties. But the flipside of the coin was that all this was new to him, uncharted territory in which Patrick, whose flat was decorated with huge framed nineteenth-century maps, Patrick, who never took a step without looking to see where he was placing his foot, felt like a stranger in a strange land: wary, unsure, and tentative.*

I knew all this and I thought I could deal with it. I thought I could show him that love wasn't as frightening as it was wonderful, that the benefits outweighed the risks, that the extraordinary connection we had would prove stronger than his fear of change. I was wrong.

The landlord was behind the bar shouting for silence. He turned up the TV until it blared with the countdown to midnight. It showed scenes of revellers at Trafalgar Square, mostly poor, drunk, freezing foreigners who were about to find out that no pubs would be open past midnight and they were about to turn into Cinderellas, packing themselves into the Tube or night buses, enjoying the time-honoured British tradition of being sexually harassed and vomited on by lager louts. Snow was thick on the ground; they were all bundled up in parkas, waving gloved hands at the TV cameras, their noses chapped and red. I would have watched them with great complacency, snug in my cosy booth in the warm pub with the man I loved beside me, if I hadn't been so scared by what I was about to do.

'MIDNIGHT! HAPPY NEW YEAR!' yelled the landlord, along with the TV presenter.

'Happy New Year!' we all shouted. The pub was a mass of bodies hugging and shouting and snapping party poppers, miniature fireworks paralleling the ones on the TV screen. Trailers of coloured paper ribbon floated down to earth, catching in people's hair, on shoulders, draping us in violet and pink and blue. Each couple turned to embrace. Patrick and I kissed and as I pulled away I looked him in the eye, determined to be brave and said, 'I love you'. No one else could hear.

He looked shocked and scared and then he said, equally brave, 'I love you too'.

My heart was a party popper. It fizzed and burst and streamers of happiness shot through my body. I could feel my toes, my fingers, all electric and tingling with joy. Patrick added, very seriously, 'I wouldn't be here if I didn't,' and I wondered if this was an attempt to qualify what he had just said, to diminish it somehow. But I didn't care. He had said the words and I knew he meant them. I knew he loved me.

There was a warning sign that evening, but it wasn't those words. It came a few hours later. But of course I was too much in love to realise what it meant.

Chapter Three

'Shall we hit the wine bar?' Davey asks.

He and I are walking up the staircase that leads out of the basement to the street, Jake is just behind us. The cold damp February air wraps around us like a clammy cloak as we step out of the security door, but I hardly notice. I'm buzzing on caffeine – I drank far too much coffee in that meeting, partly to keep awake, partly just for something to do – and also I'm shocked that Davey is so casually suggesting going to a wine bar in front of Jake, who I've just learnt is his sponsor.

'Uh . . .' I say, stalling for time in case Jake wants to voice his objections.

'You must be dying for a glass of wine,' Davey says affectionately. 'I know that was really intense for you. I'm so glad you came.'

He squeezes my hand, woollen glove over woollen glove. The sensation is a flashback to childhood; wearing knitted mittens and running hand-in-hand through the playground with your best friend that week.

'I'm really glad too,' I say, but actually I am berating myself for worrying about what Jake might think. Davey's been sober for over a year, he's fine with coming to the pub while others sink pints, and it's his decision, anyway, not mine. I'm not responsible for him.

'I *would* love a glass of wine, actually,' I add a touch too loudly.

'It's fine, Rebecca,' Jake says, interpreting my hesitation effortlessly. 'Davey can't live his life in a bubble. And remember, you're not responsible for him, nor am I. None of us can be responsible for anyone else.'

This eerily perceptive echoing of my thoughts a mere moment ago, combined with his preachy words, which sound more like an extract from an AA booklet than normal spontaneous conversation, set my teeth on edge. No wonder Davey's preaching at me; he's picked it up from Jake and all his sermonising. He's probably unconsciously resentful of it – God knows I would be – and so is passing it on to me instead. I decide that Davey definitely needs weaning away from Jake.

'Great!' I say in an over-bright tone. 'Wine bar it is, then!'

Ex-alcoholics are fabulously cheap drinking companions. Davey has a ginger ale and Jake an orange juice and soda. I insist on paying, being deliberately macho about it. I'm not going to let Jake dictate how this evening will go; paying is a way for me to redress the balance after his mini-lecture, establishing some psychological dominance of my own. Davey, naturally, is completely oblivious to all this manoeuvering, bless his sweet heart.

'My best friend and my sponsor!' he declares, beaming, as I set down the drinks and pull up a chair next to him. 'I've been wanting you two to meet for ages!'

'Davey's talked a lot about you,' Jake says to me.

I'm not quite sure how to read this. There's something about Jake that triggers some latent paranoia I didn't know I had. I decide that the best way to handle this is the direct question approach. 'Oh yeah? What did he say?' I ask, sipping my wine and looking straight into Jake's eyes, which now seem more green than grey. He's taken his jacket off, revealing a faded green sweater underneath, which brings out the same shade in his irises. I examine the sweater more closely, and observe that it isn't faded at all; that's just the weave. It must have been very expensive to look so naturally distressed.

'All good things,' Jake says, giving me that curly smile again.

'Bollocks,' I say, smiling back.

Jake, to his credit, bursts out laughing. 'OK, not *all* good things,' he admits.

'I'm glad to hear it. I wouldn't want you to get a false idea of my character.' I sip some more wine and move the focus of the conversation on to Jake. 'So how did you end up as Davey's sponsor?' I ask.

'I was at his first-ever meeting,' Jake says. 'Davey was really brave. A few of us went up and talked to him afterwards, to welcome him and offer support, and he and I just got talking.' He smiles at Davey. 'We got on very well, and after a while Davey asked me to be his sponsor.'

'Everyone has one,' Davey explains. 'It's like the personal face of AA. You have someone to ring up if you have problems, or feel like having a drink, or want to talk through the different steps.'

I nod. The sponsor thing sounds very sensible. But what I'm realising is that Davey has had a very close relationship with this man for over a year, and in all that time he hasn't breathed one word about Jake's existence to me.

'I should get going,' Jake says, finishing up his drink. 'I'm sure you two have things to talk about. It's great that you came to the meeting, Rebecca. I know you're very important to Davey, and your support will be very helpful to him.'

Jake, I think, needs to be in control of any situation he's in. It's as if he's giving Davey and me permission to talk about the meeting, when we were clearly intending to do so already.

Jake's pulling on his jacket. He clasps Davey on the shoulder in farewell, raises a hand to me, and walks out the door.

'He's great, isn't he?' Davey beams.

I choose my response carefully. 'As long as he's good for you, that's all that matters,' I say.

'You make it sound as if we were going out!' Davey says, taking off his glasses and polishing the lenses on the tail of his shirt.

'Well, you're obviously really close.'

'He's been amazing to me,' Davey says seriously. 'He's helped me so much.'

'I didn't realise you were drinking that much,' I comment, throwing out a line.

Davey bites. 'I wasn't really,' he says. 'It was more that I was relying on alcohol to avoid my emotional problems.'

'Right. I mean, I didn't think you could have been knocking back a bottle of Bell's a night, or you'd have been a wreck when you came into work.'

We had all speculated on this, ever since Davey had announced that he was in AA: no one believed that Davey had really been hitting the bottle that much. More to the point, as I've said, no one believed that he was truly an alcoholic at all.

'No, no. I wasn't half that bad. But I was using alcohol as a crutch. And now it's gone, I can see things a lot more clearly. There's Step Four, which is making a fearless moral inventory of yourself – I'm working on that, with Jake. And then you have to tell someone all the things you've done wrong. That's Step Five.'

'What on earth have you done wrong?' I say blankly. 'Nicked some sweeties out of someone else's locker when you were ten?'

At least Davey cracks a smile. 'It's really about Jenna,' he says. 'I treated her so badly. I was so scared of losing her that I pushed her away and broke her heart.'

'That's not AA, though,' I suggest daringly. 'That's just what you'd want to do anyway, isn't it? I mean, you still love her and you want her back.'

'She's seeing someone else,' Davey says, looking doleful.

'You should still go to her and tell her,' I say firmly. 'You never know. She really loved you. Maybe this guy's just a rebound.'

'I can only do that when I trust myself not to do it again,' Davey says. 'That's why AA's helping. You sort of look over everything you've done and work out why, so that you can clear the decks.'

'Couldn't you have gone to therapy for that?'

'But I had a drinking problem, Rebecca.'

41

Damn. I thought I was getting close. I bite my lip and finish off my wine.

'Anyway, that's not really why I asked you to come along to the meeting, to talk about me,' Davey says. 'I wanted you to see how good AA is, how well it works, because I think you're addicted to Patrick the way I was addicted to alcohol, and I was hoping that the AA programme, the Twelve Steps, might be something you could use to get over that.'

'I am *not* addicted to Patrick!' I say firmly. 'I am *grieving*. That's *completely different*.'

Davey looks as if he's about to contradict me. I glare at him. There's a long pause.

'OK,' he says finally. 'Whatever you say.'

I get home at ten. New York is five hours behind us, so that makes it five pm over there. Patrick won't be home from work for a couple of hours at least, so I can ring his answering machine with impunity.

I'm always nervous dialling the number. I'm scared of him picking up – not because he might think it was me, but because hearing him live, miraculously connected to me across thousands of miles of dark cold sea, would be such a terrible temptation. Several times I've rung for the sweet, illicit pleasure of hearing his recorded voice, but been taken aback by hearing him say 'Hello?' instead. And then it's so hard not to say, 'Patrick, it's me, Rebecca, do you still love me? I miss you so much . . .' Instead I just hit some keys at random on the phone to make it sound like it was a bad connection or a malfunctioning fax machine, and then hang up, my heart pounding.

Tonight I get the machine. Once isn't enough. I ring back again, but manage to limit myself to just that one more time. Then I play back the last eight messages I have from him on my own answering machine. Four from when things were still OK. These all start: 'Hi, darling, it's me', and are generally apologies for not having rung sooner. Still, they all end with: 'I love

42

you'. I taught him how to say that. Painfully. The other four are the ones he left after that last awful visit to New York, when we were on the rocks and he didn't feel confident or right saying 'It's me' any longer, and had to start with 'Hi, Rebecca, it's Patrick' instead. His voice sounds bruised, as if I had been pummelling his Adam's apple, and he finishes off by saying 'I do love you', low and drained, not sure whether I will believe him.

I can't bring myself to erase those messages. I have to be able to hear him telling me he loves me, even if it was over five months ago.

But I'm under control. I can stop any time I want to.

By one in the morning Will was so drunk he'd fallen off his chair twice and Lucy needed help getting him to the minicab office. She and Patrick lugged him out of the door. It was lucky Patrick was so strong; Will must have weighed about eighteen stone and by this stage he was pretty much a dead weight. Patrick came back ten minutes later looking exhausted, and flopped down in his chair.

'One for the road?' he said.

'Sure.'

After midnight Patrick had joined Will on the whisky shots. I hadn't really noticed how much they'd been drinking, but now I looked at the table and saw that it was jammed with empty glasses. It was hard to believe that six of us had drunk all that, even considering Will's legendary capacity.

'Maybe we've had enough,' I said doubtfully.

'Nah, one for the road,' Patrick insisted, standing up. 'You two want anything?'

Davey and Jenna looked at each other and shook their heads, giggling. They were so sweet. 'We should get going too,' Davey said.

'Let's wait for them to finish,' Jenna said, kissing his ear. 'There's no hurry, is there?'

Patrick came back from the bar with a gin and tonic for

43

me and a glass of whisky for himself, which he drank down almost in one gulp.

'Way to go, Patrick!' Jenna said, clapping her hands.

I polished off my drink too, though more slowly, and we all stood up and rummaged for our coats. I was feeling pretty drunk by this time; my head was spinning and the floor was swaying gently beneath my feet. Still, everyone here was in the same condition, or worse. And Patrick would take care of me. Patrick always looked after me when I was a little tipsy.

We kissed goodnight outside the pub: lots of hugs and Happy New Year's and I'm-so-glad-we-did-this-what-fun-and-how-nice-to-be-able-just-to-walk-home's – before Davey and Jenna finally headed off. I turned to take Patrick's arm, but it wasn't there. It was on the ground, with the rest of Patrick. The snow was so thick that he hadn't hurt himself, and he was still conscious and deeply embarrassed by his fall. He hauled himself up, saying 'Sorry . . . sorry . . .' and I realised that Patrick was very drunk indeed, more drunk than I had ever seen him before.

I am lucky in that I tend to sober up fast if I need to take care of someone else. The cold air was helping me too, though it seemed to have knocked Patrick out. I got an arm around his back and braced him as we started to walk down the street. He kept saying 'Sorry . . . sorry . . . bloody snow . . . sorry, darling . . .' and then he fell down again at the next corner. Thank God for the snow. It cushioned him to some degree. I don't know what I would have done if it hadn't been there; I would have been too scared to keep going, because he might have hurt himself badly when he fell. He grabbed on to the iron railings of the house beside us and managed to get himself up on his feet again. He didn't want my arm to steady him, but that was no surprise to me. Patrick equated being helped with anything, no matter how small, with failure. He even looked uneasy when I helped him make the bed.

I got him across the street, thanking my lucky stars that the snow meant that there was even less traffic on the roads than there usually was on New Year's Eve. Still, I was already counting off in my head the distance between here and his flat. Two streets straight, three left, two right. I thought we could do it. But Patrick was moving slower and slower; each step was clearly an effort for him, and increasingly I was taking more of his weight. My arm was beginning to hurt, the socket of my shoulder was wrenched by the awkward angle. Despite the cold, I was sweating with the effort of holding him up. We made it to the left turn and started to cross the road when I felt him slipping. I grabbed at his coat, but too late; he was falling and I wasn't strong enough to catch him. He went down as if his legs were jelly, crumpling over them, landing on his hands and knees. There were no cars coming, but I was terrified. I bent over and tried to pull him up, but he wouldn't budge.

'Patrick!' I yelled. 'Patrick, get up!'

I wondered if I should slap him to try to sober him up, but I knew how angry that would make him. 'Patrick, please . . .' I knelt down next to him. 'You're in the middle of the road, you're scaring me, please, please *get up . . .'*

It felt like for ever before he reacted, and that was only to shake his head. I thought he was refusing, and I started to cry, but then I realised that he'd been trying to clear his foggy brain. He clambered unsteadily to his feet, helped by me as best I could, and we staggered off again. Every step was an achievement. I was concentrating on the next, and the next, refusing to think how far we had to go and how many times we would need to cross the street. We didn't see a single car, and we were only two streets away from his home when he tumbled over again, putting out his hand to steady himself on a lamp-post, missing, and sliding down it to sit with a bump in a pile of snow.

I was calmer now. We were so close to home. I was sure I

could get him up again. I bent over, saying, 'Sweetie? We're nearly there, OK? Nearly there. Just hang on. Take a breath and then I'll get you up again and we'll be home before you know it.'

He was fumbling in his pocket, muttering to himself. Finally he produced his keys, which he held out to me. I took them, thinking he was just making sure that I would be able to let us in.

'Go,' he said. 'Go, it's cold, you shouldn't have to look after me ... I'll be fine ... just go and get into the warm ...'

He was slurring his words but his grammar was intact. Typical Patrick. 'No, I'm not going to leave you,' I said, 'don't be silly ...'

'GO!' he said loudly. 'Too cold ... I'll be fine ... see you soon ... too cold for you ...'

It was so silly and poignant and typically Patrick, as if he were Captain Oates walking out into the blizzard to die. I kept expecting him to add, 'Save yourself!'

'No,' I said again. 'I'm not leaving you here. Come on, it's only a short walk now.'

He fought me for a good five minutes, the stubborn bastard. But he was too drunk to stop me overruling him — which had never happened before, and would never do so again — and I managed to haul him up once more and get him moving. I don't remember much about that last stretch, but I know it was bad. I burst into tears when we were finally inside the flat. Thank God Patrick lived on the ground floor and there weren't any stairs to climb. He staggered into the living room under his own steam, and collapsed on the sofa. I saw him leaning forward ominously and went to the kitchen to get a bowl, but by the time I'd found a big one it was too late. By then my patience was exhausted. I wasn't bloody cleaning that up. I went through into the bedroom, stripped off my clothes, took some aspirin and got between his clean flannelette sheets. 'Happy New Year', I thought *viciously. 'Happy bloody New Year'. My worry for him had dissipated into cold hard anger and I passed out with my teeth clenched tight.*

The next morning Patrick was apologetic, contrite, and very understanding as I cried on his shoulder and told him how much he'd scared me. He promised it would never happen again, and he meant it. But it's odd, when I look back, that I focused on his extreme drunkenness as the object of concern, rather than trying to discover the reason for it. I was so wilfully blind almost all the time Patrick and I were together. I deliberately overlooked things I should never have ignored. I kept hoping that if I closed my eyes all the things I didn't want to see would magically dissolve away. And one of those things, of course, was that Patrick had had to get monumentally, extraordinarily, atypically drunk to cope with the fact that, for the first time in his life, he had told a girl that he loved her.

Chapter Four

Finn and Barney are fighting again. I can tell as soon as I walk into the office. We're basically a happy little bunch, and any residual tension can usually be dispersed by a bruising game of table football, punctuated by plenty of foul curses to let off steam. The one exception to this rule is Finn and Barney's fraught sibling relationship. Davey sometimes calls them Cain and Abel when things are particularly bad, and no one's ever accused him of exaggerating.

Finn and Barney are very posh indeed. They share a double-barrelled surname which is impenetrably hard to pronounce, their parents have a gigantic ancestral manor house in Somerset full of inbred golden labradors, and all their friends have those unbelievably stupid nicknames that really posh people give each other from birth. Finn and Barney have them too – Finn is Plug, and Barney is Beetle. Neither of them admit to knowing why they got landed with those particular nicknames – either that, or they're just not telling. I think they have some sort of mutual destruction pact going. I have now become completely used to answering the phone to a cut-glass accent saying:

'I say, is Plug there? Tell him it's Wobbly calling.'

Barney doesn't mind at all, but Finn hates it. Finn is doing the best he can to live down his background: he lives in Notting Hill, wears trendy black sweaters and even trendier grey mole-skin trousers, rides a Vespa to work and has Londonified his accent somewhat. Barney disdains Finn's attempts to make himself over: he says you can take the boy out of SW1 but you can't take SW1 out of the boy. Barney lives in Chelsea, wears stripy shirts with cufflinks, dates blonde gigglers called Tuppy and Wiggles, and sounds like the Sandhurst graduate that he is. When he's being particularly bossy we call him Major Barney.

In a way it's surprising that the two of them get on as well as they do – most of the time. When I was first hired by WebMasters, I thought that Finn and Barney had their relationship perfectly worked out. Finn was the younger arty one, Barney the business brain. Finn was fun and wacky and Barney was sober and cautious. But the more I got to know them, the more I saw how their characters actually elided into one another, their surface differences much less pronounced than their underlying similarities. Maybe they make such an effort to seem unlike one another because they're all too aware of how much they have in common and thus needed, from an early age, to establish themselves as distinct, discrete personalities. If you stripped away Finn's trendy haircut and silver identity necklace, or Barney's smart suits, you would see how much the brothers looked like one another. Barney might actually have the edge in the handsomeness stakes: his nose is straighter, his eyes a brighter blue, his hair a streaky gold compared to Finn's faded dirty blond. If you didn't see them side by side you'd think they were identical. It's only when they are together than you can notice the subtle differences between them. Barney's an inch taller, too, which Finn hates.

Today the atmosphere is heavy with tension. It hangs in the air like thick New York summer humidity, palpable and oppressing. I sigh. If we're lucky, the boys will have a blow-up and the clouds will pass. Sometimes they engage in a violent game of table football, cursing, spinning the handles, rocking the table back and forth till they've blown off their head of steam and they're best friends again. Sometimes, however, it lasts for days; they sulk and refuse to talk to each other, like kids fighting in kindergarten, making the office a misery for everyone else until, miraculously, something shifts in their power balance and they're laughing and shouting insults at each other and generally behaving once more as though they were twins. I exchange glances with Davey as I sit down at my desk. He rolls his eyes. I haven't seen much of Davey since the AA meeting a few nights ago; it's been a bit uncomfortable for both of us. But on the Finn/Barney nexus we are united. There's always a silver lining. At least Finn and Barney's latest scrap will give Davey and me a neutral ground on which to meet, like warring parents brought together by mutual exasperation at their kids' latest piece of bad behaviour.

I go over to the state-of-the-art espresso machine and load in some coffee. Finn and Barney spoil us rotten. It's one reason why I would never think of leaving WebMasters, unless the Falkland-Smythe brothers start attacking each other with machetes on a regular basis. The perks here are top-class. Fab coffee machine. The best filtered water. An open-plan office with shiny wood floors, huge windows and high ceilings. No clock-watching; although we all put in long hours, we can set our own schedules – as long as our work's up to scratch we can come in and leave when we want to. The kind of relaxed atmos-phere that means we can swear horribly, play pool, or hang out on the buttery-soft leather armchairs in reception, catching up on the latest trade mags, without the bosses ever shooting us disapproving looks. When Barney interviewed me he said bluffly that at WebMasters they 'worked hard and played hard', and, unlike most bosses, he actually meant it.

Stewart, one of the other designers, comes over and extracts a new carton of milk from the fridge. Under cover of the loud alt-country music that's blaring from the speakers, he says, 'Boys, play nicely. Little birds in their nests agree.'

I snatch a glance over to Finn's desk. I can't see Barney from here – as befits the business manager, he's tucked away at the back of the loft, behind a pillar, to have a little peace and quiet from the often-raucous outbursts of the designers – but Finn's face says it all.

'*Very* Mr Rochester,' I comment.

'Poor Finn, he should have been born a brunette,' Stewart

says. 'At times like these he gets *so* pissed off that he isn't dark and brooding.'

Stewart isn't gay. He just has a tendency to talk like he is. Ironically, the couple of times I've seen Stewart with women he fancies, he drops his normal way of speaking and comes across as being so butch – doubtless to compensate – that he freaks them out. They can't run away fast enough. I have been trying to think of a way to tell him about what he's doing wrong without mortally offending him.

'Blonds don't brood properly,' I agree.

'Nah. They just look sulky. Not half as menacing.'

'What is it this time?'

'Dunno.' Stewart runs his hand over the top of his head, making his short gelled hair stick up even more. Stewart will be very handsome in five years' time, when he hits thirty. Right now his fine bone structure and baby-smooth skin make him seem even younger than he is. Which is probably another reason for his super-macho act with the ladies.

'Barney was in at the crack of dawn, seeming fine,' he continues, 'and then baby bro came in looking like the wrath of God and the dark hand of gloom descended on our happy band. They haven't said a word to each other yet and I know they've got to have a talk about the Shelby account. She's coming in this afternoon.'

'Oh, that'll be OK. She's got a thing for Finn. As long as he flirts with her a bit she won't notice if he and Barney are on the outs.'

'*Right*,' Stewart says. 'Finn's in *such* a flirty mood right now. No problems there, then.'

'Eek.' I shoot another glance at Finn. His forehead is so creased his hairline is practically blending into his eyebrows.

'Rise above it,' Stewart says with a shrug as my espresso comes bubbling out into the cup like liquid black gold. 'Oh, we're out of cinnamon again.' He shakes the cinnamon dispenser in my face.

'You boys and your girlie drinks,' I say. 'Is it my turn to stock up?'

'It was your turn two weeks ago, madam.'

I have a rule about not turning into the office wife, making sure that the men have milk and expensive biscuits and cinnamon and cocoa for their poncey cappuccino dusting. When I took the job here Barney told me that there wasn't an office manager – the politically correct way of saying 'secretary' nowadays – as we didn't really need one; we all answer the phones and make coffee for visiting clients, while the cleaning lady sorts out supplies of loo paper and soap. Fair enough, but I was well aware that as the lone girl in the office, the housewifely tasks would devolve on to me at the speed of light unless I made it clear from the start that I wasn't tying on the metaphorical apron. Barney, being a relatively unevolved Sloane male, did evince a certain wistfulness in the early days that I wasn't magically making sure that his special chocolate almond wafers were always available in what he calls the 'tuck cupboard', but he soon settled down when it became clear that I was pulling my own weight as a web designer, which, after all, was the job I was hired to do. After his heavy hints fell on stony ground, he gave up and the office settled back into the rota system which had functioned perfectly well before my arrival: people chalked up their requirements on the big blackboard and nagged at the rota person until they eventually raided petty cash and went off to the posh deli. I am always careful to be the slackest of all in this department so nobody thinks they can rely on me.

Still, it's clearly time for me to pull my weight. I make a point at lunchtime of copying down the blackboard list onto a Post-it note and removing two twenties from the petty cash box.

'Make sure you get a receipt,' I mouth to Stewart, two seconds before Barney called across the office, 'Make sure you get a receipt, Rebecca!'

'Yessir, Major Barney sir,' I call back, saluting.

Finn's out somewhere, probably in the pub having a solitary

lunch and brooding about his brother's latest iniquity, so he isn't around to be cheered up by this. Shame. The Major Barney line can always be relied on to bring a smile to Finn's face, and God knows he could do with one today.

I'm crossing Clerkenwell Green on my way back from the deli, a bag filled with cinnamon, chocolate almond wafers and various other pricey goodies swinging from my hand, the receipt – thank you, 'Major Barney' for the unnecessary reminder – stuffed in my trouser pocket, when I spot Finn. He's sitting on one of the benches, smoking a cigarette, and looking as close to a character from a Dostoevsky novel as is possible when you're wearing a silver identity necklace and a leather biker jacket with red stripes down the sleeves. Maybe this was how a costume designer would dress one of the brothers Karamazov for a twenty-first-century adaptation. I am just about to alter my course and try to sneak around him unobserved – I really don't want to be drawn into whatever's the latest trouble between him and Barney; God knows my own problems are currently absorbing all of my attention – when he looks up, spots me and waves, a long train of built-up ash dribbling from his cigarette to the bench in a rather poignant trail of powdery grey detritus. I have no choice but to keep walking towards him.

'Got any biscuits?' he says. 'I haven't had lunch.'

I hold out the bag. He rummages in it and extracts, out of all the different biscuits he could have chosen, his brother's favourite chocolate almond wafers.

'Great,' he says, ripping open the packet.

'You don't even *like* those, Finn,' I say.

He shrugs. 'Barney does,' he says childishly.

'Oh well, then, feel free. Gobble away at something you don't even want just to deprive your brother.'

'That's just what our mother would say,' Finn comments nastily through a gritty mouthful of almond crumbs.

This strikes me on the raw, because as the words popped out

of my mouth I was indeed conscious of sounding exactly like a nagging mum. And just as I swore, when I joined WebMasters, not to turn into the office wife, I also made a resolution not to be office mummy either. I didn't want all the boys running to me for a bit of motherly patting on the head whenever they stubbed their toes on the furniture.

'Well, I'm not your fucking mummy, and I'm still saying it. Which means that you're behaving exactly like a spoilt brat,' I snap.

'*Whoah!*' Finn's head jerks back. He dabs at his chin, which has some crumbs on it. 'I'm *not* being a spoilt brat,' he says defensively. 'Barney's the spoilt one. He's always got to have everything he wants. Pronto.'

'On the double,' I say, echoing one of Barney's most over-used phrases.

Our eyes meet, and we can't help laughing.

'I'm sorry,' Finn says. 'I know I'm being a bloody nuisance. He just really pisses me off sometimes.'

'Understatement of the week. What is it this time?'

I wish I hadn't asked. I don't want to get over-involved in the Finn and Barney spats. Finn, to his credit, mutters, 'Never mind. It's not your problem.'

He reaches for another biscuit, hesitates, then holds out his hand for the bag instead. I give it to him, and sit down on the bench while he examines the contents. Finally, he removes a packet of shortbread. He puts the chocolate almond wafers back in the bag and opens the shortbread, clearly making a point to me. I say, 'I'm not the office policewoman, you know. It's nothing to me if you eat all of Barney's biscuits.'

'No, but when you get back, he'll ask you for them, and if the box is half empty he'll ask you why, and that would be like making you snitch on me.'

I'd thought all this out for myself already, but I'm impressed at Finn's sensitivity. Under all the bluster and childish posturing, he isn't a bad sort. But then, you could say that about most men.

'He can be such a cunt,' he says moodily, attacking a short-bread finger. 'And our parents always take his side. Barney Knows Best.' He capitalises the last three words with a derisory inflection. 'Want one?' He holds out the box to me.

'No thanks,' I say wistfully.

'On a diet?'

'I'm a woman, aren't I?'

'You girls,' Finn says caustically. 'Always counting calories. It's a bloody bore. I'd really love just once to take a girl out to dinner and have her order extra potatoes.'

'Right,' I say, 'and I expect you take a lot of fat girls out to dinner, do you?'

'What?' Finn looks baffled.

'Typical man,' I say bitterly. 'You complain about girls dieting, but you want to date perfect size tens who don't have any tummies.'

'I don't know what you're getting arsey about,' Finn says, looking at me. 'You're not fat.'

'Thanks very much.'

'No, you know what I mean. You've got a great body.'

I can't help feeling complimented by this, even though I'm cross with him. 'That's because I don't eat shortbread fingers and I work out loads, and I never order extra potatoes,' I retort.

'I work out too,' Finn says. 'I go to the gym.'

'That's the difference between us. You can still eat shortbread fingers. But I could do yoga every day and I'd still need to watch what I eat.'

There's a relief in talking about this with a man I'm not attracted to. You can be so much franker than you are with a potential boyfriend, with whom you have to pretend that no, you're not watching your weight, you just don't feel like chocolate cake today. It's only after six months of dating a man that I feel comfortable letting down my guard and allowing him to see all the little tricks I use to make sure that I don't blow up to the size of a house.

'Yoga?' Finn laughs. 'No wonder you have to be careful what you eat.'

'I used to run four times a week and I still couldn't eat what I wanted,' I say crossly. 'Girls just have slower metabolisms. Anyway, yoga's a great exercise. You ought to try it. All the male teachers at the centre I go to have amazing bodies.'

Finn sniffs, being the old-fashioned kind of unreconstructed male who doubtless thinks that all male yoga teachers are mauve-wearing, same-sex dating muesli eaters.

'You should try it,' I add. 'It might calm you down a bit. God knows you need it.'

'I *am* calm,' Finn says, lighting another cigarette and dragging on it as hard as if he's imagining sucking the marrow from his brother's bones.

I look at my watch. 'I need to get back to the office.'

I don't really: I could sit and eat my egg salad (no carbs, fat-free mayonnaise) here with Finn, but he's getting on my nerves.

'Are you coming?' I ask, standing up.

'Nah. I've got a couple more smokes to go before I can get my head round sitting in that office with Barney again. And then I've got that Shelby woman coming in, and she always expects me to shower her with compliments. I need to build up my strength with nicotine.'

'You should ask her out to dinner,' I say meanly. 'She could do with ordering extra potatoes.'

'Do you mind?' Finn looks horrified. 'That bag of bones! Anyway, I'm off women,' he adds, lapsing back into his previous state of gloom. 'Stupid trollops, the lot of them.'

I don't say anything. I just look at him.

'Sorry, Rebecca,' he says, when he realises. 'I don't count you – I mean, you're a mate . . . oh, fuck it! Sorry.'

Someone has clearly just dumped Finn. I don't blame her. As I walk back to the office I even find myself sympathising with his older brother – which is not an emotion I recall ever having felt before in relation to Barney – for having to deal with Finn.

56

Barney is super-polite all the rest of the day, even refraining from cross-questioning me as to why his precious box of Almond Galettes is two biscuits short of a packet. That's how Barney deals with his spats with Finn: he turns up the courteous meter several notches, as if compensating for Finn's bad attitude. It may not be completely genuine – I'm aware this is how siblings work, trying to score points at each other's expense – but it's much nicer to live with than Finn's juvenile broodings. It occurs to me for the first time that Finn's nickname might well be Plug because he needs his mouth blocked up on a regular basis.

I saw Patrick again, shopping in the supermarket. I rounded the corner of the aisle and there he was, with his back to me. He was talking to a girl and I wanted to kill her. I still wanted to kill her even when I realised that he wasn't Patrick. He put his arm around her and she reached up to smooth back a stray lock of his hair. I wanted to be doing that. I wanted to take off the elastic band around his ponytail and slide my fingers through his hair, touch the nape of his neck, draw his hair back, slip the band over it again, wind it around the thick hank of hair, fastening it away again. Patrick's loose hair signifies abandon to me, and to him too, I think. I used to pull it out of his ponytail when we were making love. I have so many memories of him running his hands through it to pull it back, reaching for the elastic band, fastening away his private face, composing himself for the day ahead, becoming remote, beyond my reach, no longer my lover. When we were making love he was all mine, every single fibre of his body was mine. And then he would leave me every morning, in body, but also in spirit. Being with Patrick was an endless series of little losses. I would keep recapturing him only to lose him again.

I would have stalked that guy in the supermarket if he hadn't been with his girlfriend.

Chapter Five

I've never seen such an obvious example of the class system in a club before. The bar is a huge square of pale stone, the counter so wide and high that the peons have to reach up uncomfortably and hand their money across it, bobbing their heads to catch the attention of the bar staff. But in the VIP area, which is a raised dais on one side of the square, that equation is reversed. The bar is at knee level, and you look down on the bar staff in what seems to you their pit below, negligently tossing them money for your drinks like alms to the poor. I'm slightly embarrassed by this, since I am privileged enough to be in the VIP section, with the peasants three feet below me, staring up and asking each other what I've done to merit entry.

Daisy doesn't share my scruples. She's sipping her free drink and beaming with that gigantic, light-up-a-room smile that makes every man she meets fall instantly in lust with her. It doesn't hurt that Daisy is tall, blonde, naturally slim, has eyes the colour of jonquils, and dresses in the kind of fashionable top that's always falling off at least one of her slim shoulders. I love Daisy very much; she's one of my best friends; but I do frequently question my sanity for hanging out with her in public on a regular basis. Any girl next to Daisy automatically becomes her sidekick, the one men talk to in the hopes of getting to Daisy, though Daisy herself never realises this. She is such a nice person that she thinks all her friends are just as pretty as she is and she hasn't yet figured out that most men want to go out with her just because of the way she looks. It means, sadly, that she gets her heart broken on a regular basis, and tonight doesn't seem like it's going to be an exception.

'Isn't he *gorgeous*!' she's saying, making big blue googly eyes at the reason we're here, up on the VIP dais, receiving an endless supply of complimentary drinks.

I look over at the current Daisy crush. Gorgeous isn't the word for it. The crush is tall, dark, blindingly handsome, and as far as I can see – which, since his clothes don't leave much to the imagination, is quite far – in mint physical condition. Clad in a dark blue silk sweater and tight stripy trousers, he might have just stepped from the pages of *Uomo Vogue*. He's called Lewis and he works for some PR company which tonight is promoting the latest trendy white rum, which means that we are drinking mojitos in such quantity that tomorrow you won't be able to buy fresh mint anywhere in London for love nor money.

'He's really cute,' I say. 'How did you meet him?'

'At a party two nights ago. I was covering it for the *Herald*.'

Daisy works for a London-based newspaper's daily diary column. Her job is to go to parties and write about the latest trend: which cocktail we should be drinking this season, which celebrities are knocking it back while flirting madly with each other, etc. etc. It sounds like a lot of fun, but I would be dead in a week if I tried to keep up with Daisy. She has a seemingly infinite supply of energy, but more importantly she has an extraordinary optimism which has so far been untainted by having to attend three to four parties a night, be chatted up by a considerable amount of sleazy publicity whores, and date men who want her on their arm as a trophy but who are rarely interested in hearing anything she has to say for herself. The men Daisy goes out with tend to prefer her to open her mouth for one specific purpose. I sound cynical, I know, but I'm very protective of Daisy. This charmer tonight seems attentive enough, but he's too good-looking, in my opinion, to be concerned with anyone but himself.

'He came up to me and started talking and then invited me to the party tonight and said I could bring anyone I wanted,'

Daisy is saying. 'And he said not to worry about writing it up if I didn't want to, just to have a good time. Wasn't that nice?'

My nasty little sceptical mind is telling me that this is exactly what a smooth operator would say to ensure that Daisy does indeed cover his launch for the *Evening Herald*. After all, if he really wanted to see her again he could just have asked her out to dinner.

'But you're going to write about it, aren't you?' I ask.

'Of course! It was so nice of him to ask me! And there's loads of celebs here.'

There you go.

'Daisy!'

The latest crush comes up to us. His teeth are so white that they glow in the semi-gloom, and his pecs are thrusting proudly through his silk sweater, standing out in 3-D so impressively that to appreciate the full effect we should be wearing those coloured glasses they used to give you in cinemas. He gives Daisy a big hug and she melts into his embrace.

'I'm so glad you could make it!' he says enthusiastically. 'Did you get in OK?'

'Yes, fine. Thanks so much for asking me.' She indicates me. 'This is my friend Rebecca.'

'Lovely to meet you,' the crush says, giving my hand a manly shake. But his eyes go straight back to Daisy. I can't blame him.

'There's someone I wanted you to meet . . .' he starts. 'Oh, here he is. Liam! Liam, over here!' He snags a man by the shoulder and pulls him through the crowd of people to the recess in which Daisy and I are standing. I realise that the man is Liam O'Connell, the very famous TV chef, and despite myself I am impressed. Liam O'Connell isn't as good-looking as he seems on screen – he's shorter, and his features are less well-proportioned than the camera makes them seem – but he's brimming with charisma and cockiness and if anything, is sexier in person than he is on TV. I have a secret rush of excitement at meeting one of the most famous TV stars in the country.

This is going to be a good story to tell the boys at work. They all think Liam is deeply cool, mostly because of his bad-boy reputation.

'This is Daisy,' says the crush. 'She writes for the *Evening Herald*.'

'All right, darling!' Liam says to Daisy, ogling her as if she were a cream puff in a patisserie window. 'God, Lewis, where do you keep finding these gorgeous birds!'

He practically snogs Daisy. She has to bend over to kiss him – Daisy's nearly six foot in high heels – but he doesn't seem a whit embarrassed by his comparative lack of height.

'This is my friend Rebecca,' Daisy says, blushing at Liam's obvious enthusiasm for her physical assets.

'Rebecca! Nice to meet you! Bloody hell, she's a bit of all right too, isn't she!'

Liam enfolds me in a tight embrace. Though he's a little sweaty, but it's all part of his sexy charm. He has clasped one hand behind my neck and is kissing me on the mouth. This man is positively charged with pheromones. You could bottle his sweat and sell it as an aphrodisiac. He's bouncing on his feet with an excess of energy.

'Great party, eh?' he says, when he finally lets me go.

'Yeah, excellent,' Daisy says.

'A bit crowded,' I volunteer, not wanting to seem too pathetically willing to concur with anything a top celebrity says. Besides, it's true.

'Oh, I love that! It means I can bump and grind against all the hot chicks and pretend it's just 'cos it's so rammed in here!' says Liam, and to my utter astonishment he swivels behind me, grabs my waist, and starts frottage-ing himself against my bum.

From anyone else, this behaviour would be so offensive that I would be reaching my arm up to chuck my drink all over his cheeky head. But somehow, from Liam O'Connell, it's strangely unobjectionable. I've seen him doing this to various unsuspecting women on TV, and their reaction was exactly the same as the one I'm experiencing now: absolute shock, shortly followed by an uncontrollable urge to giggle. There's something utterly pure about Liam's sex drive. Like a bawdy seaside postcard, it's all in the spirit of good honest fun, based on the assumption that the woman he's grinding himself against is deriving as much silly enjoyment from it as he is. I don't even mind that he's got his palms firmly around my hips, although with practically any other man this would have me wiggling away at the speed of light to prevent him from feeling my love handles.

I don't know quite what to do, apart from laugh. Grinding back seems a bit too much. I just stand there and sip my drink as best I can with the assault on my rear end shaking me up, and finally Liam stops, plants a smacking kiss on the back of my neck and says: 'That was great for me. Bit quick for you, though, babe? I'll take it slower next time round, I promise.'

'Do you mind if I describe you in print as incorrigible, Mr O'Connell?' Daisy says, faux-primly.

'You can describe me as anything you want, gorgeous. As long as you don't say that I only lasted fifteen seconds with your mate,' Liam responds.

'Incorrigible it is, then,' Daisy says.

'Liam's one of our top clients,' says the crush. 'He's a bloody nuisance. We keep trying to sack him, but he won't take the hint.'

'I can't leave my lovely Juliet, that's why,' Liam sighs. 'God, I love that woman. Is she here, Lewis?'

'Over there.' Lewis points to a spot deep in the belly of the crowd.

'Jules! My lovely Jules! Excuse me, ladies, I've got a hot date to snog a redhead,' Liam says, grabbing our hands with both of his, kissing each of them theatrically, and then disappearing in the direction Lewis indicated.

'I have to do some circulating.' Lewis says this to both of us, but he's clearly addressing Daisy. He strokes her bare shoulder. 'You're not heading off any time soon, are you? We've got a couple of jugglers in twenty minutes doing tricks on the bar with Ruger Rum bottles. You don't want to miss that.'

'No, no, I'll be around,' Daisy says eagerly.

'Good. Catch you later, then.'

He weaves his way back through the crowd, Daisy staring after him worshipfully. 'Isn't he *lovely*?' she breathes.

'Yeah. A bit smooth for me though.'

'Oh, just because you like them a bit rougher round the edges . . .'

Someone else comes up at that moment to greet Daisy – a fellow journo, I think.

'Rebecca, this is Jamie,' Daisy says, introducing him.

'Hi, Jamie,' I say dutifully.

'Hi, nice to meet you!' Jamie yells over the noise, pumping my hand.

Jamie seems pleasant enough, but I don't feel like talking, so I just mime that I can barely hear him, give him a smile, and peel myself out of the conversation. I am trying to remember whether I set the video for *Law & Order* tonight. It's an American import shown on Channel 5, a series I became addicted to in New York during that last fortnight that I spent with Patrick, where everything was falling apart entropically.

Entropy: the inexorable and steady deterioration of a system or society. Its antonyms are order and tranquillity. No wonder I was so attracted to a show called *Law & Order*, on which you hardly ever find out any major details about the lives of the investigators, and whenever anyone starts an episode in a seemingly happy relationship they inevitably end up with their lives in tatters and the discovery that their nearest and dearest has been cheating on them with their best friend, or has hired a hit man to put a bullet through their brain. I swear to God that show kept me sane when everything else around me was falling apart.

A harassed waitress comes by with yet another tray of drinks and I snag one gratefully. It's in a long glass, a white spume frothed into tall peaks, like a Mr Whippy ice cream or egg whites whipped into meringue.

'Frozen daiquiris!' Lewis says, reappearing beside us. 'We hired a machine specially! The club thought it would be really tacky, but we talked them into it and now they think they want to buy it, which is a bit disappointing, because we were fantasising about keeping it in our office.'

The daiquiri is magical: smooth, foamy, hardly hinting at the alcohol it must contain.

'It was Juliet's idea,' Lewis continues. 'That's Liam's agent. She was on holiday with her boyfriend in New York and had these margaritas at—'

'Benny's Burritos?' I ask, hardly imagining I'll be right.

'Yeah!' Lewis looks impressed. 'How did you know?'

'I used to go there all the time when I was in New York,' I say.

'God, you must meet Juliet, she raved about that place,' he says. 'Oh, great! The jugglers are coming on!'

As the jugglers climb on to the bar, I applaud louder than anyone else. They've saved me from anyone noticing the tears pricking at my eyes. How ridiculous, how self-pitying it is that when you've lost someone, the smallest, most stupid things can trigger a wave of nostalgia and misery so powerful that you can start crying in front of a packed bunch of A- to C-list celebrities at a pretentious launch party. Patrick and I loved Benny's Burritos. I would meet him there at the bar after he finished work. For me, a frozen margarita with half a shot of raspberry syrup: for him, Dos Equis with a tequila chaser. The lighting was the pinkest I've ever seen, so flattering it would make a reanimated corpse look like a sweet sixteen-year-old. Once I was a little late and Patrick was sitting at the bar reading a Ross MacDonald, and I burst out laughing and produced another Ross MacDonald from my pocket, which I'd been reading on the subway. The barman gave us free drinks because he said we were clearly the perfect couple. Oh Patrick, you fucking moron. How could you ever have let us go?

The jugglers are standing on the section of the bar that borders the VIP area, which is appropriate: it's closest to the celebrities, so they get the best view, and raised up so that the plebs below can see them. They're tossing around bottles of rum as if they were plastic skittles. The bar staff are still serving, which I find an impressive feat of nerve, considering that glass bottles are flying back and forth above their heads. Maybe they all played lacrosse at school and are completely inured to having heavy objects hurtling above them.

The jugglers drop to their knees and throw bottles back over their heads to one another without being able to see where they're going; the crowd gasps, draws back even further, then bursts into applause. Practically everyone is staring up at the performers with wide-eyed expressions of wonder. It's lovely to watch grown, hardened, cynical media whores reduced to a state of childish delight.

I look over at Daisy and see that Lewis has his arm around her and is whispering seductively in her ear. She's giggling happily at his words, cuddling into his embrace in that way women do when they're pretending they're not, looking away from him at the jugglers to maintain her cool, but nestling her hips against his to counteract the false impression given by the direction of her gaze. Suddenly I feel very tired. I have a hard time nowadays watching happy couples, even though I have a strong instinct in this case that this happy couple will last only until nine o'clock tomorrow morning, or until Daisy's article about tonight appears in tomorrow's edition of the *Herald*. Daisy doesn't need me any more. She wanted me to come with her, partly to get me out of the house, but also partly to provide her with company until the crush showed up. Well, both of those objectives have been achieved. My work here is done. I would go home straight away, but my bladder is bursting from all the free drinks, and now's the best time to hit the toilets, when everyone else is held captive by the show.

I slip away, forging a path through the crowd, and descend the stairs to the toilets. They're extremely swanky, with a black-tile floor and those trendy granite sinks shaped like bowls, poorly designed for anything as mundane as washing your hands, but beautiful to look at. And as I thought, they're empty. All the cubicle doors are ajar.

No, I'm wrong. There is someone in here. I see movement through the open jamb of the handicapped toilet. It's Liam O'Connell. He's kneeling down in front of the loo seat; he's lowered the lid and is busily cutting up some lines of coke on its shiny black surface with a razor. His T-shirt has ridden up over his back, and his hipster trousers are pulled down further still by his kneeling position, exposing a large tattoo along the small of his back, just above his tight round buttocks. It's done in curly Gothic lettering, a word I can't read because of the sideways angle, but I can't help staring to see if I can make it out.

He looks up, sees me, and says, 'Want some coke, darling?'

For a moment, I'm tempted. Do drugs with Liam O'Connell. Have an even better story to tell the boys at work tomorrow. Knock out, for a few brief minutes or hours, any sad memories of Patrick in a chemically-induced, rushing high. Then I realise that if I do coke I may not sleep tonight, at least not till the early hours of the morning, and I shudder in horror at the thought of sitting up alone (because I'm not going back with Liam to his bachelor pad), grinding my teeth and trying to drown my over-active brain in alcohol.

'No, thanks,' I say. 'Knock yourself out, though.'

A girl tumbles through the door. Blonde, very pretty and strangely familiar, her clothes are half-draped over her long thin body in a way that suggests you could just pull on one of the silk cords dangling from her dress and the whole thing would simply fall off.

'Liam! You in here, sweetie?' she calls, her voice slurred by mojitos or daiquiris, or both.

'Come right in, gorgeous,' Liam yells.

'Who are *you*?' she asks, looking me up and down as if there's some class system for the ladies' loos and I've just crashed the VIP toilets.

'Just someone who's here to use the loo for the purpose it's actually designed for,' I snap, going into the furthest cubicle from the handicapped one.

Over the sounds of my own wee hitting the water below, I hear her and Liam sniffing deeply and then making the following comments on the experience:

'Wow, fantastic!' [her]

'Fuck, this is good stuff!' [Liam]

'Coke makes me feel *so fucking sexy*, baby!' [her].

Then they start throwing each other around the cubicle. I hear the walls shaking. As I flush the toilet and leave I see them in a state of extreme disarray through the half-open door of the handicapped toilet. I was right about her dress. I've realised now why she looks familiar; she's a DJ on Radio One. I think she does the breakfast show. She's going to need a lot of aspirin if she's on air tomorrow morning.

'Want to join us?' Liam shouts at me.

'*Liam!*' the DJ protests angrily.

'What, baby? You don't think I've got enough juice for both of you?' Liam mumbles into her Wonderbra.

I exit the toilet, fishing my mobile out of my bag. I have to send Daisy a text message. This is top-of-the-range gossip for her; even if she can't report nine-tenths of the sordid details in the paper, she can still hint at Liam O'Connell and Ms Breakfast Show getting jiggy with it. Which, by the way, has not upset me one iota. That's one couple I can watch making out without any hint of jealousy on my part. I wouldn't for a moment classify them as happy in any meaningful sense of the word.

Chapter Six

It's dark outside and a light rain is drizzling down; no, scarcely down, to be precise. I don't actually feel it falling – it's more a light mist, humidity made visible. After the hurly-burly of the club – the scent of rum, loud music and shouting, bright-eyed people – Hanover Square is as silent as the grave by comparison, dark and damp and smelling of drains. I hurry down to Oxford Street, which isn't much better. Shuttered high-windowed shops, brand-new goods gleaming behind illuminated panes of glass, poignantly inaccessible. That's just my perspective tonight, though. I'm in the kind of mood to put the worst possible interpretation on everything around me. Rain isn't merely rain: it's the state of my soul. A bus that comes an hour late is a symbol of how unimportant I am to the cosmos. And even someone as famous as Liam O'Connell flirting with me isn't flattering so much as a reminder of how alone I am, how hopelessly I want what I can't have, because I'd trade ten world-class celebrities begging me to be theirs for one phone call from Patrick telling me he can't live without me.

Depression was guaranteed to hit me at this point of the evening. That's the way it is nowadays. I start off well: dressed-up, made-up, the sparkly glitter pencil I bought in New York outlining my eyes, a glass of wine at home to get me in the party mood, big kisses for Daisy or whoever I'm meeting, a bright tone of voice. I last about an hour on average. And then reality sinks in. This is not going to be the magical evening that transforms my life. I'm just out with a girlfriend at some stupid party, surrounded by idiotic superficial people attaching much too much importance to the fact that they're in the VIP area.

I'm not going to meet a nice guy here; the men at these kind of events are only interested in girls who look like Daisy, tall blonde trophies, and I can't even have a good conversation because the music's too loud. But even if it wasn't a stupid launch party, I would be equally discontented. If I met a nice guy I wouldn't know what to do with him. I am still in love with Patrick and no man I meet could compare with him. There's really no point to my going out at all. I might as well just stay at home with my red wine and my TV thrillers, marinating in self-pity.

I decide to get a bus home rather than descend into the bowels of the Tube. The bus is slower, but I only have to get one, rather than two trains, and besides, it's bright down there in the Underground. Out here on the street the darkness is merciful. And I'm in no hurry to get home. I never am these days.

People are huddled at the bus stop, squeezed under the fibreglass shelter, commenting occasionally on the unreliability of the electronic display board which is supposed to chart the slow lurching progress of the buses down Oxford Street towards the stop. Practically everyone is texting or on the phone, as if to demonstrate to the rest of the world that though, right now, they're alone, they are still connected to the world: there are people out there who care about their precise location, who will be plunged into gloom if they don't hear from them on a regular basis. Feeling that primitive need myself, I check my phone to see if Daisy's texted me back. Of course she hasn't – she probably hasn't even noticed her phone beeping in her excitement about Lewis. The bus arrives and we all climb on; the heater's cranked up and the upholstery smells warm and damp, like a wet animal. As the bus bumps off again I lean my head against the glass, not caring that it's uncomfortable. Find me a bed of nails and I'll lie on it. I'm busy punishing myself for being so unlovable that Patrick didn't want to be with me.

It was Lewis's mention of New York that really tipped me over the edge. One of my biggest sources of anger with Patrick is that he took New York away from me. I loved that city. I loved living in it, when I visited, not as a tourist, but as a proper inhabitant. Patrick's bank had put him up in a wonderful apartment on the edges of the Village and the meat-packing district, an apartment with a doorman – the luxury! – a gym in the basement and a roof garden. I could swan around town from the security of Patrick's deeply cool apartment, feeling like a real New Yorker.

I got to know the neighbourhood in a way he couldn't, because he was working so hard at the bank. I found a good dry-cleaner for his suits, a great Thai restaurant that delivered till midnight, and a dark sexy bar that served great martinis and curly fries and was packed on the weekends with new couples making out on the black leather banquettes hidden in the crepuscular gloom of the fire-lit back room. And, of course, I also found Benny's Burritos, with its pink lighting and fantastic, pint-sized blended drinks. I walked along the river, which was just a couple of blocks from Patrick's apartment, down to the Winter Garden at the World Financial Center to watch bandbox-pretty Korean couples having their wedding photographs taken on the staircase among the giant palm trees. The brides tiny and perfect in their frothy-as-a-frozen-margarita white dresses, the grooms 1950s-smart in white satin, the exquisitely made-up bridesmaids in pale salmon-pink. I took yoga classes in the trendy New York studio where women unrolled mats with the Gucci logo in the corner and male models did handstands next to me, their tanned muscular legs gleaming with sweat. I tried to Rollerblade in Central Park and fell over so much that Patrick's colleagues looked at my bruises and joked that he was beating me up. I stayed in on rainy days and watched terrible American daytime TV, shows where hillbillies confessed to sleeping with their brothers and seducing their best friend's grandmothers, or ones where real judges who had left the bench for the Hollywood dollar judged cases where ex-best-friends accused each other of kidnapping their dog or failing to make car payments. I befriended the doormen, who recommended Cuban-Chinese restaurants in Spanish Harlem which I never ate at because Patrick was always working too hard and I didn't want to trek all the way up there on my own.

And of course, I spent each visit deep in the fantasy that I was living with Patrick now, not just on a fortnight's holiday but for the rest of our lives. I loved waking up with him every morning – well, I didn't wake up so much as grunt good morning to him as he rolled out of bed at seven-thirty, keeping one sleep-clogged eye open to catch a glimpse of him naked as he dropped his post-shower towel and put his suit on, before falling back to sleep as soon as he'd kissed me goodbye – and curling up in bed with him every night. I loved the domesticity of picking his shirts up from the dry cleaner's, keeping the apartment stocked with the bagels he toasted for breakfast, and having him cook me dinner on the rare occasions that we didn't order in. I loved wandering around the city every day knowing that evening I would be seeing him; he wouldn't be ringing me to say he was exhausted from work and was just crashing at home in front of the TV. For those two weeks he was all mine.

But it terrified him. Patrick, who'd never had a girlfriend before in any meaningful sense of the word, who'd spent his life running from the kind of close connection which, as he'd seen all too well in his own family, could cause profound pain and loss and heartbreak, knew that I wanted something from him that he didn't know how to give. I tried to make sure he had the space he needed. I'd do a yoga class in the early evening so that he came home first, rather than me. I made friends with a couple of his female work colleagues and deliberately hung out with them some evenings, much as I hated wasting one of my precious nights at home with Patrick. I did everything I could think of to make him feel at ease with the situation, but it wasn't enough.

Suddenly I think about Liam O'Connell. God knows he's a slut, but he seemed so open, so much fun. If Liam fell in love, he'd be jumping around telling the world about it, proposing in an instant. Liam would never think that all love affairs are doomed to disaster, so you should break them off as soon as you get in deep, take the pain now in order to stop yourself getting hurt even more in the future. I've seen Liam on TV, whipping up a gorgeous-looking meal from the unpromising, scuzzy contents of some hopeless bachelor's fridge, roaring with laughter while he does it, making a silk purse out of a pig's ear. It may be partially coke-fuelled and over the top, but by God, Liam seems to see the positive side to things. Someone catch you doing coke? Ask her if she wants some and suggest a three-some to her a few minutes later. No harm in asking, right?

Liam is the anti-Patrick. Patrick always expected things to end badly. And with us, he made sure they did.

I look up and realise that it's nearly my stop. When I start thinking about Patrick, time squeezes itself up or stretches out to infinity. It's like doing acid: I step into a parallel dimension where everything's elastic and the colours of my memory, or fantasy, are worlds brighter than the drabness around me. I can lose myself for what seems like hours and snap back to real life to realise that only a few minutes have gone past, or, as now, while away a forty-minute bus ride without even noticing the time flying past. I pick my way down the steps in my uncomfortable high heels and get off at the stop next to Highbury Fields. I walk across the park, feeling, as always nowadays, that I don't care if I get mugged or raped. Bring it on. What more horrors can the world inflict on me? There's a lurking sensation that I would almost welcome being attacked. I would have some real physical symptoms to explain the pain I'm feeling. And maybe Patrick would find out and fly back home to visit me in hospital and realise that he can't live without me and . . . and . . . you get the picture.

My phone beeps: a text message. I fish for it in my bag. It's Daisy. Good stuff!!! it says, referring to the gossip. I'm in love!!! Call u tomorrow!

I find myself actually hoping that Daisy will get her heart broken by the crush, so that I don't feel too alone in my doomed single state. I am a truly awful human being. But I don't think I could bear it if Daisy, too, like practically everyone else I know, was happy and settled. I need her to be out there with me in the half-world of the emotionally unattached, because if someone as gorgeous as Daisy is single, that at least means that I look less of a failure.

I would bear it, of course, if I had to. One thing I've learnt since the breakup with Patrick is that you can bear anything, even if you get so beaten down by it that you don't think you can keep going. You still get up every morning and go to work and see your friends and take a certain, half-hearted pleasure in shopping. Though I must say that living in the nineteenth century, where one could actually die of a broken heart, must have had its advantages.

I'm through Highbury Fields now. No mugging for me tonight – it's almost a disappointment. As I turn into my street, I try very hard to hope that Daisy will live happily ever after with Lewis, but I can't. I'm not that strong or nice. It was bad enough being without Patrick after he went off to New York, but at least people knew I had a boyfriend. Now I'm the sad single girl who's probably left it too late to snap up a decent man, because they're all taken. I don't know where they went. It's not like there were hundreds of nice men years ago competing for my attention while I deliberately picked out the one commitment-phobe in the bunch. Or is it?

I get into work late the next day. I didn't sleep well. But no one cares about my tardiness; there are no client meetings I need to attend today and I can just stay on till the early evening and make the time up. The atmosphere is strange today. Barney is nowhere to be seen – most unlike Barney, who's a complete workaholic (maybe Davey should do an intervention on *him*) – and Finn is brooding silently, which again is unlike Finn. His sulks and moods are typically quite theatrical; he'll kick the furniture and swear and challenge everyone to titanically-fought-out games of pool. Finn withdrawn and taciturn is something I have never seen before. Usually when Finn and Barney aren't getting along, the air in the office feels packed in so tightly that something needs to burst. Today it's heavy and sluggish, weighed down by Finn's uncharacteristic moodiness.

I exchange glances with Davey over the top of my monitor. He looks at Finn and shrugs, indicating that he has no idea what's going on. I'm quite glad in a way. In normal circumstances it would be obvious how depressed I am, but the latest Finn/Barney spat provides a welcome distraction. Nobody's going to notice how miserable I am and ask me if I'm all right; they'll just assume that I, like everyone else, am feeling ground down by the pervading gloom.

'I can't take much more of this,' Davey says at lunchtime. 'They never used to be this bad.'

'How d'you know it's the two of them?' Vijay, another of the designers, asks.

Vijay is the most recent person to be hired. He's only been here a year, and like the rest of us, he defers to Davey for readings of the Finn/Barney nexus; Davey's known them both for years. He was a scholarship boy at the posh school every male member of the Falkland-Smythe family has been attending since the dawn of time.

'It's always the two of them,' Davey says. 'If Finn's in this kind of mood, Barney's behind it.'

'I couldn't work with my brother,' Vijay says, biting into his fried-egg sandwich.

'Do you fight?' I ask, trying not to look at the egg yolk running down his chin and into his goatee.

'Nah, we get on too well. We'd never get any work done. We just behave like six-year-olds when we're together, y'know?' Vijay dunks the sandwich in a pool of ketchup and takes another bite.

His goatee is smeared with bright red gunk now, as well as the egg. It's revolting.

'So do they,' I point out, fighting the urge to hand Vijay a paper napkin.

'But they're pissed-off six-year-olds fighting over whose turn it is to be king of the sandpit,' Davey says. 'That's the difference.'

'Finn bit my head off this morning when I asked him if he wanted a coffee,' Vijay complains. 'I mean, fucking hell.'

'It'll blow over,' Davey says. 'It always does.'

'I don't care,' I say. 'It's nothing to do with me.' I know my voice comes out very flat and emotionless. Davey shoots me a concerned glance but he doesn't manage to make eye contact; my head is ducked over my plate.

'That's because you've got a desk right across the other side of the room,' Vijay says enviously. 'You've got the pool table between you and him. I'm next to him and I tell you, it's like sitting next to the black hole of Calcutta. It's really knackering.'

'Yeah, but when Finn's up he's great,' Davey says a little defensively. 'He's got the best energy ever. You just have to take the rough with the smooth.'

Vijay folds the last of his sandwich into his mouth. A last dribble of egg yolk joins the previous traces coagulating in his goatee. I practically have to sit on my hands to stop myself reaching for the napkin dispenser. I am not his mother. Even if his chin looks like the aftermath of a bloody fight in an egg factory, I am not responsible for clearing up the mess.

'Veej,' Davey says, to my great relief, 'you've got a bit of egg . . . there . . .' He points to Vijay's chin.

'Oh yeah? Thanks, mate.' Vijay takes a paper napkin and dabs it delicately at the corner of his mouth, removing a tiny smear of egg. His goatee is still as stained as ever. I watch Davey debate the options: tell Vijay to wipe his whole chin, or let him walk out of the sandwich bar and back to the office in that state. I know Davey very well. He's got that little boy sense of humour that would think it was hysterical to see how long Vijay would go without realising what a mess he's in.

'Here you are!' shouts a voice.

We swing round, recognising the posh clipped tones of Major Barney. He's standing in the doorway, shouldering it open, as his arms are full; he's carrying a big cardboard box and beaming from ear to ear.

'Finish up, chop chop, and back to the office!' he says. 'We're celebrating!' He takes a closer look at us. 'And for fuck's sake, Veej, clean yourself up. You look like a chicken gave birth on your chin.'

'What are we celebrating?' I ask, but Barney's already gone.

'New contract?' Davey suggests. 'I don't think he had a meeting this morning, though . . .'

'*Jesus*,' Vijay mutters, examining the smeary napkins he's using to wipe his chin. 'I can't believe you cunts didn't tell me I had all this crap on my face.'

'Davey thought it was funny,' I say.

'And Rebecca didn't want to tell you because she hates it when everyone calls her Mummy,' Davey adds.

We grin at each other. Things have been tense between us ever since the AA meeting; I know Davey's itching to ask me if I've taken down those photos of Patrick, and I've been avoiding him assiduously because I don't want to answer. It's nice when we have these moments that remind us of how deep our friendship goes, even if it's temporarily in an uncomfortable holding pattern.

'What was in the box?' Vijay asks, sticking his fingers in my water glass and cleaning the final traces of egg off his goatee.

'*Veej!*' I protest. 'Jesus, men are *disgusting*.'

I bitch at him all the way back to the office. There, however, it turns out that the box Barney was carrying was a case of Veuve Clicquot, already chilled, and all thoughts of water, whether drunk or used to clean off goatees, disappear from my mind. Barney's unloading the bottles and fishing out glasses from the kitchen cupboard. We only have water tumblers, but no one cares; you get a lot more champagne into a tumbler than a flute.

'Gosh, I shouldn't have got the Widow!' Barney says happily. 'Terribly bad omen!'

'What?' says Vijay blankly. 'What's all this about? Did we suddenly score a contract with IBM?'

'Gather round, everyone!' Barney says. 'I've got some really brilliant news!'

We're all in the small kitchen area, glasses brimming, ears cocked. The only holdout is Finn, who's lurking at the edge of the pool table, clearly wanting to keep a distance between himself and Barney.

'Hold on a minute,' Barney says, looking at his watch. 'We're waiting for someone . . . should be any minute now . . .'

Several sighs rise from the assembled group. A couple of people take quick swigs from their glasses while Barney's head is ducked over his wrist. It's asking too much of human nature to have us all standing here with glasses of champagne and prohibit us from dipping into them.

A loud beep comes from the intercom. Barney dashes over to buzz in the mystery guest. We all lift our glasses to our lips (apart from Davey, who's on soda water and clearly finds this less of a burning temptation).

'I mean, come *on*,' Stewart, who is standing next to me, mutters in my ear, slurping champagne. 'We've got a case of the stuff to get through, we need to get started!'

Barney is hovering near the door, his expression both nervous and exultant. I'm beginning to guess what this is about, but before I can share my inspiration with the boys and rack up points for women's intuition, a woman appears in the doorway. She's tall and slim, with a long fall of artfully-streaked chestnut hair, and she's wearing a pale-grey trouser suit, rather corporate but undeniably elegant. At her throat is a string of pearls which are obviously real – women with her sort of grooming don't wear fake – and she, too, is looking rather nervous, or as nervous as someone that poised can look.

'Darling!' Barney says, kissing her on the lips.

'I *knew* he was getting engaged!' I whisper to Stewart.

'Engaged?' Stewart says blankly. Men are such idiots.

'Everyone,' Barney says, throwing one arm around the woman's shoulders and favouring us with a huge smile, 'this is my fiancée Vanessa! I just popped the question yesterday, and I wanted you all to share the happy news with us!'

In the rush of congratulations and whooping that follows, I have time to wonder about the very odd way that Barney has chosen to make the announcement. Why at work, in the middle of the day? Was he really so desperate to share his happiness with his employees that he couldn't wait until this evening to invite us all out to the local wine bar? Then, for some reason, I turn my head and catch sight of Finn. He looks as if he's just been punched in the stomach by the current heavyweight champion of the world and is trying to pretend that it doesn't hurt.

Barney and Vanessa are still standing in the doorway, being hugged, clapped on the shoulder in best manly style (Barney) and shaken by the hand (Vanessa). Finn is trapped. I can tell he wants to flee the scene. Davey has taken in the situation as well.

'More champagne!' he says, unwrapping the foil on another bottle. 'Come on, everyone, you've got a lot to get through!'

This is the perfect distraction from the happy couple; we all flock to have our glasses refilled. Barney and Vanessa, still locked together and smiling at each other ecstatically, move over too, Vanessa caressing Barney's face. The doorway is clear. Finn makes for it. Vanessa looks over at Finn and starts to say something, but he's already exiting. I look at the small crowd around the table, and then at the empty doorway. And, surprising myself, completely negating my own rule about not being the stereotypical girl in the office who takes care of everyone's feelings, I bend down, snatch a bottle of Veuve Clicquot from the case, and sneak out to follow Finn.

Chapter Seven

Finn hasn't gone far. He's sitting on the stairs about halfway down, his head in his hands. Our office building, a converted warehouse off Old Street, has been lavishly refurbished, and the staircase is made of wide polished boards in dark wood with a reddish sheen, shiny and expensive, the walls high, white and bare. Finn, in his trendy black cargo trousers and close-fitting T-shirt, looks like a fashion photograph in this stripped-down setting – until you see the expression on his face. He looks up as I descend the steps and I can tell that he thought, from the sound of my heels on the wooden boards, that I was Vanessa coming to find him. His disappointment would be unflattering if it wasn't so poignant.

I sit down next to him and start to open the bottle. 'Sorry I'm not her,' I say, popping the cork.

'That bitch. I wouldn't give her the time of day,' he says unconvincingly, reaching for the Veuve Clicquot.

Finn has clearly drunk champagne directly from the bottle many times before; he is a posh boy, after all. He negotiates a long, deep pull at the neck without choking or sneezing from the bubbles, then he hands it over to me. I try to emulate his example, but can't do it with his nonchalant ease. That's OK, I'm happy to keep practising.

'You didn't know that Vanessa and Barney were getting married?' I ask after a while.

'I only just found out they were fucking *seeing* each other!' Finn corrects me angrily.

I raise my eyebrows. This is even worse than I thought. 'Did he know you liked her?'

'He *knew* that Vanessa and I were together for ages!' Finn explodes. 'That's what he knew!'

'Look,' I say, handing him the bottle, 'I can keep guessing and pissing you off still more, or you can tell me what's going on, or I can just roll back up there and toast the happy couple. You pick.'

Finn sighs. 'I'm sorry, Rebecca,' he says. He attempts a half-smile in my direction. It's grotesque, like watching a gargoyle try to look like it doesn't have a care in the world. I flinch. Finn takes another drink, heaves a slightly burpy sigh, and starts, 'I was going out with Vanessa for two years, OK? And we were really – well, I thought we were really – no, we *were*, we were really into each other. Then we broke up about a year ago, no, nearly two years now, and it was hard, but I always sort of thought we'd get back together. I didn't even know that she was seeing Barney till last week. I barely knew Barney was seeing *anyone*, he hardly breathed a word to me about a girlfriend. Mind you, he was always a bloody secretive bastard. But *this* – I mean, without any warning or anything – and getting *married* to her, the cunt . . . He's spent his whole life trying to beat me, he's always had to beat me, even when we were little and he was better at everything than I was. God, he really hated it when I turned out to be a good fast bowler at prep school – suddenly I wasn't just Beetle's younger brother any more, I was someone in my own right and he couldn't bear it. He used to hide the bits of my train set in different places so that I could never find them all at once and play with it properly . . .'

I cough, feeling that this monologue has drifted significantly away from the main subject under discussion. 'Finn?' I say, as he drifts to a halt, lost in contemplation of all the wrongs Barney has inflicted upon him. 'Why did you and Vanessa actually break up?'

Finn shrugs. 'The usual stupid crap,' he says.

'But—'

'Look, I don't want to talk about it, OK?'

I pause. 'And how did Barney get in touch with her after you broke up, do you think?' I ask, unable to imagine Barney doing anything quite as nefarious as going through his brother's address book to track down his ex-girlfriend.

'They're old family friends,' Finn says bitterly. 'We bump into each other all the time in the country – our parents and Vanessa's are pretty much joined at the hip. They even go on holiday together. They were so happy when Vanessa and I were going out. Bloody hell.' His voice is quavering. I sense he's on the verge of tears, and I make an elaborate show of drinking and wiping off my mouth so that he will have time to recover himself.

'I can't believe he would do this to me,' Finn says eventually.

'It's pretty bad,' I agree.

'And the *way* he did it. I mean, walking in here with her and announcing it to everyone so that I couldn't make a big fucking scene. I *know* that's why he did it in the office. Bastard. And her. She should have had the decency to tell me in private. Bastards!'

'No great loss, then,' I say hopefully.

'Bloody bitch,' Finn says. 'I'm miles better off without her. Bloody cow.'

But it's obvious that if Vanessa came down the stairs right now to tell him that she'd made a terrible mistake, Finn would fall at her feet and forgive her everything.

Frankly, I don't think Vanessa is making a terrible mistake at all. It seems reasonably clear to me, from the brief glimpse I've had of her, that she and Barney are very well-matched. They look alike; not physically, but in the way they present themselves to the world. They're smart corporate young things in their expensive business outfits, a twenty-first-century power couple. They look as if they want the same things, the same kind of life. Vanessa and Barney are a much more obvious fit

81

than Vanessa and Finn. Finn, with his deliberate eschewing of the formalities of his upbringing, his counter-culture clothes, his dropping of the posh accent – though I notice it's coming back now, under stress – seems much more suited to a trendy Portobello Road girl who does something arty, wears elaborately deconstructed mini-skirts and listens to the kind of alternative rock music Finn favours. This is the kind of girl I've seen him out with. Vanessa wears pearls non-ironically, for God's sake. How much can she and Finn really have in common?

The bottle's nearly finished. I hand it to Finn, assuming he needs the last few drops much more than I do. 'I'm really sorry, Finn,' I say.

'Yeah. Well.' There's a long painful pause. 'You should probably be getting back up there,' he says. 'Toast the happy couple.'

'No rush. There's a whole case of champagne. Even that lot won't have polished it off by now.'

Finn makes an ambiguous humphing noise. Another awkward pause ensues.

'I don't know what's the right thing to do,' he says finally.

'I don't think there *is* a right thing to do,' I say. 'I mean, I don't know what to tell you.'

'I've got to have it out with them,' he says, but without showing any sign of rising and storming back upstairs.

'Maybe later, on your own,' I say.

'Yeah. I can't face everyone right now.'

Yet another long silence. The trouble is, I don't have any words of comfort for him. It would be too soon. When I broke up with Patrick people told me that all wounds heal in time, and that I would find someone else, and this too shall pass. It just made me want to poke them in the eye with a sharp stick. I don't want to inflict any of those clichés on Finn. They don't help; they're more for the benefit of the speaker, feeling under pressure to trot out some words of wisdom, than the listener. No one ever looked at the friend who was attempting to comfort them and said: 'My God, you're right! There *are* plenty more fish in the sea! Why am I making such a big deal over this one?'

So I just sit there and wait to see if he wants to say anything else. People usually do. But the enormity of this particular situation seems to be weighing so heavily on Finn that he's slumped under it, his shoulders bent over, his head sunk into his arms, a ball of misery. I don't want to abandon him, but I feel useless without anything to say.

To my great relief, my phone starts to ring. I assume that it's Davey, checking to see where I am, but when I look at the display panel I see that it's Daisy.

'Hey!' I say.

A heaving gulp of despair issues from the phone. I make an apologetic face at Finn and get up to walk further down the stairs. There's a couple of leather chairs in the narrow lobby and I sit down on one. This is clearly going to be a saga of a phone call.

'Daisy?'

'I'm never going to see him again!' she wails.

'Daisy, are you sure? What happened?' I brace myself: I know she's talking about Lewis.

'We had such a lovely time last night . . . he was so sweet and nice and he said such lovely things to me . . . oh, Rebecca, if you could have *heard* him, honestly, he was so amazing . . . and then this morning he just said "See you around" and kissed me goodbye, and I *knew* then, I just *knew*, because he didn't ask when he could see me again or call me or anything . . .'

'Sometimes men do that,' I say encouragingly. 'I mean, they go but then they come back. It's like that rubber band thing from that dating book you were telling me about.'

'Yes, but this was so *definite*. I mean, it wasn't I-have-to-go-into-my-cave-now-but-I'll-ring-you-when-I-come-out, it was so-long-and-thanks-for-the-shag.'

'You've done this before, Daise,' I point out. 'Panicked, I mean, and then they ended up ringing after all.'

'I know, but you know when something starts well, and you know it's started well, I mean, he does all the right things and rings you the day after and kisses you goodbye properly, like he can't wait to see you again, not just a quick peck on the lips, anyway, you *know* when it's started well. And this was just – he's never going to ring me again. I *know* it.'

I check my watch.

'Daisy,' I say patiently, 'it's three in the afternoon, and he only left this morning. I mean, give him some time before you start doing your nut.'

'Yes, but I rang him to—'

'You *rang* him?'

I want to beat her around the head with my mobile phone. Doesn't she know not to ring a guy the very next day? Men *are* a bit like rubber bands: that book of Daisy's was spot-on with that analogy. They like to bounce back in their own time. You can't just ping them around whenever you get insecure. They don't like it.

'I wanted to tell him the article was definitely going in,' Daisy says in a small voice. She knows she did the wrong thing.

'Ever heard of email?' I ask. 'And anyway, Daise, the paper comes out mid-afternoon. He'd have got a copy by five and then *he* could have rung *you* to say thanks . . .' I decide to shut up now. This is emphatically not what Daisy wants to hear.

'Well, I know I shouldn't have,' she wails, 'but I did, I rang him, and he just said "Great! Thanks so much!" and then I didn't know what to say, so there was this awful pause, and I said "So! Well, that was what I was ringing about!" and he said "Yeah! Thanks!" and didn't say anything else and there was another awful pause and then I said "So, see you around then?" and he said "Sure!" and then I hung up and wanted to kill myself. I mean, that's it, isn't it? He's never going to ring me. I made a complete tit of myself.'

She starts sobbing. I can't just leave her like this. But there's Finn, halfway up the stairs like that children's song, metaphorically

84

and actually stranded in a state of extreme unhappiness.

'Daise,' I say, 'do you want me to come round? You're at home, right?' I can't imagine that she's making this phone call from the office.

'Oh, would you? *Please?* I can't face being alone right now—'

'Only the thing is, I'm with Finn—'

'Finn from work?'

'Yes, and he's having a really bad time—'

'I *need* you!' Daisy sobs.

'His brother's just announced that he's getting engaged to Finn's ex-girlfriend, who Finn's still in love with, and Finn barely knew that Barney and the ex were going out.'

Daisy's weeping stops abruptly as she takes in the enormity of the situation. '*Fuck*,' she says, her own suffering temporarily suspended in contemplation of Finn's personal tragedy.

'Yup.'

'He must be really—'

'Yup.'

'That's terrible.'

'Yup. Would it be OK if I brought him round too?'

'Misery loves company,' Daisy says, starting to sniff again.

'Great. I mean, not great, but see you in half an hour.' I hang up and go back up the stairs.

'Wait here,' I say to Finn, which is probably an unnecessary instruction. He doesn't look as if he has the will-power to even adjust his sitting position.

The office is loud with raucous laughter and the song stylings of Madonna's latest album. Davey and Vijay are deep in a game of table football; Vanessa is chatting to Stewart, Barney's arm thrown proprietorially around her shoulders; and the rest of the team are gathered round one of the computers playing a game that, from the brief glimpse I have of it as I pass, seems to involve killer nuns enveloping big green aliens in lethal fireballs.

Barney spots me as soon as I come in. 'Rebecca!' he calls. 'Where did you shoot off to?'

'I went to see how Finn was doing,' I say rather coldly.

Vanessa's pretty face contorts into a mask of concern. 'Barney,' she says, 'maybe I should—'

'I don't think so, darling,' Barney says masterfully. 'Not right now.'

'But—'

'Give him time to simmer down, eh?'

Vanessa seems unconvinced. Stewart, obviously unaware of the situation, looks, confusedly, from Barney to Vanessa to me, receiving no enlightenment from any of us. 'Where *is* Finn?' he says.

'He's taking the rest of the afternoon off,' I say, removing two bottles from the case. Half are gone already. 'Barney, see you tomorrow, OK? And congratulations.'

'Thanks,' Barney says a little uncertainly. 'Is Finn, um . . .' But he can't find an appropriate way to finish the sentence. He knows perfectly well what answer he'll get if he asks me whether Finn's OK, so he just lets the words trail off and says bluffly instead: 'Nice of you to look after Finn, Rebecca.'

'Fellow-feeling,' I say.

This isn't quite true, because Patrick didn't dump me for anyone else, but there's no point being too precise with Barney; he has no idea what's going on in any of his staff's personal lives. I scoop up my bag and coat and wave goodbye to Davey, who doesn't even notice; he's too busy trouncing Vijay. A bottle of Veuve Clicquot in each hand like twin trophies, I navigate my way around the pool table. I shoot a glance back at the happy couple. Vanessa is watching me go, her forehead furrowed; as she raises her hand to push back a stray lock of hair, I see the engagement ring on her finger, about the size of the Rock of Gibraltar but considerably more prismatic. I can't help envying her – not the marriage to Barney, of course, or even the engagement per se, but the fact that she has two men fighting over her, both apparently willing to make the arrangement permanent. I couldn't even keep one.

Finn looks up again as I come down the stairs, with the identical hoping-against-hope expression he had before, and the identical sagging of his features in disappointment when he realises I'm not Vanessa.

'Come on,' I say.

'Where are we going?'

'To get pissed with my friend Daisy.'

Finn shakes his head. 'I can't do with seeing anyone else,' he says. 'I'll just go home.'

'Come on, Finn. You can't be alone right now. You need a shoulder to cry on.' The pathetic expression on Finn's face shows the truth of this statement.

'Why do we have to go round to your mate's?' he says in a small voice, like a little boy asking why he needs to eat his greens.

'Because she just got dumped too. We're all going to cry on each other's shoulders.'

Finn cheers up a little at the news that Daisy isn't happy either. She was right. Misery does love company. 'I dunno,' he says, however. 'I'm not up to much right now.'

'None of us are. Come on.'

He hums and haws, but finally hauls himself to his feet. 'All I want to do is get pissed and pass out,' he warns me.

'Great. Then we won't have to talk to you.'

'Why are you being so nice?' he asks unexpectedly.

I shrug. 'I don't know. It's a one-time offer. You might as well make the most of it while it lasts.' I start off down the stairs, still not completely sure that he's coming until I hear his boots clattering on the treads behind me.

'You should've got three bottles,' he says. 'One each. It sounds like we're going to need 'em.'

Chapter Eight

In what turned out to be the first ever Exes Anonymous meeting, I quickly learned that there are two basic rules for success. One: impose some sort of structure, otherwise it will degenerate all too quickly into a morass of self-indulgent sobbing and recrimination, with no positive, potentially-healing outcome. Two: limit the alcohol consumption, or at least make sure that the participants haven't been drinking large quantities before the proceedings kick off.

Our inaugural meeting completely fails to follow either of these simple rules, and as a result is an unmitigated disaster. By the time we get to Daisy's, she's already been hitting the white wine and is a maudlin, sobbing wreck. The Veuve Clicquot disappears in a terrifyingly short time, followed by more white wine (me and Daisy) and some whisky Daisy finds in the kitchen (Finn) and we sit around for hours, watching bad television, while Daisy cries about Lewis and Finn slumps in the armchair, eyes fixed to the TV, barely grunting out two words for the entire time.

Oh yes, the third rule, but just as important as the first two: ensure that each participant has an equal time to talk. I am actually really looking forward to unburdening some of my ongoing, Patrick-related misery, but don't get a chance. Daisy is far too busy relating all of Lewis's many and varied charms to bother even to make a token gesture of asking me how I'm feeling. Thus I become increasingly ratty and unsympathetic, which she barely notices, being half-drowned in Pinot Grigio and going under fast. We finally call it a day, or a night, at about ten, when I realise that I am so soused myself that unless

I leave promptly I will pass out on the bathroom floor. Daisy is very upset when I announce that I'm going and begs me to stay the night, but I hate waking up somewhere I don't live, and besides, I would have to put on the same cigarette-and-alcohol-reeking clothes I am currently wearing. When I raise this latter objection, Daisy says I can borrow anything of hers I take a fancy to, but this is sweetly naive of her, since nothing in her capacious wardrobe would fit me without my resembling a size twelve sausage squeezed into a size eight skin.

I gather up Finn and we head out into the night for the Underground, parting company at Oxford Circus, where we take different tube lines. Finn is oddly good company, in that he doesn't talk himself but doesn't seem to expect me to say anything either. It's blissfully relaxing and reminds me of why I like hanging out with guys. They don't feel the same need girls do to keep the conversation in constant motion.

At Oxford Circus, he says gruffly, 'Thanks, Rebecca.'

'It's OK.'

'No, really, thanks. I didn't want to be alone. I hope Daisy gets over that wanker.'

'Time heals everything,' I say. 'Allegedly.'

'Yeah, right.' He pauses, then says, 'It sort of helped, actually. Hearing someone else go on about their ex.'

'I don't think you and Daisy have quite the same level of trauma,' I say. 'I mean, Lewis was only a one-night stand.'

'Yeah, but it's about the pain you're feeling, isn't it? You can't have, you know, a sliding scale of who gets to feel worse. Basically we're all in the same boat.'

This is pretty impressive. Finn obviously has hidden depths.

'Well, night, then,' he says, giving me an awkward hug.

We pull apart and I'm just heading off for the Victoria line escalators – Finn's going to Notting Hill and needs the Central line – when he calls, 'Rebecca? I was thinking . . . maybe we should do this again some time?'

'Really?' I am surprised.

'Yeah. Like I said, it sort of helped. Maybe you and Daisy could come over to mine next time.'

'OK,' I say a bit dubiously. I'm glad that Finn and Daisy seemed to derive some healing benefits from the evening, but it was a washout as far as I'm concerned. 'See you tomorrow.'

'Yeah,' Finn says, pulling a face at the thought of work and Barney.

On the platform I see someone who looks a little like Patrick. A black guy, oddly enough, but with those same slanting eyes and his hair pulled tightly back from his face. Or maybe he doesn't look like Patrick at all. Maybe it's just that I am realising, free from the constraints of hanging out with someone and having to seem relatively sober, that by now I am very drunk indeed.

I think I'm dreaming when I see him on TV. Dreaming, or so drunk that I am projecting Patrick's face on to every man I see who bears even a sketchy resemblance to him. So I do something that, in my alcohol-soaked state, seems perfectly reasonable: I scrabble around for a video and shove in the first one that I find. I want to verify this sighting tomorrow, when I've sobered up.

I have cable. I got it after Patrick and I broke up; I was used to his hundreds of cable stations in New York and I think it was a way of telling myself that I didn't need him for anything, that I could have all the things I'd enjoyed with him even without him, that, although I felt he'd taken New York away from me, it was some small way of asserting my independence. Pathetic, of course. But now I channel-surf; it's too early to go to sleep, even though I'm half-passed-out with the drink. I'm scared of falling asleep too early and waking at that terrible pre-dawn hour when everything seems even more negative and all the dark thoughts rush in so fast that I have no strength to fight them off. If I can stay awake till midnight I should sleep through the night.

So I flick through the channels, looking for something, anything, that will distract me even minimally from my thoughts of Patrick. But instead, there he is, on an MTV wrestling programme called Tough Enough II, of all places. It's one of those reality shows where fifteen young hopefuls try out to become a professional wrestler and one is eliminated each week.

You might be expecting Patrick to be one of the young competitors, but you'd be wrong. You don't know Patrick. He'd never be on television allowing himself to be seen in a position of weakness. No, he was the wrestling coach. The resemblance was extraordinary. He could have been Patrick's older, more pumped-up brother. Dark, slightly slanting eyes, those high Tartar cheekbones, long brown hair caught back in a ponytail. His stance, always quiet and always alert. A bouncer, not searching out trouble but constantly aware of its possibility. Arms folded over his chest, legs slightly apart, light on his feet despite the heavy muscles. The cracks around his eyes, the sweet creases in his cheeks as he smiles. Watching him smile is the worst of all. I felt so proud when I made Patrick smile or laugh. It was my personal triumph every single time.

No, that's not the worst. The worst is when he's wrestling and his hair comes loose and falls in straight lines all over his face. Only I saw him like that, as abandoned as Patrick will ever be, his face as open as if he were truly free, my hands pulling back his hair so I could watch his eyes looking straight into mine. When we said goodbye at the airport he didn't want to take off his dark glasses. I knew if I looked straight into his eyes I could make him cry like I was crying.

I couldn't take my eyes off the wrestling guy. The way he spoke, the way he moved, shoulders always a little bunched, step cat-like. He looked after the kids in training with such a fatherly concern, laughing with pride every time they executed a perfect move, his face tightening up in frustration

when they messed up. Always fair, always the boss. That was
Patrick. You could be in a group with twenty of his friends,
and Patrick was the quietest of all of them, and their alpha.
They joked about it. They were lost when he went away.

I managed better than them at first. I lived on the phone
calls and the next time we'd see each other. I had my friends
who he hardly knew, who I'd been cultivating, knowing that
he was leaving and that I would need a rush of people to
come in and, piecemeal, do their best to fill the gap he'd left.
I did a good job. And now Patrick's friends are the ones who
know how he's doing, who fly over to New York to visit him,
and I am out of the loop.

One of Patrick's work colleagues in New York, Todd, rang him
up when I was staying there and left a message on the answering
machine which started: 'How do *you* spell "hangover"? I spell
it D-U-M-B-A-S-S.'

I always think of this when waking up feeling as if, on some
wild whim, I spent most of the preceding evening with my
head clamped in a vice. Slowly I realise that no, I wasn't being
tortured by the Mafia last night: I did this to myself. There's
no point asking why. I just crawl into the bathroom and take
two Solpadeine, remembering how excited the New Yorkers got
when I explained this concept to them. Caffeine, codeine and
paracetamol – the miracle pill. I always made sure that I had
a good supply whenever I visited Patrick. And yes, everything,
every tiny little thing, makes me remember Patrick. I can't drink
a cup of mint tea without thinking of how he'd never had
herbal tea in his life before he met me, and how surprised he
was when he realised he liked it. I can't look at myself in the
mirror without remembering how much Patrick liked my
bottom, which, naturally, I hate. He said it was his favourite
part of my body. I think I would have fallen in love with him
just for that comment alone.

Before I go to work, I can't help turning on the TV and

video and watching a snippet of the MTV series, just to confirm that I wasn't insane last night and hallucinating Patrick's face onto another man's body. The good news is that I wasn't. Bobby Thunder, the wrestler, does look a hell of a lot like Patrick. But that's the bad news, too. I have a really hard time turning off the TV. Then I realise that when I get into work I can look up Bobby Thunder on the Internet. So that's what I do. I Google Bobby Thunder and find a whole raft of websites devoted to him. He lives in Lima, Ohio and he's married with two children. Typical. Even Bobby Thunder, macho wrestler, doesn't have a problem with commitment.

I spend a lot of time that day surfing the many and varied Bobby Thunder websites. Bobby has been the Hardcore WWF champion twice, and the European champion three times. European champion? Does that mean I could actually get to see him wrestle? I indulge in a lively fantasy of meeting Bobby and having a one-night stand with him. Would I have to tell him that he reminded me of Patrick, though? I immerse myself in a carefully imagined scenario where I play a beautiful, mysterious European woman, with a tragic past, to Bobby's straightforward American hunk. Bobby will be deeply intrigued by me; I'm like no one he's ever met before. The fact that I can't fall in love with him because my heart has already been taken will make him even more fascinated by me. It will be a wonderful, doomed love affair, both of us understanding that anything more than passionate sex can never exist between us, but still torn apart by our own conflicting emotions. It's Monica Bellucci meets Robert Mitchum at the WWF European Championships.

I check the TV schedule online – no more WWF *Tough Enough II* for a week. Thank God I have that taped episode to keep me going. I consider ordering a Bobby poster over the Internet. I could put it up in my bedroom. Maybe it would be a good transition from Patrick; gradually wean myself off him, taking the photographs of him down one by one and replacing them with Bobby pictures.

'Rebecca? What *are* you looking at?'

It's Davey, who's come up behind me. I am so absorbed in Bobby's gleaming body, the sturdy frame packed into tight black shorts and a T-shirt with the arms cut off – God, how I love that look on muscly men, you get a little glimpse of their armpits and pecs through the gap, because their arms are so big the sleeve holes need to gape slightly to accommodate them – that I've been oblivious to anything going on around me for the last hour or so. Finn and Barney could have been having a knock-down, drag-out fight *à la The Quiet Man* all over the office and it would barely raise one of my eyebrows.

'Oh, just surfing for ideas,' I say airily, quickly closing the latest Bobby Thunder window.

'Was that *wrestling*?'

'You never know where inspiration's going to strike. What's up?'

'What's *up*!' Davey's voice rises to a moderated shout. Luckily the Bastard Sons of Johnny Cash are playing on the stereo, one of my alt-country American discoveries, and they're pretty loud. Davey goes unheard under the steel guitar. 'You took off with Finn yesterday, and he was obviously in a real state about the whole engagement thing. What was that all about? What's been going on? Why didn't you ring me last night and tell me everything?'

I fill in Davey on the Barney/Vanessa/Finn situation. Davey's round brown eyes open impossibly wide behind his glasses.

'Fucking *hell*,' he says.

'Yeah, it's pretty bad.'

'And doing it like that, without even warning Finn . . .'

'I know. He'd only just found out that they were seeing each other. He had no idea they were getting engaged.'

We both look over at their respective desks. Barney looks as relaxed as always; you'd never know he'd just stabbed his brother in the back. Finn is working hard, fingers flying over the computer keys. He hasn't said a word to Barney all morning, at least as far as I've noticed. The atmosphere, in fact, is eerily normal.

'I hope we don't get a Cain and Abel situation here,' Davey says. 'Not to sound selfish, but this is the best job I've ever had. I don't want Finn and Barney trying to kill each other, or breaking up the company, or both.'

'Cain and Abel with an extra love triangle,' I say.

'What do you mean?' Davey asks. 'There was always a love triangle. What do you think that was all about? Only one woman in the world and they were both fighting over her.'

'She was their mum, Davey.'

'Yeah? And how do you think the human race got propagated?'

'Good point. Ick.'

'Ick indeed. It's one of the questions kids are banned from asking in Sunday school. "Please, Vicar, who did Cain have babies with?"'

'I never knew you went to Sunday school.'

'It was never relevant before.'

I sigh. 'I know what you mean about the whole job thing,' I say. 'I don't know what it'd be like if Finn wasn't here.'

'You think Finn would be the one to go?'

'Yup. He'd storm out.'

Davey thinks about it. 'You're right. And if it was just Barney running things it wouldn't be nearly as much fun.'

'Yeah. Barney's a real capitalist pig. All the cool things would gradually disappear to be replaced by the profit motive.'

'How's Finn doing?' Davey asks, terrorised by this picture of the football table and pool table being removed and replaced by lines of desks staffed by Barney clones, busily thinking up new ways to brown-nose the boss.

'I dunno. Haven't talked to him today. He did say he wanted to have me and Daisy round so we could have another whinge session about our exes.'

Davey practically pings with excitement. 'That's it!' he says. 'Exes Anonymous! That's exactly what you need!'

'What?' I say blankly.

'A support group! Like AA, except for people who've been dumped! You could all take it in turns to qualify and give each other mutual support so that you can move on with your lives!'

'Qualify?'

'It's what we call it when you talk about the problems that brought you to the group.'

'I'm not sure, Davey,' I say. 'I mean, we got together last night, and it was a complete shambles. Daisy just cried and Finn didn't say a word.'

'But obviously he felt it was helpful, or he wouldn't have suggested meeting up again.'

I have to admit this is true.

'And what about you?' Davey asks.

'What *about* me?'

'What did you say?'

'Nothing,' I say bitterly. 'I couldn't get a word in edgeways. Daisy just went on and on for hours.'

'Well, *exactly*! That's why you need some sort of structure, like we have at AA.'

'I dunno . . .'

'Rebecca, this is a really good idea. It kills a lot of birds with one stone. Finn gets over Vanessa and doesn't leave the company, you get to talk about Patrick – you know you told me that you didn't feel you could talk about him to your friends any more because they weren't being supportive . . .'

I have to admit that the idea of being able to force a group of people to listen to me rambling on about Patrick is immensely seductive. Davey sees my weakness and pounces.

'There you go! You couldn't do it with just three people, of course. You need more. And some strangers. It shouldn't all be people you know.'

'What do you suggest I do?' I say coldly. 'Go out into the

street and stand there with a placard saying: JUST BEEN DUMPED? CALL 7263 4948 TO WHINGE IN COMPANY!'

Davey clicks his tongue impatiently. 'Don't be silly. Just put an ad in *Time Out*. I bet you'll be deluged with people.'

I'm unconvinced by this idea. 'Think of all the weirdos that might answer!' I object. 'It could be a nightmare!'

'Look, just think about it, OK?' Davey says, turning on the charm.

I agree just to shut him up. That evening, however, I watch my tape of *Tough Enough II* again and again and again. Even when I'm so tired I'm falling asleep on the sofa, I can't bear to turn it off. It feels as if I have Patrick so close to me that I can almost reach out and touch him. The part where his students try to play a prank on Bobby and discover that he's booby-trapped his room, knowing they were coming, and is hiding in the cupboard to spray them with the fire extinguisher . . . it's quintessentially Patrick. Nobody ever managed to steal a march on him. Bobby stands there, hands on hips, that I-gotcha smile on his face, quiet, in control, and I can picture Patrick with precisely the same expression. He'd never instigate a prank, but if someone tried to play one on him, he would always turn the tables. I stumble into bed at one-thirty, worn out, dumb with misery, my whole body aching with exhaustion, nursing myself to sleep, as always, with a fantasy of Patrick coming back to me. My dreams are confused mixtures of Bobby and Patrick and when the alarm goes off I crave sleep again. I want to sleep for the rest of my life so that I can dream about Patrick and not have to wake up to reality without him.

I don't need Davey to tell me that I'm not coping well.

Another Patrick sighting. I was with Daisy, coming down the escalator for the Bakerloo line in the Piccadilly Circus tube station, and he was passing me on the opposite escalator. Something about him caught at me, that one extra-thudding heartbeat of recognition before I realised it wasn't him and my breathing settled down again. His hair was drawn off his face in a ponytail and he wore a dark navy sweater under a leather jacket, with jeans. His jaw was Patrick's, sharp and strong, but it was odd – he hadn't shaved under the jaw. I caught sight of all these short, brown hairs just below the bone, and this dissimilarity made me remember Patrick still more, the contrast highlighting the accuracy of my memory.

Patrick was always smooth-shaven, apart from his goatee. He was a little gritty late at night, maybe, if I ran the edge of my finger along his chin, but that was all. He never gave me stubble rash. I could rub my cheek against his and feel nothing but softness. His hair was as silky as a child's. I remembered how it felt, loose in my hands, and I found myself straining as best I could to watch the man on the escalator as he rose away from me, because even this imperfect copy of Patrick was a connection to him.

I pretended to Daisy that I was looking at a poster on the opposite wall. She didn't notice anything odd. How could she not? How could she not see how much that guy looked like Patrick? It was extraordinary to me that she wasn't struck by the resemblance as much as I was. People can be so self-centred sometimes.

Chapter Nine

I am out of control on the whole Bobby Thunder thing. At the weekend, MTV, as if reading my mind, showed the entire first series of *Tough Enough* from midnight onwards. I don't even want to say how late I stayed up watching it. Of course I taped the entire thing. Twelve episodes of Bobby, making thirteen in all that I now have on video. It's like being a binge eater. I keep watching them even when I know them by heart, even when I have seen them so often that I feel sick and my eyes hurt, because when I turn off the TV I feel more alone than ever. I thought Bobby might be a good transition stage for me, but instead he seems to be intensifying my grief for Patrick, ratcheting up my memories of him until they're so acute they stab into me at entirely unexpected moments, just as they did when we first broke up: at a film with Daisy, hanging out with Davey and the boys after their football game. Occasions when I think I'm fairly safe because I'm being distracted by outside sources. The slightest reference, the slightest resemblance of any man I see to Patrick, and I'm spiralling back down into the black pit of loss once more. On Sunday night I re-read all the emails he'd sent me, which is something I do only in dire need. I manage not to ring him, because it's the weekend and the likelihood of him answering the phone is very high. But that's the only self-control I demonstrate. The rest is pure indulgence, a masochistic luxuriating in everything that's bad for me.

By the following Monday I am really beginning to panic. I can't talk to anyone about what's happening to me. I am too ashamed; it's quite literally too stupid for words. I know that if I mention the name of Bobby Thunder, anyone I talk to will burst out laughing – unless they see him, unless they realise how like Patrick he truly is – and it's something they will never let me forget. I'll be teased about it for the rest of my life. I'm too proud to bear that, and frankly I'm also worried that I may be going a little mad. I'd like nothing better than to sit down with Daisy or Davey and show them the *Tough Enough* videos, but I know they might well think that I am going insane.

I'm not sleeping well, and I know I don't look my best. Davey usually picks up on that, but mercifully all of Monday he is very distracted, completely absorbed by work, and I manage to avoid any adverse attention from him. Tuesday is a different story. He's sitting on my desk when I come in for work, waving a magazine at me.

'What is it?' I say, taking off my coat. From across the office I can't see the cover. I assume it's one of those boys' magazines with some sizzling pictures of the latest hot TV starlet dressed only in a skimpy bikini and posing in some awkward squatting position while being interviewed about how seriously she takes her acting career.

'I did it!' Davey chants. 'I did it for you!'

'What?' As I approach, I realise that he's holding a copy of the latest edition of *Time Out*. 'You *didn't*,' I say, realising exactly what he means.

'I did! It looks great! Here!' He flips through the magazine and points to the ad which he has thoughtfully marked with one of those little Post-it stickers.

I open my mouth but no words come out. Instead I make burbling noises.

'I set up the hotmail account for you so that you don't have a lot of weirdos knowing who you are and where you work,' Davey smirks. 'I'll help you weed out the loonies.'

'*Davey*,' I say, still at a loss for words.

'Don't be angry with me,' he begs, suddenly changing tone from smug to nervous. 'You don't have to do it if you don't want to. I just thought it might help, that's all.'

He looks at me pleadingly. Davey always resembles a little boy when he has that expression, with his eyes saucer-like behind his glasses and his round chubby cheeks. That's why he works so hard at the austere designer clothes and black-framed glasses; he knows that his natural appearance is that of an overgrown twelve-year-old.

'I'm not angry,' I say. 'I'm scared.'

I didn't mean to say that. It takes me so aback I have to sit down.

Davey's eyes soften with understanding. He reaches out and squeezes my shoulder. 'I know,' he says. 'It *is* scary. But you need to open up and talk about it. I know you're having a really hard time getting over Patrick, and I'm doing this for you. Not Daisy, not Finn, you. You're my best friend, and I—'

'What's not Finn?' says the person in question.

We haven't noticed him come up. I start. But Davey says, 'Here,' and hands him the copy of *Time Out*, pointing out the ad.

Finn reads it and then stares over the magazine at me.

'I didn't do it,' I say quickly. 'It was Davey.'

'I thought it would be a good idea,' Davey says. 'You know, like AA, but for people who are having a hard time getting over their exes.'

'Jesus,' Finn says.

'I *know*,' I say, sensing support from him. I don't want to do this. If Finn nixes it too, that will help me to fight off Davey.

'It's a *great* idea,' Finn says. 'We can have the first meeting at mine, if you want. That way if there are any loonies they won't know where you live, Rebecca.'

'Are you *serious*?' I say.

'Totally. Fuck, I can't wait to tell everyone what a fucking bitch Vanessa is. She's tried to ring me twice to "talk to me about the situation", can you believe it? Bloody cow. I just hung up on her.'

I am speechless again. This is clearly my day for complete inarticulacy. I never expected that Finn would go for this.

'Have you had any responses yet?' Finn says.

'Let's check!' Davey suggests enthusiastically. He turns my computer monitor towards him and goes to the hotmail website, entering the address he made up for me.

'Blah blah blah, loading . . . Yes! Two emails! Brilliant!

"Dear Rebecca, I would love to be part of your Exes Anonymous group. I am still struggling with the aftermath of a very painful divorce and really need the kind of support this could provide."

'Ooh, that one sounds good. Let's check the other one.

"Dear Rebecca, When my ex-girlfriend left me I thought I would never be able to love again, but since I have accepted Jesus Christ into my life, my heart is full. I have realised that the love He gives to me and all the world is—"

'Nah,' we say in unison.

'I could just write something about the group being full for now,' I suggest.

'Yeah, you don't want to be cyber-stalked by a Jesus freak,' Finn agrees.

'It must help a lot to be a Christian,' I say wistfully. It would be lovely to have a full heart.

Davey and Finn cast me a perplexed glance (Davey) and a frankly scornful one (Finn) but otherwise ignore this comment.

'Right,' Finn says masterfully. 'How many people should we have in the group?'

'No more than ten, I'd say,' Davey pronounces.

'So there's me, Rebecca, Daisy – Daisy'll come, won't she?'

'I would have thought so,' I say, feeling that the reins of the situation are being taken from my hands – not that I ever had a firm grip on them to start with.

'That leaves seven others.'

'Six,' I say. 'Davey, you should come too. You're still hung up on Jenna.'

Hah. Rebecca's Revenge, or The Tables Turned. Davey gapes at me.

'I don't know . . .' he says feebly. 'I sort of talk about that in AA as it is . . .'

'It's not the same,' I say firmly.

'But there probably shouldn't be too many people in the group who know each other . . .'

'Coward,' I say.

'Wimp,' Finn agrees.

'Maybe later,' Davey mutters. 'I don't think I'm really ready yet . . .'

'Pathetic,' Finn says.

'Pushing us into something he isn't up to doing himself,' I say.

'We'll show him,' Finn says.

'"We?"' I say. 'What's this "we" shit, white boy?'

Davey giggles. Finn says, 'What?' blankly.

I click my tongue. 'Davey, d'you want to tell him, or shall I?'

'The Lone Ranger and Tonto are riding across the prairie,' Davey begins, 'when they come round a bend and see a huge bristling mass of Indians—'

'Native Americans,' I say.

103

'OK, Native Americans,' Davey says, rolling his eyes, 'and—'

'What d'you mean, a "bend"?' Finn says. 'A "bend" in the prairie?'

'Well, you know, they go round a corner or something—'

'*Round a corner?*'

'*Anyway*,' Davey continues crossly, 'they realise they're being ambushed, OK? And the Lone Ranger looks at the hundreds of Native Americans with spears at the ready and says, "Geez, Tonto, we're in big trouble this time!" And Tonto says—'

'What's this "we" shit, white boy?' I chorus along with him.

Davey glares at me. 'And rides down to join the rest of the Native Americans,' he finishes.

'"Down"?' Finn says evilly. 'I thought they'd just turned a bend.'

'Fuck off, both of you,' Davey says, very cross. 'I wash my hands. You're on your own with this.'

'Oh no, Davey, please, you said you were going to help—' I plead.

'Yeah, come on, mate,' Finn says. 'You don't have to come to the meeting if you don't want to, but at least help us sort out the crackpots.'

I think Finn and I are scared of being left on our own with this. Davey's got much more experience in support meetings. The kids aren't ready to go it alone; we need Daddy holding our hands.

'All right,' Davey says, pretending to be magnanimous when I know very well that the truth is that he'd hate to be left out. 'But actually, I'm not the only person whose help you need.'

We both stare at him. Davey looks at me.

'I think you should go and talk to Jake,' he says.

If I felt I had any choice in the matter, I would have avoided Jake like the plague. I don't like his holier-than-thou attitude, or his intimacy with Davey. I don't like feeling self-conscious when I drink in front of him and I don't like his being so tolerant when I drink in front of him either, as if he were a smug do-gooder watching others sinning, safe in the knowledge that he's closer to salvation than they are. And most of all, I don't like the nagging sense that I may be misjudging him because I am jealous of his friendship with Davey.

There's only one reason I take up Davey's suggestion – I have absolutely no idea how to run a self-help meeting. I'm nervous that people may be all over the place emotionally, and I don't know how to manage that. Visions dance in my mind of the meeting descending into an uncontrolled sob-fest, as complete strangers pour out their guts all over Finn's living room. Even as a metaphor this is horribly unpleasant. We need some sort of structure to stop the meeting melting down into anarchy. I'm big on structure and order – that's why I love my yoga classes; they give me a much-needed sense of balance and focus right now. You learn what every single part of your body should be doing during any given position. Downward Dog: hands down, index finger and thumb exerting a slightly stronger pressure; forearms turning outwards, elbows straight, upper arms in, taking the shoulder blades into the back; head hanging heavy, collarbones widening; back lengthening, thigh bones to the back of the thighs; knees opening like windows; calves back and pulling down to the ankles; feet pressing evenly, big toe mounds reaching down to extend the inner leg. You can see why it's such a comfort. For at least a few hours a week I can have the surety of knowing precisely what I'm supposed to be doing.

Patrick earthed me. I'm not sure exactly how *that* metaphor works; I don't remember my Physics GCSE in any detail, but I know that electricity needs to be earthed, or it's dangerous. Patrick grounded me, physically and mentally. His body felt like home to me. When I was with him, I knew where I belonged. Now I am unrooted, floating free, and I don't want to be free. I want to be tied down to Patrick. He was my love, my rock, my security . . . OK, I need these meetings. I will admit that, if only to myself. Naturally, to everyone else I'm pretending that I'm only going along with this because of Davey and Finn's enthusiasm for it. But, when I come out with maudlin stuff like that recent effusion, I can see that Exes Anonymous might have something to offer me after all. I loathe being maudlin and ever since Patrick and I broke up, it's been my default state.

So two days later, Finn and I are sitting in a brightly coloured coffee shop with Jake holding forth on the principles of AA. The wall opposite me is yellow, the ones on my left and right are bright blue. Curlicues and swirls of yellow and purple swish across the walls. The chairs are orange and blue and the tables are a crazy mosaic of patchwork primaries. Doubtless the design concept was to cheer up the customers and yet discourage them from staying too long. Well, the latter part is working for me. It's like being trapped on a set for a kids' TV show.

'The two primary principles of AA,' Jake is saying, 'are to stay sober and to help other alcoholics achieve sobriety, so you could apply that to your own group. Remember, it's not just about each individual, it's about the group as a whole, like a living organism. You're there for yourselves but you're also there for each other.'

'Good stuff,' Finn mutters as he scribbles. He's actually taking notes. I can't believe how much Finn is into this.

'And how should we run the meetings?' I ask.

Jake's green eyes fix on mine. Reluctantly, I have to acknowledge his charisma. He's effortlessly in command of this meeting, a still, calm centre to the group. I wonder whether it's his years in AA that confer this authority on him or whether he's just naturally a bossy bastard. Whoops, there I go again. I hope he's not picking up on how scratchy and hostile my feelings for him are.

'These are going to be closed meetings, obviously,' he starts.

'Wait a minute . . .' Finn says, perplexed.

'Meetings where only the actual members can come,' I clarify, not wanting to let Jake do all the information dissemination.

'Oh yeah. Well, obviously,' Finn says.

'So there are a few different things you can do,' Jake says, 'but basically at each meeting, you need someone to moderate. One format is that the moderator will open the meeting and then call on someone to qualify – that means talking about the problems that have brought them there. So that person will give an opening statement, and then anyone else who wants to speak can raise their hand afterwards and the moderator can call on them. Or you can do what we call a round robin – you go round the room and everyone gets a chance to speak.'

'What if people don't want to?' I ask.

'They can just say "I pass".'

Phew, I think.

'And you could have themes for the meetings,' Jake continues, warming to the task. 'The person who qualifies first has a particular theme that they talk about, and afterwards everyone can say how they feel that relates to them.'

'Like what?' Finn asks, still scribbling away.

'Serenity,' Jake suggests. 'Acceptance. Facing up to life. Letting go of old ideas. Gratitude.'

'Gratitude?' I say dubiously. This is all sounding a bit hippy-dippy for me.

'Gratitude for having found the group and the courage to change,' Jake says, looking at me again. 'AA is about changing your life in a very fundamental way, facing up to your demons and moving on.'

I glance over at Finn's notebook and see that he's drawing Vanessa with horns, a tail and a pitchfork. Very therapeutic, no doubt.

'You might need what we call a "spiritual timekeeper",' Jake suggests. 'To make sure that people don't just talk and talk. Five minutes is the usual amount of time.'

'What do we do, set an alarm clock?' Finn asks.

'Kitchen timer would be easier,' I say.

Jake looks slightly taken-aback. 'I don't think that's a great idea,' he says, obviously trying to be tactful. 'You could just appoint someone to point at their watch when the person who's qualifying runs over time.'

'I know!' Finn says. 'Cards! Like football! You get a yellow card after the fourth minute, to tell you you need to wind it up, and a red card at five!'

'That's great,' I say enthusiastically.

I think Jake may feel we're not taking this seriously enough.

'You can always call me if you have any problems,' he says. 'I'd be happy to give advice. I'm sure some things are going to come up that you're going to need help handling.'

I bridle. 'Like what?' I say coldly.

'Relapses. Interventions. Deceit. Remember, addicts are very good at lying. When I was drinking, I'd tell so many lies it would actually have been easier in the end for me to tell the truth. Or you might get inappropriate behaviour in the group.'

We look baffled. Jake elaborates.

'Lots of relationships form in AA,' he says, 'but you've got a different situation from us – you've got people who are addicted to love. So ideally, you don't want anyone in the group going out with anybody else, and, given what you're talking about, that might well happen. Actually in AA we say no relationships for the first year. No new relationships, anyway.'

'Great,' Finn says gloomily. 'Not only are we moaning about being single, we have to bloody stay that way.'

'You're going to have to work a lot of things out,' Jake says. 'That's why I said you can ring me if you need to.' He hands us each a sheet of paper. 'Have a look at that while I go to get another coffee,' he says. 'Anyone want anything?'

Finn orders another caffè latte, but I'm too immature to let Jake buy me a drink. He's good-looking, poised, centred, and he knows more than we do about all this: I can't see him as an equal and I refuse to let him play big brother, which he obviously gets off on – look at him and Davey. So though I really do want another cappuccino, I shake my head. Cutting off my nose to spite my face: a Rebecca Havers speciality.

Finn and I have a look at the leaflet as Jake goes upstairs to the coffee bar.

The Twelve Steps of Alcoholics Anonymous

1. *We admitted we were powerless over alcohol – that our lives had become unmanageable.*
2. *Came to believe that a Power greater than ourselves could restore us to sanity.*
3. *Made a decision to turn our will and our lives over to the care of God as we understood Him.*
4. *Made a searching and fearless moral inventory of ourselves.*
5. *Admitted to God, to ourselves and to another human being the exact nature of our wrongs.*
6. *Were entirely ready to have God remove all these defects of character.*
7. *Humbly asked Him to remove our shortcomings.*
8. *Made a list of all persons we had harmed, and became willing to make amends to them all.*
9. *Made direct amends to such people wherever possible, except when to do so would injure them or others.*
10. *Continued to take personal inventory and when we were wrong promptly admitted it.*
11. *Sought through prayer and meditation to improve our conscious contact with God, as we understood Him, praying only for knowledge of His will for us and the power to carry that out.*
12. *Having had a spiritual awakening as the result of these steps, we tried to carry this message to alcoholics, and to practice these principles in all our affairs.*

Finn and I finish reading and look at each other. I sense that we are both concerned about the same thing.

'This God stuff . . .' Finn finally says, a doubtful tone to his voice.

'I *know*,' I agree.

'I'm not sure . . . it sounds so preachy . . .'

Jake comes back down the stairs, carrying two gigantic cups of coffee. Actually, they're not so much cups as orange bowls with handles. He's wearing a grey crew-neck T-shirt and jeans, both of which fit him so well I'm sure he paid a fortune for them. The girls at the next table look at him admiringly. He's a handsome bastard, no question about it.

'Let me guess,' he says, setting down the cups. 'You're worried about the whole God issue.'

We nod like two children in front of the teacher.

'Don't get too hung up on that,' he says. 'You can see God as anything you want to. The higher power we talk about can be whatever that means to you. Lots of people like to think of it as the group. The group, as an entity, is stronger than any one of you. It's your support mechanism, it gives you strength. That's the point about AA, and why it works so well. We're none of us trained therapists but we all give each other strength because we know what we've all been through individually.'

'Hmmn,' I say dubiously.

Jake gets even more serious than he has been so far during this conversation, which is saying quite a lot. 'You *have* to work the steps,' he says. 'They are the reason why AA's been so successful for millions of people. Work the steps and keep working them. That's what it's all about.'

'Him,' I mutter.

'What?' Jake says.

'Him,' I say. 'God as "Him". Hasn't anyone heard of feminism in AA?'

'God is whatever that means to you,' Jake says.

'Well, you could write "It" then, couldn't you? Or "Her"?'

Finn rolls his eyes at Jake in manly solidarity at this feminist nonsense, but Jake doesn't return the eye roll, which perversely annoys me further still. Can anyone really be as above normal human fallibility as Jake presents himself as being? I don't believe it's possible.

'Work the steps,' he says again. 'You know what we say at the end of meetings, Rebecca. "Keep coming back, it works if you work it." Remember?'

Finn stares at me. 'You've been to an AA meeting?' he asks in disbelief.

'I was just supporting Davey,' I say quickly.

'Thank God,' he says. 'I mean, thank God you're not, you know . . .' He looks at Jake. 'No offence, mate, but we're going to be sinking some booze at these meetings. I mean, bloody hell, standing up in front of a group of complete strangers and talking about your deepest feelings – I'm going to need some help from Mr Single Malt with that one.'

For a second, Jake's façade of composure actually cracks. I could hug Finn for having managed that. All he says, however, is: 'You might want to keep the alcohol to a minimum, Finn. Remember, you're trying to achieve emotional sobriety.'

'One step at a time, eh?' Finn says cheerfully. 'Right now, all I'm going for is getting that evil witch out of my head.'

I look down at Finn's notepad. The top page is completely covered with caricatures of Vanessa. Finn has moved on from the devil-girl motif to sketches of her riding a broomstick, covered in spots and grotesquely fat. No wonder his mood has improved. What a great idea, I think. Maybe we can incorporate some art therapy into the group sessions.

Chapter Ten

Finn's flat is much smarter than I pictured it would be. Which was probably my own lack of imagination. Finn dresses in a pretty hip way, and it would only have been logical that his decor would be an extension of that. It's sleek and modern, with thick rugs on the floor, shiny Swedish-designed modular furniture, and big comfy sofas, all done in white and black and grey. The sleek wooden cabinets and a few big prints on the walls are the only touch of colour. You would know as soon as you walk in the door that this is a bachelor pad. I nearly burst out laughing when I go to use the loo. Finn's bathroom announces all too clearly that there's no woman in residence: a scanty shelf of products – mouthwash, aftershave, shaving gel – all arranged neatly with space between them. There's no body lotion or bath foam or any of the myriad girly products with which a woman's bathroom is always cluttered. I do understand why men are reluctant to move in with their girlfriends. We bring a chaos to the bathroom and bedroom that men can never understand. Patrick was perpetually baffled by my using the word 'need' to describe my constant additions to my extensive shoe and perfume collections.

We've all brought drink. Finn's point about the importance of lubricating the emotional wheels with a hefty dose of alcohol was well taken. By the time I stand up to open the meeting we've had a couple of drinks each and the embarrassment we're feeling at what we're about to do has dissipated somewhat. Half an hour ago our nerves were jangling like wind chimes; now they've settled down to a low, barely audible hum.

There are seven of us altogether. Besides Finn, me and Daisy, we have four comparative strangers, the only ones whose emails in response to Davey's ad weren't entirely barking. The loudest one is Charlotte, a super-Sloane in unflattering tartan trousers, who I am already finding rather intimidating. Then there's Ben, who seems fairly average, Jennifer, a pretty little redhead in her early twenties, and Jim, a sad middle-aged man in a ratty grey cardigan and beige nylon-blend trousers with a permanent crease down the front. There is something very tragic about Jim. Merely to look at him depresses me utterly. I am sure that his story of love and loss is going to be both heartbreaking and horribly banal.

Three men to four girls – not a bad ratio at all. Obviously the newspaper surveys are right – men in the UK *are* getting a lot better at talking about their feelings.

'Hi,' I begin, clearing my throat. Thank God for the wine I've drunk. Even with it, it's unexpectedly hard to start pouring out my heart to people I know, let alone ones I don't. 'I'm Rebecca, and welcome to the first ever meeting of Exes Anonymous.'

'Aren't you supposed to say: "I'm Rebecca and I'm addicted to my ex?"' asks Daisy.

'What?' I glare at her. I had this speech all worked out, and now she's ruining my flow.

'You know, that's how they start in AA,' Daisy explains. '"Hi, my name's Daisy and I'm an alcoholic." And then everyone says "Hi, Daisy" back.'

She's right, damn her. I really don't want to say it. But here I am, and everyone's staring up at me expectantly. (I'm standing up. It seemed more dignified and authoritative.) 'OK,' I say through gritted teeth. 'I'm Rebecca and I'm addicted to my ex.'

'Hi, Rebecca,' everyone choruses dutifully.

'Welcome to this group. Um, we're all finding our way a bit here, but thank you all for coming, and hopefully over time we'll work out a format and a way of doing things that everyone feels comfortable with. For this first meeting we're going to have Finn here start off by talking about his feelings towards his ex – that's called "qualifying" – and then anyone who wants to talk can have five minutes to say whatever they want. If people don't want to say anything, they don't have to, but the rule is that you can't interrupt when other people are qualifying. Nobody should be judged for what they might say. But after everyone who wants to speak has had their go, I thought we might have a discussion about useful things we can do to help us get over our, um, emotional addictions. Oh yeah, and one more thing,' I add, remembering. 'There's a confidentiality rule. You're not supposed to talk about anything people say here with anyone else. What you hear here stays here. We're going to try to run these meetings on a sort of AA template, and that's a big rule in AA, to create a space where everyone can be safe and truthful.'

Charlotte, the posh girl who had a bad divorce, claps enthusiastically at this. No one else does, but Charlotte seems undeterred. She's oozing with self-confidence. Poor Jim, who's sitting next to her on the sofa, huddles his shoulders up to his ears even more than he was doing before. Jim's unspeakably shy; he's barely got a word out tonight apart from mumbling his name as he came in the door. If we shook him and Charlotte up together we might get two people with reasonably normal levels of self-esteem.

'So,' I say, 'Finn, will you start us off?'

Daisy looks sulky. She wanted to start, but I vetoed it. From my long friendship with Daisy, I know her tendency to go on and on and yes, on still further, about her relationship miseries. I thought that beginning the meeting with an endless ramble through the low points of Daisy's emotional life would be bad for group morale. Of course, that wasn't how I put it to her. I said that Finn was in crisis because of the Vanessa/Barney engagement and needed urgent help and support. Daisy had to admit the logic of this, but she's still pouting.

'Um, should I stand up?' Finn asks.

'I don't know,' I say, sitting down on a floor cushion.

'I think I'd feel a bit of a prat standing up,' Finn says.

'Oh, but it might help,' Charlotte chips in. 'You know, psychologically.'

'I'm not giving a speech, though,' Finn says.

'I don't want to stand up,' says Ben. He's come straight from work and is the only man in a business suit; clearly he works in a conventional office, as the suit is grey and the tie nondescript. But his hair is spiked up with a little too much gel, as if the top of his head is attempting to explode out of his conservative outfit. 'I wouldn't get a word out.'

'Shall we take a vote?' Charlotte suggests.

Charlotte clearly wants to take charge. I imagine her in ten years' time, living in the countryside with a merchant banker husband, ruthlessly whipping the Women's Institute and the church charity fête into shape.

'Why doesn't everyone do what they feel comfortable with?' says Daisy, bless her.

'But I think a vote would be—' Charlotte starts.

'I think I'll stay sitting down, then,' Finn says, ignoring her.

God, I forgot how awful the politics of meetings can be. Not just self-help meetings, any bloody meetings. Thank God for Daisy. She's very good at keeping everyone happy. I tend to go in the other direction and just boss everyone around. Basically I'm just an inferior version of Charlotte. It's a dispiriting reflection.

'Hi, I'm Finn, and I'm addicted to my ex,' Finn starts.

'Hi, Finn,' we all chorus.

'She's called Vanessa, and she's an evil psycho-bitch who messed with my head and ruined my life,' continues Finn with gusto. 'And now she's fucking engaged to my brother. Can you *believe* it? I'd only just found out they were going out. Bastards. Complete and utter fucking bastards! I hate their guts.'

I'm not sure how therapeutic this is – aren't we supposed to be trying to be positive? But everyone else is nodding their heads enthusiastically, or looking sympathetic, so Finn has clearly hit a chord. He continues in this vein for the rest of his alloted time. Every one of Vanessa's iniquities is covered, or at least I assume they are. Finn gives such a thorough summary that I can't believe he's left anything out. Vanessa's stingy: she expected him to pay for everything. She was forever criticising him and complaining. She's selfish, self-obsessed and vain. She thinks she's the most gorgeous creature in the world and expects constant compliments. Etc., etc., etc. Finn is on a roll. He's loving every minute of this.

When he finishes, he's beaming with pleasure. Charlotte claps again. 'Jolly good!' she says.

'OK—' I start.

'I think we should thank Finn for sharing,' says Daisy.

'Any time,' Finn says happily.

'Right,' I say, 'who wants to go next?'

I look around the room. Jim ducks his head and stares at his lap. Jennifer fiddles with a strand of curly hair the colour of marigolds and looks terrified when I momentarily catch her eye. I glance over at Ben, but before I can make reassuring, encouraging eye contact with him, Charlotte bursts out with, 'I will!'

She is totally going to take over these meetings if I don't stop her.

'Can people raise their hands if they want to talk?' I say, in a probably hopeless attempt to hint to her not to be pushy. 'OK, Charlotte, off you go. You've got five minutes.'

'Yeah,' Finn says. 'Yellow card on four, red card on five.' He produces two coloured pieces of paper. 'I'll be timing.' He looks at his watch. 'Right, Charlotte, three – two – one – go!'

'It's not a sprinting race, Finn,' I mutter.

Charlotte of course stands up.

'Hi, everyone, my name's Charlotte and I'm addicted to my ex-husband,' she says with jolly-hockey-sticks enthusiasm.

116

'Which is pretty bloody odd, considering what an utter creep he is. He was playing the field from the moment we got married. I found out a year ago that he was snogging one of my bridesmaids at our wedding, can you believe it? And he'd make a beeline for every single nanny that came in the door, even the black ones.'

Aaaaaaaaah, goes a voice in my head. *Aaaaaaaaaah*. I look frantically at Daisy and see that she looks as panicked as I feel. What the hell do we do? I've just announced that there's a rule about not interrupting! For an awful, guilty moment I feel relief that there are no black people here, because then I would feel I *have* to interrupt, to show Charlotte how unwelcome that kind of comment is, so that the poor hypothetical black person didn't feel that they were surrounded by a bunch of closet racists.

The thought whirls through my head at lightning speed and when I tune in again to Charlotte's stream of words, praying that she isn't coming out with stuff that will require an interruption, she's saying, '. . . because I always thought he had a thing for blondes. But I soon realised, black, white, yellow . . .'

Oh God, I think.

'. . . red, green, as long as they had a pair of tits he didn't give a damn what colour they came in.'

Is this OK? I exchange glances with Daisy again. She grimaces in confusion. It isn't really OK. If I were black I think I'd be really pissed off with Charlotte. But would I? Damn it all, it's hard for white liberal anti-racists to work this stuff out on their own sometimes.

'And it wasn't as if I was madly in love with him,' Charlotte continues. 'But we have two little ones – Camilla and Piers – and I expect I stayed with him for their sake. More fool me.'

Charlotte's children *would* be called Camilla and Piers. I stare at her square figure; her large spreading arse; her deepset, tiny blue eyes, so small you'd completely miss them if they weren't heavily outlined with navy pencil; her thin mouth, slicked with pale pink lipstick. I wonder despondently how on earth Charlotte, who is by nobody's standards attractive – she has a nice head of thick blonde hair, but that's about it – has managed to find someone who wanted to breed with her, while I, looking considerably less like the back end of a bus, am still single, my eggs remaining resolutely unfertilised. Yes, her husband was constantly cheating on her, but *still*. What the hell is wrong with me?

'Finding out about him snogging Veronica was the last straw,' Charlotte says. 'I mean, the nannies were bad enough, but all husbands shag their nannies, don't they? Or at least try to. But *Veronica*. And at our *wedding*. Somehow it was completely ghastly to think of him doing that with, you know, someone like us.'

Ben, whose accent is more Essex than the Home Counties, is staring at Charlotte with thinly disguised contempt. I can't blame him. If Charlotte once uses the word 'common' we're in big, big trouble.

'I took my revenge, of course,' Charlotte says grimly. 'I cut all the crotches out of every single one of his suits. It took *forever*. You'd be amazed how long it takes to cut through really good material. And then I absolutely took him to the cleaners in the divorce. Daddy's a judge, so he should have known better than to mess with me. He hired a really good divorce lawyer, but so did I, and of course Daddy knows *everyone* and Jolly's lawyer didn't want to get on the wrong side of him . . .'

Can Charlotte's husband really be called Jolly? It must be a nickname like Plug and Beetle, in which case he's probably changed it by now. I can't imagine him still being jolly after Charlotte had finished with him.

'But I still get angry *every single time* I think of him,' Charlotte's saying. 'And I simply don't trust *anyone*. It's been two years and every time I think about Jolly, or I have to ring him about picking up the little ones, my blood *boils*. So I thought that this meeting was an absolutely brilliant idea. I really need to get over all of this.'

I wonder whether Charlotte will continue referring to Camilla and Piers as 'the little ones' even when they're hulking great teenagers chucking bread rolls at each other during charity balls. Probably. I come out of my reverie and realise that Charlotte has finished and is sitting down. She's looking as cheerful as ever; everyone else is staring at her, transfixed with horror. Maybe it's a good thing that comments on people's qualifications are banned.

'Didn't even need the red card!' Finn says, trying for a jokey tone of voice and only partially succeeding. 'Well done, Charlotte!'

'Oh well, Daddy's a lawyer,' she says jovially. 'I learnt to be concise when I was just a little one, or he wouldn't pay a blind bit of attention to anything I said. No point in going on and on, is there?'

'Um, great, Charlotte, thanks for that,' I say. 'Who's next?'

Paradoxically, I think that Finn and Charlotte's fluency and ease have scared everyone else off. I know that's how I feel myself; they were so sure of themselves, so eager to relate their stories, that I feel too intimidated to follow them. I'm nervous about stammering or repeating myself and seeming infinitely less articulate than they were. Looking around the room, I realise that I'm right. Jennifer's hair-twiddling is positively manic; Jim has practically curled into a ball and is playing dead, as if he were being menaced by a bear; and Ben is staring in a faux-abstracted way at his bottle of beer, refusing to catch my eye. I look rather desperately at Daisy, hoping she will volunteer and save me having to qualify.

She pulls a face at me. 'Um,' she says. 'I would but I feel a bit funny about it. Sorry . . .' she casts an apologetic glance around the room '. . . it's just that, you know, I barely know anyone here, and I just feel a bit awkward—'

'Oh, I *know*,' Jennifer bursts out, her voice high-pitched with

119

relief. She blushes, the freckles on her nose seeming more pro-nounced. Jennifer is the cutest little thing; with her red curls, snub nose and pale skin, she looks like the Raggedy Ann doll I played with when I was little, brought to life. She's wearing trousers cropped at mid-calf to show off stack-heeled boots, a faded pink T-shirt with a picture of the game Twister on the front, and dangly plastic earrings: she looks like a fashion photo from *Cosmo Girl* magazine.

'I mean,' she says, 'I was already nervous before I came, and now . . .' She blushes even deeper. 'It's like Debbie says, I feel really embarrassed—'

'It's Daisy,' Finn corrects her.

'Oh my God, I'm sorry . . .' Jennifer looks overcome. 'You see, I haven't even got everyone's *names* sorted out yet, and now I've got to tell you all about, you know, personal stuff that's really upsetting me . . . I just feel like an idiot . . .'

'Oh no, you mustn't, we all feel like idiots,' I reassure her, just as Daisy says 'You don't have to do anything you don't want to do . . .'

'Pluck up!' Charlotte says loudly. 'Just dive in, the water's fine!'

I roll my eyes at Finn, who grimaces. If Charlotte keeps up the jolly-hockey-sticks, Head-Girl-reassuring-shy-Fourth-Formers attitude, she's going to drive us all crazy.

'I've got a great idea!' Daisy exclaims. 'Trust exercises!'

'What?' I stare at her.

'You know!' she says. 'Like actors do when they start a rehearsal. We can all do trust exercises to make us feel more relaxed!'

'What does that involve exactly?' Ben asks nervously. 'Do we have to sing?'

'No, no . . .' Daisy jumps up. Her eyes are sparkling. Ben, I notice, has removed his gaze from his bottle of Becks to ogle at her worshipfully. I can't blame him. 'It'll be fun, come on! It's exactly what we need to do!' She looks around her. 'Look, let's push all the furniture back against the walls, to make a bit more room . . .'

Daisy's enthusiasm is very infectious. Also, I think the people who haven't qualified yet are so grateful to have a distraction that we are even willing to throw ourselves into unspecified trust exercises – which in any other context would terrify us – rather than get up in front of everyone else to talk about our pain. In ten minutes, we have cleared a decent amount of space in Finn's living room and are standing around like kids in PE class, waiting for Daisy to tell us what to do next.

'Right,' she says briskly. 'Everyone form a circle around me.' We shuffle into place.

'Now, I'm going to make myself all stiff, like a board, and Rebecca, you grab my shoulders, and then you all pass me around the circle.'

'OK,' I say dubiously, leaning forward and grabbing Daisy's shoulders. I can feel the sharp bones through her thin sweater. As soon as I touch her, she lets her weight fall against me. Though her feet are still planted on the ground, she's heavier than I expected, and I stagger a little. Ben, next to me, reaches out and grabs Daisy's waist.

'You have to take my weight!' Daisy says crossly. 'It's a trust exercise! I have to feel completely confident that you won't drop me!'

Ben levers Daisy's stiff body over to Jennifer on his other side. Jennifer looks terrified. She lugs Daisy from Ben as if she were supporting a thick sheet of glass which might shatter in her hands.

'Gotcha, Daise,' Finn says cheerfully, hoisting Daisy over to Charlotte in one smooth move that boosts all our confidence. I'm worried about what will happen when Charlotte passes Daisy to Jim; but Charlotte, catching my eye, swivels Daisy as far as she can so that I can grab on to her too and prevent Jim taking all the weight. Jim is barely touching Daisy – he's too scared, I assume, of accidentally grabbing her in the wrong place and getting his face slapped.

'OK,' Daisy says when she's back in my grip again. 'Who's next?'

'I'll go,' Finn offers. 'At least I'll get some girls feeling me up.'

Ben sniggers. 'Better than paying for it, eh?' he says.

'Yeah, ladies, feel free to let your hands wander,' Finn leers, and he and Ben high-five each other.

'Shut up, Finn, you pig,' I say. 'Anyway, you're not doing it, you're too heavy.'

'Sod that, it's a trust exercise!' Finn says. 'I trust you! Come on!' and he jumps into the middle of the circle, makes a face like a little boy diving into a swimming pool, goes stiff and falls heavily against me. Thank God Ben is standing next to me. We both grab him, barely managing to keep him on his feet.

We wrestle Finn's body around the circle, sweating and grunting.

'I swear you're making yourself extra-heavy,' Daisy says crossly, as she and Jennifer stagger under his weight. 'Here, Charlotte . . .'

'This is so much fun!' Charlotte says happily, her brawny frame seeming to have no trouble supporting Finn. All that hockey and lacrosse she no doubt played in her youth must have made her arms like thews of oak. 'It's just like school!'

'Jesus!' Ben says, leaning over to help me support Finn as he comes round again, as Jim is barely taking any of his weight. 'If we'd tried this at my school the boys would have been feeling up the girls' tits and any boy who didn't would have been called a big fat poof.'

'Your turn, you big fat poof,' Finn says happily, and they laugh again.

'Oof, Ben, you weigh a *ton* . . .' I grunt, my knees buckling.

'Solid muscle, darling,' he says.

Thank God Jennifer is next. She's as light as a feather. And then it's me. It feels awkward and suddenly I understand the trust aspect of this; I can sense Jennifer's nervousness, Finn's blithe insouciance, Charlotte's hearty grab, and poor Jim's claw-like, unsteady grip – and yet they all manage not to let me fall. Ben, despite his bravado, is a gentleman, making sure that I can feel him supporting my lower back while I'm technically being held up by Jim, so I don't get scared that Jim will drop me. We all take turns until only Jim is left.

'I'd really rather not,' he mutters, ducking his head. 'Sorry . . . if you want me to go . . . I mean, if you want me to leave . . .'

'No! Jim, it's fine, really!' Daisy says immediately. 'Shall we do a different one?'

'Now, Jim, you really should try—' Charlotte starts, but Ben cuts her off.

'Yeah, Daisy, what's next?'

'Everyone lie down in a circle with your head on each other's laps,' she says gleefully.

'I really think Jim should have a go,' Charlotte says. 'All for one and one for all!'

'He doesn't have to if he doesn't want to,' Jennifer says, blushing.

'Yeah, Charlotte, put a sock in it,' Finn says briskly.

I think Charlotte is going to take violent offence at this, but clearly I completely fail to understand the communication strategies of the upper classes. Charlotte bursts into laughter at this insult.

''Nuff said,' she says cheerfully. 'Bossy me!'

Daisy marshalls us down to the floor. I find myself lying with my head on Ben's lap, which I don't mind, and Jim's on mine, which I do. He has dandruff. Still, as one of the organisers of Exes Anonymous, I expect it's only fair that I draw the short straw. Jim's head is wobbling like one of those nodding dogs that people hang from their rear-view mirror. Poor man, he must be bitterly regretting ever having come here. I bet this is his first and last time.

'What do we do now?' I say.

'Just lie here for a bit,' Daisy says.

'I feel silly,' Jennifer says.

'I feel *great*,' Finn says, predictably. 'Daisy, if you want to edge your head down a bit, that'll be fine with me—'

'Finn, you *naughty boy*!' Charlotte says reprovingly, and she sounds so like a school matron ticking off a saucy pupil that I start giggling, then Ben follows suit, and in a few seconds we are all howling with laughter, the tummies we're resting on bubbling up and down with giggles. It's such a relief. We're all still stressed and anxious by the content of this meeting and the artificiality of sharing our feelings with a bunch of strangers. But the laughter lets out all the tension and anxiety until we're laughing just for the sake of laughing. I can feel Ben's stomach muscles contracting beneath me, and notice that he's in pretty good shape. Maybe it's not so bad that I've got Jim on my own tummy. At least he's in no position to judge me for my little Buddha belly.

'Oh my God, that was *hilarious*,' I say, sitting up to wipe the tears from my eyes.

'Were we supposed to be doing something?' Jennifer asks, sitting up too, red in the face with laughter.

Daisy looks smug. 'You always start laughing,' she says. 'That's the point. To get everyone laughing.'

'Excellent!' Ben says, running his hand through his spiky hair. During the prop-people-up game, he took off his suit jacket and rolled up his sleeves, and he now looks a million miles away from the rather formal yuppie he seemed at the start of the evening. We are all flushed and giggling, apart from Jim, who looks, if possible, more nervous than ever. Maybe he wasn't laughing at all; maybe I just thought he was because his head was bouncing up and down with my own tummy contractions.

'Daisy, this was a brilliant idea,' I say respectfully.

'Yeah,' Finn agrees. 'How do you know all this stuff?'

'I did an article on it ages ago,' she explains.

'Are there any other exercises?' Ben asks.

'I know a great game called Squeak Piggy Squeak!' Charlotte suggests.

I catch Jennifer's eye and we both collapse in giggles. Now that Charlotte, too, is flushed, she does look a little like a blonde pig. I think playing a game like that with her would send me over the edge into screaming hysteria.

'Nah,' Finn says, jumping to his feet. 'I know exactly what we're going to do! Ben, mate, give me a hand, eh? I need to shift the kitchen chairs in here.'

'Sure,' Ben says, hoisting himself up. 'What are we doing?'

Finn beams. 'What about a nice round of Musical Chairs?' he says.

'I can't believe Charlotte won *every single round*,' I say crossly as Daisy and I are walking back to the tube station.

'It's because Finn and Ben were being too polite to shove her out of the way,' Daisy says.

It's true. Finn and Ben, though very competitive, and fine about knocking each other to the ground to get the one remaining chair, lacked the ruthlessness required to shove a woman they hardly knew out of the way. Charlotte, on the other hand, had absolutely no scruples about jostling them.

'And also,' I add meanly, 'she has such a big bum that as soon as she got it anywhere near the seat she was covering the entire area.'

'Oooh! Nasty but true!'

'I'm glad she and Finn spoke,' I say, bringing up something that's been concerning me, 'but didn't you think they were a bit . . . well, angry? I mean, I know it's only the first meeting, but shouldn't we be talking about our pain, not just using it as an excuse to mouth off about hating the people who dumped us?'

'No, no,' Daisy says at once. 'It's very important to be angry. Aren't you angry with Patrick?'

I ponder this. 'Not that much,' I confess.

'You have to get angry. It's one of the crucial five stages of grief. Oh, bollocks.' She stops and fishes in her bag.

'What?'

'I forgot to hand these round . . .' she says, bringing out a sheaf of papers. 'I did a search on the Internet, and found some great stuff about grieving. There's a site called Suddenly Single, and they list the five stages of grief that you're supposed to go through . . .'

In the light from the streetlamp I squint at the paper she hands me.

'See? Anger's the second one. Though this other site I found says it's the first.'

'I'm just really depressed,' I say.

'Well, depression's there too . . . but you're not doing them in order, then. Maybe that's why you're stuck. I was going to read them out and see if we could all work through the five stages.'

'That sounds like a good idea,' I say, folding up the paper and putting it in my bag. 'We could do that next week.'

'Mmn, it might break the ice. I mean, we can't do trust exercises every week, and this might be a way of getting everyone else talking. It's such a big thing to stand up and just start going on about your breakup – you don't know where to start sometimes – and this might be a way of focusing it a bit. You know, we could all say this week we're going to talk about Denial, or Anger, or whatever.'

'Jake said it would be a good idea to have themes for the meetings,' I remember.

'Oh yeah, Davey's guru! What's he like?'

'A bit of a know-it-all,' I say, feeling this isn't being quite fair to Jake.

'Is he New-Agey?'

'God no. He's very trendy and good-looking. I just think he's a bit full of himself, that's all.'

126

'I like Ben, don't you?' Daisy says.

'Where did that come from?' I ask, swivelling to look at her. We're entering the tube station, and she's reaching in her bag for her Travelcard, so I can't see her face. 'You don't fancy him, do you?'

'God no! He's not my type! Much too straight! But he's pretty cool, I think.'

I observe Daisy narrowly as we pass through the barrier. She looks like she's telling the truth.

'He and Finn really bonded,' I observe.

'Yeah, that was nice. We need the men to stay. It would be really sad if it was just girls whinging about useless men.'

'Jesus, yeah,' I agree. 'Then it wouldn't be Exes Anonymous at all, it would just be a Men-Are-Bastards meeting.'

'I know. I love that men are in pain too about being dumped, it makes me feel so much better.' Daisy giggles. 'That sounds awful, but you know what I mean. I miss Lewis so much . . .' She sighs. 'I really wish I'd talked in the meeting now. Oh well, I'll be super-keen for next week, you wait and see. I'll go first, if you want.'

'OK,' I say a little curtly.

I hope my true thoughts don't show in my tone of voice. I'm realising that I'm actually pretty ambivalent about Daisy's presence at Exes Anonymous. The rest of us are struggling with real, nasty breakups from people we were with for a long time, and here's Daisy using it to vent about a one-night stand that went pear-shaped. It feels as if she's putting her pain on the same level as mine.

God, I'm a bad friend. Who am I to judge Daisy's pain and say that it can't compare to mine? But it can't. I'm sorry. I'm still possessive about my pain. I don't want to let it go; I still want to wallow in it, because if I stop hurting when I think about Patrick, I will have lost the intensity of those happy memories too.

To distract myself, I choose the best remedy I know: bitching about mutual acquaintances. 'Jim's a sad case,' I say.

'I know. He's scared of his own shadow.'

'And he pongs, too.'

'Really?'

'Yeah. You weren't sitting that close to him. It's not actually being unwashed or anything, he just smells old and musty, like clothes that have been in a damp cupboard for ages. And he has dandruff, did you see?'

'Oh, yuck.'

'I know. I had to dust off my sweater after he'd had his head on my tummy.'

'Oh, *yuck*!'

'Mmn.'

'Well, I sort of felt sorry for him,' Daisy says, confirming her status as the nicer one of the two of us, if any proof of that were needed. 'He seems so depressed. That's stage four,' she adds.

I'm glad that the next stop is Oxford Circus. It's annoying me to hear Daisy talk so knowledgeably about the stages of grieving: she's never had a relationship that's lasted longer than a few months. What does she know about real grief? We kiss goodnight and I get out of the train, saying I'll ring her tomorrow.

Not a terrible night at home. At least, not the full range of my Patrick fetishes. I manage not to ring him, or listen to the messages on my machine, and I don't watch the Bobby Thunder video, but I do spot a man who looks very like him on the *Law & Order* repeat I've taped, a Filipino guy playing a pharmacist. He's tall and handsome, with the requisite ponytail and dark slanting eyes, and has a quiet, restrained poise about him that reminds me of Patrick even more than Bobby Thunder; he looks so competent in his white coat, so calmly sure of himself. He's only on screen for a minute or so but his image floats before my eyes for the rest of the episode, distracting me from the complicated evolution of the plot. At the end I crack, rewind the tape and watch the tiny segment with the Filipino pharmacist again and again. Then I fast-forward and find out his name in the credits. Johnny Lee. If I grow really weak I can always Google him and see if there's a photograph on the Net.

This isn't my fault. I wasn't looking for men who resemble Patrick; I deliberately restrained myself from putting on the Bobby Thunder video and gorging on that. I just happened to stumble across a guy who is almost the spitting image of Patrick. I can't be blamed for that.

I wonder whether this obsession with men who look like Patrick is actually a healthy sign – replacing the original object of desire with transitional fixations – or just an indication of my total and utter unwillingness to loosen my death grip on my memories of Patrick. I have a feeling that the group might tell me that it's Option B. But I am never, ever, going to talk about this with the group. It would be far too embarrassing. My behaviour, I know, is almost pathological. And besides, I don't want to give it up. I'm not ready. And right now it doesn't feel as if I will ever be ready. I'm in stasis. It may not be comfortable, but it's familiar; and maybe, in its way, that *is* a kind of comfort.

Chapter Eleven

Every time I get home and see the light flashing on the answering machine, my heart leaps. The triumph of insane hope over hard-won experience. I still think it might be Patrick. I spend so much time fantasising about a message from Patrick, asking how I'm doing, whether I still miss and love him, that it would almost be an anticlimax if it ever came. Almost, but not quite.

The message – there's just one – is however, to my considerable surprise, from Jake. 'Hi, Rebecca,' he says. He has a great voice, low and throaty. Much better than Patrick's. Patrick had – has – a light tenor, which was never that sexy. I used to listen to his voice on my machine in the early days of dating and wish that it could be deeper and huskier, the kind of voice that would send shivers down my spine. And then it didn't matter any longer. After the first time we had sex – the best first sex I've ever had in my entire life, probably will ever have – everything about Patrick turned me on. I even loved his flaws: his unsexy voice, the wariness in his eyes, his ugly T-shirts. Which is the best definition of love I know. There are many things about Patrick I would have liked to alter, hypothetically, but if a genie had offered me the chance to change them I wouldn't have touched a thing. Apart from his fear of loving me, of course.

I realise that Jake's entire message has run through without my hearing it; I've lost myself in thoughts of Patrick. I press the PLAY button again and listen to it properly this time.

'Hi Rebecca,' he says. 'This is Jake, Davey's friend. I know you had your first meeting last night and I was wondering how it went. I thought you might want to talk about it. When we

130

start in AA there are always a lot of people who've been there for ages and know the ropes . . . but you guys are all new to this, so there aren't any more experienced people there, or ones who can sponsor you, so there might be some stuff you want to iron out, or need some help with . . . Anyway, I'd be happy to give some support if you need it. Feel free to give me a ring any time you want to. I could sort of be your unofficial sponsor if you like. Well, um, that's about it. You've got my number, feel free to use it.'

That's actually a pretty nice message. Unpatronising and not at all pushy; much better than I would have expected from Jake. I consider his offer while I take off my coat (I always listen to my messages first thing when I walk in the door, just in case one might be from Patrick), kick my shoes into the corner under the coat rack (ditto), and pour myself a glass of wine. I don't need to wind down too much. It was a fairly easy day at work. Finn has been utterly ignoring Barney since the engagement announcement, lost in his trademark brooding gloom, but today, after his outpouring at the EA meeting yesterday evening, he's been positively cheerful – though, naturally, still sending Barney to Coventry. He's been bouncing around the office, challenging all comers to table football, and winking at me periodically as if we share a juicy secret. Which, in a way, we do. Only Davey knows about the EA group, and he doesn't expect me or Finn to tell him what went on at the meeting. We could confide in him about our own situations, of course, but the group rules forbid talking to outsiders about anything else, and Davey is too close to Finn and Daisy for me to feel comfortable discussing the group dynamic with him. No one would know: Davey is the soul of discretion. I could complain about Daisy and Finn and whoever else I wanted to until the cows came home, and Davey wouldn't breathe a word to them. But that would be cheating. We have to do this properly if we want it to work. Having been emotionally blackmailed into doing this whole EA experience, I find myself, very unexpectedly, wanting to give it

131

a chance; well, at least not sabotage it from the very beginning.

Which is why I am tempted to ring Jake. That would be appropriate, whereas talking to Davey would not. Jake is an outsider; he barely knows Finn and me; he's been in AA for donkey's years, sponsored several newcomers, and knows all about how the process works. In fact, I probably *need* to talk to him. Questions for my own benefit aside, I have no idea about what to do with the Twelve-Step process and how to introduce it to the group. And then there's the list Daisy printed off the Internet. It's on my coffee table. I pick it up and have another look at it.

SUDDENLY SINGLE?

THE FIVE STAGES OF GRIEF

Death of a spouse or the breakup of a marriage or long-term relationship can trigger similar responses in people. Each person mourns a loss differently.
However, there are five common stages of grief that a person goes through when mourning the loss of a relationship. These were adapted from Elisabeth Kübler-Ross's *On Death and Dying*. You may not experience these stages in one fluid order. You may go through some of the stages more than once. Sometimes an event will make you experience one of these stages again. For instance, cleaning out the basement and finding an old shirt of your deceased spouse or hearing your ex-partner is to remarry might cause reoccurrence of certain stages.

The five stages of grief are:

1. Denial – The 'No, not me' stage

This stage is filled with disbelief and denial. If your partner has died you still expect him to walk through

132

the door. If your partner has asked for a breakup you think that she will change her mind.

Cf. my perpetual, pre-falling asleep fantasies about coming home and finding Patrick waiting on my doorstep. In this fantasy he always wears the sweater I gave him for our first Christmas together, which he didn't like because it fitted him too well (Patrick was much too self-conscious about that kind of thing), but made him look unbelievably handsome. And I know, as soon as I see him wearing that sweater, that he's come to ask me to get back together with him. I handle it coolly, of course: I don't let him see how my heart is racing with excitement. I make him plead for hours until I finally relent.

2. Anger/Resentment – The 'Why me?' stage

Anger at the situation, your partner and others is common. You are angry with the other person for causing the situation and for causing you pain. You may feel anger at your deceased partner for dying. You may feel anger at your partner for asking for a divorce and breaking up the family.

OK, I've done this, if only very briefly. I was angry at Patrick when we broke up. I sent him a couple of furious emails pointing out what a bastard he'd been to keep me hanging on when he knew in his heart that he was never going to change and let me in. Particularly when he moved to New York. If he'd had any decency he would have broken up with me then, instead of initiating a miserable, drawn-out long-distance relationship. It was completely selfish of him. He couldn't let me go, even if it would have been the kindest thing to do. But the rage faded almost immediately. I think I was in such denial that I didn't have any time left over to be angry.

3. Bargaining – The 'If I do this, you'll do that' stage

You try to negotiate to change the situation. If you've lost a spouse to death you might bargain with God, 'I'll be a better person if you'd just bring him back'. You might approach your partner who is asking for the breakup and say, 'If you'll stay I'll change'.

Yup, I recognise that one. But while we were going out, rather than after we'd broken up. I did it constantly. If I give him more time and show him how much I love him, he'll realise that he can't lose me and make a massive effort to open up his heart to me ... I don't think I'm doing it now, though. I'm too busy being depressed.

4. Depression – The 'It's really happened' stage

You realise the situation isn't going to change. The death or breakup happened and there is nothing to bring the other person back. Acknowledgement of the situation often brings depression. This could be a quiet, withdrawn time as you absorb the situation.

I don't think I'm depressed in the right way. It isn't an acknowledgement of the situation. It's just ... being depressed.

5. Acceptance – The 'This is what happened' stage

Though you haven't forgotten what happened, you are able to begin to move forward.

Hah! Dream on.

Suggestions for if you find yourself suddenly single:

Avoid long-term legal decisions. If you are in an emotional state, it's better to put these off until your thinking is less cloudy.

We could all take a leaf out of Charlotte's book on that one, I think. No cloudy thinking there. Just ring up Daddy and make sure you've got plenty of leverage over the divorce lawyers so that you can financially screw your ex-husband into the ground.

Nurture yourself. You need to care for your spiritual, emotional and physical health. No one else will do it but you. Eat healthily, exercise regularly and take vitamins. Allow yourself to grieve and give yourself as much time as you need to adjust to what has happened.

I've done all that. I exercise and I eat healthily and I take calcium and folic acid and multivitamins every morning. Oh yes, and milk thistle to help my poor liver cope with all the abuse I'm throwing its way. But how much time is enough to adjust? I look round at all the photographs of Patrick and know that even the thought of taking them down, going cold turkey, would send me into panicked withdrawal. At least I'm not going to stumble over any possessions of his that will trigger extra grieving: I posted everything he had left in my flat back to him the day after we broke up. It was a pitifully small collection. One sweater, one pair of boxer shorts, one T-shirt, two books. Patrick had probably forgotten that he ever left them here; it was I who insisted that he leave something, and I'm sure he only did it to shut me up. But boxing them up and FedExing them to New York did at least give me some small, nasty satisfaction.

I sigh. I remember exactly what the sweater and the T-shirt and the boxer shorts looked like: I almost remember how they smelt. (Not the boxer shorts, of course. Those were clean: I'm not a pervert.) But I used to get that T-shirt out of the drawer and bury my nose in it as if it were Patrick's body. Those last few days in New York, when I knew that we weren't going to make it, I would lie in bed with my face pressed up against him as he slept, inhaling his scent, trying to fill myself up with it so that I would remember it for ever. I always loved the way Patrick smelled. He hardly ever wore aftershave; it was just eau de Patrick, his own particular chemistry, and whenever we met up after a long absence I would hug him and bury my head in the hollow of his neck for the exquisite pleasure of smelling him once again and knowing that I had come home. It was ironic that Patrick, so physically repressed except for when we made love, was the man to bring out all of those animal instincts in me. I greeted him partly by sniffing him, like one dog with another. And I could sleep with my head in his armpit and be intoxicated by the smell. Was it like that for him too? He once mentioned that he could smell me on his sheets and that it was sad to have my scent but not my physical presence, so maybe it was.

Aaagh, I'm wallowing in stupid memories again, and I'm sick of them. It's like having a sugar binge: you stuff sweets down, one after the other; the pleasure's only momentary but your teeth ache for hours afterwards. I need to do something constructive to change my mood. So I pick up the phone and ring Jake.

He isn't in. I leave a message. But I do feel better.

'I don't think I was ever really in denial,' Daisy is saying. 'I sort of *expected* him to dump me. Maybe I made it happen, because I didn't believe that he would really want to go out with me, and he picked up on that. I mean, he realised that I didn't value myself enough and took me at my own estimation. He had everything – he's gorgeous, he has a good job, he's really charming and dresses well and he's very clever – I

136

just didn't believe that I deserved someone like that for a boyfriend.'

Jennifer, who's sitting next to me, snorts in disbelief. I turn my head and grin at her in mutual recognition of Daisy's totally illogical lack of self-esteem, and she ventures a small timid smile back at me. I notice that Ben and Finn are also rolling their eyes at each other incredulously. It's very hard to get your head round the fact that a tall, beautiful, fashionably attired blonde with a fabulous job could actually be crippled by having such a low opinion of herself.

'So, you know, maybe that's my problem,' Daisy continues. 'I'm not going through the five stages and so I'm not moving on. I don't really feel anger or resentment either, because I'm too willing to believe that I deserve the treatment I get. I mean, if someone doesn't ring me, I think it's all my fault. *And* I do the bargaining part too much. I'm always too willing to change for someone. I just sit around for hours after a date, thinking what I could have done differently. Maybe if I'd worn a different outfit, or been more lively, or less lively, or more stand-offish, or less stand-offish . . .' She sighs. 'You know when you just go over and over everything you've said to someone, and everything they said to you? And you torture yourself thinking: If only I'd done this, or done that, then maybe everything would have worked out?'

Finn holds up a yellow card. He loves those cards. I'm disappointed, actually. This is really good stuff that Daisy's coming out with. I identify with it so closely. I want her to keep on talking about it, partly because if she really nails this one, I won't feel that I have to talk myself. I'm scared of qualifying. And yet, I feel a huge pressure building up inside me that won't be satisfied until it bursts out of my mouth.

'Well, that's about it,' Daisy says. 'I think I need to work on my denial and my anger, which sounds pretty stupid when you put it like that, but would probably really help me. I tend to be much too positive, I think, I always try to see the good in everyone. And I need to look after myself more, be a bit more on the defensive and get in touch with my negative feelings – God, this is sounding really like therapy-speak now. I'm going to shut up and let someone else make a fool of themselves – no, sorry, I didn't mean that, I just meant *I'd* made a fool of myself – oops, red card, I'm really going to shut up now.'

We all clap. It's become a convention now after someone qualifies.

'Who wants to go next?' I say, hoping that Jim or Jennifer will raise their hands. But of course they don't; they just sit there looking panicky at the thought of having to say anything on their own. Even Ben, who came in all cocky and confident, him and Finn doing lots of shoulder-punching by way of greeting, isn't meeting my eye. And Finn and Charlotte, of course, have already talked. They both look like cats who ate the cream: how they love a good healthy venting of their anger towards their exes. Finn and Charlotte have no problems at all with Stage Two.

'All right,' I say reluctantly. 'I'll go.' And though I don't want to talk about Patrick, I feel a huge release flood through me at those words. Finn looks at his watch and fiddles with a tiny button on the side.

'Three – two – one – go!' he says, pressing another button.

Finn is definitely taking this whole timing thing much too seriously.

'Um, hi, my name's Rebecca and I'm addicted to my ex,' I start.

'Hi, Rebecca,' they all say supportively. Charlotte's voice, naturally, is much louder than anyone else's.

'I really identified with what Daisy was saying about wondering what would have happened if she'd done something differently,' I continue. 'I've been doing a lot of thinking about that myself recently. For me it's more things that I put up with, which I now think I shouldn't have, though I'm not sure what that would have changed. I think maybe it would have meant that I would have broken up with Patrick earlier – that's my ex. But maybe, if I'd stood up for myself more, it would have meant that we had a better relationship and he would have worked harder at it. Um, for those of you who don't know, I was going out with Patrick for two years and then he got posted to New York with the bank he works for, and he was going to be gone for at least two years. And he didn't ask me to go with him, or talk about getting engaged, which I obviously found really difficult. Now I really regret not having said that I would break up with him if one of those two things didn't happen. But I couldn't, I just loved him so much and hoped that it would work out and he'd realise how much he missed me . . . but he didn't. We hardly saw each other – he said he was working really hard and couldn't get back here, and I was too proud to push and insist that I should go over there a lot, and also I felt that *he* should come back and visit *me*, because he was the one who'd gone away . . . Anyway, as soon as we broke up I found myself realising all the things I'd done that I wished I hadn't. I'd made a real effort to get to know all his friends, and his family, and he didn't do the same for me. He was sort of awkward with my friends and never suggested going out with them.'

I see Daisy nodding at this. I know she always felt that Patrick was uncomfortable around my friends, who were louder and more raucous than his. He was polite with them, but not much more than that; he made it clear that he was hanging out with them for my sake, rather than because he actually liked them for themselves.

'We tended to do things much more on his terms – watch the kind of films he liked, listen to his kind of music. I mean, I liked those things too, I wasn't martyring myself, but it was always me extending myself to take an interest in *his* interests, rather than the other way round. I was the one making all the effort. He made me go to a football game once and I always said he'd have to come to the theatre with me, in return, but he was so pissy about it that I never ended up making him go. I mean, we did have a lot in common, but somehow it was always in Patrick's comfort zone. If he wanted to watch *The Simpsons*, I'd watch it with him, but if I was watching *Friends*, he would pick up a book instead until it was finished. I was just so happy when he was happy. I would have done anything to make him happy. And he'd make it so clear that stuff like *Friends* didn't make him happy that it was never worth insisting on. But now I look back and that small stuff was really significant of the big stuff, you know? Those things were tiny little cracks that were incredibly indicative of the fact that Patrick was never going to step towards me, it was always me stepping towards him . . .'

Finn holds up the yellow card. I'm pathetically grateful. This is proving even harder than I thought it would be.

'When we broke up, I wrote to him about this,' I go on. 'I sent him two emails about it. I was so angry. Because when we broke up, he said that he didn't really want to be in a proper couple. He said that he didn't want to double-date or have dinner parties.'

Daisy draws in her breath sharply in disapproval. I've never told her that before. I probably never would have done, if it hadn't been for the group.

'And I just thought: all those times I hung out with your friends, all those times I had dinner with your ghastly family, and you *never* made the slightest bit of effort with mine . . . I thought it was my fault for not being right somehow, or trying hard enough, and it wasn't me, it was him, he's just so fucked up. When we broke up I told him he was completely messed up because he couldn't have a proper relationship and he wouldn't have one-night stands, and it was *so true*. I should have spotted that years ago, but so should he, he just kept me hanging on completely selfishly because he couldn't bear to lose me, but he treated me so badly—'

Finn's producing the red card. I stop dead.

'No, finish off if you want to, Rebecca,' Daisy says instantly, and everyone else is nodding.

'No, that's fine,' I say quickly.

I'm done. I'm more than done. I feel completely drained and on the verge of tears. I want to cry, actually; it would be such a release. But I'm too proud. I choke back the tears as they all clap, and pray that the attention will turn to somebody else so that I can sit here in silence for a while and let my emotions settle down to a more manageable level.

'Does anyone else want to talk?' I mutter hopefully. Jim and Jennifer duck their heads immediately. 'Ben?' I say.

'Maybe next week. I'm still building up the courage, you know?' he says honestly.

'Take your time, mate,' Finn says supportively.

'Actually, I'd like to say something,' Charlotte says. 'I think we should be able to comment on what other people have said.'

'I don't know,' I say doubtfully. 'They don't do that in AA.'

'But we're *not* AA,' Charlotte points out. 'We're making up the rules as we go along here. And I think that if we have comments we should be able to make them.'

'Yeah,' Finn chips in. 'It could be helpful.'

'Just as long as people are supportive,' Daisy says. 'I mean, we're not trained therapists or anything, we need to be careful of each other's feelings.'

'Yes,' Jennifer says unexpectedly. We all turn to look at her. She blushes so deeply her freckles almost disappear under the flush of blood to her cheeks. 'I mean, it shouldn't be critical,' she adds in a tiny voice.

'Well, I have something to say to Daisy,' Charlotte says, ignoring this. 'The man you were just talking about – how long did you know him for?'

Oh God, I see exactly where this is going.

'It was a one-night stand,' Daisy says, bravely telling the truth, though I'm sure she, too, gets Charlotte's drift.

'Because I thought this group was supposed to be about getting over your exes,' Charlotte says, 'and I really don't think that this counts as—'

141

'Hey, Charlotte!' Finn interrupts. 'Remember, no criticism!'

'But—' Charlotte's prominent jaw is thrust out, her small blue eyes narrowed.

'Yes,' I say, having collected my own emotions and stuffed them down into a dark little place from which I will retrieve them later, when everyone's gone. 'No judgements. People have to be free to talk without being, um, judged.'

This is despite the fact that secretly, I agree with Charlotte. Still, I know whose side I'm on. I have to defend Daisy in public.

'I just don't think a one-night stand is comparable to eight years of—' Charlotte starts again.

'It's not *about* that,' Jennifer says. We all stare at her again. The blush is even stronger, the bright red of her cheeks clashing with her hair, but she persists. 'It's not about who suffered more, is it? It's about how much pain you're feeling. And I thought what Daisy said about the Five Stages was really helpful.'

Daisy looks unutterably grateful. I am deeply impressed that little Jennifer has had the nerve to stand up to Charlotte. It's like watching a mouse put itself in the path of a charging rhino.

'Me too,' Finn says.

'Yes, me too,' I chime in. 'It made me realise that I wasn't feeling angry enough. I was in the beginning, but I'm not angry now, and I should be.'

'I made copies of the Five Stages for everyone,' Daisy says, pointing to a small pile of papers on the table. 'I thought we could try to work through them together.'

'Great,' Finn says, taking one and stuffing it into his pocket. 'Thanks, Daise.'

'Yeah, thanks,' chimes in Ben, smiling at Daisy in a way that says, 'don't worry about Charlotte, we're on your side'.

Charlotte snorts, but we all ignore her.

'Why don't we have a theme for next week?' I suggest. 'We could all talk about the Five Stages and how we feel we're doing with them.'

'Great idea,' Finn says.

The meeting breaks up a short time afterwards. Daisy offers to help me clear up, but I refuse. I need to be on my own. It felt like something broke inside me when I talked about Patrick like that. I didn't mean to do it. I meant to talk about how much I loved him and how good he was for me, and then all of that anger poured out instead. I feel horribly unbalanced, as if I were drunk and the floor was tilting beneath my feet. I put the glasses in the dishwasher, stack the empties into a cardboard box, and then, when I have no clearing-up left to do, I wait for the tears to come.

But they don't. I can't cry. I have a great lump in my throat which hurts when I swallow, and I still can't cry. I go into my bedroom and sit in front of the huge photo of Patrick, trying to summon up memories of that holiday in Portugal. But what comes instead are flashbacks to all the times he sat silently when we were out with my friends, refusing to relax and enjoy himself, all the times we ended up seeing the films he wanted to see instead of the ones I did, all the times I rang him in New York only to get his answering machine, and all the times I exerted myself to be bright and cheerful and interested at dinner with his family, who were pretty much the seventh circle of hell, and whose politics, infighting and ability to bear grudges made mine seem like the Waltons by comparison.

I am really angry now, and I don't know what to do with all this rage; it's fizzing up inside me like a geyser beginning to explode, hot stinky bubbles of sulphur coming to the boil. I climb up on to my chest of drawers and wrestle the photograph off the wall but I'm so worked up that I lose my footing and slip, and the photograph falls out of my grasp. I end up on the floor with a sore leg from where I whacked it on the chest of drawers, bits of shattered plastic lying all around me, and a bruised arm from the corner of the clip frame, which fell on top of me as I went down. Thank God I didn't get it framed professionally, or it would have been glass in the frame instead of plastic. I could have been cut to pieces.

Now I do burst into tears, lying there amid the wreckage. My leg hurts and my arm hurts and my entire body is throbbing from an excess of violent emotion. I cry hard, the tears wrenched out of me, big angry gulps which convulse my chest, and when I can't cry any more I am still aching all over. I don't know what to do with myself. I need something but I don't know what it is. Finally, I pick myself up off the floor, ignoring the mess around me, and limp over to the phone. I need to talk to someone. I mean to ring Daisy, but instead I find myself reaching for my address book and dialling Jake's number.

Chapter Twelve

The Palm House is as packed and humid as a late-night dance club under the railway arches behind Waterloo station. Steam pipes squeak and hiss, emitting streams of vapour every few minutes. It reminds me of those 1940s detective novels where in the third act the hero always ends up trapped in a basement which the villain is proceeding to flood with gas. Usually chained to a wall next to a beautiful blonde.

Though not chained to a wall – something I wouldn't completely rule out under the right circumstances – I *am* in the company of a beautiful blond. I notice the looks other women are giving Jake, who seems completely unaware of the attention he's getting. Either that, or he's so used to it that he just takes it for granted. Despite my softening towards him, I can't help but feel some enduring, latent hostility. Maybe that's because he's so good-looking. As pleasant as it is to be out with a man who is so handsome, I am aware that the looks we're getting are more along the lines of what-is-he-doing-with-her? rather than wow-what-an-incredibly-gorgeous-couple. A mother with two small children and a hubby in tow is blatantly flicking her hair and smiling in his direction, totally ignoring her harassed husband's attempts to stop their two sprogs falling down the gaps in the narrow iron staircase we're all ascending.

This excursion to Kew Gardens was Jake's idea. When I rang him, he suggested that we meet up, and said he tries to come here most weekends. It was a schlep to get down here – I'm so used to living in my little North London bubble that encloses Highbury Fields to Clerkenwell – but I must admit that it was worth it. I'm even getting a free facial steam cleanse from the humid, greenhouse air of the Palm House. My pores will be as open as a twenty-four-hour petrol station by the time we leave.

It's typical of Jake to do something as healthy for the soul as coming to Kew Gardens on a regular basis. Jake's a walking, talking embodiment of all the virtues; clean liver, clean lungs, clean mind. He makes me feel inadequate by contrast. Jake has done all his work and made peace with his demons, whereas I am still struggling under their weight. And then, of course, there's his previously mentioned insane handsomeness. No wonder I have a hard time warming to him.

We haven't talked about anything important yet, just made idle chit-chat. Jake wanted to come straight to the Palm House, and now I understand why. It's so calming in here: the steam, the enormous, leafy palm trees which reach up to the glass roof as the sun pours down through it, casting bright reflections on to the green leaves. Despite the Sunday-afternoon crowd, I can feel my mood softening, the tension releasing. By the time we have threaded our way along the iron catwalks and back down the circular staircase at the other end, I feel so peaceful that I can hardly remember what was so urgent that I needed to call Jake late at night, almost sobbing with stress and unhappiness.

'This place is beautiful,' I say.

'Isn't it? You can see why I come here so often.' He smiles at me, a light breeze lifting his hair. The sky is a clear blue and the glittering green lawn outside, after a long rainy winter, is velvety soft, as thick and high as the pile of an expensive carpet. We can bitch all we want about England's weather, but it does mean that come spring, we have the lushest, greenest grass. I want to take my shoes off and scrunch my bare feet into it, feeling the blades cling and catch between my toes, but I would be inhibited to do something that childish in front of Jake. He's so poised, so together, that I feel I need to be on my best, adult, behaviour around him.

146

'So tell me what's been going on in your group,' he says. 'You sounded pretty upset on the phone.'

'Well, it wasn't just the group – no, I suppose it was,' I admit. 'It brought up a lot of stuff for me.'

He nods, obviously having expected this. 'Do you want to sit down?' he asks, gesturing to a bench under a spreading oak tree which casts a huge pool of shadow at its base. The sun is so warm that I can already imagine how fresh and cool that shade will feel in the heat of summer.

'No, thanks, I think I'd rather keep walking,' I say.

'OK. Let's head this way.'

We stroll across a swathe of lawn bordered with white daffodils, their centres the pale yellow of new primroses, the petals trembling slightly in the breeze. An urgent academic type passes us, walking fast and muttering to himself. There's a rucksack strapped to his back with a folding umbrella sticking out of it, the whole contraption looking like a home-made jet pack, as if he were a mad scientist planning to launch himself into the sky.

'I don't know . . .' I start, and then pause. I do know. 'I spoke for the first time last meeting, and it brought up a lot of issues . . .'

Jake nods again. 'That must have been scary,' he says.

'Very,' I say gratefully. 'I just have all these things I know I should be doing to get better, and I'm not doing them, and the group really reminds me of them and I get very confused . . .'

'What sort of things?'

We pass some cherry blossoms, and some pink-and-white petals, caught by the wind, float off the trees in a gentle rosy cloud. The roots of the trees are puddled with fallen petals, like pink shadows on the grass. It's so ridiculously pretty that it seems unreal, as if we've walked into a Monet.

'I have these photos of Patrick – that's my ex – all over my flat . . .'

And now that I've started, I can't stop. I tell Jake all about the candles, the photos, the big one in the bedroom, about how I broke the frame and hauled all the broken pieces of plastic down to the garbage, but still kept the photo, propped up now against the dresser, with its edges curling so that I can barely see the picture. It's humiliating, but such a relief. I don't think I could ever have said this in group, with six people staring at me and pitying me. Jake is different. Firstly, we're walking, so I don't have to look at him while I recount this. And secondly, I don't even like him. Well, not that much. He's just a good listener, someone who has been through the wars himself, who has counselled a lot of people before and to whom my story, though pathetic, can hardly be the most shocking thing he's ever heard. In that way, it's like confiding in a therapist. Only it's free.

By the time I've finished, we're across the gardens and walking past the petting zoo. The air is full of children's piping cries, squeaky with excitement, as they queue up for their turns. But the children actually in the pen with the animals are quiet, enchanted, solemnly stroking the shaggy chocolate pelts of the miniature ponies. The smell of fresh hay and horse dung is rich in the air. More kids are slumped on the grass around the zoo, drugged into happiness by their close encounters with the animals, their chatter momentarily stopped by sweets and ice cream from the snack pavilion.

'I've got an idea for you,' Jake says.

'What?'

'Get an exercise book. Just a cheap one, like you used to use for school. Not a notepad, because the pages'll come away from the binding. You know, one of the old-fashioned ones with the staples in the middle.'

'OK. And?'

'And every time you have an obsessive thought about your ex, draw a line in it, just a short one.'

'You mean, like prisoners counting off the days?'

He laughs. 'Yeah, exactly. But every time you think about your ex, you have to draw a line. I know it sounds crazy, but it does work. I used to do that when I had obsessive thoughts about drinking. Sometimes you just sit there with the book for ages, drawing line after line, and sometimes you just add one or two. It's a real release.'

'OK,' I say again, doubtfully.

'You'll fill up pages and pages at first. But then, gradually, you'll find yourself using it less and less. And there's something – I dunno, something satisfying about seeing all those pages full of lines. It makes you feel as if you're getting all the bad thoughts out.'

'Do you still do that?' I ask. I'm not sure how much I'm allowed to ask Jake about his alcoholic past, and not sure, either, how much I want to know. It *is* like talking to a therapist, in the sense that I need Jake to remain strong and relatively neutral: I couldn't deal with him spilling his guts to me the same way that I'm doing to him.

'Not so much,' he says easily. 'But I still have all my notebooks in a drawer of my desk.'

'"All your notebooks"?'

He laughs. 'Yeah, I got through quite a few.'

'Was it . . . um . . .' I'm shy about this, but feel, to be polite, that I ought to at least put some token questions to him, so this conversation isn't one hundred per cent Rebecca-whinge. He can always field them if he wants.

'It was pretty bad,' he says. 'I fucked up a long-term relationship, and I fucked up my job. I thought I was the coolest guy in the world, and alcohol just encouraged me in that delusion. It took a lot of self-inflicted crap to make me realise that I was only human. The drink made me very grandiose.'

Two cyclists pass us, talking softly to each other, the wheels of their bikes crunching lightly on the gravel path.

'But I can't blame the drink,' Jake continues. 'It was me, using it to feel like something I wasn't. I've pretty much given up the fantasy of being Superman now.'

149

'That's a shame, in a way,' I say without thinking. 'I'd love to feel like Superman.'

Then I think I've just jammed my foot so far into my mouth that it will never come out. To my great relief, Jake turns to give me one of those grins that make his mouth curl up so appealingly.

'Yeah, it was pretty good,' he says. 'I miss it sometimes.'

We're walking along the river path. The Thames is flat and dirty green, with seagulls swooping and crying over its surface. Planes pass constantly overhead, coming and going to Heathrow, but in the last hour I have become so used to them that I have tuned them out. Instead, I hear the sound of the seagulls and bicycle wheels on gravel and children's high yelps of excitement.

'And how's the group going?' he asks, signalling that he's finished talking about himself. I am grateful. He gave just enough to make me feel that we're in the same boat, but not too much. I know from Davey that Jake's been mentoring people for a long time now, and his experience shows.

I give him a brief summary of the two meetings, with a rundown of the participants. He loves the trust exercise part; he laughs and laughs when I tell him that we finished up with Musical Chairs.

'Sounds like it was very successful,' he says.

'Yeah . . . Not everyone's talked yet, though. In fact there's one guy – Jim, the weird one – who never opens his mouth.'

'Oh, don't worry about that,' Jake says immediately. 'You'll find that some people will keep showing up but hardly ever talk. Just don't push them to qualify. They have to feel comfortable about it. Remember, the group's going to be made up of a whole range of different personalities. You're going to have ones who are pretty silent and ones who try to talk too much . . .'

'*Exactly*,' I interrupt. 'There's one woman, Charlotte, who just can't keep her mouth shut. She's basically trying to take over the entire thing.'

'She'll probably settle down,' Jake says reassuringly.

'So you don't think I should have a word with her?'

'Nope. Not yet, anyway. It's much too early. And you'll be surprised how much even the most annoying people can contribute. There's one guy in my regular meeting who's a bit of a nightmare most of the time – he's loud and obnoxious and sets people's teeth on edge. But every so often he'll come out with something amazing and profound that really moves me and gets me thinking. This is partly a tolerance exercise, you know. That sounds a bit wanky, but it's very good for you.'

I sigh again. 'That *does* sound a bit wanky, to be honest. But I take your point.'

Jake laughs again. He has a lovely laugh. 'Sorry. I do tend to get a bit preachy sometimes.'

'No problem,' I say, though I don't really mean it.

'Let's go into the lily house,' he says, indicating a small building on the left side of the path. 'It's lovely in there.'

We pass through the doors and into a tropically heated zone; like the Palm House, it's so steamy that I feel my jeans become instantly stiff and heavy with moisture. In the centre is the water-lily pool, a flat black circle of water, its surface constantly, delicately dappled by tiny invisible bugs, pattering on the surface like miniature raindrops. The flowers spike up from their frame of flat green leaves, candy pink, orange, pale chartreuse, as spiky-petalled as their leaves are soft and rounded. It's strangely hypnotic; the people around the pool are speaking softly, as if they were in church.

'I've got the feeling there's something else that's on your mind,' Jake says perceptively. 'About the group.'

'Well . . .' I take a breath and tell him about Daisy. 'I just feel that she's riding on our coat-tails,' I finish. 'And I feel bad about thinking that. But her experience – it's just not equivalent to anything that the rest of us are going through. And we wouldn't have let her into the group if she hadn't been a friend of mine. I mean, if she'd emailed us saying that she'd had a bad time with a one-night stand, we wouldn't have thought that was enough for her to come to meetings.'

'Hmn,' Jake says. 'Look . . . let's go outside, this was a bad idea, we can't talk properly in here . . .'

It's true: the elderly ladies next to us keep turning curiously to eavesdrop. One thing I always notice about being old is that you have absolutely no shame about being caught listening to other people's conversations. When I catch their bright beady eyes they just smile and nod at me, and cock their heads at an angle, hoping to hear more.

Jake finds us an unoccupied bench outside, and we sit down. 'OK,' he starts, 'I think what you're describing with your friend is what we call in AA a "high bottom". That's the name we give to someone who realised early on that they were an alcoholic, without having to end up lying in the gutter in a mess of their own puke, or drive drunk, or alienate all their friends and relations. Maybe they just got badly drunk a few times and decided that alcohol was dangerous for them, and that they needed support to stay away from it. And, to be perfectly frank with you, there *are* some people in AA who are a little snobbish about their own experiences – the ones who really hit bottom in a bad way, who've had to claw their way back up again and rebuild their entire lives. But mostly, there's an acceptance of whatever any particular person has been through. All you need, when you decide to come to AA, is the awareness that you're an alcoholic – whatever that means to you. It's number three in the twelve traditions of AA – has Davey ever mentioned them to you?'

'No.'

'Never mind. You don't need most of them. But number three goes: "The only requirement for AA membership is a desire to stop drinking." So if your friend thinks that she has a problem getting over her exes, enough of a problem for her to want to come to the group, then she does, and you shouldn't judge her. I doubt she would ever say to you that she thinks she's suffering as much as you are. But remember, everyone's problem is different, and everyone's problem is the same.'

That helps tremendously. I take a deep breath and feel my annoyance with Daisy melting away.

'Did that help?' he says a little anxiously.

'Yes, it did. It really did. Thanks so much, Jake.' It's the first time I have ever thanked him, and it's completely sincere. I'm very glad I rang him.

A billowing tomato-red kite is floating in the sky, its colour seeming even more artificial because there are practically no flowers in the gardens yet, just the pale daffodils and delicate pink clouds of cherry blossoms. The colour of the kite is like a promise of the summer to come: bright red roses, purple tulips. I find myself actually looking forward to summer. Which is wonderful, because it's the first time for ages that I have looked forward to anything. A pair of lovers walk by, their arms entwined; like us, they're wearing mostly black, and they look incongruous among the suburban families so prevalent here. The man ducks his shaved head to kiss the woman, and I wait for the usual catch of envy and loss under my breastbone. But it doesn't come. I feel almost easy watching them embrace. It's a minor miracle, the kind that you can build on. And Jake helped me reach it. I am more grateful to him than I can say.

Chapter Thirteen

CHARLOTTE

'I've only just realised how terribly unhappy I am – completely thanks to this group. Fantastic, isn't it? Ironically, I was actually an awful lot better off before I started in bloody Exes Anonymous. I was holding it together very well – you know, divorce settlement sorted out, life back on track, kids doing not too badly, considering. And I've spent a lot of time over the last few weeks resenting this group with every fibre of my being. But the trouble is, once I start a thing, I have to finish it. Public school upbringing, I suppose. No shirking a task once you put your hand to it. My headmistress was terribly hard on quitters. She didn't mind, really, if you did a bad job, as long as you were trying and you got the job finished as best you could.

'So there was never any question of me just dropping out, though by God, I wanted to. I had to face up to the fact that it was me who'd answered that ad in *Time Out* in the first place. Some part of me must have wanted to go through this, God knows why. I think on the surface I told myself it'd all be healthy venting, you know? Lots of isn't-he-or-she-an-absolute-bastard, downing a few drinks, exchanging horror stories and cheering ourselves up by having a damn good bitch about how atrocious our exes were. And then Daisy brought along those bloody Five Stages of Grief, and I couldn't stop thinking about them. I even threw out the list, but by then I had them all in my head, programmed in. I knew I was stuck on Anger. I knew it. I'd been through the whole Denial thing already, when he said he was leaving. I'd kept thinking, "it can't be happening, he'll wake up one day and decide he's changed his mind and tell me he was a bloody fool and he's sorry, and everything will be back to normal again." And there I was, just angry. Furious. Livid. I couldn't get over it. I don't know if I've done Bargaining yet. I suppose I have. I think I did that earlier too. If I give him a bit of time to go and live with that wretched common tart he thinks he's madly in love with, enough time to break up our whole happy family and cause the children so much pain, well, after a while he'll realise what an idiot he's been, and what a walking cliché he is. Having a mid-life crisis and running off with your secretary, how pathetic! He's just a joke to everyone!

'But he didn't come back. He stayed with her. And he kept telling me that she was the love of his life and that he'd never been so happy. And I just got angrier and angrier and one day about two weeks ago I burst into tears and couldn't stop crying and barely got out of bed in the morning – thank God for the au pair, who's super, and lovely Nadia, the cleaning lady, I'd have fallen apart without them – and I realised I was well and truly into Depression.

'I'm not even that angry any more. It comes and goes, but basically I'm just bloody depressed all the bloody time. I try to pull myself together for the sake of the children, but I don't think I'm doing a brilliant job, frankly, and none of my friends are any help. My mother just keeps telling me to buck up and get on with things, and she thinks it's my fault for letting him go – as if there was something I could have done to keep him when he was packing up and telling me that he was moving in with that cheap little tart! – and my friends are terrified it's going to rub off on them. You know – now that William's bolted, their husbands are going to look at him and decide to run off too. Well, after he got taken to the cleaners in the divorce, I'm sure all their husbands are too bloody terrified of losing everything to even think about screwing their secretaries.

But still, I'm a bit *persona non grata* at the moment. The skeleton at the feast. And telling them I'm depressed just makes things worse. They don't want to see me as it is, let alone if I'm sobbing all over their shoulders about how unhappy I am. I have to keep a stiff upper lip.

'So I expect, deep down, that's why I decided to come to this group in the first place. I loathe getting all beardy-weardy and psychological, but I'm sure I actually felt the need to have a good sob and talk about how depressed I was with people who wouldn't ostracise me for it . . . I haven't got to Acceptance yet. God knows how long that'll take. Years, I imagine. Years of arranging the kids' holidays with him and working out when he gets to see them and if he can bring the cheap tart to school sports days and who gets them for Christmas. God, I don't know if I can face it. I really don't.

'So Daisy, you ought to be jolly proud of yourself. I'm on Stage Four. Bloody Depression, I hate it. My doctor wants to give me some happy pills but I won't hear of it. I'm damned if some little pill's going to tell me how I feel. You know, I said I wasn't angry any more, but I am. I'm angry at this damned group. Sorry. I will keep coming back, though. Because I know that if I don't, I might be stuck in this depression forever, like I was stuck in anger before I came. God, it's hard though, isn't it? It's the hardest thing in the world. I could kill him for making me go through this. I really could.'

I get into work on Monday to find a white envelope propped up against my computer, addressed to Miss Rebecca Havers in elaborate, black cursive writing. Miss? Who says Miss anymore? Looking around, I see that similar envelopes are leaning against the computer screens on the desks of everyone who hasn't made it into work yet. I wave the envelope at Davey, who's always at work early nowadays. Ever since he gave up the demon booze, he's become an early-morning riser.

'What's this all about?' I say.

'Open it and see,' he says, strolling over to my desk.

I sit down on the corner of my desk and rip open the envelope. Inside is a thick white rectangle of card, the writing on it so deeply embossed that the effect is three-dimensional. No expense spared here.

In honour of the engagement of
Barney Falkland-Smythe and Vanessa Carpenter
Mr and Mrs Falkland-Smythe
have the pleasure of inviting:
Miss Rebecca Havers
to a weekend House Party
at Grange Manor, Yeovil, Somerset
Friday, 10 July, to Sunday, 12 July

RSVP

'Oh boy,' I say, looking around for Finn. He's nowhere to be seen. 'Are we all invited?'

'Yup,' Davey says. 'Should be interesting, shouldn't it?'

'Does Finn know?'

Davey nods. 'He opened his and went out straight away.'

'I love when people are so posh that they don't have a street address,' I say. 'Daisy used to work at a really expensive safari company and she said that practically all the clients either lived at The Manor House, Little-Pilkington-on-the-Wold, or had a SW1 or SW3 postcode. If someone rang up for a brochure and didn't have one of those addresses, she knew they wouldn't be able to afford the safari.'

'Did she send them the brochures anyway?'

'Yup. But they never booked.'

The door swings open and Finn strides into the office. Covert glances slide his way; he is walking with such a focused, unwavering gait that he clearly has some important goal in mind.

157

We assume that he's going to head over to Barney's desk and throw the invitation down in front of his brother with a caustic comment, but instead he comes right over to me and Davey.

'Rebecca,' he says, 'I've got something to tell you. And Davey, too.'

'What?'

'You have to promise not to tell anyone in the office.'

I look at Davey. We both nod. 'OK.'

Finn's jaw is set and his short fair hair is sticking up in places, as if he's just been running his hands through it. He looks even more counter-culture than usual; he's been dressing in a deliberately alternative way – faded leather trousers and bright T-shirts printed with slogans like 'Malibu's Most Wanted' or 'Girls Gone Wild' – ever since the wedding announcement, as if to proclaim his utter disdain for Barney and Vanessa's bourgeois values. I think he's been spiking his hair with more moulding wax than usual, too. The expression of determination on his face is very much at odds with his slacker style. I'm extremely curious to know what he's going to say.

'Daisy's going to be my girlfriend,' he says.

I stare at him, completely taken aback. I've never picked up on any sexual tension between him and Daisy, and Finn isn't the type Daisy usually goes for; though Finn's good-looking enough for Daisy, which is saying quite a lot considering the standards of beauty Daisy herself sets, she tends to prefer men who are much smoother and more persuasive. Lewis was the classic Daisy type: a slick charmer ready to shower her with compliments. Finn, by comparison, is much more rough around the edges – direct, no-nonsense, and certainly lacking airs and graces. I can't imagine Finn buttering up a girl to get her into bed. Except maybe literally.

'Um, wow. Is this a unilateral decision?' I ask. I'm sure that if Daisy had any interest in Finn, I'd have heard about it by now. Daisy is incapable of keeping that kind of thing to herself; she's like an oil gusher. Once she's struck, she just keeps on pouring herself out. If she fancied Finn, she'd have been talking non-stop about him.

'No, not really,' he says impatiently. 'It's just pretend, for this sodding house party weekend. I just went outside and rang her on my mobile and she said OK, she'd do it.'

Davey and I stare at him, stricken dumb.

'I can't face being there all by myself with Barney and Vanessa canoodling and being all lovey-dovey,' he explains.

'But you won't be by yourself, mate,' Davey says. 'We'll all be around.'

'Yeah, but there'll be loads of their friends there too, and they all know that Vanessa and I used to go out. I have to have a girlfriend there or they'll all just feel incredibly sorry for me.'

'How big is your parents' house?' I ask, amazed, imagining a mansion large enough to accommodate everyone from the office plus a bevy of Barney and Vanessa's friends.

'Oh, gigantic. We could put up an entire regiment. I think we did, during the Civil War. But that's not the point. I need you guys to promise you'll go along with this.'

'But why Daisy?' I'm still trying to get my head round this.

'Because she's a good mate and she knows it won't mean anything.'

'Yeah,' I say cynically, 'and because she's a gorgeous blonde who'd make anyone feel psychotically jealous.'

'Daisy's not my type,' Finn says.

'Daisy's *everyone's* type,' Davey corrects him.

'And then what?' I ask. 'Does she have to pretend to be your girlfriend at the wedding too?'

Finn looks nauseated at the thought of Barney and Vanessa's nuptials.

'We can cross that bridge when we come to it,' he mutters.

'Are you going to kiss?' I say, wondering why I'm being so prurient.

'No, we can just cuddle a lot and stare into each other's eyes,' Finn says practically. 'We just negotiated that over the phone.

159

I mean, neither of us actually wants to get off with each other, so we're sorted.'

'And what about sharing a room?'

'Oh, I've worked that one out. She can have the bed and I'll sneak in my old sleeping bag and kip on the floor. No one will know.'

'God, Finn, I really don't know if this is such a good idea.' I object. 'I mean, we're supposed to be getting over our exes, not trying to make them jealous. This is *not* part of a healthy recovery process.'

Davey coughs loudly and nods behind me. I glance over my shoulder and see Barney coming our way.

'Everyone got their invites, then?' he asks bluffly.

'Um, yeah,' Davey and I say. Finn just stares at his brother, his face expressionless.

'It should be a great weekend! Nessa's so looking forward to getting to know all of you better!' Barney says, his smooth, pinkish face beaming as if Vanessa didn't already know his brother very well, in the Biblical sense at least.

No one can think of anything to say, so Barney is forced to continue. 'And Plug, old man, it'll be a great opportunity to bury the hatchet, eh?' he says, clapping Finn on the back. 'What's done is done! The race is to the swift, and all that! Oh, and Nessa's got a lovely girl lined up for you, apparently. A friend she was at school with. Super girl, in PR, good family. Nessa's told her all about you and she can't wait to meet you.'

I meet Finn's imploring eyes and nod slightly, to let him know that I'll go along with his and Daisy's masquerade. I can't let poor Finn be subjected to the humiliation of Vanessa trying to set him up with some friend of hers as a sort of consolation prize. Finn looks unutterably grateful. 'Actually,' he says icily, 'I've already got a girl of my own. You can tell Vanessa that her matchmaking services won't be needed.'

'Really?' Barney is clearly amazed and relieved. 'Well, super! Fantastic! Look forward to meeting this totty of yours! I've told

Dad to make sure the croquet field's rolled and to put down plenty of poison so we don't get those bloody moles running havoc all over the place. Oh yes,' he says to me and Davey, 'and bring your swimming cossies, eh? G and Ts by the pool. Can't wait.'

Oh God, I think, swimsuits. I may be thinner than I used to be, but I'm not in Daisy and Vanessa's super-skinny league. I'm going to look gigantic next to them. I must go to Harvey Nicks and splurge on a really nice bikini with a tummy-control panel.

Barney wanders off to pass on the swimsuit message to everyone else.

'Thanks *so* much, guys,' Finn says in heartfelt tones.

'Just take care of Daisy, OK?' I say. 'She gets upset really easily. I don't want this messing with her head.'

'Hey, no problem!' Finn looks very surprised. 'I'll treat her like a queen!'

I don't know why, but I somehow think there's more to this story than Finn's telling. I decide to ring Daisy as soon as I get home and find out if she's really all right with this. If she isn't, if Finn has emotionally blackmailed her into agreeing, I'll back her up if she wants to change her mind. Daisy's so vulnerable. I can't have Finn riding roughshod over her feelings.

I have Daisy's number on speed dial on my home phone, but for a moment I think it isn't working. I hear the number dialling but no ringing tone immediately afterwards, just a long pause. I'm about to hang up and try again when I hear her voice.

'Lewis?' she says nervously. 'Is that you?'

'Daisy?'

'Who's that?'

'It's me, Rebecca. I just rang you but I didn't hear the phone actually ring . . .' My words tail off. I realise what has just happened: Daisy was picking up the phone to ring Lewis at exactly the same time that I called her.

'This is an intervention,' I say firmly. 'I know what you were up to. You have to burn that number so you won't be tempted to ring it.'

A deep bubbling sob comes down the telephone. 'I was so upset . . .' she weeps. 'Finn rang me today and asked me to do this pretending-to-be-his-girlfriend thing, and of course I said yes, I mean, I couldn't let him down. But all the rest of today I've been thinking, he wouldn't have asked me if I *had* a boyfriend, it's only because I'm single, and now I've got to go and pretend to be happy when I'm not. It's like some awful parody of what I want, you know? I've been crying all afternoon and then I just got this irresistible urge to ring Lewis and ask him what's wrong with me, I mean, why he never rang me. If I just knew I could fix it, there must be something I did that he didn't like, but I don't know what it was, and maybe if he just *told* me . . .'

Daisy really is making an enormous deal out of what was, after all, just a one-night stand. Look at me: I'm not sobbing all over her about how much I miss Patrick, and our relationship was practically a marriage compared to Daisy and Lewis. But as soon as I have that unworthy thought, I realise that Daisy, at least, is open about her feelings, unashamed to admit how much pain she's in. I, on the other hand, have always bottled everything up, and the only person I'm truly confiding in right now is an AA sponsor rather than, as would be much more appropriate, my closest friends. Daisy's way must surely be a lot healthier than mine.

So I bite my tongue and let Daisy's sobs and stream-of-consciousness wind to a close. When she's finally worn herself out I say, 'Are you sure you're OK about doing this thing for Finn? If you want to back out, I'll talk to him for you.'

'Oh no, I couldn't let him down,' she says immediately.

'Really?'

'Yes, I couldn't leave poor Finn all by himself with that evil bitch trying to mess with his head. I mean, we've heard the answering machine messages.'

This is very true. Last meeting, Finn brought along a tape of the messages Vanessa had left for him. This is one of the things that's so great about Exes Anonymous; you can indulge in the kind of obsessive behaviour which your friends would normally discourage, in the hopes of finally working through your problem. Or, to put it in less therapy-centred vocabulary, you can play back all the pleading messages your ex has left you to get feedback from everyone else in the group about whether yes, she is still trying to manipulate your emotions, or no, you are reading too much into her words and all she wants you to do is leave her alone before she has to get a restraining order. We had all agreed that Vanessa's messages fell into Category A: Messing With Finn's Mind. Although she was ostensibly just trying to reconcile Finn and Barney, there was a pleading, seductive quality to her words, hinting at unresolved feelings she might still have for Finn, that had sent his head, understandably, spinning.

Thinking of the messages, I find myself increasingly coming round to Finn's loopy idea. A fake girlfriend will protect him to a large degree from the mixed signals that Vanessa's sending him.

'But what about you?' I ask Daisy. 'Isn't this just going to keep on upsetting you?'

'Not when Finn's kept up his end of the bargain!' she says happily.

'*What?*'

'He didn't tell you?' Daisy says blithely. 'He's going to come out with me next week to this party Lewis is going to be at, and pretend to be *my* boyfriend to make Lewis jealous! Tit for tat! Or do I mean quid pro quo?'

'Daisy,' I say hopelessly, 'we're supposed to be *getting over* our exes, not obsessing about them.'

I look guiltily around me at the photographs of Patrick propped up around the living room and the Bobby Thunder video that's lying on top of the TV. I'm like a fat girl who binges in secret ticking off another fat girl for binging publicly, while the latter course of behaviour is clearly more healthy. After all, we all know that fat girls overeat; it's much better for them to do it out in the open than engage in some sordid late-night two-cheesecake gorge session.

'Just talk about this at the next meeting, OK?' I say.

It's so easy to give other people good advice, and so hard to take it yourself. Still, when I put down the phone I realise that I haven't had a Patrick sighting since the last EA session: nearly a week. And I haven't rung him and hung up, either, or even listened to his messages on the answering machine. This is definitely some sort of progress.

It's so hard to be addicted to your ex. If you're a drunk or a junkie, you know you have to go cold turkey. I'm not saying that's easy, but at least it's simple. The worst, in a way, must be Overeaters Anonymous, because you always have to eat; your demon is always with you, sitting right there on your shoulder, murmuring seductively, 'Go on, you're so unhappy, just treat yourself to a little Black Forest gateau, one slice won't hurt . . .' Unlike drink or drugs, its power is never lessened by the years you put between yourself and its effect on you. But I remember something Jake said to me in Kew Gardens – that you should concentrate on your actions rather than beat yourself up for your fantasies. Control the actions, and the thinking behind them will fall into place.

Thinking about Jake, I find, calms me down. He has that survivor's serenity; life messed with him – he clearly went down in flames, reading between the lines of what he's told me – and yet he managed to rise from his ashes. I feel as if I could say anything to him. Not that I would. There's plenty of really embarrassing stuff about Patrick that I would never say. And how can I tell a man, any man, that I'm scared I will never have sex that good again, that for the rest of my life I'll be remembering Patrick's naked body, Patrick's eyes, Patrick's – I'm not going to think about that particular part of Patrick or I'll get miserable and frustrated, but I think you get my drift – and comparing every man I meet to him? I can't. Still, Jake feels like a beacon of sanity to me. I realise that Jake symbolises the person I would like to be.

God, what a change from my first impression of Jake. I've done a 180 degree turnabout. That'll teach me to make snap judgements of people. The trouble is, once you start trying to improve your character, it's the Augean stables: you keep finding more and more flaws and as soon as you sort one out, another pops up in its place. I think I have the wrong metaphor – it should have been the Hydra instead. Never mind. Like Jake says, one day at a time.

Chapter Fourteen

BEN

'This is really hard to say, so I'm just going to dive right into it. I sort of stalked my ex. Not in a psycho way or anything – I didn't threaten her or nail her cat to her door – but I expect I did stalk her. That's what she called it, anyway. I hung around her place the whole time and rang her mobile constantly and even went round to her office and hung outside there. I couldn't help it.

'We had this unbelievable connection. When I met her, the first thing she told me was that she'd just come out of a bad relationship, so I went really slow. I didn't want to scare her off. We hung out a lot but I didn't try anything. I was getting her to trust me. I've never done that for a girl before in my life. I was so into her I'd have waited as long as she wanted. And finally, we went away for a long weekend. I booked separate rooms, so she wouldn't feel pressured, but we had such a great time – we were both into hiking and we went for these long walks every day and got back in the evening completely knackered, it was great, and we talked about everything, I really let down my guard with her, and on the Sunday night – we were staying till Monday – I walked her up to her room and we started kissing and one thing led to another and we just . . . well, it was amazing. And after that we were a couple. It was like magic. Like someone had flicked a switch and turned us into this perfect couple. We practically never spent a night apart. I couldn't believe it. It was like everything I'd ever wanted had fallen into my hands. I was insanely happy, I loved her so much, and she loved me, I know she did . . .

'We were practically living at mine, it's a bigger flat, hers wasn't up to much, but she'd complain about having to go back and get her things all the time. She left more and more of her stuff at my place but she'd always forget things and get ratty about it, and I finally said that we should buy somewhere together – of course I'd been wanting to do that for ages, but I didn't want to rush her – and she was really into it. We went round all the estate agents and looked at a million flats. I was so happy. I even pretended to myself that we were married. I've never been so happy in my life. I really wanted to marry her, but again, like I said, I was trying not to rush her. So we found the perfect place. I wanted it to be perfect for us. It was me who made us keep looking and looking, there were loads of flats she liked but they were never good enough for me, and at last we found this maisonette – God, that's a stupid word – with a garden. It needed some work but I knew we could make it really nice, and we talked about it that evening and decided we'd put the offer in first thing the next morning.

'But when I woke up, she was gone. And most of her stuff had gone. She must have used garbage bags to carry it all out, she had so much at mine by then. I tried to pretend to myself that it was a joke. I know that sounds crazy, but I couldn't let myself believe that it was over, that she'd really left. I went round to her flat, but she wasn't there, so I went to her work to wait for her, but they said she wasn't coming in that day, she'd rung to say she was sick.

'She was gone for a week. I don't know where she went. I didn't know many of her friends, we'd hardly seen them or talked about them, we were so into each other it was like the rest of the world had disappeared, we didn't really see anyone at all. So I didn't know how to find her. I kept ringing her work, but they were offish on the phone. I knew she must have told them not to tell me where she was, or when she was coming back. So I just waited – outside her work, outside her flat. I couldn't believe this was happening. I kept telling myself that she'd just got nervous and needed some time. Her last boyfriend had treated her really badly before finally dumping her and I knew she'd felt uncomfortable with me because I was so nice to her. She could never believe she deserved to be treated well. So I knew she was probably freaking out because everything was going so brilliantly, but I thought that if I could just see her and talk to her and hold her again she'd come round and realise that I really loved her and would do anything in the world for her. I'd give her more time if she needed it, we didn't have to move in together if she thought that was going too fast, we could just go on as we were, I'd never have put any pressure on her . . .

'Finally she turned up. She was staying somewhere else, with a friend, but she went back to work. She had to. I knew she had to, so I was concentrating on there rather than the flat. I know I sound like a stalker, but I couldn't do anything else. I had to talk to her. I was so sure I could make her see that everything would be all right. But she completely blanked me. It was like there had never been anything between us. She even told me I was making a big deal out of it and that I should just let it go. I really thought I was going to go mad. She must have told everyone at her office that I was dangerous or something, because they'd just hang up when they heard my voice, and the security guard said he'd call the police if he saw me hanging around there any more. But I had to see her, I just had to. I wrote loads of letters and emails to her – I spent any time that I wasn't hanging around her office writing and writing. I skived off work so much I got a formal warning. And I never got an answer. She changed her mobile number so I couldn't ring her. And finally I saw her again outside her office and she screamed at me to go away and she burst into tears, and I started crying too, and we just stood there, crying and crying, and then she ran away from me, and I've never seen her again.'

Jim's looking as sad as ever, a symphony of sadness in sludgy earth tones. Grey cardigan, thinning around the elbows, over a beige shirt. Brown corduroy trousers. Brown hair, streaked with grey, dull at the ends and greasy at the scalp; I imagine if he ran his hands through it, flakes of dandruff would pour out like confetti over his shoulders. Even his skin looks grey. His upper body is an S-bend, his shoulders hunched forward and his chest hollowed into such a deep concavity that I wonder he can breathe at all; it looks as if his narrow ribcage is pressing right into his lungs. He always looks uncomfortable to be here, perching on the edge of whatever chair he selects as if he were ready to make his escape at any moment, refusing all offers of alcoholic refreshment that might loosen him up a little, fiddling nervously with his glasses. And yet he keeps coming back faithfully, week after week. It's like a minor miracle.

'Do we actually need to follow this?' Jennifer asks, holding up her copy of the Twelve Step list. I emailed it to everyone a few days ago, so that they could all have a look at it before the meeting.

'I don't know,' I say. 'I just thought it might be helpful. I mean, AA has worked so well for millions of people, it seemed like they must be doing something right.'

'Step One,' Finn reads aloud. 'We admitted we were powerless over alcohol – that our lives had become unmanageable.' He looks round, waiting for comments.

'Well, we must all feel powerless, mustn't we?' Jennifer says bravely. She's talking more and more at meetings now, and blushing less when she works up the courage to say something. 'Or we wouldn't be here.'

'*Unmanageable*'s good,' I say reflectively. 'I felt I was really caught in something I couldn't get out of without help.'

'God, yes! I felt I wasn't coping at *all*!' Charlotte chips in. Her voice is always several decibels louder than everyone else's. 'More salmon, anyone?'

We're at Charlotte's tonight. She insisted. And she's put the rest of us to shame as hosts. Charlotte has rolled slices of smoked salmon around cream cheese, cut the crusts off chicken sandwiches, dissected a wide assortment of raw vegetables for crudités, even torturing a few poor carrots into those odd half-flower, half-cactus shapes as garnish, and brought home the entire cheese counter of her local delicatessen. There's tea and coffee in smart Thermos pots, wine in the fridge, and a bar at the far corner of the living room stocked with what looks like pretty much every form of alcohol available to humanity, if you except the gimmicky drinks like flavoured vodka and alcopops. Charlotte's living room is yellow and white: the carpet's thick enough to lose a stiletto heel in, the sofas are lush and comfortable and the cut-glass bowls that hold flowers are glittering like cubic zirconia and dusted within an inch of their lives. The serving trays are silver and the china plates – large oval ones for the canapés, small round ones for the guests – all match. They are decorated with a motif of small painted flowers in yellow and green which would be more suitable for a country kitchen rather than a lavish town house in Fulham, but that's Charlotte's social class for you, always pretending that they're in the country even when they're not. Clearly Charlotte wasn't exaggerating when she said that she took her husband to the cleaners during the divorce. On the evidence of all this luxury, the husband would have been lucky to come out of it with a couple of unmatched socks and an old pair of boxer shorts.

'We admitted we were powerless to control our feelings for our exes,' Daisy suggests, 'that our lives had become unmanageable.'

'Our addiction to our exes,' Ben corrects her.

'OK. "We admitted we were powerless to control our addiction to our exes – that our lives had become unmanageable." How's that?'

'Um, fine,' Finn says, 'but what—'

'I'm making a Twelve Step list for us!' Daisy says cheerfully. She's in very good spirits this evening; I wonder why. 'What's number two?'

'"We came to believe that a Power greater than ourselves could restore us to sanity",' Ben reads.

'I quite like that, actually,' Jennifer says in a small voice. 'It's like there is someone out there that cares about me.'

'Maybe you should come to church with me this Sunday,' Charlotte suggests to her. 'We have an absolutely lovely vicar.'

'Ooh, I don't know,' Jennifer says nervously. 'I'm not much of a one for church. But I like the idea, you know, of someone looking out for me.'

'Jake says the higher power doesn't have to be God in the literal sense,' I volunteer. 'It can be whatever God means to you. Or it can be the group.'

This seemed like a great idea at the time. But now I look round the assembled members of EA and wonder whether I can possibly let go and fall, metaphorically at least, into their supportive arms, let alone allow them to restore me to sanity. There's Charlotte, with her Alice band and bright beady eyes, who's probably going to use this whole discussion as a springboard to drag us all off to church; Ben, who looks like a photocopier salesman with his grey suit and spiky hair, and who I hardly feel I know yet; Jennifer, nervous of her own shadow; Jim, who probably only comes here because he's lonely and wants some company – for all I know he goes to different support meetings every night of the week and doesn't say a word at any of them – and Finn and Daisy, who, far from being in recovery, are busy planning their double-headed scheme to make both their exes madly jealous. Broken reeds, the lot of them.

'That's really nice!' Jennifer exclaims. 'It's like saying your friends want what's best for you!'

'And know when you're doing things that are just going to drag you back into the past and mess with your head,' I say pointedly to Daisy.

She flicks her tongue out at me so fast that only I see her do it.

'I don't see why we have to follow this Twelve Step thing at all,' Ben says rebelliously. 'Why can't we just do what we've been doing? I mean, just come along and talk about our exes?'

Everyone turns and looks at me. I'm the one who brought the list into discussion; I'm the one who has to defend it.

'Because AA's got a programme that really works,' I explain. 'I thought if we followed the steps, it would work for us too.'

'But we're not alcoholics,' Ben objects.

'That's why Daisy's making up a list for us. Like theirs but different.'

'I must say, I like the idea of some structure,' Charlotte chips in. 'Steps to follow and all that. It feels a bit amorphous just turning up to a meeting and having a whinge.'

'It's not a *whinge*, Charlotte,' Finn says crossly. 'It's an honest statement of our feelings. Maybe if you thought about it like that, and not as a whinge, you'd actually talk about what you felt and not just about how pissed off you are with your ex-husband and how much money you got in the divorce.'

Charlotte's mouth falls into a perfect 'O' as she stares at him. Jennifer, sitting next to me, emits a tiny giggle.

'I resent that!' Charlotte says, as soon as she's got her breath back.

'Finn's actually got a point,' Ben says. 'You don't talk much about your feelings, Charlotte.'

I notice that Ben's accent gets a little more Estuary English whenever he speaks to Charlotte: he drops his 'Ts', turns 'isn't it' into 'innit' and 'wasn't it' into 'wunnit', and sits back with his legs spread wide, like annoying men on buses who take up more than their fair share of seating space. I don't know if he's doing it consciously, but I assume that he's making the point that he's not intimidated by Charlotte's extreme poshness.

'Depression is a feeling!' Charlotte says crossly. 'I said I was depressed!'

'Yeah, but it's only one feeling, innit?' Ben says. 'There's got to be more down there you're not letting on about.'

'Well, I'm very upset about my divorce!' Charlotte says. 'Is that what you want to hear? I'm upset about my children living without a father in the house, and I feel very alone!' And she bursts into tears.

We all stare at her in horror. Ben looks as guilty as if he were Charlotte's cheating ex-husband. It's little Jennifer who gets up and goes over to put an arm around Charlotte, hugging her and whispering gently in her ear until she sniffs and clears her throat and wipes the tears away with a cocktail napkin and apologises to everyone for making such a ghastly scene.

'Charlotte, it's what we're here for,' Jennifer says. 'We've all cried. Well, most of us. *I* have.'

'I have,' Ben says quickly, as if this will make him feel less responsible for upsetting Charlotte.

'I have,' Daisy says.

'I nearly have,' I say, not wanting to be left out.

Jim is, as usual, staring at the floor, so we all look at Finn instead.

'I haven't yet,' Finn says, 'I'm an emotionally constipated mess, all right? Everyone happy?'

'Oh, nobody meant—' Jennifer starts.

'He's joking, Jennifer,' I say.

'Oh, right.' Jennifer smiles at Finn apologetically.

'I think Charlotte just did part of Step Four!' Daisy says, holding up her list. 'She started to "make a searching and fearless emotional inventory of her feelings"!'

'Um, do you need the "emotional" in there?' Finn asks. 'Isn't it redundant?'

'Oh, yes,' Daisy says, looking at the list and crossing out 'emotional'.

'Aren't you supposed to be a journalist?' Finn says.

'I'm a *lifestyle* journalist, Finn,' Daisy says, not at all cowed by his sarcasm. 'Lifestyle journalism is all about piling on the adjectives. Anyway, we should all be really pleased for Charlotte. She's had a breakthrough. Yay Charlotte!'

Egged on by Daisy, we all clap.

'I could help you with that list, Daisy, if you like,' Jennifer says shyly. 'You know, try to work out one for us.'

'Great,' Daisy says. 'I've got your email, so I could send you a first draft and you could have a look at it.'

Charlotte is still looking very upset. I can tell that Jennifer and Daisy are trying to distract attention from her.

'Actually, I've got a bit of a headache,' Charlotte says, sitting up a little straighter. 'I always do when I let go and blub. I think I need to take some aspirin and lie down.'

We all jump to our feet as Charlotte apologises seventeen ways to Sunday for her appalling hospitality and tells us we're welcome to stay on without her, which of course we refuse. Failing to convince us, she insists on packing up all the food in neat little Tupperware containers and parcelling it out to us before she finally surrenders to her headache. It's the spirit that built the British Empire.

'Anyone want to come to the pub?' I say as we leave Charlotte's house.

'Yeah, all right. Did you have anywhere in mind?' Ben asks.

'I dunno, there must be one around here somewhere . . . maybe near the tube . . .' I look doubtfully down the quiet leafy street.

'Actually, Finn and I've got somewhere to be,' Daisy says, looking a little embarrassed. 'We're, um – Finn's coming with me to this opening I have to do a piece on. Those things are so boring if you don't have company.'

I wonder for a moment why she's explaining in such detail, and then realise what's going on: Finn's doing fake-boyfriend duty tonight. Daisy's clothes – or comparative lack of them – are designed to have the same effect. Her jeans are painted on, her heels are vertiginously high, and her skimpy top is falling off her lean, fake-tanned shoulders even more than usual.

If Finn and Daisy are otherwise occupied, the last thing I want is to be stuck having a drink with the rest of the ill-assorted group. I say quickly, 'Actually, it's later than I thought . . . and we'll probably take ages to find a pub . . .'

'Yeah, maybe we should just leave it,' Ben agrees equally fast. Not very flattering to me; but I doubt he wants to come out for a drink if his buddy Finn isn't there to add some testosterone to the mix.

We all say goodbye, which is embarrassing, because we then turn out to be going in the same direction. It's always uncomfortable to be stuck keeping people company after you've made your official farewells. I've noticed that we usually try to stagger our departures so that we can be by ourselves immediately after the meetings, when our emotions are still running high and we need time and solitude to settle down. Now we have to walk to the tube station making awkward conversation. Ben sensibly slips off as soon as he spots a newsagent's, saying he needs to buy cigarettes: I bet that he waits a good ten minutes before entering the Tube, in the hopes that we will have left already. Jim says he's catching a bus. I don't quite believe this: I think he's pulling a Ben. Hopefully they won't bump into each other at the station.

I catch the tube with Daisy, Finn and Jennifer, whose original shyness seems to revert outside group meetings; she sits in total silence until Earl's Court and then mutters a quick 'see you next week' before jumping off the train. I start to lecture Finn and Daisy about taking the proper steps to recovery instead of deliberately stalling it with schemes to make their exes jealous, but they put their fingers in their ears, close their eyes, and make bubbling noises with their lips to avoid listening. When they get out at Notting Hill Gate they blow raspberries and waggle two-fingered signs at me, which is not appreciated by the mother with two children sitting opposite. And I stay on the tube until Paddington, where I change to the Bakerloo line – I'm going to a late-evening yoga class, which I can just make since the meeting broke up early.

I'm spilling over with envy for Finn and Daisy. Now I'm alone, I can acknowledge that to myself: my reproving words to them were just a cloak to hide my true feelings. I want what they've got. I want to walk into the restaurant Patrick's friend runs with a gorgeous man on my arm who's all over me, wait smugly for the news to get back to Patrick and imagine him racked by fits of jealous misery. Why the bloody hell couldn't I have thought of that first? Look how happy Finn and Daisy are at the prospect!

I reach for my phone and text Davey.

```
Doing step 4 on inventory of worst feelings it's
horrible
```

I send it as soon as I clear the ticket barrier at Maida Vale. Davey fires one back almost immediately.

```
What r they?
```

That's a no-brainer.

```
Jealousy revenge I wnt 2 hv fake boyfriend 2 & make
Ptrick suffer
```

Davey's response comes back so fast that I am barely over the zebra crossing outside the station.

```
OK to have feelings just don't act on them
```

Yeah, yeah. Sounds easy, is in practice impossibly hard. I am just thinking about my answer when he shoots another one at me:

```
Yr not asking me 2 b fake bfriend, r u????!
```

I am in such a state that I do consider this seriously for about a minute. It would really annoy Patrick, who was always a little jealous of my friendship with Davey. But then I decide that even thinking about this clearly means that I am tipping over the border into insanity. Davey is my best male friend. It would really mess us up to try a stunt like that.

No no don't worry. I text back.

Good!! he answers.

I'm nearly at the yoga studio now, but I manage another one to tease him.

Why, don't u fancy me?

Davey's comeback is terse:

R u drunk?

Tchah, no sense of humour . . . I text:

No. just going to yoga actually

GOOD!! he answers. WILL HELP U CALM DOWN! TALK TOMORROW!

Ooh, capital letters. I must have really wound him up. I resign myself to lying to Davey tomorrow; I will have to reassure him that I don't have fake-boyfriend plans of any sort. If I admit that I do, not only am I not going to get any support from Davey on this one, but he will actively try to talk me out of it.

Daisy is another matter. I'll ring her tomorrow and discuss things with her. Because seeing her and Finn tonight has put a cunning plan into my head. I know it's wrong. I know it's not healthy. But I can't wait to put it into action. And because I know it's wrong, I make a trade-off with myself: if I go ahead with this, no watching Bobby Thunder until it's done. It may be a primitive bargain, but I do believe in making a sacrifice if you want something really badly . . . particularly something you know is bad for you . . .

Chapter Fifteen

Patrick was always bad at going out to dinner with me. He was awkward, and the conversation rarely flowed that well. It was as if he knew that intimate dinners tête-à-tête with your girlfriend were a required part of having a relationship, so he was prepared to bite the bullet and do his duty, but couldn't quite bring himself to enjoy it. I found that dinners out worked best when we'd just seen a film and could talk about that; preferably an action film, which Patrick loved. Fortunately, I did too. Talk about catharsis. We'd go to the latest Jet Li thriller, watch tiny Jet kicking the crap out of a series of menacing blokes twice his size, and then retire to dinner beaming with vicarious satisfaction. Actually what worked best was getting out a video: we would curl up on Patrick's revoltingly stained but gigantic sofa, put on Cliffhanger *or* Predator *and, usually, start snogging. The way we preferred to watch videos was lying full-length on the sofa, me in front, Patrick behind, his head propped up on a couple of pillows, his arm resting over my hip. Eventually his hand would stray up or down and before we knew it Sylvester Stallone or Arnold Schwarzenegger's shoot-outs became mere background noise, while the real action was taking place on the sofa cushions. We always kept condoms on the bookshelf next to the sofa. Patrick wasn't good in public, but he made up for it so well in private that I happily put up with the trade-off.*

There's a tale, I think in Thomas Malory's Le Morte d'Arthur, *about a knight who wins a trial of strength and courage and is rewarded with the hand of a fair lady. The only catch is that the fair lady is under a spell, doomed to turn into an ugly graceless hag every day. The knight is given a choice. He can have her beautiful by day, so that he's envied by everyone, but a hag when he's alone with her: or he can have the beauty for his eyes only, and be mocked by others for the awful old bag he's married. That was almost how I felt with Patrick. No one but me knew how happy he made me, because he didn't show his affection when we were out with other people. And no one but me knew how beautiful he was under his nondescript clothes. He was like a box of chocolates: his clothes were just packaging that I ripped off impatiently and threw on the floor. Every time I unwrapped him, he was the best present I'd ever received. His skin was like milk, his arse tight and firm, his buttocks as round and full as cherries. I wanted to braid his hair into a cable and climb up it as if he were a tower I had to conquer.*

Oh God, I can't go on remembering Patrick naked. I never did conquer that tower. Every time we got close, every time he was inside me and the world melted away, I thought I finally had him, and I never did; he always slipped from my grasp again. He had never learnt to trust a lover and he wouldn't let me teach him. I think of all those times we were out together in the Seven Dials, that restaurant his friend Matt managed. Matt would come and sit at the table with us at the end of the evening, drink a Jagermeister with Patrick and tell him how lucky he was to have such a lovely girlfriend (I was very fond of Matt, as you can imagine) and Patrick would invariably look nervous.

Girlfriend. That word. It took him a year to be able to use it. And I would watch Patrick relaxing with Matt in a way he never did with me, except after we'd had sex. It was with his friends that Patrick could really let go. They didn't want anything from him, just to hang out, sink some beers, talk about the footie. Patrick would push his chair back a little from the table and watch them all bantering and laughing and yelling at the sport on TV, and his expression would be one of utmost contentment. He never had to give anything with them that he didn't want to. He didn't have to open up. He could just be Patrick, their alpha, quietly drinking and enjoying their company.

I wished so much that he could have been like that with me. I tried to talk about films and football and all the stuff he liked, and, as a result, shoved my own tastes under the carpet. Whenever he took an interest in my life, it was always in an over-polite tone of voice, as if he were fulfilling an obligation rather than genuinely trying to join me in my world.

I should never have put up with it. I know that now. I should have broken up with him a long time ago.

'Nice place,' Jake says.

I'm late. I wasn't going to run the risk of turning up before him and find myself sitting at the bar, chatting to Matt and looking like Desperate Rebecca Waiting For a Man. Tonight I am cool and sexy and sought-after, or at least that's my cover story. The fact that I am actually falling apart underneath my red lipstick and my strapless top is a deep dark secret, from Matt, at least. I can tell Jake I'm falling apart; in fact, it might be a very good tactic, because the more Jake and I lean across the table towards each other in serious conversation, the more Jake takes my hand to express sympathy and concern, the more Matt will think . . . well, you know what I'm doing. If you can't beat them, join them.

Daisy was jubilant after her night out with Finn at that party Lewis's company was organising. Apparently Finn was a fake-boyfriend model of perfection; who knew that he had so much acting ability? Daisy said he held her hand and stared into her eyes and steered her around the room with his hand in the small of her back, the way that men always do with trophy girlfriends, as a mark of possession. Any time you see a gorgeously dressed girl in clothes a little too small for her, look behind her and you'll see a man with his hand on the curve of her spine. These girls dress outrageously when they're out with their boyfriends because they know they'll be safe from other men's drunken advances, and, of course, because they want to make their boyfriends feel that they're out with the woman every other man in the room is dying to be with.

Lewis, by Daisy's account, fell completely for her and Finn's little show. He came up to her in one of the brief moments that Finn wasn't surgically attached to some part of her, asked her how she was and how she'd been, told her that he'd missed her but had been really busy, and, even when Finn returned, said he'd love to get together some time and could he ring her?

Daisy was ecstatic. Finn insisted that they leave on the early side, to make Lewis think they were desperate to jump in the sack, and as they were leaving, Lewis waved at her and made an I'll-call-you gesture with his hand. He hasn't rung yet, but it's only been a couple of days: Daisy has high hopes. So, when Jake rang me last night and said did I want to meet up and talk about how the meetings were going, I immediately suggested dinner at the Seven Dials and rang up the restaurant using a fake French accent ("'Ello, can you tell mee eef Matt weel be zere tomorrow night? Oh, zank you so merch. No, zank you . . .' girlish giggle '. . . I do not weesh to leeeve mah name!' More girlish giggles, hang up smartly) to double-check that Matt would be working tonight. No point in setting this up to find out that Matt isn't there to fall for my cunning plan.

I see Matt as soon as I walk in the door, over at the back of the restaurant, talking urgently to a couple of the waiters. I wave at him with a big smile and look around the restaurant for Jake. He's at a table by the wall, looking very sharp indeed in a snug-fitting matt black shirt, subtly embossed with black circles in a slightly shinier finish. He stands up to greet me – nice manners – and I see that he's wearing faded jeans under the shirt, also fairly snug. The black shirt makes his greenish

181

eyes seem grey and he has a light tan, probably from all those afternoons spent in Kew Gardens; his hair seems a couple of shades lighter, too, the blond streaks more pronounced. There are two heavy silver rings on his long fingers which gleam dully in the muted lighting. I couldn't have picked a better fake boyfriend. Wait till Matt reports back to Patrick on the hunk I was having an intimate dinner with.

I catch sight of myself in the mirror behind the table. I look pretty good, actually; a big silk rose looks beautiful in my dark hair and I've made a real effort with my make-up. I have smooth skin, pink cheeks, big dark eyes; well, they should be – I've used about half an eyeliner pencil on each of them. And I've found this new long-lasting, dark pink lipstick. You put on the colour and then you top it up with a clear coat that makes it last all night, even through dinner. This is the best I'm going to look, and I have to say, surveying myself quickly, that it's not half bad. I certainly don't seem like a girl who's pining away from a terrible obsession with her ex-boyfriend which is driving her to watch, in an endless loop, lousy wrestling videos featuring a bloke who looks very much like him.

'I'm glad you like it,' I say to Jake as we sit down.

'It's very nice. And I like places that are sort of tucked away, so you have to know where they are. I'm not a fan of those big vulgar restaurants with their frontages out on the street yelling: "Come and get me!" I like a bit of . . . well, subtlety, I suppose.'

Oh dear, maybe my rose is a bit over-the-top. Does it shout: 'Come and get me?' Never mind, I think. It looks pretty. And besides, I'm not interested in seducing Jake, I'm just using him to make a good show for Matt's benefit.

'I didn't know what to order you, sorry,' Jake says. 'For a drink, I mean.'

'Rebecca! It's been too long, baby!' Matt swoops down on me from behind with a glass of Lillet, a vermouth which I always used to drink when I came here. I'd forgotten about it till now. 'How are you doing?' he says. 'I've missed you!'

I give him an awkward little hug; I can't get up from my chair as there isn't really room. The restaurant is very small and the tables are crammed in quite close together. 'I'm great,' I say.

'You've been neglecting us,' he says disapprovingly.

'Well, I wanted to leave it a while, you know . . .' I say. 'Let things settle down . . .'

Matt nods understandingly. 'It's shitty,' he says. 'I was really sad to hear about you and Patrick. Still, water under the bridge, eh? Those long-distance things are always really tough.'

It didn't *have* to be long-distance, I think in a rush of anger; Patrick could have *taken me with him*, the emotionally constipated *bastard*. But I smile and agree and say, 'Oh, Matt, this is Jake.'

'All right, mate,' Matt says, shaking hands with Jake.

I know I'm safe. Matt is straight: he's not going to ask Jake and me about our relationship, or how long we've been together, or anything embarrassing like that. Straight men don't do that. Matt will just assume that we're going out, ask Jake some manly questions about his job and try to talk to him about football. If Matt had been gay, I could never have come here; I'd have been rumbled in five minutes.

'I'm rushed off my feet at the moment, but I'll catch you guys later, when things have settled down a bit, yeah?' Matt says. 'We'll have a post-dinner drink and catch up. Rebecca, I'm going to send you over something I know you'll like.' He winks. 'Oh yeah, have the salmon if you like salmon. It's really great tonight.'

Two minutes later a plate of fried artichokes arrives. I moan faintly. They are my favourite food in all the world and I always used to order them here. 'I can't believe Matt remembered.' I exclaim, digging into them. 'It's been almost a year since I came in here.'

'Old friend?' Jake asks, squeezing some lemon over the artichokes.

I have to play it carefully here, so that Jake doesn't suspect anything. 'Yeah, more a friend of my ex's, originally,' I say lightly. 'That's how I first met Matt, but we really get on.'

'I can tell. He was so happy to see you.'

'Yes, he's great,' I say, a warm rush of happiness flooding through me.

It's lovely to feel that Patrick's friends liked me for myself, not just as the chick on Patrick's arm they had, perforce, to try to get along with. I always knew they liked me, but this is the first time that I've seen Matt since the breakup, and it's great to be reminded that the affection we felt for each other hasn't just turned itself off like a switch, as if it were conditional upon me and Patrick still being a couple.

'So, how have you been?' Jake says, looking serious.

I consider this. 'Better, I think,' I say. Of course, I can't tell him about tonight, which I doubt he would consider an improvement. But generally, I do feel better. 'I've been doing what you suggested,' I say. 'You know, drawing lines in an exercise book every time I have an obsessive thought.'

He grins. 'How many pages?'

'Eight and counting,' I admit.

'Great. That means you're being honest.'

Jake so often surprises me; I keep expecting him to reproach me for evidence that I am still deeply addicted to Patrick's memory, and instead, when I admit it, he finds a positive twist to the situation. I see now why Davey speaks his name in a hushed whisper of admiration. Jake is a really great sponsor: encouraging, morale-boosting, a rock of support.

'Wow,' I say. 'I thought you'd tick me off.'

'That's not what I'm here for. If it looked like you were in trouble, I'd try to talk to you about it, but I would never tick you off.'

I pull a face.

'What?' Jake says, grinning. 'That was so sweet – you look about twelve when you do that.'

'I quite like being ticked off, in a way,' I confess. 'I expect I associate it with someone caring about me. Like Davey, when he gave me such a hard time about . . . you know . . . the photographs . . .' I mutter these last two words, still deeply embarrassed that Jake knows about them. 'Oh, I took them down, by the way, I cleared them all out two days ago . . .'

'Good,' Jake says. 'As long as you felt ready.'

'I *think* I did . . .' I say. 'Well, I managed to do it, which is the important thing . . . Anyway, I was really pissed off with Davey for having a go at me about them, but to be honest, it sort of felt nice at the same time.'

Jake roars with laughter. 'So you want me to give you a sort of metaphorical spanking?' he asks, still laughing.

God, I wish that Matt had been passing the table just then! It would have sounded so good!

'Patrick would never tick me off, even when I needed it,' I say. 'He'd say I needed to work out my problems on my own, and that no one should be responsible for another person.'

'But you were in a relationship,' Jake says.

'Exactly. And I think that part of being in a long-term relationship is that you support each other, and if your partner wants help working on their problems, you should give it to them.'

'Well, of course.'

'Sometimes I'd smoke too much at parties,' I say. 'I don't really smoke, but occasionally I'd really go through the fags at a party, if I had a friend who had them, and once or twice I'd actually buy a packet before going. I'd always leave them there, but I'd smoke quite a lot of them. And then I'd wake up in the morning smelling of smoke and feeling sick and I'd regret it. I asked Patrick if he saw me smoking just to remind me that I'd feel shit in the morning, but he never would. I thought, if he really cared about me, he would have.'

185

'You can't be sure of that,' Jake says.

'No, but you see what I mean? He wouldn't get involved, he wouldn't try to help me, even when I asked him to and promised that I wouldn't get cross if he did.'

'Would you have got cross?' Jake asks, grinning.

I giggle. 'Maybe a bit, if I'd been drinking. But I would have thanked him for it afterwards.'

Oh, why did I have to throw in the bit about having been drinking? I am always so nervous that Jake's going to decide I'm an alkie and try to do an intervention on me.

'You know that quote: "no man is an island"?' I continue, since Jake doesn't seem to have jumped down my neck about alcohol abuse. 'Well, Patrick did his best to contradict that. He was as close to being his own island as he could possibly be. Self-sufficient. It was the single most important principle of his life to need nothing and no one. I can't blame him, coming from his horrible family, but it made things really hard for me.'

Jake nods sympathetically.

'And now, looking back on things, I feel that it was all my fault for not realising that Patrick was never going to be able to break through that wall he'd built around him and really love me. I should have figured out a year and a half ago that it was never going to work, and instead I hung on and on and wasted so much of my life just hoping blindly. I feel like such an idiot. That's the trouble – when I look back, I just keep blaming myself for not ending it sooner. I closed my eyes to every single warning sign.'

'You're not closing your eyes now,' Jake says gently. 'That's the most important thing of all. Believe me, a year and a half is nothing. Loads of people in AA spent decades closing their eyes to their problem.'

'What about you?' I say.

Jake looks taken aback. 'What *about* me?' he says.

The salmon arrives. We both ordered it on Matt's recommendation. It's wonderful: pink and buttery with a golden crust, on a bed of slowly braised lentils that, like the salmon, are melting enough to cut with a fork but still maintain a delicate texture and bite. I sigh in appreciation as I take my first mouthful. But I'm not distracted enough by the food to let Jake off the hook. I want him to talk about himself a bit, exchange some confidences in return for mine. I've ordered a glass of white wine, but I'm sipping at it, because Jake isn't drinking at all and I'm determined not to get silly and giggly with the wine while he maintains his own sobriety and thus keeps the upper hand.

'I meant, what about your own situation?' I say, taking a tiny gulp of wine. 'Are you seeing anyone? How does that work with you being in AA?'

Jake seems uncomfortable, but he nods. 'Fair enough,' he says, understanding why I'm asking. 'Well, I wasn't seeing anyone when I was first in AA. I've been sober for six years now, and it took me quite a long time to settle into that. It's a whole new life, a whole new way of being in the world.' He takes another forkful of salmon. 'Mmn, this is good,' he says in parentheses. 'And then I did get together with a girl I met in AA. Louise. It was pretty serious for a while, but we always had problems. Louise was newly sober when I met her, and we tried to hold off on seeing each other because you're not supposed to start a new relationship in your first year of sobriety. There are guys who deliberately hit on girls who are at their first meetings. It's pretty nasty, preying on women who are three days sober. You're so vulnerable when you first come to AA, you're stripping down all your defences and building them up again. Going after people new to AA's like being a paedophile.'

I raise my eyebrows.

'Well, maybe that's a bit too strong,' he corrects himself. 'Let's say it's like a teacher hitting on their underage students. The power imbalance is just too pronounced to be healthy.'

'So you and Louise didn't get together for a while?' I prompt.

187

'No, but the attraction was always there. She was really gorgeous, and so clever and sharp. And when we finally did, it was great, but it was always hard going. She was very moody and volatile and I think in retrospect that she'd deliberately act out and be wild because she knew I'd be there to catch her. We ended up tearing each other apart. It wasn't pretty. So after that I've been a bit wary of getting involved with anyone else.'

I can just picture Louise: one of those skinny, stunning, temperamental girls who appear not to care what they're wearing but always manage to look superb, who throws tantrums at parties or slumps on the sofa chain-smoking and pouting and has a circle of male admirers perpetually surrounding her, each one sure that he's the only one who can succeed at the near-impossible task of making her happy. Louise is the kind of girl men see as a challenge: she's never fully available, her attention is almost always turned inwards on what she thinks are her fascinating mental problems, attracting a slew of men who want to be the one to figure her out and finally be rewarded when Louise's large, kohl-outlined eyes turn to look at them with the same interest she has previously focused only on herself. It never happens, of course. The Louises of this world remain constantly self-obsessed. But they're never short of men who love a girl who isn't really present even when she's with them.

I have never been able to be like that; I'm much more likely to play the role that Jake did – trying to be the fixer. But I am very envious of the Louises. I just don't know how to be like them. I have the very strong instinct that if I threw tantrums or sat on the sofa, pouting, no one would want to touch me with a bargepole. You have to be the genuine article to get away with being a Louise. Oh yes, and naturally thin. Moody and temperamental doesn't work on anyone apart from skinny chicks who live on coffee and cigarettes and look as if they're being consumed by their own mesmerisingly tortured psyche, the complexity of which no one but themselves will ever truly comprehend. If I tried a series of Louise-type antics, I'd just look fat and sulky.

'So, she was a bit of a bird with a broken wing?' I say, probing at Jake's defences.

'Yeah, I guess so.' He grins, but the smile doesn't reach his eyes, which are distant and sad. 'Only I didn't manage to mend hers, and she broke at least one of mine before we said goodbye. Like I said, it wasn't a happy situation.'

I feel uncomfortable now that Jake has been so open with me. Perhaps this is like your therapist confiding in you about the problems in her marriage; you think you want to get to know them, but you're not sure what to do with the information once you have it. I lead the conversation back on to more general lines. 'So there's a lot of dating in AA?' I say, taking my last bit of salmon.

Jake, I notice, eats slower than me. Self-control in all things. I'm always impressed by people who can take a lot of time to eat their food.

'Oh yeah,' he says, grinning again, and I am happy to notice that this time the smile is much more genuine. 'It's like a dating service sometimes. I've heard that in the States people go to AA even when they're not alcoholics, just to meet people.'

'God!' I laugh.

'I know. Crazy, isn't it?'

Jake is one of the least fidgety people I have ever met. He doesn't push back his hair or twist his rings or rearrange his cutlery. He just sits there, calmly, making me feel like a perpetual motion machine by contrast as I fiddle with my wine glass and refold my napkin on my lap.

'How was everything?' the waiter asks, removing our plates.

'Lovely, thanks,' we say in unison.

'Some dessert, perhaps?'

I'm really glad that Jake asks for the dessert menu. I am always too embarrassed to order it on my own, particularly when I'm eating with a man. He picks the rhubarb crumble and, after deliberating the options, I go for ice cream.

'No chocolate mousse?' he says, looking a bit disappointed. 'I thought you were going to get that, you were ooh-ing and aah-ing over it so much.'

'I thought it might be a bit rich after the salmon,' I explain. 'And anyway, I practically always have ice cream. Childish tastes, I suppose.'

I'm almost tempted to change and have the mousse just to please him. That's what I would have done with Patrick. I was torn between the ice cream and the mousse, too, as Jake knows; it wouldn't be self-sacrifice to pick it. Then I remember that I'm not altering my own decisions to please a man any more. When I did that kind of thing for Patrick, I used to think that I would be rewarded for it somehow. But I never was, and I couldn't blame him; it was my own fault for setting up trade-offs in my head of which he couldn't have been aware.

And Jake doesn't seem at all aggrieved by my tacit refusal to call the waiter back and change my order. That's the thing I'm learning; stick to your guns, and no man will resent you for it. But become a pushover for them, even without their asking, and they'll just keep pushing you over and over again without ever realising that they're doing it.

'So how's Davey doing?' Jake asks.

I feel my eyebrows arching in surprise. 'I thought you saw him all the time,' I say.

'Not really. We go to different meetings. I'm an early-morning guy, generally. He'll ring if he's got something he needs to talk about, but I haven't heard from him for a couple of weeks.'

'He's pretty good,' I say. 'Work's going well. I was trying to get him to come to meetings, you know, to talk about Jenna, but he doesn't seem to be up for it.'

Jake nods understandingly, but doesn't comment, which is a relief. I wouldn't have been comfortable if he'd come out with some therapy-like platitude about everyone having to find their own path in life.

The desserts arrive, and a minute later, so does Matt. 'How's everything?' he says.

'Yummy,' I say happily.

'This is really good,' Jake says through a mouthful of rhubarb crumble. 'I thought it was a bit dodgy ordering rhubarb out of season, but it's very tasty.'

'Nice presentation,' I add, looking at the crumble, which comes in a small ramekin, its top flashed under the grill and dusted with powdered sugar. 'It's a *petit pot*.' I pronounce this with a deliberately poncey French accent, and Jake laughs.

'*Petit pot de* rhubarb crumble,' he says, grinning at me, and our eyes meet in mutual amusement.

'Yeah, very classy,' I say, smiling back.

I was just being flippant, but the result is that we do look exactly like a couple sharing a silly joke. I see Matt noticing this and my heart swells with pleasure. Very smugly, I imagine him passing this information on to Patrick. 'Rebecca looked really happy, mate. The boyfriend seemed pretty nice. Good-looking guy, too. I'd say she was doing very well.' Vindictively, I hope that Patrick throws up again at the news, just as he did when we were breaking up and the conversation got so hard and deep and painful that he had to run to the bathroom to spew his guts.

'Cointreau for the lady,' Matt says, putting a glass down in front of me.

'I can't believe you remembered after all this time!' I say, very impressed.

He winks at me and hooks out a chair with his foot, pulling it up so he can sit with us. The restaurant is beginning to empty out now, and the tables on either side of us are unoccupied.

'I've brought some Laphroaig,' he says, placing a bottle on the table. He looks round and snaps his fingers at a passing waitress. 'Jenny, a couple of whisky glasses, please,' he says.

'None for me, thanks,' Jake says.

I'm actually glad at this moment that Jake doesn't drink. I

have sat in this restaurant so many times with Patrick and Matt sharing a few snorts of Laphroaig that to have Jake and Matt replicating the same behaviour would be horribly painful.

'Whisky not your thing? Can I get you anything else, mate?' Matt says hospitably.

Jake shakes his head. 'I'm fine, thanks.'

He doesn't go into any detail or belabour the fact that he's not drinking, just keeps it simple. It's amazing how well that works. Matt doesn't press the point, just says: 'Oh dear, more for me,' and fills his glass with a couple of fingers of whisky.

'So, Rebecca, how's everything been?' he asks cheerfully. 'You're looking gorgeous as always.'

'Thanks,' I say, never averse to being complimented.

'Work good?'

'Great. The company's doing really well.'

'Nice one!' Matt says, raising his glass and drinking some Laphroaig in a little toast.

'And what about you, Matt?' I ask. 'Business seems to be flourishing.'

'Like the green bay tree,' he says, winking at me. I'd forgotten that habit of Matt's; it's very endearing. Matt has the knack of making everyone he meets feel instantly at home with him. He's the epitome of hail-fellow-well-met, the perfect personality for a restaurant manager. 'That's the way of the world, sinners always flourish. Cheers.'

He clinks his glass with mine. 'And have you heard from Patrick at all?' he asks. He glances at Jake. 'Sorry, mate, I'm assuming . . .'

'Oh yeah, I know about Patrick,' Jake says, smiling at me.

Matt naturally interprets this in precisely the wrong way. 'Good, good. I was worried I'd put my foot in it there. Opening my mouth without letting the brain engage first, always been my problem,' he says cheerfully.

'We haven't been in touch at all,' I say. 'It seemed better . . .

I mean, we didn't have anything to say, or not anything constructive . . .'

Matt nods understandingly. 'I gotcha. Clean break. Better, probably.'

'How is he?' I ask. I shouldn't, but I can't help it.

'Oh, doing OK. Doesn't ring that much, the bastard, but that's Patrick for you. I went over for the weekend a couple of months ago. He was good. He's cheered up a bit since . . . well, you know. He's running again, seriously, did you hear?'

I shake my head.

'Did a half-marathon a while back. He was making very good time but he had to go back to help that bird he works with. Apparently they've been training together and she got a bit winded . . . well, that's Patrick for you, he went back when he saw she was in trouble and helped her along. Buggered up his time as a result, though.'

'Anita?' I say, though I know exactly who he's talking about.

'Yeah, that's right. Nice girl, very friendly.'

BITCH BITCH BITCH, I want to shout. That *bitch*. I always knew she fancied Patrick, though she behaved perfectly in front of me when I went over to visit. And now she's moving in on him. I could never have done a half-marathon with him; three miles were always my limit. I didn't even know she was a runner. I imagine her taking it up just to have something in common with Patrick. I want to kill both of them.

Matt looks as if he knows he's said something he shouldn't – his big jovial face is starting to crease with worry – and I know my expression must have given me away to some extent. I have to retrieve the situation.

'Half-marathon!' I say lightly. 'Bloody hell! I don't know how anyone can be bothered! I always get so bored after a few miles.'

'Boredom wouldn't be the first thing on my mind,' Matt responds. 'I'd be too worried about the heart attack. Patrick was always nagging me to go to the gym with him, but I could never be arsed.'

I really wish Matt wouldn't keep dragging Patrick into the conversation; just when I've recovered from one reference, he drops in another one. I can't help remembering Patrick working out in the gym of his apartment building, or doing his exercises after he came in from a run. I always made sure I was in when he came back, so I could watch him. Just the sight of Patrick in his running clothes would turn me on, let alone the sight of him doing press-ups on the living-room floor . . . sometimes it was all I could do not to jump on top of him then and there, and the only thing that held me back was knowing how much he would hate it. After the time I tried to slide under him when he was in the press-up position, thinking it would be sexy, and he asked me what on earth I thought I was doing, I learnt that you never interfered with Patrick when he was working, or working out, two of the things he took most seriously in life. For an Englishman, he had an amazingly American Protestant work ethic. If you made a pass at him at the wrong time, you would just get snubbed and retire feeling completely unattractive. I hope that Anita has tried hitting on him when he's training and got that blank, one-eyebrow-raised stare that sends you reeling away, consumed by insecurity.

'I'm not one for the gym, myself,' Jake says. I think he sees that I'm poleaxed and need help. 'It feels a bit artificial.'

'What do you do, then, mate?' Matt says. 'You look pretty fit.'

'He walks,' I contribute. 'All around Kew Gardens for hours and hours until you're completely exhausted.'

This is of course a completely gratuitous interruption for Matt's benefit, designed to look like happy inter-couple teasing. Jake rises to the bait perfectly. 'Oh, come on!' he says, smiling at me. 'That's a wild exaggeration! It was only about an hour!'

'Well, it felt like hours,' I say. It didn't, but I want to keep the teasing going. Matt looks at the two of us with obvious approval.

'So how long—' he starts, and I'm terrified that he's going

to ask how long we've known each other, and Jake may realise he thinks we're a couple and deny it, and my whole carefully constructed house of cards will come tumbling down.

'Matt,' I say quickly, 'I think someone needs you at the bar . . .' I point behind his shoulder to one of the waitresses, who is indeed looking in our direction but doesn't seem in any hurry to attract Matt's attention. Still, it does the trick. Matt gets up with a muttered apology and I ask him for the bill as he goes. I feel that my work here is done.

Chapter Sixteen

Jake insists on paying the bill, saying that it was he who asked me out. I don't remember it quite that way; my version of events would be that I rang him, asked if we could talk, and then steered our mutual diary consultations cunningly round to the conclusion that it would be easiest to meet up for dinner. But in this case I'm happy to let him pay, when any other time I would have insisted on splitting the bill; it looks so much more like a date when the man pays. Matt also, according to Jake, gave us a whopping discount, so I don't feel too guilty about letting him get out his credit card.

The restaurant is warm and glowing and golden as I hug Matt goodnight, accept his whispered: 'You've got a nice one there!' with a happy smile, and pass through the door that Jake is holding open for me. It's not cold outside, but it is dark and slightly damp, and I shiver a little.

'How are you getting home?' Jake says.

I look at my watch. It's eleven-thirty. 'I'll walk down to Leicester Square and get the Tube,' I say.

'But you're cold,' he says. 'You'll freeze. I'll give you a lift.'

I start to protest, and then think: 'Why put him off? Why not just accept, if he's offering?' Louise wouldn't have told him that he didn't need to bother, because she wasn't actually that cold. Louise would doubtless have taken it for granted that he would drive her home. A fundamental change in behaviour starts with the very smallest things and works its way up.

'OK,' I say, 'that'd be great. Thanks.'

Jake starts walking down a narrow side street off Seven Dials, where, presumably, his car is parked. The shops are all shuttered up, and the street is dark for central London, with only a faint trace of unnatural orange glowing from a street light down the next corner. My heels click along the pavement, sounding unnaturally loud. A door opens and a spill of golden light pools out on to the pavement as a couple exit a restaurant, the woman linking her arm through the man's. All the times I have walked through London streets, going home alone after a late night out with friends, feeling inferior to the couples I pass, melt away temporarily; here I am out with a good-looking man, and I feel socially respectable again, not a sad lonely woman unable to get a date.

'Where do you live?' Jake asks.

'Highbury,' I say. 'And you?'

'Clapham Junction.'

'Oh my God, I forgot you were down south. Are you sure you want to drive me? That's completely the wrong direction for you.'

Clearly I need much more practise in channelling Louise. Here I am, falling automatically into guilty apology, instead of just accepting his offer of a lift as my due.

'No, it's fine,' Jake assures me. 'I like it, actually. I love driving around London late at night. When I was first sober, I couldn't sleep very well, and I used to go out, get in my car and just drive around. Often it would be at two or three in the morning. I'd wake up, realise that I wasn't going to get back to sleep again, throw a sweater over my pyjamas and pick up the car keys. It became a habit I really enjoyed. A pleasure I couldn't have had when I was drinking. I'd just drive, without really knowing where I was going, explore areas of London that I'd never been to and would probably never go to . . .'

We stop by a silver Golf and he clicks off the alarm, then opens the passenger door for me.

'Wow, great manners,' I say, climbing in.

Jake shuts the door and goes round to the driver's side. 'It's how I was brought up,' he says as he turns on the engine.

197

'Holding doors, walking on the street side of the pavement. Girls used to think it was patronising, but in the last few years I've noticed they don't care about that any more, they like to have a man who's being attentive . . .'

'Absolutely,' I say. 'I used to be very bolshie about it when I was eighteen, and now I like it. Actually, more than that. I get pissed off if a bloke lets a door fall back in my face.'

'A return to chivalry,' Jake says lightly as the car turns into Cambridge Circus.

'So did you take an *A–Z*?' I ask.

'What?'

'When you were exploring London during your night drives?'

He laughs quietly. 'Never. It was like a point of pride. Or an adventure. I'd get lost for ages and then finally come across a street I knew and find my way back home again.'

We fall silent. I'm imagining Jake out driving in the small hours of the morning, the car slipping through a dark maze of narrow residential streets, not knowing where he was going or how to get home, and finding a certain strange peace from that, a paralleling of his situation in what he describes as a strange new world without drink to rely on, no rules, no security. I think that for me to drive around like Jake did, with no map or compass, would make me feel lonelier than I have ever done in the past; lost, adrift in an uncharted sea, with no one waiting for me at home to worry if I would ever make it back. It tells me something about his character, his ability to withstand the weight of solitude – or rather, to accept that weight and let it settle on to his shoulders without fighting it and making it still worse. And it reminds me of something that I can't yet bring to the surface. I file it away for future reflection.

As we reach Highbury Corner, Jake asks for directions and I give them to him, but we speak quietly, with the minimum of words, reluctant to break the peaceful silence between us, the almost trance-like sensation of the car moving smoothly through night-quiet London. Flares of orange street lamps and red and green traffic lights sliding over the windscreen and slipping away into the dark again. I'd forgotten how much I love being driven, a passenger with no responsibilities. It's like being a child again, curled up in the back of the car as Mummy and Daddy drive you home. I could sit here for hours, drugged by the movement and the companionable silence.

I'm almost sad when we reach my house, sad that the drive is over. I wanted to keep on travelling through the night, keep driving, with no destination in mind, just perpetual, silent motion. I wonder if Jake is feeling this too, because he doesn't move, just sits there behind the wheel, not speaking. Finally I say, 'Thanks so much for the lift.' My voice falls into the silence, shattering it, and I wish I hadn't spoken.

'Oh, no problem.' He shakes his head as if he's emerging from water as deep and dark as the shadowy night streets, and opens his door. I'm still fiddling with mine, trying to work out where the lock is, by the time he's rounded the car and is opening my door for me.

'Oops, I forgot you were going to do that,' I say, getting out. 'Thanks again.'

'Were you OK with tonight?' he asks.

'I'm sorry?' I look at him blankly.

'Going back to a restaurant where you used to go with your ex,' he clarifies. 'It must have brought back a lot of memories.'

'Yes, it did,' I say smoothly, completely prepared for this. 'But that's kind of why I picked it. I decided that since we were going out to talk about things I should look my problems in the face, and I'd always avoided going back to the Seven Dials and seeing Matt because it was too painful. So it felt very cathartic to admit it was difficult for me, and do it anyway. It was almost like reclaiming the past.'

Jake nods understandingly. I've fooled him. He has no idea why I really picked the restaurant or paraded him under Matt's nose like a matador concealing his true shiny steel purpose under a bright red cape. Momentarily, I'm disappointed that Jake can be fooled, that he's not omniscient after all. And then I feel a surge of relief that Jake *is* human, not some perfect AA-programmed truth-seeking robot.

'Well, good night,' he says.

'Good night.'

We smile at each other awkwardly. If this had been a date we would pull in closer, shifting our feet, trying to sense if the other was hoping for a kiss; but it isn't a date, and a handshake feels too formal, a hug a bit too intimate, so we just smile again and Jake turns away to the car.

'We should go out again sometime,' he says. 'I had a really nice time tonight . . .' He pauses, as if about to add something else, and then seems to change his mind.

'Great,' I say. 'Me too.'

He waits until I have unlocked the front door before pulling away. I go upstairs, into my flat, kick off my shoes, wonder whether to have a glass of wine and decide that no, I'm in a good place emotionally, I don't need to drug myself any further. I turn on the light by the sofa and realise at that precise moment that I am very attracted to Jake. It's nicely appropriate that it hits me as I turn on a light, because that's exactly what it feels like, a blinding flash of revelation. I stand there in shock, wondering how I could have been so stupid. Patrick has been dazzling me; his memory was so bright in my eyes that I couldn't see anything beyond him. And now, for some reason, I can: I see Jake at Kew, Jake tonight over the dinner table, looking impossibly handsome and so unlike Patrick that he never called up any memories which would have made me nostalgic . . .

My main emotion is a near-paralysing sense of relief. Secretly, I was afraid that I would never be attracted to anyone again. I knew that was ridiculous, but I was still scared. And now here I am, definitely – I check by calling up an image of Jake as he looked tonight, and verify the instant clamping in the pit of my stomach – yes, definitely sexually interested in another man. My God. I feel insanely happy. I wonder whether that was why I disliked Jake so much when I first met him; was it because I was attracted to him, and didn't want to be? Did I feel it was somehow disloyal to Patrick, and did that make me incredibly hostile to Jake, disguising my true emotional reaction to him? And . . . I think about what else I'm feeling, and realise that I feel – free.

All these thoughts and speculations have raced through my head so fast and furiously, smashing themselves one on top of the next before I've even had time to assimilate each one as it hits me, that I'm dazed with the cumulative shock. I don't know how much time has passed, but I think it can only have been a minute at the most. And while I'm still standing there, frozen, my arm still half-extended as it comes back from reaching for the light switch, the doorbell rings.

I know it's Jake. For a split-second I want to hide. I can't pretend I'm not here, but I could always say later, if he asked me, that I'd been in the bathroom and hadn't heard it. But instead I find myself crossing to the living-room window, which faces on to the street. My intercom is fuzzy and for anything beyond the bare minimum of communication, i.e. letting in the pizza delivery guy, I throw up the window and talk directly to whoever it is standing below me in the tiny front garden.

The window frame sticks and I have a violent momentary rush of frustration with it, heaving and cursing, before I get it open. Illogical, because Jake will wait at least long enough for me to put my head out of the window; he's not going to ring and run like kids playing knock down ginger. But when you're attracted to someone and he's right below you in the street, ringing your doorbell at midnight, logic is not the first thing on your mind. I drag the window up and lean out. Jake's head is right underneath me; I could drop a penny on him and watch it bounce off his scalp. I notice how thick his streaky blond hair is. Thank God for that. I have a big prejudice against those sad little balding spots that you just know are going to widen tragically with age.

'Hey,' I say, incapable of any comment more articulate than that.

He looks up. 'Oh, hey,' he says, clearly also tongue-tied.

'The intercom doesn't work very well,' I say.

'Oh, right.'

We stare at each other, the angle awkward, and are temporarily stalled. What I'm thinking is: *of course* I fancy him, for God's sake! How could I not have realised that! Just look at him! I never believed it was possible when friends told me that they had suddenly realised they fancied someone they had been working with for the best part of three years, let alone when you see romantic comedies where the two stars are obviously destined to fall into each other's arms in the closing reel but remain wilfully blind to their mutual attraction long after the audience is fidgeting in frustration and muttering: '*Kiss* her already, you big idiot!' I look down into his green-grey eyes and feel as if I could fall straight into them. Then I worry that I must look enormously fat from Jake's perspective. Daisy always says not to let anyone photograph you from below, because it makes you look as if you have three chins even if you don't. I wiggle around a bit to try to get my face at a better angle, and Jake says: 'Um, could I come in?'

'Oh, um, sure! Sorry.'

'If it's OK with you – I mean, if you're not too tired . . .'

'No, that's fine. I'll, um, just buzz you in.'

I extract myself from the open window and rush across to the entry panel at the front door, my heart pounding as if I'm standing much too close to the speakers at a rock concert and can't hear anything but the insistent beating roar of the bass line. What is Jake going to say? What am I going to say? My breath must reek of Cointreau; is that going to revolt him? What am I doing being attracted to a non-drinker in the first place; is that some kind of subtle masochism? Luckily, Jake is pretty fit and makes it up the stairs quickly enough to prevent me from indulging too much in the kind of speculation that sends your head spinning so fast that you feel you're about to go insane. Thank God I took down the photographs. Otherwise I'd be scrabbling around now, trying to collect them all and shove them under the sofa, then I'd keep Jake waiting and look all flustered when I finally opened the door . . .

Jake seems larger standing in my flat. Men always do. On your own turf, where you're used to your own proportions, a man, even a smallish one, is noticeably larger. They fill up the armchairs and leave their enormous unsightly shoes lying around (men's shoes may look reasonable when worn but are invariably ugly when off, unlike women's, which can look even prettier without a foot filling them, like a delicate little stiletto-heeled work of art). The effect of Jake's presence on me is as if he were breathing in too much oxygen; sucking in all the air and leaving none for me. I don't know what to say.

He closes the door behind him, but remains standing there, staring at me. I can't read his stare; it could mean many things. It isn't immediately lustful, though, for which I'm hugely relieved. I don't think I could cope at all if Jake just tried to snog me passionately; I think I would have a heart attack or swoon away. My reflexes are not what they were. Patrick has worn them down, and they need a slow, steady building of strength to restore them to their old settings.

'Rebecca . . .' he starts.

I just look at him and nod. I'm incapable of speech right now.

'I'm sorry to barge in on you like this – I just got into my car and I was about to drive away when I realised there was something I really needed to say to you . . .'

I manage to widen my eyes a little in encouragement. My range of motion is temporarily very restricted. I feel like an actress I saw in a blockbuster movie recently, a forty-year-old who had just made a triumphant return to the screen, all the reviews ignoring her acting abilities to focus instead on how stunning and young she looked. She'd had so much Botox injected into her face that she was completely incapable of any facial expressions. Her forehead wouldn't wrinkle, the skin around her eyes wouldn't move, she could barely smile; all she could do to signify high emotion was to roll her eyes.

'I don't think it's appropriate . . .' he continues, '. . . I don't think I can go on acting as your sponsor – I mean, I think I'm very conflicted about it and tonight really brought that home to me – I didn't actually realise until tonight that this was going to be awkward for me. I sort of had an inkling of it at Kew but I thought I could deal with it and now I think I can't . . .' He breaks off. 'Can I sit down?'

'Oh yes, sure,' I say, gesturing to the sofa. I'm as confused as he seems to be; if he's saying that he doesn't want to meet up with me any more, why is he asking to sit down, rather than just giving his speech and shooting out the door? I have a lurking hope that I know where he's going with this, but I won't anticipate, I won't help him along. I will just let him say his piece and not make a fool of myself by imagining him to be making a declaration that may be very far away from what he's actually come to say.

He sits down on the sofa, looking ridiculously handsome. I never quite believe that men that handsome will be attracted to me; it's probably long association with Daisy. If, during your formative years, you hang around with a tall skinny blonde, you are always going to feel gigantic by contrast, convinced that your small pot belly, which some people actually consider cute, in reality only needs udders to make it a dead ringer for a cow's. I have actually been out with a large quantity of pretty good-looking men in my time, but I persist in regarding this as some kind of fluke. So Jake's extreme good looks, as well as, naturally, getting my blood racing, are also a source of insecurity for me. I can't believe I'm actually thinking that I might be in his league.

'This is all very sudden,' he starts, 'and it only really hit me tonight . . .'

I am too dazed by what Jake says next to be able to remember it all as I would like to. One of my greatest regrets is that I didn't rush to the stereo and bung in a tape to record the whole thing. I could have played it back to myself forever, whenever I felt insecure or unattractive or lonely, and it would never have failed to make me feel as clever as Dorothy Parker and as gorgeous as Gina Lollobrigida, because Jake tells me how perceptive and funny I am. He says that from the moment he saw me he thought I was one of the most beautiful women he had ever seen. He says he's been struggling against his attraction to me, because he felt it was inappropriate, since he was giving me advice about my situation, and he says that he still feels that he shouldn't be declaring himself to me at all because he's worried that I'm not over Patrick. But he couldn't resist. He needed to say something because he is so attracted to me that whenever he sees me all he can think about is how much he wants to kiss me, and he realises that means he's scarcely in a good position to give me impartial advice about getting over someone else.

He looks at me the whole time he's talking, as if finally he has given himself permission to do so. I am probably hallucinating by now, but it seems to me that there is a golden glow around him, as if he's more distinct and real than anything else in the room, that the sofa and the wall behind him and the lamp to his left are receding away in an unfocused blur, leaving only Jake sharp and real in front of me.

He says I'm sweet and caring and that I make him laugh like he never thought he would laugh again. He says he's been very closed down since his failed relationship with Louise and that he wasn't looking to meet anyone, that I've taken him completely by surprise and that he doesn't know what to do with the feelings I've aroused in him. He says he thinks about me constantly and is always overjoyed to hear my voice when

I ring him. He says whenever he's with me he never wants to take his eyes off me, he just wants to keep looking and looking at me because he can't believe how beautiful I am. I would probably remember much more of what he said if I hadn't been in such a haze of lust and longing and excitement, but I know that he finishes up by saying that this entire evening has been very difficult for him because he kept having the urge to reach across the table and touch me, hold my hand. He says he practically had to sit on his hands to stop himself doing it, because he was worried that it would be wrong, that he was taking advantage of my vulnerability, but he felt that there was an incredible connection between the two of us and though he told himself that that was just self-delusion, he couldn't help feeling it anyway, which is why he couldn't just get in his car and drive away but had to come and talk to me tonight and see how I felt, and if he's totally deluded and this is all making me feel horribly uncomfortable I must just tell him at once and he'll go immediately and never bother me again.

Finally, he stops. I wanted him to go on talking forever. Never in my life has anyone made this kind of speech to me, and probably no one ever will again. It's one of those very rare, truly free gifts, no strings attached. I am in such a state of shock that I can't speak for a while after he finishes, and then I realise that he's staring at me imploringly, begging me to say something, to give him some kind of reassurance that he hasn't just made a complete idiot of himself. I've never seen Jake vulnerable before. He looks even more handsome like this, with all his usual guards down. I open my mouth but nothing comes out. What I really want to do is slap myself sharply around the face, but I don't think Jake would find that very encouraging.

'I don't feel . . .' I start, haltingly. More than anything I want to get up from the armchair and manoeuvre around the coffee table and sit down on the sofa next to him and feel his arm slide around me, but I'm paralysed to the spot.

'Yes?' Jake says nervously.

'I don't mind . . . I mean, I don't think . . .'

Maybe I shouldn't be trying to start with a negative; it doesn't seem to be coming out right. I expect I ought to launch into a speech as long and articulate as Jake's, but I know I am utterly incapable of that right now.

'I do actually find you really attractive,' I say, realising how stupidly prim that sounds. 'But I only realised that tonight, so I'm still a bit shocked by all of this. I mean shocked in the sense that I didn't expect this, you know, not shocked as in . . .' I tail off. I have no idea where I'm going with that. Best to leave it alone. 'But I'm just . . . I do, I am really attracted to you too, and I didn't expect to be attracted to anyone else ever, or not for ages, so this is all a big surprise to me . . .'

Jake gets up and instead of walking awkwardly around the coffee table, he takes one huge stride across it and ends up directly in front of me. It's very manly and decisive of him, but the sight of him looming over me is more than I can take. It's literally as if he's saying, 'Here I am. Take me now.' And I don't think I'm quite ready for that. I shrink back a little in the armchair, but the next second he's dropped to his knees on the carpet and is reaching out to take my hands. I give them to him as shyly as a schoolgirl being asked out by her first big crush. I can barely look at him; he's so gorgeous, and he's right in front of me, mutely asking me for so many things, none of which I'm sure I'm able to give. He bends his head and kisses my hands. That's much better. Now he's not looking at me, I can look at him. I eat him up with my eyes: his thick silky hair, his strong silver-ringed hands, his wide shoulders. I realise I want to unbutton his shirt and cup my hands over those bare shoulders, feel the caps of muscle over the bone, bury my head in his neck and smell his skin, kiss him in that little hollow of the throat where I can see his pulse racing. Desire is growing in me like one of those speeded-up nature films where the flower suddenly opens and bursts into full-blown life.

Jake is kissing my wrists now, pushing up the sleeves of my

top to bare my skin. I pull one hand away. He looks up at me, worried, but I reach out and run my hand through his hair, and it's like an electric current surging through both of us now that we're connected in a circle; my hand on him, his on me. I am infinitely glad that his hair is so different from Patrick's. It means that I don't have any sense memories flooding up to ruin this moment. I bury my hand in the nape of his neck. I want to pull him towards me and kiss him, but I'm not quite brave enough yet.

Patrick has definitely scarred me. In the old days I would be all over Jake by now. Look at how I finally seduced Patrick, when I got frustrated, after a few weeks that seemed like an eternity, that he still hadn't kissed me; I kicked off my shoe and played footsie with him under the table at that bar we went to with his friends. I watched his face freeze and then flush with excitement, and then announced, unilaterally, without even asking him, that I was going back to his place that night to watch some crappy video we'd been talking about earlier. Hah. As if we ever watched that video. I did all the initial work. And now I'm too nervous to even kiss Jake.

We stare at each other, Jake's face still below mine. He raises my hand and puts it behind his neck to join the other one, and then comes to his knees so his face is level with mine. I want to scream and run away, but even more than that, I want to kiss him. So as he leans into me, my hands tighten on the back of his neck, encouraging him to come even closer. I shift a little on the armchair so I can sit up straighter, and Jake's lips finally meet mine, delicately, brushing against me, giving me plenty of time to say that I don't think this is such a good idea after all, and then, tentatively, deepening the pressure.

I close my eyes and wrap my hands even tighter into his hair. I feel his mouth part mine, his teeth tugging gently at my bottom lip, his tongue lightly tracing the outline of my mouth, and I want him very badly indeed, my whole body is now desperate to press myself against him, and I sit up even straighter in the armchair as his arms slide around my back, pulling me towards him, and now we're kissing as if we'll die if we don't, and Jake is pulling me off the chair so that I half-fall to my knees facing him and we're both kneeling up with our arms wrapped around each other and he's kissing the corner of my mouth and tracing a line of kisses all the way down to my neck, which always makes me go weak at the knees, which is obviously a considerable handicap in this position, because I stagger with sheer pleasure and collapse backwards on to the armchair. Jake grabbing me just in time to make sure that I don't whack my head on it, and he falls on top of me and the armchair slides back a little and suddenly we're on the carpet with our bodies still wound tightly round each other. I'm trying to get Jake's shirt open so that I can kiss his neck, which is difficult as I only have the use of one hand because the other is caught between our bodies, but I don't care, I'll get that bloody button undone if it kills me, and finally I wrest it free and sink my head into the soft skin of his neck. I hear him moan with pleasure, and then he grabs me and rolls me over so that I'm on top of him, only his legs get caught under the coffee table when I'm halfway over and we're momentarily stuck before he can work his feet free, and then I'm lying on top of him on my living-room carpet, my elbows propped either side of him, and I start to giggle, and he starts to laugh, and then we meet each other's eyes and it stops being funny because I can feel the whole length of his body underneath mine and I move my groin just a little bit, almost experimentally, and he groans and grabs me and pulls me even tighter before sinking his tongue into my mouth and we kiss properly, passionately, our bodies grinding into each other's, though of course I'm trying to hold my stomach in so he doesn't realise how fat I am.

After an eternity we come up for air and take deep breaths. I slip off him so that I can lie next to him and feel a little less self-conscious for a moment, We curl up next to each other on the carpet, grinning moronically, caught in that cycle where you can't stop kissing but have to pause every now and then to look at each other. We smirk with satisfaction and wonder in amazement that we've been lucky enough to have found each other, that we've found someone who wants to be in our arms as much as we want to be in theirs, someone who can't think of anywhere in the world he would rather be right now than lying next to you on your living-room carpet, kissing your eyes and your nose and yes, your mouth again, and though I close my eyes I can feel his smile against me as he kisses my lips and twines his hands through my hair. I run the pad of my finger over his mouth and slide it through his lips, pressing it against his teeth until he sucks it in. Neither of us are smiling now, Jake's eyes are shut as he concentrates on the feel of my finger in his warm wet mouth. I watch him, his eyelashes thick on his cheeks, his hair messed up and falling over his face, and I feel a brief, terrible sadness that he's not Patrick, but I shove it deep down inside me, I won't let it ruin the bliss of this moment. I pull out my finger, slowly, and replace it with my mouth and we start kissing again. I want to be suspended here forever, beyond time, just lying here on the carpet in Jake's arms, feeling that maybe the world is finally falling into place for me.

Chapter Seventeen

JENNIFER

'For ages I wanted to kill my ex, literally kill him. I used to fantasise about going up to him and shoving a gun in his face and saying, "This is how much you hurt me. This is how much I suffered," before pulling the trigger. But that never seemed like enough. I mean, it was never really that satisfying as a fantasy. So then I'd extend it. I'd imagine I had him tied to a chair in his flat, and I'd make him beg for mercy, and then finally I'd go up to him and put the gun up against his chest and watch the expression in his eyes as he realised that I was actually going to do it. But then I'd always get to that point, and I wouldn't know what happened next. I would kill him, but what would I be left with? Just his dead body. And I'd still be as angry as ever. Nothing would have changed. Killing him wouldn't free me from all the unhappy feelings I had, or the sense of betrayal. The only logical thing to do next would be to kill myself too, but that was so miserable, it didn't cheer me up at all.

'So I'd imagine myself beating him up. I'd picture myself as this kick-boxing action figure, incredibly tough, and I'd walk into his flat and find him in bed with his new girlfriend. I'd grab her by the hair, punch her in the face and throw her across the room. Then I'd turn to him – he'd be completely incredulous and angry – and I'd beat him up in front of her. I'd kick and punch him until he was on the ground covered in blood and curled up in a ball begging me to stop. Then I'd give him one final kick in the balls and walk out looking really cool, you know, all dressed in black with my hair pulled back and not a mark on me.

'But I still couldn't imagine what I did after that. You know what I mean? There I'd be, standing in the street, and I'd want to be all righteous and revengeful and washing my hands of the whole mess, but I'd still be really unhappy. It didn't make me feel any better, which was the whole point of fantasising about it in the first place. I still try. I still try to find a way of imagining being really violent and it giving me some sort of satisfaction, but it never does.

'I think I wanted to have violent fantasies because the rest of my wishes were so pathetic, you know? They all involved him waiting for me after I got out of work, holding a big bunch of flowers, saying how sorry he was and that he'd realised what a big mistake he'd made and that he couldn't live without me. I'd pretend to be cool for a while and make him crawl, but of course I'd always take him back. I make up things like that before I go to sleep. It's like I'm a grown-up kid telling myself bedtime stories, and even though I know they're just fairy tales, they calm me down.

'But I don't want to be like this. I don't want to rely on fairy tales to get me through. I thought that if I talked about it today it would help – you know, get it all out. And I was really embarrassed to think about standing up in front of all of you and talking about wanting to beat up and kill my ex. I thought at first you'd all think I was a psycho. And then I thought, no, we all think like this, we all have these feelings, I bet there isn't a single person in the room who doesn't close their eyes at night when they're feeling really lonely and there's nothing left to distract them from their unhappiness, who doesn't wish that they were killing their ex or hurting them in some way to sort of pay them back for the pain they've caused . . . For ages I used to go to sleep with the light on, and music playing. I couldn't bear being alone in the dark. I didn't sleep very well, I'd wake up after a few hours and think it was morning because the light was on, and start getting up before I realised. That was awful because there's nothing as bad as waking up at three or four in the morning and not being able to get back to sleep. You have the worst thoughts of all then. You just feel worthless and miserable and alone and like no one will ever love you again. But I still couldn't turn the light off.

'I can now. That's like a victory for me, really. Being able to go to sleep in the dark.'

'So you actually think this is a good idea?' Davey asks me incredulously.

'Well, why not? What harm's it going to do?' I smile at him blithely as I put on my jacket.

'What *harm*?' Davey is so wound-up that he can hardly get the words out.

'Yeah. Daisy and Finn put on a bit of a show for Vanessa and Barney and Finn gets to keep some dignity while all the blokes there gawp at Daisy and tell him how lucky he is . . . it's just a weekend away, Davey, it's not like they're getting married or anything.'

Davey takes off his glasses and polishes them on the hem of his shirt, something he only does under extreme stress. 'I can not believe,' he mutters, 'that you can not see how destructive and dishonest this plan is. Finn has to confront his feelings, not run away from them. And Daisy's messed-up enough as it is. The last thing she needs is to pretend she has a boyfriend when she doesn't. It'll just upset her terribly because of the gap between appearance and reality.'

'Oh well,' I say cheerfully, 'maybe when they start pretending, they'll realise they were secretly in love all along and they'll fall into each other's arms, like a romantic comedy. Wouldn't that be great?'

Davey replaces his glasses and stares at me as if I have lost my mind. 'Have you lost your *mind*?' he says. 'What's wrong with you? Finn and Daisy are completely incompatible!'

213

'Are they?' I pick up my bag and we walk out of the office, heading for Exmouth Market. I can't really focus on this conversation very well. My head is full of Jake. He has crammed himself in there, squashing my brain into such a small area of my cranium that I'm surprised I can actually use it at all. I'm constantly forgetting things I know perfectly well, like which section of my wallet my Travelcard lives in, or that I need to put on mascara in the morning to stop my eyes looking bald. I can barely drink coffee because it over-stimulates me, and I'm buzzing quite enough already. If I try very hard I can ignore Jake's presence in my skull for about thirty minutes at a time, and I use these brief opportunities to plough ahead with work. It's amazing how much I can actually get done during thirty minutes' concentrated activity. But then, as I mentioned, I am highly stimulated at the moment.

Davey is telling me all the reasons why Finn and Daisy are incompatible. Finn needs someone who will stand up to him, apparently, which Daisy will never be able to do, because she rolls over for men; she should be with someone who will take care of her and make sure she doesn't ignore her own needs. Daisy can be a flirty flibbertigibbet (that was Davey's exact phrase, believe it or not) and that would drive Finn crazy because he's insecure, doubtless from spending his entire lifetime feeling inferior to Barney. Daisy needs someone stable and quietly confident who will understand that her flirtatiousness is just part of her friendly nature, and who will trust her to let off steam without being paranoid that she's going to fall into bed with every man she giggles with at parties. It probably all makes sense, because Davey always makes sense, but I hardly listen. I tune in now and then for the latest brief snippet of in-depth psychological analysis while the other ninety-nine per cent of my mind is occupied with calling up a memory of exactly what Jake said to me on the phone this afternoon.

'Are you even *listening?*' Davey says indignantly.

I wrench myself away from the part where Jake said how much he was looking forward to seeing me.

'Yes, of course,' I say in a reassuring tone. 'Finn needs someone less flighty, Daisy needs someone more stable. It sounds very easy when you put it like that, doesn't it? Maybe we should advertise for a boyfriend and girlfriend for them in *Time Out*, too.'

Davey stares at me suspiciously. 'If I didn't know better,' he says, 'I'd think you were on something.'

'Life is the only happy pill I need,' I say sweetly. I mean this to sound jocular, but I'm so happy at the moment that it comes out much too sincere.

'You've certainly cheered up recently,' Davey says. 'The meetings must be going well.'

'Brilliantly. We're all so in touch with our feelings that we could write entire books about them. And Jake's being a lot of help, too.'

Hah! I have managed to get Jake's name into the conversation! I've been dying to talk to Davey about him for over a week now. Daisy knows, of course, but she hasn't met him, so it's not quite the same; I can't gloat over his many manifest perfections and expect her to agree. Davey, on the other hand, is the ideal person to discuss Jake with, but Jake and I have agreed not to mention the alteration in our personal relationship to Davey yet. I really want to, but I'm terrified of jinxing anything, which is why I agreed so readily when Jake suggested that maybe we should just feel our way through this precarious new situation together for a while, without bringing in our mutual friend. I can see the wisdom in this. I would just burble away to Davey about Jake all day, probably creeping him out, and Jake was concerned that Davey might be less likely to approach him when he needed sponsor-type advice if he thought, for instance, that Jake might share pillow talk with me about urgent counselling interventions he had already had to stage for Davey.

'Jake's great, isn't he?' Davey says happily.

This is so ironic. I have spent what feels like ages loathing Jake's name. Every time that Davey sang Jake's praises I would pull faces when his back was turned and sing 'La la la' in my head to try to drown out the annoyance I felt that Davey had practically put this near-stranger on a pedestal, hanging him with metaphorical garlands and bringing him metaphorical offerings. If they had been Catholic, I could see Davey conducting a vigorous campaign after Jake's death to get him on the fast-track canonisation process which is usually reserved only for the Pope's close friends and deeply dubious cardinals. But now, the more Davey praises Jake, the happier it makes me. Perspective is everything.

'He *is* great,' I agree, though, unlike Davey, I'm thinking about the way Jake lightly bites my earlobes, or his soft breath on my lips just before he kisses me. Jake is very good at taking his time.

'He's so understanding,' Davey says.

We turn into Exmouth Market. I love this little street. Despite being on the edge of the City and only a short distance from King's Cross, it has a cosy neighbourhood feel: lots of cute little restaurants and cosy, slightly dilapidated bars. The creeping incursion of chain restaurants has been mainly avoided – there is a Pizza Express, but, despite being a chain, Pizza Express has always managed to avoid the stigma that usually entails. Davey and I make for the bar we always go to, about halfway down the street, a rickety little place with French and Spanish beer signs on the walls, crumbling paintwork, a small pool table at the front and a few coveted, red vinyl booths at the back. Its clientele are scruffy trendies from Islington, but it has a Hoxton Square vibe about it: the clothes they wear are deliberately stained and distressed, the trousers dragging over their limited-edition trainers, the T-shirts highly prized vintage designs for which they paid a fortune. The girls' hair is as straggly as the boys', the only difference being that the girls mostly have their hair in bunches, decorated with fake flowers or brightly coloured bobbly hairclips purchased from children's shops. Looking grown-up isn't done much in these circles. There are late-thirty-year-olds here dressing like disaffected teenagers.

All the booths are taken – there are only three and people tend to get here early to claim one. Davey and I sit at the bar and order a red wine for me and a cranberry and lemonade for him. The service is as erratic as ever, and I have to ask for olives three times before the would-be pop star/DJ behind the counter finally processes my request and dips the ladle into the gigantic jar to scoop out a saucer of oily, wrinkled black olives. They make my red wine taste sour, but it wasn't very good red wine anyway, and I love these olives. Drag flesh off with teeth and spit stone, drag flesh off with teeth and spit stone. My mouth puckers with the combination of tastes.

'How are you doing, Davey?' I ask. I'm full of the milk of human kindness at the moment, brimming with it like a glass which needs just one more drop to make it spill. I want everybody to be happy and in love.

'What, generally?' he says. 'As opposed to worrying about this lunatic upcoming house party?'

'Yup, generally. How's life in Davey World?'

'Pretty good,' he concedes. 'I love my work, you know? How many people can say that? I really love my work.' He pushes his glasses up his nose. 'And everyone seems happier. I didn't realise how bad the atmosphere was in the office until everyone cheered up.'

'You can't take care of everyone,' I say.

'I know.'

'No, you don't. You worry too much about other people and not enough about yourself.'

'Davey's the best!' Daisy says, coming up and wrapping her arms around him from behind. 'He rocks!'

I remove my bag from the bar stool I'd put it on to reserve it for her. Daisy's in no hurry to sit down, though. She stands there, tall enough in her ubiquitous heels that she can lean her head almost on top of his. Her blonde curls tumble over her face, and her eyes are outlined and smudged with a bright blue pencil which intensifies their colour so that they pop like twin neon lights. Daisy is one of those girls who is beautiful and slim enough to be able to wear the latest make-up or dress fashions as if they had been invented just for her. I've seen that blue eyeliner in magazines for the last two months, but wouldn't have dreamt of trying it myself. I'm thirty-three and now I stick to what I know suits me, rather than being buffeted by every passing gust of fashion wind into buying the current must-have pair of shiny satin combat trousers with ankle ties, which would inevitably make my bottom look as wide as Kent and my legs like a knock-kneed six-year-old's. I swear that designers invent these things as a cruel joke, to see how many poor women are bullied into wearing them by *Elle* or *Vogue*, and then have a good giggle when they see the sad cows walking down the street looking like rejects from an avant-garde circus. It's all about consumption, of course. They keep designing new stuff to whet our appetite, and we collude in it because it gives us an excuse for yet another shopping expedition, worshipping at the altar of Selfridges or Harvey Nichols. For a moment I think that this whole Higher Power idea might not be such a bad one after all if it would save me from compulsive shopping.

'God, both of you are as buzzy as bees today!' Davey says, unwinding Daisy's arms from around him and swivelling to give her a quick hug. 'Did someone put happy pills in your morning coffee?'

'Lewis rang me!' Daisy announces, completely blissed-out. 'It really worked! The whole thing with Finn!'

She leans over to the bar and says: 'A Stella, please,' to the barman, who blinks, dazzled by her gorgeousness, and moves uncharacteristically fast to fill her order. Which is to say, he moves, rather than just leaning against the bar for another five minutes until eventually she has to remind him of what she wanted.

I sigh. I don't see this Lewis thing as bringing anything but more pain for Daisy. He's been turned on by the fact that she's seeing someone else – or so he thinks – and now he's chasing after her once more. It's just the dog in the manger syndrome. As soon as he knows he's got her again, he'll dump her just as fast as he did before. Maybe I'm being unduly negative; maybe Lewis really did realise that he was serious about her when he saw her out with another man; but I strongly doubt it.

'And he sent me a saucy text too!' Daisy cackles happily. 'Want to see?'

'*No*, thanks,' Davey and I say in unison, pulling faces of disgust.

'Oh, it's not that dirty . . .' Daisy says wistfully.

I shake my head. Obviously, she wants to prove her source of happiness to independent witnesses, but I draw the line at reading rude text messages.

The barman puts Daisy's Stella down in front of her and she chinks it with our glasses. 'To being happy!' she says, winking at me.

'Daisy . . .' Davey begins, but he doesn't finish the sentence. He glances at me and I shrug. There's no point saying anything.

'So, Rebecca, what have you been up to lately?' she says naughtily. 'Been doing anything fun?'

'Oh,' I say demurely, 'nothing much. Just hanging out.'

'Seen anything of Jake?'

God, she's pushing it. Daisy is so fizzy with excitement that she wants everyone around her to be on a perpetual high as well. Naming Jake to me with Davey present, she knows, will cause me to blush and stammer, and she wants to inject a note of conspiracy and sparked-up, hidden meaning into even a simple meeting-of-friends-after-work-for-a-drink.

I manage to restrain myself from accidentally on purpose

spilling some red wine down the designer jeans that I know cost her a small fortune, and say instead, 'Olive, Daise?' handing her the bowl. Playing for time, always a good tactic.

She takes an olive but goes straight back on the attack again. 'So, Jake been round at all recently, has he?' she says.

'Yeah, he's been saying some stuff that might be very useful to the group,' I respond, catching her eye and narrowing mine at her in the closest I can get to a death threat.

'Oh yeah?' Daisy asks faux-innocently. 'Like what?'

'Oh, the need to be supportive . . . you know, bear in mind the idea of the group as an entity stronger than its individual parts . . .'

This is meant as bait for Davey, and it works marvellously. He launches into an impassioned diatribe on the AA philosophy, which shuts Daisy up for a few minutes. Unfortunately, he then gets on to the many wonderful qualities of Jake, how he's learnt so much from him, how inspiring Jake has been, which allows Daisy a perfect opportunity to say, 'Yeah, I think Jake's been inspiring Rebecca a lot as well. Hasn't he, Rebecca?'

'Oh, I think I've managed to give Jake a few ideas too,' I say, finding that I'm actually rather enjoying this banter.

'Yeah,' Davey says immediately. 'That's the whole thing about AA, or, obviously, your group, too. There's always give and take. You can learn things from the most unlikely people.'

I wouldn't say that Jake had actually taught me anything so far. We're just so happy to be ripping each other's clothes off right now that we haven't exactly been experimenting with sophisticated positioning or esoteric props. Still, for a moment I imagine Jake tying me down and running ice cubes over my body, or vice versa, and a shudder of such desire runs over me that I actually wobble on my stool and nearly send myself flying.

'You all right there?' Daisy asks evilly.

I was determined not to ask about Lewis, but it's my last hope before this conversation becomes too much for me. I want

220

so badly to boast about Jake, to witter on about how happy I am and how fortunate I feel to have connected with him, and Daisy is doing such a good job of playing the evil temptress that I can feel her lures pulling at me, winding round me, compressing my chest until the urge to burst out with my news will be unstoppably squeezed up and up until it explodes out of my mouth.

'When are you seeing Lewis?' I ask.

She knows what I'm doing, but like me, she can't resist. We are both caught by our own desires and don't want to break free.

'Tomorrow night!' she says blissfully. 'We're going to dinner.'

'When did he ring?' I ask.

'Yesterday.'

I tut. 'You should have said you weren't free this week. You mustn't make it too easy for him.'

'Oh, poo.' She sticks her tongue out at me, but a second later doubt flits momentarily across her pretty features and I can tell she knows I'm right. 'I wanted to see him,' she says defensively. 'And it's a proper date, not just meeting up at a party he's organising.'

Neither Davey nor I comment on this, and after a moment she says brightly, 'Now, what about you, Davey?'

'What *about* me?' Davey asks blankly.

'We need to get you sorted out with someone! I know lots of nice girls who'd love to go out with you!'

'God, no, Daisy, I hate set-ups. You know that.'

'Nothing too heavy,' she assures him. 'We could just all meet up for a drink and you could see how you get on.'

Davey looks distinctly underwhelmed by this idea.

'Come on, Davey!' Daisy says. 'It's been ages since Jenna! Time to move on and get your life going again!'

I know this state of mind. It's the I'm-so-happy-with-my-man-that-I-want-everyone-around-me-to-be-happy-too syndrome. She beams at me, making me complicit with her, adding me to the list of people who are blissfully in love and will empathise with the wish to set everyone else up successfully as well.

'We could go out with a few other people,' she suggests to Davey, 'if you felt uncomfortable. Make it a group outing so it doesn't look too obvious. Like, we could invite Rebecca and . . . I don't know, maybe Jake?'

Daisy is going much too far with this. I notice that Davey has finished his cranberry and lemonade, and I order another round. The sooner he needs to go to the loo, the sooner I can sit on Daisy's head, or pummel it against the bar, or whatever it takes to stop her hints about me and Jake. This is all so new, and, as I said, I'm terrified of jinxing it. I'm at that stage where I want to text him all the time, just to prove that he's there, or rather here, in spirit; in my life, just at the other end of a mobile phone. I'm dizzy with joy to have found someone after all the pain and uncertainty, not to mention the utter conviction that never again would I meet someone who would make me think that my life wasn't a series of doors slamming shut in my face, but full of prospects opening up to the sky.

Chapter Eighteen

ME

'I was watching *How To Lose A Guy In 10 Days* the other night and apart from thinking what a fucking amateur Kate Hudson was in that film – I mean, if you really know what you're doing, it doesn't take ten days to lose a man, you can do it in ten seconds – it made me realise how much I hate romantic comedies. I actually turned it off halfway through, and I never turn films off. But the thing about romantic comedies is that they're based on one of two moronic ideas, neither of which ever happen in real life. Either the hero and heroine hate each other and go at it like cats and dogs, only to realise much later that they're attracted to each other. Or one or both of them is blocked in some way, and have problems committing because they always try to please everyone. They've either got an alcoholic father – like in *Runaway Bride* – or they're cold hard businessmen who can only date prostitutes – like in *Pretty Woman*. But suddenly some magical therapeutic thing happens to make them get over it and they rush back to Richard Gere or Julia Roberts and fall into their arms because everything's been resolved and now they can get married, which is even more bullshit, because these things never happen in a lightning flash. I mean, sometimes the person does get over it, but it takes years, it's a long, slow, painful process to change your entire idea of yourself and your life. It doesn't happen just because a friend or your long-lost dad says the right thing to you at the right moment which then flicks a switch in your head so immediately you're different. Even when you do get over it, if you do, it takes ages and you usually end up with someone else, not the person who made you realise what your psychological problems were in the first place.

'I remember years and years ago I watched *When A Man Loves a Woman*. Meg Ryan's an alcoholic in that, and Andy Garcia's her long-suffering husband. A friend of mine who had a big problem with drugs was with me, God knows why we were watching that film in the first place, but we just couldn't help cacking ourselves with laughter at how stupid and Hollywood and miraculously neat that whole film was. You know, Meg Ryan has loads of problems, goes into therapy, works out why she drinks too much, and what feels like two weeks later she and Andy are holding hands and working through her problems together and he's accepting his share of the blame and everything's smelling of roses . . . I mean, no one ever cleans up that fast, or that easily. It takes years and years and your marriage probably breaks up in the meantime and you relapse again and again. This film was more like a marriage guidance 'ideal scenario' training video than anything resembling real life.

'And anyway, what I always want to know about romantic comedies is: what happens after they end? It's easy enough to fall into someone's arms, but what happens after that? I mean, after *Pretty Woman*, wasn't Richard Gere secretly unbelievably jealous and insecure that Julia Roberts had been tarting around for years? And didn't Julia Roberts, after *Runaway Bride*, start having affairs because she was still shit-scared of committing to one man for her whole life? We're all fixated on the getting-together part of it, and we all 'ooh' and 'aah' when the couple finally kisses, but that's not the end, it's barely the beginning. And this whole crap about love being enough. Love is *not* enough. It's only the start. If love had been enough, Patrick and I would still be together. We broke up still in love with each other, and that just made it worse . . .

'And don't even get me *started* on bloody pop songs!'

*

'Whew!'

'Yeah . . .'

'Wow.'

'Mmn . . .'

'Did I . . . were you . . .'

'What?'

'Well, at the end – when you said "Yeah, fuck me like that" – I was worried that you meant that, you know, I hadn't been doing it the way you liked before . . .'

'No, no.' I'm collapsed on the bed, arms and legs starfished, replete with afterglow, but I manage to get muscle command to one arm and prop myself up on my hand so I can see his face. 'I could see you were about to come, so I was talking dirty for you.'

'Oh.' He laughs sleepily. 'Good. Good technique. It really worked. Mmn.' He bends down and kisses me, not a serious, passion-stirring kiss but a slow plant of lips to lips, a memory and a promise. Then, reassured in his manly abilities to satisfy a woman, he too allows himself to collapse next to me.

'I tried not to bite you,' I say, reaching up for a pillow and pulling it under my head.

He laughs again. 'I tried to keep biting you.'

'It was great.'

'Mmn.'

Jake and I are really good at this. Not just the sex itself, but the during-and-post-coital exchanging of information. What we like, what we don't. Put your hand just there, no, a bit to the left, I don't like it when you bite my neck, I love it when you bite my neck, hang on, I need to put a pillow under my bottom. We've done more what-pleases-me Q & A in a few sessions than Patrick and I did in our entire relationship. I did try to ask Patrick in the beginning. I've always believed you should do that in the early stages, otherwise you can fall into patterns your partner doesn't enjoy but, after a few months, is too embarrassed to tell you about because you'll exclaim in horror, 'Oh my God!

You never liked that? Why didn't you tell me?' But to all my queries, Patrick would simply reply that he loved everything I did. And he never asked me in return. That wasn't Patrick's way. He preferred to work it out for himself. In many respects he was extraordinarily sensitive to other people's feelings, and this was a prime example. He watched and listened and experimented and gradually he got so good at working out what pleased me, without ever asking a single question, that he could have written a user guide to my body. It took him about a month of study to pick up everything he needed to know. He was a fast learner.

Jake rolls over on to his stomach. I look at him now that I can, properly, a long lustful gaze, because his face is hidden: the thick fair hair, the long line of his back, the smooth skin, the firm arse, the hairs on his legs fading the further down they go, till, by the bottom of his calves, they're the pale gold of his hair. One arm is stretched towards me, and I stare at his hand and feel a reminiscent tremor low down in my belly, remembering how his fingers felt inside me. Music is playing on his bedroom stereo, a slow, subtle, sexy trip-hop that was perfect for our mood. We had dinner at a Japanese place where the food comes on conveyor belts running around the bar and you select the plates you want, which makes it feel like a snack bar until you count up the plates and see how much money you've spent. Then we went to see a French movie with subtitles, about a man and a woman in Paris who meet through an ad she places in a contact magazine, asking for a guy who wants sex without strings. Gradually they fall in love, but because it's a French movie and psychologically accurate, rather than an over-romanticised American one, they realise that being the kind of people they are, people who would choose to meet up for specific, anonymous sex, they are incapable of turning what is between them into a serious relationship, and, understanding this in mutual, wordless agreement, they part. It was beautiful and sad and true.

Then we came back to Jake's, put a sexy, moody CD on and started kissing on the sofa. Apart from the sofa kissing, it was an evening I could never have had with Patrick. Japanese food was too weird for him. And he wouldn't ever willingly watch a film with subtitles, or one which didn't have a predominantly male cast who spent the entire time facing each other down in a series of increasingly macho stand-offs before shooting, high-kicking or pounding the crap out of each other. On TV, Patrick watched *The Simpsons*, the football and the rugby. He liked camping, Led Zeppelin, solitude, cold weather, and meat-and-two-veg for dinner. I prefer raw fish, posh hotels, sunshine, dance music, parties, and arty movies where the characters talk about philosophy and nothing much seems to happen but by the end you realise that delicate psychological changes have altered them almost imperceptibly. We were not very compatible, apart from horizontally.

'Shall I turn off the music?' Jake mumbles into his pillow.

'No, it's nice.'

'It'll turn off by itself at the end of the CD.'

He half-sits up with what is clearly a heroic effort, and reaches up to turn off the light. Leaning over, he kisses my shoulder and then curls up for sleep, his back turned to me, his warm smooth bottom pressing gently against my hip. I pull the sheet up over our lower bodies. It is white and starched, feeling fresh and clean over our overheated skin. I arrange another pillow under my head, inching back a little till it butts against the headboard and provides me with some support into which to nuzzle my nape. The headboard is a smooth sweep of leather which matches the big armchair on which most of our clothes are strewn. The duvet cover is white, piped subtly at the seams in a dark brown. Jake's decor is bachelor elegant, male but not obtrusive, expensive but not flashy. Patrick had flannelette sheets in a green plaid pattern for winter and ancient beige cotton ones, the bottom sheet fraying gently along the corner elastic, for summer; his bathroom was rarely cleaned, his clothes lay in piles all over the tatty carpet and his sofa had more stains on it than the upholstery of a ten-year-old tube seat on the Northern line.

I fit in to Jake's flat much better. Superficial as it may sound, I like being smart and fashionable and dressing up to go out and having the things around me reflect that. I used to buy sweaters for Patrick in the early days of our relationship, sweaters like the ones Jake wears, expensive fine knits that show off his body, in colours that bring out his eyes. Patrick would put them on, look breathtakingly handsome, shrug, look uncomfortable and take them straight off again. He wore a suit for work and the rest of the time jeans and oversized T-shirts or loose plaid shirts rather like his flannelette sheets. So no, we didn't make an obvious match. We weren't style-compatible like the couples you often see, the lovely streaked blonde and the tall dark handsome man in his and hers Gucci. You would never have looked at me and Patrick and thought 'They look so right together'. I would be tittupping along beside him in my heels and short skirt, a fake flower in my hair, while Patrick strode along in his lace-up boots and over-pale jeans. It was only when we had all our clothes off, and no one else was around, that we became that perfect match.

Jake and I like the same music and the same films. We're clothes-conscious; we look like people who could share the same moisturiser and his and hers versions of the same scent. But we don't fall into each other when we have sex. We don't lose ourselves in each other and find something new and strange, rare and magical, instead. We're always two separate beings, and though we work together for mutual enjoyment, our pleasure, when we find it, is separate too. Before Patrick, I would have thought this was the best I could ever hope to achieve. And maybe, in the long term, this is better.

From: Daisy
To: Rebecca; Finn; BenDavison44@hotmail.com; Jenny@penny.demon.co.uk; charlotte_gavan_duffy@virgin.net; jim.watts@argot.co.uk
Subject: More Grief Stuff, how cheerful!

Ooh, Charlotte, just found this on the Net and thought it was really good stuff for you. It's from a single parents' website – it's the Five Stages of Grief again, but with advice on how to handle the kids. (I like 'guerrilla single parenting', btw!) I cut the stages bit 'cos we all know that by now! And yeah, everyone and especially Charlotte, I know I'm in Denial, OK? I know I spent a lot of time last night saying I wasn't, but he still hasn't bloody rung, and I am. Fuck it. Actually I think I'm in Anger right now. And Bargaining. Anyway, this helped a lot. Have a read of the attached, I thought we could talk about it next week. Wish me and Finn good luck on this weekend's girlfriend imposture thing. I'm getting all my sexiest clothes together to make Finn's ex madly jealous!!!
Daisy xoxo

Suddenly Single? The Five Stages of Grief

By Single Parent Central,
the home of Guerrilla Single Parenting

Death of a spouse or the breakup of a marriage or long-term relationship can trigger similar responses in people. Each person mourns a loss differently. However, there are five common stages of grief that a person goes through when mourning the loss of a relationship. These were adapted from Elisabeth Kübler-Ross's *On Death and Dying*.

Suggestions for when you find yourself suddenly single:

*   Avoid long-term legal decisions. If you are in an emotional state it's better to put off long-term legal decisions until your thinking is less cloudy
*   Drive carefully. It's easy to become distracted when you are grieving so use care when you get behind the wheel

*   Seek support for your kids and yourself. Your kids are grieving along with you and will need support. It might be wise at this point to have separate grief sessions apart from your children if you're experiencing anger and resentment

*   Maintain rituals. The children will most likely feel insecure and abandoned at first. Maintaining the same patterns of holidays, birthdays, Saturday outings, et cetera will give them a sense of normalcy and consistency

*   Nurture yourself. You need to care for your spiritual, emotional and physical health. No one else will do it but you. Eat healthily, exercise and take vitamins. Allow yourself to grieve and give yourself as much time as you need to adjust to what has happened

This information is free to reprint in any format, provided that the information at the bottom, including this, remains intact. Reprinted from *Single Parent Central*, www.singleparentcentral.com, which offers information and resources to single-parent families.

From: charlotte_gavan_duffy@virgin.net
To: Daisy; Rebecca; Finn; BenDavison44@hotmail.com; Jenny@penny.demon.co.uk; jim.watts@argot.co.uk
Subject: RE: More Grief Stuff, how cheerful!

Bloody good stuff, Daisy! Guerrilla single parenting indeed! That bit about maintaining rituals for the kids really hit home. Hope you & Finn & Rebecca have a blast this w'end. Knock 'em dead! Just try not to get too squiffy. In vino veritas and all that. You don't want to get tiddly and start blurting out your super-cunning plot to all and sundry.

See you next Wed, dying to hear how it all went
Charlotte

From: Jenny@penny.demon.co.uk
To: charlotte_gavan_duffy@virgin.net; Daisy; Rebecca; Finn;
BenDavison44@hotmail.com; jim.watts@argot.co.uk
Subject: RE: More Grief Stuff, how cheerful!

Well I don't think this weekend is a good idea at all but I've
said my piece and I hope you and Finn get through it OK
Daisy. I'm working on the Twelve Step list for us but I do like
the Five Stages of Grief too. I'm in depression at the moment
I think, which would be good if I thought it meant I was near
the end, but they're right about you going through the stages
more than once I'm sure.
Jennifer

From: BenDavison44@hotmail.com
To: Rebecca; Finn; Jenny@penny.demon.co.uk;
charlotte_gavan_duffy@virgin.net; jim.watts@argot.co.uk;
Daisy
Subject: RE: More Grief Stuff, how cheerful!

Yeah, good one, Daise. Like Jen, the 5 stages've been more
help than the 12 steps to me, I get messed up by that God
stuff (and I think I'm the only one who got baptised out of all
of us!). Finn, mate, keep strong, OK? It's just one weekend,
after all, and if I walked in with a bird like Daise on my arm I'd
be smirking all over my face (hope that's not sexist!). Daise,
are you available for hire?? I'd love to arrange to bump into
my ex with you! Just tell me what your price is (I'm a bit skint
at the moment so no diamonds, OK?) and it's a done deal.
See you guys Wed for a full report.
Ben xx

From: Rebecca
To: Finn; Jenny@penny.demon.co.uk;
BenDavison44@hotmail.com; charlotte_gavan_duffy@virgin.net;
jim.watts@argot.co.uk; Daisy
Subject: RE: More Grief Stuff, how cheerful!

Oi, Ben, what about asking me or Jennifer or Charlotte
to pretend to be your girlfriend? Why does everyone
want Daisy? Don't bother to answer, I know exactly why . . .
Sigh . . .
I'm on making-sure-Daisy-doesn't-get-too-squiffy duty,
Charlotte. Pray for me, I've got the hardest task of anyone this
weekend . . .
R
xxxx

From: Finn
To: Rebecca; BenDavison44@hotmail.com;
Jenny@penny.demon.co.uk; charlotte_gavan_duffy@virgin.net;
Daisy; jim.watts@argot.co.uk
Subject: RE: More Grief Stuff, how cheerful!

Daisy's a BLONDE, Rebecca. Gentlemen prefer and all that.

From: BenDavison44@hotmail.com
To: Finn; Rebecca; Jenny@penny.demon.co.uk;
charlotte_gavan_duffy@virgin.net; Daisy;
jim.watts@argot.co.uk
Subject: RE: More Grief Stuff, how cheerful!

I second that (e)motion.

From: Daisy
To: Rebecca
Subject: Men are BASTARDS

Well, if gentlemen prefer blondes, why is Finn all traumatised over Vanessa (brunette), and, much more to the point, why was Lewis always making googly eyes at that redheaded cow he works with???
I can't believe he still hasn't rung. It was such a wonderful night and the last thing he said to me was 'Ring you tomorrow'. Bastard. Feeling suicidal. So glad we're getting out of London. I'm not going to take my mobile so if he rings over the weekend he won't get me and he'll get freaked thinking I'm off with some other man. Which, actually, I am! Good idea??
Have you noticed Jim hasn't replied to any of the emails? They haven't bounced back though, so he must be getting them.
Can't believe someone's too shy even to EMAIL for God's sake.
Daisy xoxo
PS: did you remember to fake tan for the pool??

From: Rebecca
To: Daisy
Subject: RE: Men are BASTARDS

Aw, sweetie, I'm so sorry he hasn't rung, but you know what men are like, man-time is different from girl-time, 'tomorrow' doesn't mean 'tomorrow' to them, it means 'when I want another shag'. Sorry.
Good weather for the weekend, did you see the forecast?
I was panicking about being seen in a bikini but since Jake I couldn't care less. Eating like a pig and feeling really happy. Sorry again about rubbing my happiness into your

wounds but I can't help it. Wish Jake was coming. But he asked
me down to Whitstable weekend after next, did I
tell you? He has a little house down there apparently,
it used to be his father's. Romantic weekend by the sea, hoorah!
Sorry, more wound-rubbing, will stop now. See you tomorrow.
Meet at Finn's with inappropriately large suitcases at 3, we're
all skiving off early to avoid Fri-eve traffic. Exfoliated
yesterday, am fake-tanning now but if I go streaky I'll kill you.
R
Xxxx

PS: yes, poor Jim, I wonder whether he gets ANYTHING out
of the group at all, why does he keep coming??

From: Daisy
To: Rebecca
Subject: RE: Men are BASTARDS

You don't streak with that stuff, that's why I got it for you. I
have tried them ALL and it's the only one that doesn't.
Wow, only two Jake mentions in your email, if you don't count
all those 'hes'. Infatuation fading, is it?

From: Rebecca
To: Daisy
Subject: RE: Men are BASTARDS

Piss off, blondie.

Chapter Nineteen

FINN

'I don't think I'm still in love with her. Vanessa. I hate saying her name. It's as if it gives her power over me when I do. You know all those primitive tribes that have superstitions about people knowing their names, or taking photographs of them? I used to think that was bullshit, but now I understand it. I hate her having all those photos of me that we took on holiday. She was really big on taking photographs. I'd love to go round to hers and clean them all out, delete all the emails I sent her, so she can't look back over them. I want to get rid of all the things she has that prove we were together. It's like, as long as she has them, we exist, our relationship exists on some plane, and it's still real. But if I could cancel them all out, that would clean the slate. Maybe Barney's made her do it already. Can't be much fun for him going through her photo albums and seeing loads of pics of me and her in Corfu and Goa and Venice . . .

'Anyway, I was saying: I don't think I'm still in love with her. I'm bloody angry every time I think about it, but that's more because of the situation. I mean, what were they thinking? Does Barney have to take every single thing of mine? He was always like that when we were kids. I can't even remember how many times he nicked my toys and broke them. And he's older than me, it's not like he even wanted to play with my toys in the first place, it was just about him being jealous. I had this amazing train set when I was about ten, and Barney brought some of his friends round and they started putting all these old stuffed toys we had on the line and crashing the trains into them, just for a laugh. One of my engines got broken and Barney just ignored me when I got angry about it – I was so pissed-off, I still get angry thinking about it now – I tried to repair it but the wheel never worked properly again and the engine ran all wonky . . .

'I don't think he wanted Vanessa just because she used to go out with me and he knew I still had a thing for her. I don't think he's, like, completely evil. But I'm sure it's part of it, even if he won't admit it to himself. He's always fancied her. Her family lives near ours and we've all been friends since we were really little. He was amazed when we started going out. Barney's always had loads of girlfriends, he's really smooth, and he's always been able just to click his fingers and get any girl he wanted. But that didn't stop him wanting what I had.

'God, this is sounding like it's much more about Barney than Vanessa. But it isn't. Or only partly. I'd be upset if she was engaged to anyone. It being Barney is just the icing on the cake. I mean, we weren't together, she had a right to be with anyone else she wanted, but she didn't have to pick him, for God's sake! And now she's ringing me up a lot. Well, you know that, you've heard most of the messages. So I'm getting these endless calls from her, saying she misses me and she really wants to talk. Meanwhile, whenever I talk to my mum she gives me all these bulletins on what flowers she's ordering for the church and what the bloody bridesmaids are wearing – like I bloody give a shit! I think Mum goes on and on about it because she knows I'm upset and she wants to remind me that it's really happening and that I have to deal with it, but you see what I mean? All the time Vanessa's ringing me she's also in cahoots with my mum and her mum, working out her wedding details. It's really fucked up.

'I haven't talked to her yet. I don't want to. Or, to be honest, I really do want to, so I don't trust myself to be cool and not

236

to start pleading with her to dump Barney and come back to me. I bet she wouldn't anyway. She'd have to give back that huge diamond. Vanessa really loves diamonds.'

'Oooh, that's lovely. Where did you get it?' Daisy coos.

Daisy has the same voice for appreciating clothes as she does for cute kittens; girlish, raising to a high pitch, her forehead corrugated with the effort of taking in all that prettiness.

'Harvey Nicks. Cost a fortune. I won't even tell you how much. But I thought I'd wear it when we go down to Whitstable, too, so . . .'

'Jake will go nuts when he sees you in that,' Daisy said approvingly.

'It's brilliant, isn't it?' I pirouette in my new bikini. It's a halter neck, made of a pale blue material like fine towelling, the sides of the bikini bottoms and the front of the top held together by big white plastic rings, Seventies-style. Sexy without being vulgar, and the cut is miraculous.

'The saleswoman said it's designed by this American woman who has big tits herself and cuts all her clothes to fit 'em,' I explain. 'This is the first time I've been able to wear a halter neck in my life.'

'It's great,' Daisy says, squinting at me critically. 'Your tits look brilliant but you're not falling out of it.'

I stretch out a towel on the grass and lie down next to her. 'The trouble is, now I'll never be content with getting my swimsuits at M & S ever again,' I sigh. 'It's all right for you, you can walk in anywhere and get a little embroidered triangle bikini without worrying . . .'

Daisy adjusts hers smugly. 'Hey, at least there are some benefits to not having much in the way of bosoms,' she says. 'I wish we could go topless.'

'Yeah, right. This is Somerset, not St Tropez. And besides, I look like I'm making a porn video every time I put suntan lotion on when I'm topless.'

Daisy giggles. 'I should put it on for you,' she says. 'Give everyone heart attacks.'

'That guy'd go first,' I say, indicating with a nod a very fat young man, who's goggling at us. He's lying on his stomach on the grass on the other side of the pool, probably to hide the rolls of fat spilling over his swimming shorts.

'His eyes would pop out of his head first,' Daisy says, 'like something in a horror movie . . . I'd love to feel up your tits you know? I'm always curious to know what big ones feel like. I don't think it's lesbo tendencies, but sometimes I see you and I think, "Cor, cop a feel of those . . ."'

I burst out laughing. 'If he could hear us he'd *definitely* have a heart attack.'

'Davey!' Daisy calls. 'Over here!'

Davey, a T-shirt over his swimming trunks, a towel slung over his shoulder, has emerged through the hedge surrounding the pool and is standing, one hand over his eyes to shade them from the sun, looking for us. Five-thirty in the afternoon and there's still enough English sun for us to sunbathe. Amazing.

'Hey, girls,' he says, reaching us and spreading out his towel. 'Global warming hot enough for you?'

'No,' Daisy says, stretching like a cat. 'I want it to be like Greece all summer.'

'Don't worry, it's coming,' Davey says gloomily, 'unless the Americans finally get their act together and realise we have an environmental crisis.'

He takes off his T-shirt. Daisy and I wolf-whistle. Davey pretends to be embarrassed, but we know he adores it. The thing about Davey is that he looks, clothed, as if he's a little porky. He has a square build and always wears rather baggy clothes, his shirt invariably cut large and not tucked into his trousers, so until he gets undressed you forget that he actually has a good body lurking under all that loose material. He plays football twice a week, and since giving up the drink he's also been hitting the gym; his beer belly has completely disappeared, revealing a nicely toned six-pack. He'll always look solid, with that large frame of his, but he's one of those people who look much better stripped-down rather than fully clothed. I notice several of the girls giving him assessing looks.

'You know what they call the six-pack in France?' Daisy asks.

'Nah.'

'The chocolate bar. Because you get those nice chunks, one on top of the other, like a giant slab of Cadbury's.' She sits up and is about to trace the outlines on Davey's stomach, but he knocks her hand away, blushing.

'Oi,' he says, 'inappropriate behaviour for someone else's girl-friend.'

'Oh, don't worry,' Daisy says, 'I'm going to be all over Finn. I'm dying to see what he looks like in a swimsuit, aren't you?'

'Kind of weird to see all your co-workers in practically no clothes,' I say. 'I'm not looking forward to seeing Barney in trunks.'

Daisy giggles. 'Wait till they see you in that bikini,' she says. 'They'll all be fiddling with themselves for months afterwards, imagining you busting out of that halter neck . . .'

'Daisy!' I whack her on the head. '*Yech!* Anyway, I'm not busting out, I'm well-contained . . .'

'Hey, nice swimsuit, Rebecca!' Vijay yells from across the pool, waggling his eyebrows like Groucho Marx, his voice slightly obscured by the mouthful of crisps he's munching on. 'You're turning me on, and you know that's not supposed to happen!'

'Oh, yuck,' I say, disgusted. I get up and dive into the pool, removing any possibility for my sleazy fellow WebMasters to ogle me for a few brief minutes. When I've done a few lengths I prop myself on the edge, smoothing back my hair, and observe that Finn has come out of the house and is kneeling beside Daisy and Davey. He is stroking Daisy's hair and she's smiling up at him.

They do make a gorgeous couple. Finn, like Daisy, is one

of those blonds who are lucky enough to tan easily (though Daisy's endless limbs are a much deeper caramel than his, thanks to her regular applications of that miracle self-tanning cream). Like her, he's lean, without any excess fat that I can see, and he's wearing a daring pair of swimming trunks, much more close-fitting than Englishmen usually sport; they look like an Italian style from the 1920s, short and stripy, like boxers, and show off Finn's narrow hips and tight buttocks to perfection. He's more hairy than I would have imagined, but not unpleasantly so. After Patrick, who was smooth as silk, I'm not that keen on hairy chests, but Finn has a nice chest hair formation: masculine without being out of control.

'Plug! Oi! Give us a hand!' Barney calls from the entrance to the pool. He's carrying a folding table which he proceeds to set up in the shade of the hedge. 'I thought we'd have some Buck's Fizz by the pool. Set us up for the weekend, eh?'

The assembled guests cheer. Finn gets up to help, shooting Barney a filthy look to which the latter is happily oblivious. Champagne, ice buckets and orange juice are produced from the house and we drink Buck's Fizz in plastic flutes. Mr and Mrs Falkland-Smythe clearly know Finn, Barney and their friends well enough to ban glasses by the pool, and I can't say I blame them. Some of the pinker, podgier young men are bawling at each other and seem half-drunk already. Or maybe that's just their manner. These are really posh English people. They went to obscure boarding schools where intellect is less important than your surname; they spent their time at university shagging secretaries who washed and ironed the red-faced boys' shirts in an effort to prove themselves good wife material; and now they hang out at discos with silly names on the Fulham Road where they order expensive champagne by the bottle, and sexually harass girls of a lower social class than themselves.

'Loads of eligible husband material here,' I say to Daisy.

'Oh God, absolutely,' she says in a parody of their accent.

The girls divide clearly into two types. The first group are the Daisy-wannabes; tall, mainly blonde, and elegant, wearing discreetly expensive jewellery, sleek and tanned – probably the real thing, unlike us. They immediately discount me as a potential rival, as I'm too curvy (a polite way of putting it) to enter their thoroughbred-racehorse stakes. But they stare at Daisy with barely-concealed envy and loathing. Daisy's got what they want. She has an instinct for being always ahead of the fashion curve, and though they can probably afford serious purchases – the latest Hermes bags or Prada shoes – by the time they've got to the head of the waiting list for them, Daisy will be off on some new fashion craze, months before it hits the streets. She just has the knack. She started out as a trainee in fashion journalism but soon announced that even though she might not be Brain of Britain, she wasn't quite vacuous enough for that; but she would have been a great success at it. I know from the looks those girls are giving Daisy that whatever she's wearing is exactly what they would like to have on, even though, to a man's eyes, it's just a simple bikini accessorised with three strands of narrow turquoise beads wound negligently round her neck.

The other type of girl is the carthorse of the posh world. With inexpertly streaked blonde hair, built low to the ground and solid as suitcases, they have given up any pretence to beauty and adopted instead the mantle of good sports, always up for a laugh, the butt of plenty of rowdy physical horseplay from the men. I bet they're a lot better in bed than the racehorses, though. They look like they'd go like the clappers. The racehorses probably just lie there and complain if the men are messing up their hair.

I share these last observations with Daisy. We clink glasses. 'All these boys want is to be spanked, anyway,' she says. 'That's what I've heard. After all that corporal punishment at public school, the only way they can get off is if you whack them on the bum and make them call you "Matron".'

'You what?' Vijay says, coming up to us with Stewart in tow. 'Did I hear you mention spanking?'

I sigh. 'Veej, Stewart, this is my friend Daisy, who's going out with Finn,' I explain. 'Daise, Veej and Stewart work with me, for my sins.'

'All right, darling,' Stewart says in his usual over-compensatory way, taking Daisy's hand and kissing it. 'Cor, top bird! Finn's a lucky man!'

I sigh inwardly. Stewart really will have to stop trying to talk like some macho East-End thug if he wants to get anywhere with the girls. It would be fine if he really were a macho East-End thug – the ladies love that hard-man stuff – but he's much too pretty, not to mention un-tattooed, for it to work. As it is, you can tell it's all front. I think he's exaggerating it even more than usual because of the super-poshness with which we're surrounded. In keeping with his fake image, he's staring blatantly at both my and Daisy's chest area. Vijay, on the other hand, is looking everywhere but at my bosoms in a way that indicates all too obviously his desire to gawk. His goatee is greasy and salt-stained from the crisps. Vijay really is the messiest eater I have ever come across.

'Nice to meet you, Daisy,' Vijay says, shaking her hand. 'I'm one hundred per cent with Stew on this – Finn's done very well for himself.'

Daisy smiles demurely. Lucky we're not Continentals, or he'd have kissed her on the cheeks and transferred all that grease to her face. Mind you, a few seconds later I notice her discreetly wiping her hand on the lounger cushion, so his hand must have been fairly oily too.

'This house is fucking awesome,' Stewart says. 'Veej and me have a room the size of a football pitch, all panelled and everything.'

'I know,' I say, noticing that we have lowered our voices slightly; we're not used to visiting country houses, unlike the other tranche of guests, and we don't want to admit too blatantly that we aren't, nonchalantly, taking this old-money luxury in our stride.

'Where are you sleeping?' Vijay asks me.

'Jeez, Veej mate, have a bit of class!' Stewart says.

Vijay actually blushes. 'No, I didn't mean – I just –' he stammers.

I take pity on him. 'I've got this cute little room on the second floor, next to Daisy and Finn. The walls are painted blue and they're sort of combed-down – I can't really describe it properly – like someone took a comb and ran it down the paint when it was fresh. It sounds weird, but it's really pretty. Anyway, I'm sharing with someone,' I add, fixing the boys with a hard stare, 'so I'm safe from midnight raids.'

Vijay blushes again. He has a big mouth and a roving eye but he's actually very sweet underneath all the bravado, and is now too embarrassed to get a word out.

'Do you know who you're sharing with yet?' Daisy asks me.

'No, she hadn't arrived when I got in, so I bagged the best bed,' I say smugly. 'Boarding school rules, as a posh friend of mine used to say.'

'I hope she doesn't make a mess in the bathroom,' Daisy says, frowning. Our rooms are linked by a shared bathroom, and Daisy has always been fussy about hairs in the sink and people who make stains in the toilet and don't seem to realise what the toilet brush is for – 'I mean, what do they *think* they're supposed to do with it apart from clean their own poo off the bowl?'

'Don't worry,' I say, grinning. 'You'll soon train her up.'

'Darling!' Finn says, crossing the grass to us.

Daisy forgets to look up until I nudge her surreptitiously and she realises that this endearment is meant for her. 'Sweetie!' she coos, giving him a big smacker on the lips to compensate for her moment of inattention.

'Darling, this is Vanessa, Barney's fiancée,' he says, his face studiously without expression.

243

'I've been dying to meet you,' Vanessa says.

She looks superb. She's wearing a thigh-length silk kaftan which clings to her elegantly, and the rock on the fourth finger of her left hand is echoed by two large diamond studs in her ears. Her long chestnut hair is wound into a seemingly careless knot at the back of her head, which probably took her twenty minutes to get right, and she exudes a subtle, floral perfume. Daisy takes one look at her and winds her arm through Finn's, pulling him against her scantily clad body.

'Lovely to meet you,' she says blithely. 'Finn's told me so much about you, haven't you, darling?'

In an odd way, Finn is irrelevant to this conversation. I see that straight away. He's just a symbol of the fight for possession between two women who formed a mutual loathing as soon as they laid eyes on each other – or probably, now I think about it, long before. The tension between Vanessa and Daisy is as thick as mud with rivalry. Even Vijay and Stewart, not the most sensitive of young men, pick up on it; they shift from foot to foot, exchange uncomfortable glances and mutter something about getting more drinks, before sloping off in the direction of the bar.

'Finn hasn't told me anything about you, the naughty thing!' Vanessa says, raising the stakes.

'Oh,' Daisy counters, dealing with this one effortlessly, 'I've been keeping him much too busy for talking to other people, haven't I, sweetie?' She squeezes Finn's arm and beams up at him. 'You know what it's like when you're madly in love,' she says to Vanessa confidentially. 'We can't keep our hands off each other! We don't give each other much time for anything else, do we, gorgeous?'

She gives a naughty giggle. In my opinion, Daisy is over-egging the pudding, but she has judged her audience well. Vanessa is struck dumb and a vivid, unflattering flush is rising on her perfect cheekbones, two clown-like spots of red.

'Actually,' Daisy says, 'I need to finish my unpacking. Finn,

244

sweetie, why don't you come upstairs with me and show me where our room is again? I've got all my clothes just thrown over the bed, and we don't want to get them all creased, do we?'

She winks at him. Finn isn't doing this half as well as Daisy. He looks at her blankly for a moment before he gets it, and then stammers: 'Yeah, yeah of course. Um, see you around, Vanessa,' as Daisy pulls him away. I give them a couple of minutes and follow, running – once I'm discreetly out of sight behind the hedge – to catch them up. Like Daisy, I have no idea how to find my room again in this giant mansion of a house, and I too need Finn to show me so that I can finish unpacking. Daisy and I just ripped our swimming costumes out of our suitcases and raced down to the pool when we arrived, wanting to take advantage of the late afternoon sun. Besides, Vanessa is doing a great impersonation of a pillar of salt (motionless and bitter to the taste), and it's too painful to watch. I am amazed to find myself feeling sorry for her.

My room has been invaded by an alien from a planet where they breed their women as tall as giraffes. She looks as if her parents starved her and gave her regular sessions on a torture rack all through her childhood; there's something very unnatural about her extreme height and thinness. After a short while, I realise that it's because she has dieted herself down to a weight that is well below what would normally be prescribed for a large-boned woman who stands five foot ten in her bare feet. I have to admire her self-control, even as I gawk at the rather unnerving result.

Still, doctors' height and weight tables are not the first thing on my mind as I enter my – our – bedroom. When I left, my suitcase was placed neatly at the bottom of my bed, thus clearly indicating that I had bagsied it. A child of five would have recognised this primitive sign of possession, and would almost definitely have respected it a hell of a lot more than Ms Alien from Planet Lettuce Leaf. Now, on my lovely bed next to the window, with the pretty view of the lawn, is a pile of her clothes, and my suitcase has been chucked on the floor next to the other, considerably less desirable bed, the one with the view of the open bathroom door.

'Hello,' the alien says, turning to see who's come in and bestowing the briefest of glances on me before swivelling back to her suitcase again. 'You must be Rebecca, right? I'm Baby Thompson. Vanessa said we'd be sharing. I took this bed. You don't mind, do you? It's just that I always have it when I sleep in this room.'

I know straight away that I have to make a stand. If I don't, this evil cow will ride roughshod over me the entire weekend, borrowing my make-up and dropping it on the floor so that all the eyeshadows go crumbly, appropriating all the hangers and discarding her dirty knickers everywhere so that I tread on them when I get out of bed. I need to establish dominance immediately. This is a situation where there can only be one alpha; parity is impossible when one of the parties has thrown down the gauntlet with such a loud crash. I have to fight her for supremacy or retreat with my tail between my legs, whining submissively. It reminds me of Daisy and Vanessa just now, two bitches snarling for possession of their territory. I've watched the Discovery Channel enough to know all about dog pack behaviour.

'I'm afraid I do mind,' I say, managing with an effort not to be too English and drop a 'sorry' into that statement, which would be a near-fatal admission of weakness. She didn't say 'sorry' for nicking my bed, after all. 'I'd already taken that bed and I'd like it back.'

Whoah. The head shoots round again and I get a glare that could melt Teflon. Her throat is so long that I realise now why the alien metaphor came immediately to mind. She looks like one of those creatures from horror films whose neck extends and extends until the jaws are snapping in your face.

Her hair is dark, cut close to her head, and her lip gloss shines like glass. She's wearing a top which looks like she tied a Hermes scarf over her upper body and a pair of yellow linen trousers hanging so preposterously low on her narrow bottom that it's as if she's deliberately parodying the fashion for low-riders. They reveal a long expanse of lightly-tanned stomach and hips. It's not the most attractive part of a woman's body, and because she's long-waisted there's an almost ridiculous amount of it. Or maybe I'm just telling myself that out of pique, because my stomach will never be flat enough to display so publicly.

'But I always have it!' she says, with such an air of entitlement that it's almost hard to argue with her. 'I sleep so much better by the window!'

'Yeah, me too,' I say, pouncing on this excuse. 'That's why I picked that bed first. I left my suitcase on it.' I stare pointedly at my suitcase, lying at a crooked angle on the floor, my dresses spilling out of it on to the carpet. I don't move to pick it up, though. We are like two cowgirls facing each other down in a Wild West saloon: this needs to be settled with words to avoid things turning nasty. Any sudden gestures would be interpreted as reaching for one's gun.

'Look, I don't think you quite understand . . .' Baby Thompson says haughtily. 'I've been staying here for years, and I always have this bed . . .'

'Rebecca?' Daisy comes through the open bathroom door, a sponge bag in her hand. 'Do you mind if I have the first shower? I want to get that chlorine out of my hair.'

The addition of a third party, a witness to our stand-off, actually heightens the bristling hostility. Baby and I barely take our eyes off each other, just flicking our glances sideways to acknowledge Daisy before returning to glare daggers at each other once again.

'I'd like you to move your things off my bed now,' I say firmly. 'I want to finish unpacking.' I say this partly because it's time for an ultimatum, and partly because I want to bring Daisy into the loop.

Here Baby makes a huge tactical mistake. 'I'm going to tell Vanessa,' she says with a flounce. 'Vanessa invited me and she always gives me this bed. Mind you, I usually share this room with her, and she's terribly sympathetic,' she adds, making it clear by her intonation that she considers me a lower-class interloper who hasn't the breeding to be as understanding as someone born with a silver spoon in their mouth.

I jump all over this one with both feet. I see your Vanessa, madam, and I raise you one son of the house. 'Vanessa?' I say, mock-surprised. 'I didn't know this was her house! Because Finn invited me, and he actually lives here.'

Daisy, bless her, delivers the coup de grace.

'Oh,' she says. 'You must be Vanessa's friend in PR, the one she was setting up with Finn! Baby, right? Sorry, he's already taken.' She beams smugly. 'Lucky me. But hey, don't be too disappointed. It looks like there are loads of single men about this weekend. Rebecca knows a couple from her office. I'm sure she'd introduce you, won't you, Rebecca?'

It's lovely work. Baby makes a noise like a kettle that's about to explode, and storms out of the room. She's so tall in her stilettos that her head almost scrapes the lintel.

'Jesus,' I say, taking a deep breath. 'Nice one, Daise.'

'What a Grade-A bitch,' Daisy says, eyebrows raised. 'Vanessa must be mad. Finn would never look at her.'

'She's quite striking,' I admit, now that she's safely gone. We heard her heels storming away all along the wooden corridor, so we know she's not eavesdropping.

'Yeah, but Finn likes girlie girls,' Daisy says. 'Ones that go in and out, not up and down. Besides, he'd never go out with someone taller than him. Here, I'll give you a hand shifting her stuff before she comes back. Did you see those trousers she was wearing? Fuck, they were so low I would have seen her pubes if she didn't wax!'

I gather up a large handful of Baby's exiguous designer thongs and chuck them on what is now her bed. 'How do you know she waxes?' I ask.

'Because we would've seen her pubes otherwise,' Daisy says, doing likewise.

'This is one of the most annoying things about being single,' I sigh, lifting my suitcase on to my bed. 'You never get a room to yourself when you stay with people. I wish Finn had asked me to be his girlfriend. I'd have had the double bed all to myself.'

'He's already sneaked in his sleeping bag,' Daisy says complacently. 'Ooh! We should have said we were having a threesome! That way you could have shared with us!'

I crack up laughing. 'Can you imagine everyone's faces?' I say through my giggles. 'Oh, and it would have been so nice to have shared with you two!'

'It's not too late,' Daisy suggests, waggling her eyebrows suggestively.

'Nah. Now I've won this bed I can't give it up. I'm staying right here to enjoy the spoils of victory.'

Finn pokes his head through the bathroom door. 'What are you two giggling about?' he says suspiciously.

'Threesomes,' Daisy and I say in unison, then we laugh harder than ever as Finn stares at us nervously, obviously wanting to ask what we're on about but too scared to, in case the answer's one he doesn't like. Men are so easy to frighten.

Chapter Twenty

I have to ring Jake. It feels like I'm breaking down, that my willpower's failing, because I want to be cool and not rush for his number every time I feel a bit insecure. I told myself that I wasn't going to call him this weekend, that I was away, busy with friends; that it would be so much more mature if I could hold out till I got back on Sunday night. (Besides, he hasn't rung me.) But I'm feeling that things are spiralling away from me, and I want to hear Jake's voice to keep me rooted, remind myself that I have someone who cares about me, who's thinking about me and waiting for me to come back . . .

This weekend is turning into a roller-coaster ride. I managed not to ring Jake after the Baby stand-off, even though I knew he would find it very amusing. It's the kind of thing you would do with a long-term boyfriend, but not someone you've only been seeing for a couple of weeks. The impulse to turn someone new into something more is very powerful with women. We start dating someone and immediately struggle to resist the urge to confide every little detail of our lives, those small niggling irritations which dispel as soon as they're shared with someone. The bitch at the post office who tells you that your package has the wrong tape on it and you can't send it like that. The bus driver who won't sell you a ticket and won't wait for you to get one from the automatic machine. The cow sharing your room for the weekend who snores, throws her wet towels over your bed and hogs the bathroom for hours every morning. I do have Daisy, of course, and Davey, but the trouble is that as soon as you have a boyfriend, he's the one you want to reach for.

We did have a lovely day. We got up late, played croquet and drank Pimm's all afternoon, then retired to our rooms for a nap before congregating for the big blowout dinner, cooked for us by the staff, aka three middle-aged ladies who live in tied cottages down the lane beyond Finn and Barney's mansion. It really is a mansion, built of soft grey stone, covered with clinging ivy. The croquet lawn is as big as a football field and as smooth as satin, surrounded by banks of oak trees and willows whose dangling branches brush the silky green floor below. The dining room has an oak table long enough to accommodate thirty chairs, whose seats are covered with a once dark-red damask now faded over the centuries to a pale rose – you can see the original colour at the edges, where the material is coming slightly away from the seams.

There are three sitting rooms, all upholstered in ancient fraying chintz. The back entrance, which everyone uses, takes you into the kitchen through a long hallway so lined with hanging Barbours and green wellies that you can barely see the walls. The wellies date back to the Second World War; the Barbours are ancient, stinky and stained with decades of blood from dead pheasants stuffed into the pockets. No amount of money can buy the aristocratic look: it's the awareness that generations of the same family have lived in this house, heeled-and-toed their muddy boots clean on the iron scraper just outside the back door, padded through the kitchen calling for toasted crumpets from the cook, and thrown themselves on to the chintz armchairs, making the springs groan.

The kitchen is as big as my whole flat, with a forty-foot high ceiling, in the beams of which can be dimly seen an enormous drying rack, winched up with a rope, which apparently they still use for towels and kitchen cloths. Its Aga is the size of an industrial boiler. Everything in Grange Manor is on a massive scale. Its centrepiece is the gigantic polished oak staircase, known, according to Finn, as the Death Trap, which glides majestically around three sides of the great oak-panelled hall and then rises in a huge well, culminating with carved flour-ishes on the third floor. A group of incredibly drunk posh boys are busy trying to slide all the way down the balustrade right now. I rather hope some of them slip and kill themselves, but they're all doubtless used to houses and banisters like this and have been practising on their own ones since they were big enough to walk (their nannies, one assumes, first removing the silver spoons from their mouths so they wouldn't fall and choke on them).

I don't like posh boys much. This is partly because they're braying, full of themselves and atrociously vulgar when they drink (Daisy and I are demure little novices in starched wim-ples compared to them), but also because they don't fancy me. I expect this is fair enough, because I don't fancy them, but it still irritates me. The higher up the social scale I go, the fewer men find me attractive. Builders love me: I'm shortish, I have tits, a reasonably pretty face, nice curly hair ... One of the horrors here, who, I promise you, is called Tooty, told me that I had 'crazy hair' half an hour ago. Curly hair is obviously non-U. Looking around, I see the proof of that. Every single posh girl here either has naturally straight hair, or has invested in that extremely expensive Japanese straightening process that burns your scalp to cinders but lasts six months, guaranteed. I think Tooty got annoyed with me because I didn't want to talk about his career as a merger arbitrageur (or possibly an arbi-trageur merger) or his Jag, or the cricket, or, finally, his penis. These seemed to be his only four topics of conversation. He went off to chat up two of the carthorse girls called Flopsy and Mopsy (I'm not making this up, I couldn't) who are currently squealing with laughter at his witticisms. Judging from his graphic gestures, he's on topic four.

I want to talk to Daisy, but she's hanging on Finn's arm, batting her green-mascaraed lashes at him adoringly. Even though I know it's all fake, it makes me feel sad. Everyone here is either coupled off, or chasing someone – even Vijay and

Stewart are flirting madly with the awful Baby and a couple of her cohorts – apart from me.

And Davey. I look over at him, sitting in an armchair. He's watching Daisy and Finn too and there's an expression on his face which I can't help recognising, even though I don't want to. Sadness, and jealousy. For a moment I think Davey's feeling the same as me – that he's wistful for a relationship, longing to have someone perching behind him on the arm-chair, winding her arm around his neck – and then I see the direction of his gaze and I realise that it's more specific than that. It's not just about having a girlfriend. He wants Daisy.

Poor Davey. He doesn't stand a snowball's chance in hell of getting together with Daisy. Even Finn is more her type: smart, a little flashy, hip, streetwise. Davey is solid and loving and secure, all the qualities Daisy has resolutely rejected in her dating life. And, as much as I adore Davey, I have to admit that he's not a great looker. Daisy has always gone for drop-dead handsome and I don't see her changing now.

I can't watch this, and I don't have anyone I can talk to about it. I don't want Davey to confide in me either, because I won't know what to say: the truth will hurt him and any-thing else will be false comfort. I love Davey so much; I don't want to see him in pain. I want to go over and give him a big hug, but something is holding me back, and I don't know what. I stand up and slip out of the living room. Eminem, surreally, is playing in the hall, the music of angry young American socially-deprived white-trash punctuated, with no sense of irony, by the cries of wildly over-privileged, sweaty, pink-faced young men complaining boisterously about their packages get-ting caught on the banisters as they slide down them. I want to go up to my room to ring Jake, and I'm damned if I'm run-ning the gauntlet of the Death Trap – I could be flattened by a falling merger arbitrageur tumbling off the balustrade – but when I go through the swinging baize doors at the back of the hall, to use the servants' staircase, I see Tooty and Flopsy (or possibly Mopsy) sprawled in a heap across the first steps, his hand up her skirt, as she giggles madly and cries: 'Tooty, you are such a *naughty* boy!'

I retreat precipitately. Sometimes coming across a really attractive couple making out can be quite a sexy experience. Seeing Flopsy and Tooty rutting, on the other hand, is enough to put you off for life.

Couples seem to be sprouting everywhere I look. I go back into the hall and slip outside, through one of the myriad sets of big French windows, into the warm, velvety night air. Leaves rustle gently in the balmy breeze and the crescent moon hangs low and pale in the black sky. I forget how polluted London is until I come to the country and the sky is black and pierced with stars, instead of the dusty violet pall that hangs over the city, dense with emissions and distant sulphur light. I take a deep breath of air cleansed by chlorophyll, smelling grass and jasmine and a faint chlorine wash from the swimming pool. How I wish that Jake was here to share this perfect, romantic night with me. I am struggling against the urge to ring him right now and ask him to drive down to Somerset. We could sleep on the satin lawn and wake in the dew. (I think I may be a little tipsy.) But what if I asked him, and he said no? I would feel even worse. This is my trouble, or one of them: I imagine great sweeping romantic scenarios for my boyfriends to execute and then am crushed with disappointment when they don't somehow psychically intuit what I want them to do. What I would really love is to hear car wheels on gravel, see headlights running brightly along the laurel hedge, and know that it was Jake, come to find me, unable to bear another night alone in London without me. I drove all night to get to you. Car wheels on a gravel road. My fantasies are made up of American ballads and country songs.

I won't ring him, because I don't trust myself not to ask him to come. Instead I compose a text message. It takes me a while to get it right.

It doesn't quite convey the full range of my emotions, but
it's the best I can do, and hopefully it doesn't sound too needy.
I press SEND and just then I see two figures come out of the
French windows further along the long hall. Light pools out
from the windows and, by the gold glow of his hair and the
slim red dress she's poured herself into, I realise that it's Finn
and Vanessa. They're speaking in low, intense voices. She touches
his arm. He pulls back a little, then lets her take it. They walk
slowly around the corner of the house and are lost to my sight.

Hmn. Well, I suppose they needed to talk sooner or later,
but I can't help feeling that a more suitable setting might have
been at eleven in the morning in a nice brightly lit coffee bar,
all chrome and hard edges, rather than a moonlight stroll in
the perfumed Somerset air. I wander back inside, clutching my
mobile to me, waiting for the double beeps that will signal a
message coming back from Jake. I shouldn't have texted him.
I'll be on tenterhooks now until I get a reply that proves he
still likes me.

The first thing I see when I enter the main living room is
Baby's back. Baby does have back, though only in the strictly
literal sense. She's wearing a halter-neck silk dress, cut very
loose, which drapes over her fake bosoms and falls so low at
the back that, as with her trousers of yesterday, one can practically see her bum crack. Almost every single one of her ver-
tebrae is on display. She's so thin they're like a rope in which
someone has tied a tightly ranked series of bony little knots.
She's swaying like a sapling in the wind on her three-inch heels.
I feel like Holly Golightly in *Breakfast At Tiffany's*: I want to
yell 'Timber!' and watch her topple over. It wouldn't take much.
Just one surreptitious little nudge to her centre of gravity.

Daisy is being chatted up by two young men. One is wearing
a stripy shirt, the other a shirt with a faint brown open-check

pattern on a white background, but otherwise they are practically identical. They both have bottles of champagne and are filling Daisy's glass as fast as she can empty it. Not exactly a subtle tactic, but often effective.

'Hey, sweetie!' I say, winding one arm around her waist. 'Where's your boyfriend?'

She pulls a face and turns slightly away from her suitors. 'Vanessa collared him,' she said. 'She "wanted to have a talk". Bitch.' She lowers her voice even more. 'I mean, if we were really going out, that'd be outrageous behaviour.'

'I saw them wandering off for a head-to-head on the lawn,' I say.

'Just as long as she doesn't try for a literal head-to-head,' Daisy says menacingly. 'She was putting on her best seductive voice and stroking his arm. She'd better not mess with Finn. He's doing so well.'

I shrug. 'I don't know what we can do about it, though, short of tracking them down and throwing a bucket of cold water over her.'

Daisy gets a martial light in her usually soft blue eyes. 'Hah! That's all you know!' she says triumphantly. 'There's *lots* I can do about it!'

I'm about to ask her what she means when Barney enters the room. His hair is flopping over his forehead and he looks unhappy and distracted.

'Barney!' Daisy calls, giving him her best come-hither smile.

Barney is unable to resist such a summons, but he doesn't manage a smile in return. He crosses the room to us and says abruptly, 'Have you seen Nessa?'

There's a moment's pause: I'm waiting for Daisy's cue, as she seems to have at least some theory on how to handle this.

'I've been deserted too,' she purrs, and now her smile is positively bewitching. 'We're going to have to console each other.' And she actually reaches up and straightens the collar of his polo shirt. I couldn't get away with that move for a moment:

it's so self-consciously 1940s vamp it can only be carried off by a woman absolutely confident of her own killer attractiveness. But like Davey said a while ago (poor darling Davey), Daisy's everyone's type. She's the gold standard of beautiful women. And tonight, fired up with a lot of champagne and the drooling admiration of every man present, she's flying. Also, I remind myself, she's playing a part this weekend, which always helps. You can do things in character that you would never manage if you didn't have a role to protect you.

Despite his distress at not finding his fiancée – and, I assume, his suspicions at who she might be with – Barney is a red-blooded male who can't help being flattered by such blatant attention from a gorgeous blonde. He coughs gruffly, widens his legs a little in the classic manly stance, and says gallantly: 'Can I offer you some more champagne?'

'Oh, I'd love some,' Daisy purrs, batting her eyelashes and staring up at him admiringly.

Barney's chest puffs out like a pouter pigeon's as he removes a bottle of champagne from the hand of one of Daisy's erstwhile suitors and tops up her glass. 'Down the hatch!' he says, refilling his own.

They clink glasses and smile at one another. I back away from the happy twosome and secure a seat on the arm of Davey's chair to get a better view of the scene. I don't want to cramp Daisy's style in any way.

'What's happening?' Davey asks.

I fill him in briefly on recent events. He looks concerned.

'I saw Vanessa annexing Finn,' he says, 'and she did look very . . . well, suggestive . . .'

'I think Daisy's planning to flirt so madly with Barney that Finn and Vanessa will feel left out when they get back,' I explain. 'Well, not Finn, obviously. Just Vanessa.'

'She's drinking champagne like it was water,' says Davey disapprovingly.

'Hey, it's free,' I say, raising my glass.

'Yes, but . . .' Davey tails off.

'Look,' I say, 'he's already smitten.'

Barney has backed Daisy against the wall and is telling her some story at which she is laughing immoderately.

'Mission Vanessa-baiting well under way,' I say with satisfaction.

I know Barney isn't Daisy's type, but I have to admit they do make a handsome pair; both blond, tall, blue-eyed and very good-looking. Barney has a very nice body under that awful Sloane uniform of polo shirt tucked into jeans. At the angle he's standing I can see his bottom, which is small and pleasantly firm.

'You know,' I say, giggling, 'our boss has a very nice bum.'

Davey regards my glass with loathing. 'You'd never have said that if you hadn't been drinking,' he says coldly. 'You'll hate yourself in the morning.'

A terrible, ear-splitting noise rings out from the corner of the room. It's like a car alarm crossed with the mating cry of a mynah bird. I start, nearly spilling my drink, before I realise that it's actually Baby Thompson shrieking with wild, flirtatious laughter.

'Fab idea!' she screams. 'Totally fab! Last one in's a sissy!'

'Baby, darling?' calls Mopsy. 'What's going on?'

'Pool party!' Baby shrieks. 'Everyone in the pool!' And she leads a rush for the French windows, closely followed by Vijay, Stewart, two of the identikit young stockbrokers and Mopsy, who is clearly one of those girls who never has an original idea herself but tags along with anyone who'll tell her what to do.

'That's it,' Davey says. 'I'm off to bed.'

'Oh Davey,' I plead. 'Don't abandon me.'

The idea of a midnight swim suddenly sounds wonderful; it's a lovely night and the water was warm enough this afternoon to barely have cooled down by now. But I don't want to be odd-one-out among these drink-crazed Sloanes; I want a companion to share it with, and Daisy is clearly not going to be available for girly gossip. Barney has placed one arm on the wall behind her head very proprietorially, and is leaning over her in a way that would make me think he was seriously chatting her up if I didn't suspect that he, too, is engaged upon a bout of making-the-significant-other-jealous-enough-to-start-throwing-champagne-bottles-through-French-windows.

'No, I'm off,' Davey says, his tone determined enough to make it clear that this is non-negotiable. He stands up. 'No offence, Rebecca, but you have no idea how boring it is to hang around people drinking past midnight. They make less and less sense, repeat themselves constantly and think they're hysterically funny . . .'

I hang my head.

'Not you,' he says, hugging me. 'Well, not much.'

I concede defeat. 'I'm getting changed, though,' I say. 'I'm not jumping in the pool with all my clothes on.'

'Wise girl,' he says, grinning at me. 'Especially in that.' He nods at my outfit. I grin back.

'Yeah, if I weren't wearing a white top I might see it differently . . .'

In the hall we are nearly trampled by a raging horde of stockbrokers Heffalumping it out to the pool and yelling upper-class war cries. We jump aside in the nick of time and then have free access to the staircase. My room is blissfully empty of Baby, so I change into my expensive miracle bikini and am just about to throw on my silk mini-kaftan over it (a cheap copy of Vanessa's from M & S) when I hear someone come into Finn and Daisy's room – Daisy, I assume, coming to change for the pool.

'Yeah!' I say, nipping through the bathroom and into their room. 'Bikini time, baby!' I strike a sexy porno pose to amuse Daisy before I realise with horror that the occupant of the room is actually Finn. I stand up straight, take my finger out of my mouth and my hand off my bottom, and mutter, 'Sorry . . . thought you were Daise . . .'

Finn is goggling at me. I feel completely naked. I remind myself firmly that it's a bikini I'm wearing, not my underwear, but I'm sure I'm blushing. If I dash back into my room to grab my kaftan, I'll be even more embarrassed; I decide that the best approach is to be jocular and all-friends-together.

'Are you coming for a swim?' I say bluffly. 'We're all going.'

He sits down heavily on the edge of the bed, his shoulders slumping, and I suddenly remember the last time I saw Finn: heading off for a private talk with Vanessa under the starry midnight sky.

'Oh,' I say. 'Hang on a minute.'

Now I do put on my kaftan. Partly because Finn is seriously upset and I should cover myself decently to show respect, and partly because I'm damned if I'm going to sit next to him on the edge of the bed with my tummy spilling over the top of my bikini bottoms.

'What happened?' I say.

Finn still doesn't speak. He buries his head in his hands instead. My own cheerfulness is evaporating fast. I realise that I was pumping my mood up in an attempt to avoid realising that Jake still hasn't texted me back. There could be loads of reasons for that, of course: he could be seeing a film, or out with friends somewhere noisy where he couldn't hear his phone, or he could even have switched it off because he wanted to have an early night. Still, I can't help being twitchy. It's so new, this relationship . . . he might be having second thoughts, and my message might have made him decide that I'm too keen . . .

'She made a pass at me,' Finn says through his fingers, jolting me back into the real world where my own preoccupations are minimal compared to what my friends are going through.

'Oh *Finn*,' I say, very shocked.

'We went out for a walk . . . she said she wanted to talk to me . . . and we ended up under this tree on the lawn, it used to be our tree, just a silly joke we had from when we were kids, 'cos we used to play under it when Barney wouldn't let us play with him and his friends because we were too small, so we said it was our tree and that he couldn't play there. Not that he cared, but it was a way of making us feel better, you know? Anyway, we sat down under the tree, and Vanessa started saying that she really missed me, and that she was in love with Barney but she still had feelings for me, and she didn't know what to do about it. Before I knew it I had my arm around her and we started kissing, and then we were – well, you know, we were rolling around and it was getting serious, and she was all over me. I'm not being arrogant or anything but it was her making all the running, because I was so taken aback and I didn't know if we should be doing this. Then she had my trousers open and I said, "Oh my God, that feels wonderful" and she said, "Yes, and it can still be like this, we can do this whenever we want", and I stopped her for a moment and said, "You mean you're leaving him?" and she said . . .' Finn's voice is even more choked now. 'She was all surprised and said, "Of course not, you know I'm marrying Barney!" and I pushed her hand away and sat up and said, "Then what the fuck are you doing grabbing my dick?" and she said, "I thought you understood, I'm marrying Barney, it's the right thing to do, but I still want you," and I felt like I couldn't breathe . . . I really couldn't breathe for what felt like ages . . . Then she started giving me this whole explanation about why she thought she and Barney were much more compatible, they wanted the same things and the same kind of life, but she couldn't stop thinking about me, she didn't want to lose me, and she had to be with me again. We always had amazing sex,' he adds wistfully.

'So what did you do?' I ask with bated breath, though I know that this story already ends well from the point of view of Finn's recovery from Vanessa. He's here, alone, in his room, obviously traumatised. If he and Vanessa had reconciled he'd be hyped up, on top of the world.

Finn sits up straight and looks at me for the first time

since my porno-babe pose. 'The group has really, really helped, Rebecca,' he says fervently. 'I think if I hadn't been going to the group, I would have tried to argue with her about the whole compatibility thing, you know? Told her that we *were* compatible, and we could have a great life together, and she was wrong to think we couldn't . . . but instead I looked at her and thought about what she was doing. I don't know if she just wanted a one-off with me, but I got the clear impression that she was actually suggesting that we get together every time she wanted her itch scratched, even if she was married to Barney, and it suddenly struck me – *this* is the woman I've been so upset about? Someone who'd get engaged to one brother and still try to shag the other one? I mean, what if I *did* convince her and she did agree to marry me? Would she be getting off with Barney whenever my back was turned? So I basically told her to fuck off and that she disgusted me and I did up my trousers and stormed off. So here I am.'

I put my arm around Finn's shoulders. He's surprisingly warm: heat is coming off him in waves. Feeling no resistance in his body, I pull him towards me and he nestles his head on my shoulder.

'You did the right thing,' I say.

'So why was it so fucking hard?'

'Um,' I say, risking a joke, 'because you still fancy her?'

Finn snorts out a giggle on my shoulder. 'This has to be the worst weekend of my life,' he says. 'I've just turned down one gorgeous woman and I'm sharing a room with another one who's off-limits. I couldn't tell any of my mates about this. They'd take the piss so badly I'd never hear the end of it.' He sighs. 'And I think it's only because Daisy's here that Vanessa went after me,' he says bitterly. 'She hates the idea that she's not the sexiest thing around. She couldn't bear to see me with someone else. I bet if I'd turned up without Daise and moped around, she wouldn't have cared so much.' He pauses. 'The group was right, you know. She loves to play games. She wants to feel she's still got me in her clutches.'

'You're better off without her,' I say firmly.

'Yeah,' Finn says, sighing again.

Silence falls, but it's very companionable. We sit there, Finn snuggling against me, his weight cosy and pleasant, the warmth of his body seeping through my thin kaftan and heating my skin. And then, from my bedroom, I hear what I've been waiting for: two short beeps that signify a message waiting for me. I jerk a little in an automatic reflex.

'Is that your phone?' Finn asks. 'It must be, mine's switched off.'

'Yeah,' I say, and I feel my body tensing up with the urge to go and check my message.

Finn senses it too. He sits up straight. 'Off you go,' he says. 'I know you want to. Is it your man?' Finn knows there's someone; I've talked about Jake in group, but without mentioning his name.

'I hope so,' I say feebly.

'Go on then.' He grabs my head and plants a kiss on my forehead. 'You're a good mate, Rebecca.'

I go through the bathroom and check my message.

London lonely without you, miss you, see you Sun! J

No kisses after his initial, but he said he missed me and was lonely . . . my body flushes with warmth as if I had his arms around me. I take a few moments to feel smug, glorying in my luck at having Jake while poor Finn is in misery next door, alone and confused. Then I pull myself together, switch off the phone so I won't be tempted to text Jake again, and stride back into Finn's room.

'It *was* your bloke, wasn't it?' Finn says, managing a smile. 'I can tell. You look like someone turned a light on in your head.'

I nod.

'Don't worry,' he says. 'I won't get pissed off that you're happy. I can be a good mate too.'

I kiss his forehead in return. 'Pool,' I say firmly. 'Get your trunks on. We're going down there and we're going to have a good time. I'm not leaving you here to sit and mope.'

He needs a bit of convincing, but I'm too tough for him, armoured now with the conviction that Jake's missing me as much as I'm missing him. I override his protests and leave him to get changed. Two minutes later, he jumps through the door, clad only in his stripy trunks, and strikes the same pose I adopted when I thought he was Daisy.

'Is this right?' he says, grinning at me. 'Oh no, wait, I need to be spanking myself too . . .'

'You tell anyone about that and you're dead meat,' I say, turning on my heel and striding out of the room before he can see how much I'm blushing. Oh well, it'll make a great story for Daisy; she'll kill herself laughing about it.

Chapter Twenty-one

I don't get a chance to tell Daisy after all; she's nowhere to be seen when we get down to the pool, but I don't realise this for a while, because the sheer spectacle is so overwhelming that I can barely even make out individual figures at first. There's a writhing mass of bodies in the bright blue water while a group of equally drunken spectators sprawl on the loungers, shouting encouragement, spilling champagne and snogging. It's like *La Dolce Vita* set in a posh English co-educational boarding school.

Eventually an orange rubber ball pops up from the midst of the huddle of bodies in the water. Everyone shrieks and pounces at it. They're playing some sort of water polo. I keep an eye on the swimmers to make sure that there are no dead bodies on the floor of the pool. This situation is a prime candidate for one of those awful tabloid stories where deeply contrite Flopsies and Mopsies testify one after another at the inquest to say they had no idea that Tooty had drunk three bottles of champagne . . . he seemed absolutely fine up until the moment his head disappeared below the surface . . . they can't believe they went on playing water polo for half an hour above poor Tooty's submerged body . . .

'Jesus,' Finn says, 'it's a fucking orgy!' He looks at me. 'You coming in?'

I shake my head. It looks much too energetic, and I don't trust those boys to behave themselves in the scrum; a couple are already tugging playfully at the strings of Mopsy's bikini as she squeals with laughter.

'I'll just drink more fizz and preserve my dignity,' I say.

'Isn't that a contradiction in terms?' Finn says, grinning. He doesn't wait for an answer. 'OK, fuck it . . . if you can't beat 'em, join 'em . . . Room for one more?' he yells, and runs hard for the deep end, dive-bombing in to the whoops of the party in the pool and the curses of a pair of snoggers near the edge, whose happy petting party has been drenched in cold water.

I go into the house to retrieve a bottle of champagne and when I re-emerge, the polo match is, if possible, even more orgy-like. Baby Thompson is so thin she can run around in only a pair of thong knickers and still not look vulgar. Her bosoms and bottom hardly even jiggle. I know this, not because I shared a room with her last night and saw her in her underpants, but because that's how she's clad as she dashes across the grass looking for the ball, which has been thrown out of the pool by an over-enthusiastic player. You could flatten your hand against her chest and barely notice her breasts getting in the way; they're like a pre-pubescent girl's. I can't help envying the elegance of her figure. Not that I want to be as thin as that, but how lovely it must be to be able to strip down to a thong so exiguous it looks like dental floss, without looking as tarty as one of the women in *Readers' Wives*.

'Bay – *BEE!* Bay – *BEE!*' the boys are yelling. As far as I can see, she's the only girl going topless. She's not the prettiest one there – far from it – but she's certainly getting the most attention. Which, I assume, was precisely her goal.

She throws the ball in and stands posing for a moment on the edge. Normally the players would be diving for the ball and the game would recommence, but the men are, naturally, mesmerised by the sight of a near-naked woman standing above them with one hand on her hip, water dripping from her nipples.

'Take it all off!' yells Vijay.

Baby actually slips both her thumbs into her G-string and gives a stripper's wiggle, causing the men to ululate like coyotes. Then she yells: 'Catch me!' throws her arms in the air and launches herself into the pool. Stewart and Vijay, who are standing near each other with their arms (and their tongues) out, disappear underneath her and only emerge some time later, Baby triumphantly clinging to them both, coughing for breath and looking like they've just won the lottery.

'She's such a *whore*,' mutters one of the girls sitting on the lounger behind me.

'I *know*. So *obvious*. She'll never get a husband that way,' agrees her friend.

It's clearly the worst thing they can find to say about anyone. They chink glasses, giggling maliciously.

I find an unoccupied lounger and look around for Daisy, longing to share this prime spectacle with her, but I can't find her anywhere. Maybe she went up the back stairs to change, and I missed her because Finn and I came down the Death Trap. Finn seems to have submerged his troubles, literally, by throwing himself into organising the game. Goalkeepers are chosen and two impromptu goals made by putting discarded towels and items of clothing on each end of the pool. I can't keep track of the score, but then I'm working my way through the champagne and feeling oddly serene, despite the mayhem happening around me. Jake texted me back; I'm at peace with the world; and it's weirdly relaxing to be lying out on a lounger under the stars, in the balmy night air, watching lots of people engaging in violent physical activity while you yourself have nothing more strenuous to do than recline with your head comfortably propped up, lift a glass to your lips and lose yourself in dreamy fantasies about the torrid reunion you're going to have with your boyfriend in less than twenty-four hours.

'What *are* you doing!' someone shrieks from behind me, breaking annoyingly into my daydream. Jake and I were having a leisurely bubble bath and he had just started doing something very naughty to me with a sponge.

It's Vanessa. She storms across the grass and on to the concrete surround of the pool. 'That's my best pashmina!' she shouts indignantly, bending to pick up one of the goalposts.

'Finn, did you put my best pashmina by the pool so people could trample on it? Look at it! It's all wet!'

Finn, leaping in the air to make a catch, ignores her.

'Finn! I'm talking to you!'

He turns his head reluctantly, holding the ball tight to his body so no one can make a grab for it. 'Come on, Van, don't make a scene . . .'

'And whose is this?' She picks up the other goalpost. 'It's sopping!'

'Oi, Vanessa, leave those alone!' yells another player. 'We need our bloody goals!'

'There are proper goals in the storeroom,' she shouts back, 'with nets. If you weren't too bloody lazy to set them up you wouldn't have had to use other people's *very expensive* pashminas!' She stalks around the edge of the pool and scoops up the other two goal markers. 'I'm taking these to dry out,' she says angrily. 'You can get the goals if you want to carry on playing.'

Finn, sighing loudly, drops the ball, heaves himself out of the pool with a flex of his biceps, and goes over to the storage shed, which I hadn't even noticed before. It's a large wooden building with a slanting roof, set back a few metres from the pool area and partially obscured by wisteria and rambling roses. He pulls open the door and flicks on the light. There's a scream from inside.

With the door open and the light on, the interior of the storage shed is lit up like the stage of a theatre, brightly illuminated against the darkness of the night. Which is very unfortunate. Because inside, lying on a pile of extra pillows for the pool loungers, are a couple desperately trying to rearrange their disordered clothing. Daisy and Barney's blond hair glows like gold in the light of the bare bulb. Daisy's blue silk skirt is round her waist, her strappy top completely off her shoulders, and Barney is shirtless and fumbling frantically with the zipper of his trousers. Their faces are turned towards the open door,

268

frozen in identical expressions of guilt and panic. Daisy's mouth, open in surprise, is a perfect 'O' of consternation.

Vanessa is on the far side of the pool, near the house, but she has taken in the scene with complete understanding. The garments she's carrying fall to the ground as she stares at her fiancé and Finn's girlfriend caught in flagrante delicto.

Absolute silence falls. And then Finn, still standing by the open door, does the last thing anyone would expect. He bursts out laughing. He positively howls with laughter, doubling over, as Daisy and Barney, released from their momentary paralysis, scramble to cover themselves.

'God,' Finn says through his laughter, 'I can't *wait* to make the best man's speech at the wedding!'

Banshee-like screams issue from Vanessa. She races round the pool and, to everyone's surprise but mine, launches herself, not on Barney, but on Finn, punching and slapping him so hard it takes two brawny stockbrokers to pull her off and he has bruises for the following week.

Chapter Twenty-two

'I really didn't mean to do it,' Daisy says helplessly. 'And Barney didn't either. We were getting drunk together in the house – Barney was upset because he'd seen Finn and Vanessa going off together, and he thought there was something going on, and of course he was right.' She looks at Finn, who has already recounted the story of him and Vanessa under the willow tree.

'I tried to tell Barney nothing was happening between the two of them,' Daisy continues, 'but he wouldn't believe me, and I couldn't blame him, because I secretly thought he was right. And Barney was in a terrible state, and I was pretending to be Finn's girlfriend, so I had to be in a bit of a state too, because that would have been the normal reaction, and besides, I was really cross with Vanessa. Partly on Finn's behalf, because I knew how much she'd been messing with him, and partly because I was pissed off on my own account. I mean, what if I really *had* been Finn's girlfriend, and she'd dragged him off like that in front of everyone? It was totally disrespectful. So Barney and I drank buckets of champagne, and I found myself really getting into my role, if you know what I mean. I sort of convinced myself I *was* Finn's girlfriend. Before I knew it Barney and I were practically crying on each other's shoulders. And then everyone went out to the pool, and we were all alone in the living room, and there was an awkward moment when we looked at each other and weren't sure what to do. I didn't realise then that I was attracted to him, but I'd been flirting with him a lot and there was definitely a bit of weird tension between us. Barney must have felt it too, because he stood up and said in a sort of over-hearty way that we should go out to the pool and not sit here getting all maudlin. Then I tripped when I tried to stand up, so he took my hand to help me, and there was a fizz and crackle when we touched – you know . . .' She glances at me. '. . . We got a bit embarrassed by it and Barney dropped my hand very quickly. So we went out to the pool, where they were already playing water polo. Barney said that they needed proper goals, with nets, and that they had some in the shed, so I said I'd help him get them out.' She sighs. 'I don't know if either of us was trying to get the other one alone. I don't really think so. But I couldn't see Rebecca or Davey, and I felt sorry for Barney, so I thought I'd stick with him and keep him company till Vanessa turned up. And I admired him for not chasing after Finn and Vanessa. He was obviously trying to distract himself, so I thought I'd help. Well, we got into the shed, and Barney couldn't find the light switch – we were pretty drunk by then – so we were stumbling around in the dark, and then I fell over on to this pile of pillows and started giggling . . . Barney was trying to help me up, then he tripped on something and fell over too, and before we knew it we were kissing. It wasn't planned or anything. I mean, there wasn't a moment that we looked at each other and went, OK, let's have a bit of a snog. And I don't remember consciously thinking that I wanted to pay Vanessa back, or anything. It happened very naturally. I do remember Barney kicking the shed door shut after a while, but we were just really caught up in the moment, and after that we didn't notice anything going on around us. I didn't even realise Finn had opened the shed door until he turned the light on. And then Vanessa started screaming . . . God, it was awful. I couldn't believe I'd done it.' She pauses.

'So what happened after that?' asks Jennifer, eyes wide. The usual rule about not asking questions while people testify is being ignored this time; it's impossible to resist when Finn and Daisy are telling such juicy stories.

'Oh, God. Rebecca took me up to mine and Finn's room, and Finn came up after a while, still howling with laughter,

271

and we put stuff on his scratches – Vanessa had really messed him up . . .'

Finn indicates a fading red graze on his cheek with considerable pride.

'. . . and we decided that Finn and I should drive back to London first thing the next morning. Rebecca said she'd stay and get a lift back with Davey, so Finn and I sneaked out at dawn.'

'How was the next morning?' Ben asks me.

'Everyone was really hung-over and miserable,' I say. 'No one got up till twelve. Then we all sat around having eggs and bacon and nobody would look at anybody else. Vanessa never came down to breakfast at all. I didn't see her the whole day. Baby never came back to bed and it turned out she'd crashed in Vijay and Stewart's room. I don't know if they did anything, but Vijay and Stewart have been boasting about it non-stop.'

'Well, they were, until I told them they were repressed homosexuals who'd jump at the chance to feel each other up,' Finn says cheerfully.

'Finn! You didn't!' I exclaim.

'I was getting sick of them banging on about being superstuds,' Finn explains.

'So, Daisy, how do you feel about all of this now?' Jennifer asks her, a serious expression on her pretty little face. 'I mean, I know you told us that you were doing this whole thing about pretending to be Finn's girlfriend, but we never got the chance to discuss it in group. And actually . . .' her voice gets stronger. '. . . I know I emailed you saying it wasn't a good idea, but I think I should have gone on about that more, because it wasn't a good idea, was it? For either of you . . .' she shoots a glance at Finn '. . . but particularly for you.'

Jennifer is clearly more on the side of the girls. But she's raised an important point. We all feel guilty that we've been ignoring the deep emotional states we're here to talk about in favour of having a lengthy gossip.

'Absolutely,' Charlotte says. 'Was it painful pretending to be in a happy relationship, Daisy, when you feel that that's exactly what you're not managing to achieve in real life?'

Ouch. Charlotte has a way of getting right to the point. I flinch on Daisy's behalf.

'Yes, it was,' Daisy says quietly. 'I think that's why I got so drunk in the first place.'

'Daise, I'm so sorry,' Finn breaks in. 'I should never have asked you to do it.'

Big significant nods from both Charlotte and Jennifer, who seem to have taken strongly against Finn.

'Oh, come on,' Ben protests, standing up for his buddy. 'Daisy could have said no if she'd wanted to.'

'No, I put her under pressure,' Finn admits manfully. 'I begged and pleaded.'

'I still didn't have to agree, though,' Daisy says fairly. 'I could have said no, or I could have talked about it with the group, and that would have given me the support to say I wouldn't do it if I couldn't manage it on my own.'

More nods from the two girls.

'Yes, it's all our faults for not seeing how stupid it was,' Charlotte agrees. 'It was a ridiculous idea. Set you both back months. We should have seen that at the time.'

'Yes,' Jennifer says, pushing her red curls back from her face and staring earnestly at Daisy, 'the group's supposed to be all about honesty, not pretending to be in a relationship when you're not.'

Finn is writhing under the lash. 'I'm sorry,' he says helplessly, 'I'm really, really, sorry . . .'

'What I didn't say,' Daisy interrupts, 'is that I only agreed to do it because Finn pretended that he was going out with me to make Lewis jealous. We went to a party of Lewis's and Finn was all over me.'

Indrawn breaths from the group.

'And it worked,' Daisy confesses. 'For a bit, anyway. Lewis

started ringing me up again and wanting to see me, but as soon as he got what he wanted, he dumped me again.'

Charlotte, sitting next to her on the sofa, pats her hand in sympathy. 'Hopefully you've learnt your lesson now,' she says. 'That man is never going to be any good for you.'

Daisy nods. 'But it's more than that,' she says, sitting up straight and looking round at all of us. 'It's not just Lewis. I realised that I was *always* going after men who were never going to be any good for me. Look at me and Barney. I mean, what was I doing? Getting off with a man who was in love with someone else – *engaged* to someone else – at their engagement party! Barney's not even my type!' She takes a deep breath. 'So *that's* what I learnt,' she continues. 'I learnt that I keep going after unavailable men. Maybe I see it as a challenge, to conquer the guys I can't have. I don't know. But this has really been a lesson for me. I'm never going to do that again. I'm never going to get off with someone who doesn't really want me. I knew Lewis didn't, not really.' Her voice drops again; this is hard for her to say. 'I knew I was just another notch on his belt. But I wouldn't let myself see it. I thought I could make him love me, but I couldn't. So I have to spend some time working out why I do this. And I'm never going to put myself in that position again. I'm not going to jump into bed with anyone. I'm going to wait and take things slowly and not just throw myself at guys and expect that they'll fall madly in love with me because I sleep with them the first time we go out. I'm going to wait, and if they don't like it, that means they're not the right ones for me.'

She's crying a little. Charlotte has her arms around her now and everyone else reaches out to pat the closest part of Daisy they can reach – apart from Jim, who, as always, is sitting a little back, looking nervous. We're so used to this by now that Jim doesn't freak us out any more.

'And Finn,' Daisy sniffles, 'you're not to feel guilty, OK? I brought this on myself. I didn't have to say yes. I agreed because you were going to do the same thing for me with Lewis.'

'I still shouldn't have done it,' Finn says instantly. 'I blame myself. I should have looked after you better.'

'No,' Daisy says through her tears. 'I should have looked after myself. But I'm going to do that from now on, and I know the group will help me . . .'

She dissolves into sobbing. Charlotte holds her firmly and lets her have her cry.

'Hey, everyone, don't look so sad for me!' she says after a while, managing a smile. 'You should be happy! I've just had a really big breakthrough!'

I wanted to talk about Jake with the group, but I didn't get the chance. The Finn and Daisy stuff took up so much time and energy that I was drained by the end of it, and Jake got put off till next week. I wasn't going to give his real name, of course; but I did want to talk about how I felt about him before we go off to Whitstable this weekend. It's our first time away together and I thought that discussing it with the group would give me a kind of framework, help me to work out my feelings – and to be honest, my fears. I'm scared of what's happening between us. I'm scared it might be too fast, too soon, that in my excitement at having a new man in my life, at the revelation that I can actually be attracted to a man who isn't Patrick, I might be throwing myself at Jake so hard I'll put him off.

I try to talk to Daisy but she's not much help; she just tells me to go for it and enjoy myself. As far as she's concerned, I have someone I like, who likes me, someone who rings me regularly and asks me away for the weekend, and that's more than she's managing, so she's not particularly interested in probing into the deep tortured recesses of my psyche. Besides, she's very excited by her whole new go-slow strategy with men. I wonder whether I should mention to her that I think Davey likes her, but, after reflection, I decide not to. Daisy has barely embarked on this new direction for her life. There are bound to be slips and stumbles along the way, and it would be terrible if Davey, so sweet and genuine, got caught up in an early attempt by Daisy to date men who are nice to her, which she then found she couldn't manage. Still, I do tell Davey about Daisy's breakthrough. He humphs and says he'll believe it when he sees it.

Jake picks me up on Saturday morning, bright and early. He was working late on Friday night, so we couldn't drive down then, and maybe he was also nervous and wanted to make this first trip away together just an overnighter. We haven't seen each other since Tuesday; I wanted to, but he said he was working very hard, and he was a little . . . not dismissive, exactly, but short with me when I asked him about what clothes I should bring. He said swimsuits, jeans and sensible shoes for walking on the beach: Whitstable wasn't at all smart. I'm not sure about this, since I read in a Sunday magazine a few weeks ago that loads of assistant fashion editors on *Vogue* have apparently bought houses in Whitstable recently, but I err on the side of caution. Men hate women who dress up too much on a casual weekend away.

So I pack my magic jeans, which I bought in New York when I was staying with Patrick. I should have bought more than one pair; when you find jeans that always, no matter how fat you're feeling, make your bottom look high and round (and, due to the clever contoured fading, not too large), you should always get multiple pairs. Since I didn't, I wear these rarely, saving them for this kind of special occasion. I add some T-shirts that are low-cut without being whorish, a couple of clingy cardigans that look casual but were in fact horribly expensive, my miracle bikini and, of course, a ridiculous amount of sexy underwear. I hesitate over the bright blue Chinese-print knickers that Daisy got me for Christmas, which fasten in bows at the hips so that your boyfriend can untie you like a present, and then throw them in. They don't take up any space, after all, and I'm dying to wear them for someone. Everything goes in the pricey brown leather overnight bag that I got at a luggage sale on Oxford Street; it turned out to be too heavy for most trips – that's the problem with leather suitcases – but I can just chuck it in the back of Jake's car, I don't have to carry it any distance, and it looks fabulously chic.

All this time accumulating sexy underwear and the perfect overnight case for romantic weekends away, and I finally get the chance to use them. I feel that the stars are finally in the right conjunction for me. I'm sick of reading about '10 Best Romantic Getaways at Quiet Country Hotels' in magazines and not going on any myself. Patrick wasn't much for Best Romantic Getaways – typical Patrick, he thought they sounded too contrived – but Jake looks as if he might well be. I spend Friday night fantasising about future weekends with Jake spent at country inns with four-poster beds, fires burning in the grates, and lovely three-course dinners. Maybe I'm finally growing up and having the kind of relationship I've always dreamt about.

Jake seems nervous, too. I kiss him when I answer the door, but he only responds perfunctorily, looking around for my luggage and saying: 'Is this all? Great!' before picking up my bag and going back downstairs. I tell myself I've earned points for packing light, but I wish he'd been a little more demonstrative. Still, this must be weird for him too.

The drive down is quiet. We listen to music and don't talk much. I want to, but I can sense that Jake doesn't, so I manage to shut up and watch the road instead. I do whoop when we see the sea, though, and Jake turns his head to me and smiles.

'Happy?' he says.

'Blissful. I've never been to the English coast before. Well, apart from Brighton when I was little, but I don't really remember it very well.'

Did that sound a bit over-the-top, I wonder? 'Blissful'? And pompous: 'The English coast'? But he's still smiling.

'It's not exactly glamorous,' he says, 'but I love it. We came down here practically every weekend when we were kids. Dad's not here that much in the summer any more, but I haven't been making the most of it. I'm not very keen on hanging out here all alone. But now – well . . .' he shoots a shy glance at me '. . . well, we'll see how you like it, OK? If you do, we can always come back.'

I have to practically bite my tongue off to stop myself from gushing, 'Oh, I'm sure I'll *love* it!' I don't want to scare him off, and besides, I remind myself firmly, I may *not* like Whitstable. This new relationship is going to be built on me being honest, not, as I did with Patrick, pretending to enjoy some things I really didn't just to keep him happy and make him think we were completely compatible. So I leave it too long to answer, which is probably a good thing; keep Jake on his toes, keep him guessing about how keen on him I am.

But I do love it. The house is beautiful. It's a small cottage in a row of pretty little houses just off the main street, with a blue-painted door and a tiny square of front garden rimmed with pebbles and sea shells: exactly what a cottage by the sea should look like. The front door leads straight into a sitting room with a light wood floor, squashy blue and green sofas, and a working fireplace with a carved iron surround. There's a small galley kitchen in the same light wood which leads to a back garden rich with the scent of salty sea water and wild rosemary, sage and thyme. Jake immediately goes to water the basil plants on the kitchen windowsill while I explore the rest of the house. The first floor has a pretty bathroom and a guest bedroom, but our room, in the attic space at the top of the house, is reached by a staircase that's almost a ladder, like being in a ship, and it has a huge bed with fresh white sheets under a wide skylight that shows the clear blue sky. I lie down and watch the clouds scudding overhead, waiting for Jake to come upstairs and find me. If I had the nerve, I would take most of my clothes off and pose in my underwear, but I don't. As I hear Jake's feet on the ladder, see his head popping up through the trapdoor, my heart beats fast. I so want him to fall on me and for us to make love straight away, like christening the house for us.

He laughs. 'You look really comfortable.'

'It's so cosy up here!' I say, trying to sound seductive without overdoing it.

'Yeah? You like it?'

'I love it.'

And, just as I'd hoped, he pulls off his boots and comes to lie next to me. I'm already getting turned on just by having him so close to me on the bed. I wait, determined that he's going to have to make the first move, but when I turn my head to look at him his face is right there and I don't know which one of us moves closer to the other, I think we both do it simultaneously, and then we're kissing, and then we're pulling off each other's clothes, and it's perfect, this is perfect. Jake, thank God, has remembered to bring condoms, and we make love under the skylight with the clouds overhead and it feels like God is in his heaven for me and all's right with the world.

I've got through my pain and come out the other side. Jake's here, his weight is pressing me into the bed, nailing me down, and any memories I had of Patrick are pushed to the back of my mind. Right now, I hope they never come back.

Chapter Twenty-three

We doze a little after sex, and then Jake gets up and announces that we're having a picnic by the sea. I would almost have spent the whole day in bed, but I take his point; it's silly to come to the seaside and then not visit it. So I drag my sluggish body, limbs heavy with satisfaction, out of bed, and pull on my bikini and a T-shirt and capris while Jake is downstairs making up a picnic basket. He brought food from London especially. Perhaps he's entered himself in some secret 'Best Boyfriend of the Year' competition and there are hidden cameras everywhere. If so, I hope they enjoyed our morning romp.

The walk to the sea is beautiful. We head down some little lanes running past pretty, homey little houses to a level crossing over some railway tracks. (I get very excited about crossing open railway tracks, it feels so 1950s.) A rusty gate on the far side leads to an overgrown path, thick with Queen Anne's Lace and waist-high weeds, which cuts across a golf course over which old men are ambling peacefully, and then past some newer, posher houses and on to the seafront. I am a bit disappointed that the beach is pebbled, but I don't mention this, particularly as it would reveal how much of a moron I am. Clearly English beaches aren't often sandy. I would have known that if I'd thought about it.

We do find a stretch which has some stubbly grass to spread our towels on, and Jake unpacks the basket. I'm starving. I fall on the pita, hummus, feta, olives and sun-dried tomato dip from Marks & Spencer's and come to myself ten minutes later. Jake is grinning at my greed.

'Isn't it funny that when you have a picnic in England now,

you always eat Greek food?' I say, to cover my embarrassment at being a total pig. 'I don't even know what English picnic food would be.'

'Pork pies and coleslaw and ham sandwiches,' Jake says. 'That's what we had when I was little.'

'*Urgh*. I'd much rather have this,' I say, wondering if I have room for a last piece of pita and hummus.

'I can tell,' he says, still grinning.

'I was hungry!' I say defensively. 'All that exercise worked up an appetite!'

'What exercise? I was doing all the work.'

'I writhed around a lot,' I point out. 'You have no idea how knackering that is.'

'Clearly not.' He plants a kiss on my neck. 'Next time you can be on top. Then I can complain about how tired I am, just having to lie there and take it.'

'Or we could do it sideways,' I suggest. 'Equal opportunity tiredness.'

I lie down on my towel to stop myself eating any more, and shut my eyes. The sun beats down on my closed lids, suffusing me in golden red. 'I really want to go for a swim,' I say, 'but I'm too full.'

'That's OK,' Jake says, 'the tide's coming in. If you give it an hour it'll be the perfect time to go swimming.'

The water turns out to be very shallow; you have to walk a long way to get deep enough to be able to swim, and that walk is pretty much what the Little Mermaid must have experienced directly after getting her legs. Every step cuts my feet. Mixed in with the pebbles are sharp bits of broken shells, and underneath them is sucky damp mud that clings to my soles, pulling me down and making unattractive squelching noises. I want to look graceful for Jake, but after three steps I give up the attempt and concentrate instead on just making it through the shallows without slipping on stones and falling on my bum. I had a vague fantasy of me and Jake creeping back down to the sea this evening to have sex, but clearly that's out. If it's high tide now it will be low tonight, so we'd have to walk for twenty minutes over this mud flat to even get close to the water. And then we wouldn't be able to do anything because as soon as I jumped on Jake, my extra weight would mean that every time he trod on a shell it would cut him so badly he'd scream with pain and drop me.

The view is beautiful, though. A hazy white mist hangs over small green cliffs, which curve to either side of the long bay. There's an island in the distance, which seems to tremble in the humid air like a mirage on the horizon. Sunshine casts a long, golden streak over the water, the sky is gull's-egg blue overhead, and soft salt water laps around me as I float on my back, while Jake waits for me on the shore. Why can't it always be like this?

I have to squint all the way back to make sure I'm heading for Jake. Even so, I make a couple of mistakes before I get close enough to see where I'm going.

'I thought you were going to sit with that bloke instead,' he says, indicating a portly man with his hairy white stomach hanging so far into his lap it looks as if he's supporting it with his knees.

'I'm really short-sighted,' I confess. 'Once I was on holiday in Australia with my friend Robert – he's gay, and he took me to this gay beach, so I went topless, because no one was going to care. I went for a swim, and when I came out of the water and thought I was walking back to Robert . . .' Jake's laughing already '. . . I went right up to this poor gay guy sitting by himself. You should have seen the expression on his face. He looked *terrified*. This half-naked woman was walking towards him, waving. He actually started shuffling himself back, away from me.'

'You should have said: "Hi, handsome! Feel like being converted today?"' Jake suggests.

'I wish I'd thought of it. Robert was wetting himself, of course. He yelled at me, "Darling, you've got the wrong fag!" and I apologised profusely to the guy, but he just waved his hands at me in a go-away-and-never-come-back gesture, so I did. That wasn't the only embarrassing moment, actually. When I went to pee in the woods there were all these naked men in there running away from me. It was really dispiriting. I just gave up in the end and peed in the sea.'

'You've led a rich full life,' Jake says.

'You haven't heard the half of it.'

I want to snuggle up to him, but I'm not sure what level of public intimacy we're at, and he isn't initiating any physical contact, so I don't. I hate these early stages of a relationship, where you don't know how much you can do, what the new person will happily accept, and what they'll feel is invasive.

'I'm going for a swim,' Jake says, jumping up.

Lucky I didn't try to cuddle him. I want to eat more food while Jake's off swimming. I'm not hungry, but this spending-the-whole-day-together is making me nervous, and that translates into greed. I manage to restrain myself by grabbing big folds of my stomach in both hands until I am revolted by my gargantuan appetite, and pull out a book instead. It's a detective novel from the shelves of Jake's father's house, which is acceptable. I know better than to read a trashy romance around a boyfriend, new or not. But you can't go wrong with Agatha Christie.

Jake is gone for an hour. First I panic, then I tell myself not to be silly, the sea is so mild that nobody could possibly drown in it, then I remind myself that Jake has been coming here since he was a little boy and knows the currents perfectly, then I panic again, irrationally, and then I convince myself that he's taking so long because he's getting twitchy at having to spend the whole day together and wants to get away from me. By the time he returns, silhouetted against the sunlight and dripping water as he bends to pick up his towel, I am a gibbering wreck.

'That was a long swim!' I say brightly.

Jake hears straight away that something's wrong. 'Did I worry you?' he says. 'I'm sorry. I always go out a long way.' He looks abashed. 'You're not the first person to get worried. I should have remembered to tell you. Sorry.'

He kneels down next to me, his handsome face full of concern, beads of water caught on his thick golden lashes. But now I'm pissed off. I assume he's referring to other girlfriends he's brought down here; and if they got anxious, then I refuse to.

'No, I was fine,' I say casually. 'I was so caught up in my book I didn't even notice you were still gone till a few minutes ago.'

'Really?'

'Yeah. Actually, I want to see what happens next . . . do you mind if I go on reading . . . ?'

He doesn't quite believe me, but he can see I'm not going to say any more. I turn back to my book, wilfully denying myself the sight of Jake towelling himself down. He stands in front of me for a long moment, waiting for me to look up again, say something else, but I don't and eventually he moves away and lies down on his towel.

I have the feeling that now it's him who wants some physical affection, but I won't give it to him. I'm cross, irrationally, I know, and I'm nervous. This is reminding me of all the times with Patrick that our wires got crossed, the misunderstandings, one of us wanting a hug or a kiss, some reassurance, and the other one spinning away on a different tangent. God, having a relationship is so hard. I'd forgotten about all the moods and the negotiations.

I bury myself in the Agatha Christie. Even though I was lying to Jake about being absorbed by it, I actually find that my lie becomes true. I concentrate so hard on the story that I manage to lose myself in it, and by the time I emerge my grumpiness has gone. That's the magic of detective fiction; it's

284

so cathartic. You can channel all your unpleasant thoughts and wishes into the pages and let your surrogates behave badly for you. No wonder I'm addicted to *Law & Order*.

I'm sitting by the fire, waiting for Jake to come back with dinner. It's too warm for a fire, really, but Jake could see how much I liked the idea, and he built a small one: just a single log burning slowly behind the grate, crackling comfortably, an occasional little shower of sparks sending a bright gold spray up the chimney. Mozart is playing in the background; I'd have put on something a bit sexier myself, but I appreciate Jake's being cultured. It's good for me. Maybe he'll help wean me off police TV shows and Agatha Christie and on to something a bit more sophisticated.

I've put on only two of the lamps and lit some candles on the mantelpiece. Not too many – I didn't want it to look as if I'd gone for an over-contrived romantic atmosphere. I actually stood by the door and checked out the impression that Jake would have when he came in, like I used to do when my mother told me to tidy my room and I'd shove everything under the bed, pull the duvet straight and then stand back to see if a first glance would give a clean-enough verdict.

Though I really wanted to wear my knickers with the bows on the hips, I balked at the last minute, thinking they might be too much. I compromised with a lacy cream set trimmed with fuschia embroidery – sexy, but not too tarty – and pulled on my miracle jeans and a simple T-shirt over them. That way when Jake undresses me he'll get a nice surprise, as the underwear is much more ooh-la-la than the clothes covering it imply. Perhaps I'm too obsessive. But if I am, I bet the rest of the female population of the United Kingdom is too. We spend so much time fantasising about perfect romantic evenings and so little time actually having them, that it's no wonder that when we're away for the weekend by the sea with a man who's built us a fire even though he didn't need to, we do our best to pull all the stops out.

The door latch clicks and Jake steps in. He looks so handsome I am unable to believe my luck. His faded old jeans and soft grey cotton sweater are a neutral frame for his sun-lightened hair and those amazing grey-green eyes. Wow. I goggle at him. He's much more striking than Patrick was. As I've said, you didn't realise how handsome Patrick was until he was naked, because he played his looks down so much. While Jake, even at an initial glance, is obviously sex on a plate. I should be thinner. I resolve to go on a diet – a serious one, this time, no messing around. And do more yoga. Maybe start running again.

'The best fish and chips in the whole of Whitstable!' Jake announces, going over to the table and unloading the paper bags he's carrying. I've put out ketchup, brown sauce and vinegar, but no plates; I wasn't sure if he would think that was being too prissy. Clearly I got it right. Jake tears open the bags and extracts newspaper-wrapped packages which he carries over to the floor in front of the fire.

'Two picnics in one day,' I say, sitting down next to him and planting a kiss on his mouth.

He looks a little startled at the kiss, but then he smiles and kisses me back. Good.

'Do you mind?' he asks, sounding concerned. 'I mean, did you want to go out to dinner? There are a couple of nice restaurants we could have gone to . . . I just thought this would be more fun . . .'

'Oh no,' I hasten to assure him, 'this is lovely. We've got a fire, we've got cod and chips, mushy peas, and pickled eggs and vinegar—'

'Oops!' He jumps up. 'And we've got wine! I forgot, sorry!'

He goes into the kitchen and returns with a bottle of white wine and a glass for me.

'Bliss,' I say, taking a sip.

The fish is tender and flaky, the mushy peas aren't too soupy and the chips are pure evil – crunchy, oil-soaked and delicious. I don't feel I can tell Jake to put them beside him, where I can't reach them easily. Men don't like it when you tell them you're dieting, not in the early stages of a relationship, anyway. Later on it's fine, but you have to wait a couple of months. Still, by visualising how awful I will feel later trying to have sex with a swollen belly, I manage not to eat too many. And I know better than to go for the pickled eggs. I love them, but they make me fart.

'Do you want to watch a video after dinner?' Jake asks. 'We've got loads.'

'Love to.'

'Just pick something out. I've seen all of them already, so you choose.'

Very smart of him, I think. Big dinner, a two-hour video to help us digest, and then a romp in front of the fire to round off the evening. I won't think about whether he's done this before with other girlfriends. Patrick hadn't really had girlfriends before me, and though I was pleased by that, because there was no one for me to be jealous of, it turned out to be a terrible sign. I remind myself of this. If Jake's had girlfriends, that's normal. It means that he can actually make a commitment. Look at the pleasure he's taking in making this day so lovely for me. I resolve not to pick holes in it.

I choose a psychological thriller for us to watch. That way we get to be a little scared together, which will heighten our adrenaline, and we won't go to sleep in front of the TV, which would make sex afterwards less likely; but it's not an action film, which would remind me too much of the kind of videos I always watched with Patrick. We cuddle up on the sofa. I go to top up my glass halfway through the film and when I come back I stretch out with my feet in Jake's lap. I like my feet. They're small and pretty and I just did my toenails for the weekend (old rose, nothing too vulgar). Jake starts to rub them, absent-mindedly at first, but when I make appreciative noises he gets down to it more seriously. I close my eyes and start to melt. There's practically nothing in the world I like more than having my feet massaged. He pulls each of my toes gently, rolling them between his fingers, applying just the right amount of pressure, and then he starts digging into the balls of my feet, hitting sore spots and breaking them down, sinking into the arches until I'm moaning with pleasure.

The film is forgotten. Jake's hands are warm and strong and I'm so busy imagining them going all over me that I don't notice at first when he stops. I make a small whimper of protest, but it tails off when he lifts one of my feet and slides the big toe into his mouth. His tongue's warm and wet, his teeth nip gently at the pad of the toe. I sit up a little in shock and stare at him.

'What?' he says, grinning at me, still holding my foot. 'You don't like it?'

'No, it's incredible,' I stammer, 'it's just that no one's ever done that before . . . I didn't know how good it felt . . .'

'Then don't interrupt me,' he says, and goes back to work.

I can't believe how erotic this feels. By the time he's sucked every single toe he's worked me up into a state of such excitement that I really think I would do absolutely anything he wanted. He pulls up my T-shirt and starts licking up my stomach, slowly, taking his time, teasing me. Impatiently, I reach for the T-shirt hem and pull it over my head to give him more access to me.

'Wow,' he murmurs, 'sexy bra . . .'

'It all matches,' I say, smug that he's noticed.

'I need to check,' he says, unbuttoning my jeans. 'I don't take anything on trust . . .'

We end up on the rug in front of the fire. I started to get creative with the wine – if Jake was going to start licking me, I was determined to up the stakes – and we didn't want it spilling all over the sofa. Wooden floors, and a rug that Jake assures me is washable, are another story. We don't make that much of a mess in the end. I don't like wine going to waste. Me licking wine off Jake doesn't seem to be banned under any sub-clause in the AA guidelines, thank goodness. And the taste of it on him is so potent I want to lick up every last drop. Even though he's showered, he still tastes a little salty from the sea. Pinot Grigio, salt and fresh male sweat. It makes me dizzy. I'm so drunk with him I could lick every inch of his body. And I almost do.

Mind you, he returns the favour.

Chapter Twenty-four

Jake farts in his sleep. I assume it's the pickled egg he ate, as he's never done that before. The window's open and the smell isn't too bad and I'm far gone enough to find it endearing, proof of his fallible humanity. I am so close to being in love with him. I'm on the edge, about to fall over. If he does just one more perfect thing, some tiny thing more that proves how compatible we are, I'll tip over the brink and start tumbling. He's lying with his back to me. I give it ten minutes and when he hasn't farted again, I snuggle myself up against his back, throw an arm over his waist and drift into sleep, my nose buried in his skin.

When I wake up I reach out for him sleepily, and it takes me a little while to realise that he's not in bed. I don't panic. I sit up slowly, propping the pillows behind me, and catch the sound of water running downstairs in the bathroom. He's showering. I decide to get up; waiting in bed would look too passive. I pull on my dressing gown and go downstairs to make coffee.

He's all dressed when he comes into the kitchen, which surprises me; it says he's not expecting to have sex this morning. I go over to kiss him, but he puts his hand on my shoulders, blocking me before I can reach up to put my lips to his. I get a rush of anxiety, but tell myself that some men aren't good in the mornings. Though Jake always has been before.

'I made coffee,' I say, and am pleased to hear that my voice sounds normal.

'That's great,' he says, but his voice is clearly distracted and tense.

I look up into his eyes. They won't meet mine. My anxiety is growing; I have a bad feeling about this.

'Look,' he says, and promptly runs out of steam.

'Have some coffee,' I say reassuringly, pouring just the right amount of milk into his mug, handing it to him with a smile, and in short behaving, I realise, like a Stepford Wife.

He takes the mug but doesn't even seem to look at it.

'We need to talk,' he says, still not meeting my eyes.

I am now in panic stations, but I try not to let it show. 'OK,' I say, going through into the living room and sitting down at the table.

Jake follows me. He takes a seat opposite me, as if we're conducting an interview. 'Rebecca,' he begins, reluctantly, 'you're a wonderful girl . . .'

That's it. It's over. I know straight away. I can't believe this is happening.

'. . . but I just don't feel that this is right. I don't know why. Maybe it's too early for me to be in a relationship.'

'*Early?*' I say, despite myself.

'Since I've been sober.'

'But you've been sober for years and years . . .'

'Yes, I know. I don't think it's that. Somehow . . . this is going to sound crazy . . .'

He runs his hand through his thick fair hair. I watch his gesture, and realise that I am never going to be allowed to run my fingers through his hair again. His body is no longer mine to touch as I want.

'. . . but I don't think we're meant to be together.'

'*Meant?*' I sound like a deranged parrot.

'You've been so good for me. You're an amazing person and I feel so grateful to have you in my life, but I just don't think we're supposed to be going out. I don't know, it's like you're my soul sister, or something. We have this deep, wonderful connection. But I sense that we're not meant to be a couple. Does that sound strange? It's the only way that I can explain what I'm feeling.'

I clamp down on the scream I can feel rising in my throat

and say instead, 'So what is it – I mean, what happened this weekend to make you think that we weren't meant to be a couple? I thought we were having a great time.'

Never argue with them when they tell you they want to break up. I know that. Every instinct is telling me to argue, though, and it's hard to resist, particularly as it's so closely tied to the need for an explanation. I'm right to want an explanation, aren't I? He owes me that! Perhaps it would be better just to give a bright smile and say casually: 'Oh, OK, if that's how you feel, there's no point talking about it any more, is there?' then never refer to the subject again. That would drive him mad. *He'd* be the one insisting on discussing it further. But I'm not cast-iron enough to do that. I have to ask. I need *something*, some reason for this complete volte-face, the fact that he was so loving and affectionate and sexy all of yesterday and now he's talking to me as if I were some freakish stalker he doesn't even want to look in the eye.

'We did have a nice time,' Jake says. *Nice!* How dare he? 'But I felt that something was wrong all along, and it hit me when I woke up this morning.'

'Oh come on, Jake,' I say, completely breaking the non-argue rule. 'We had a brilliant time yesterday. Don't rewrite history.'

He makes a gesture with his hand as if he's pushing something away. 'There's no point going back and forth on this,' he says. 'I just really wanted you to understand. I was hoping you'd feel the same.'

'Feel the same? How could I have had any idea what you were thinking? We were all over each other yesterday!'

Jake looks profoundly uncomfortable. 'Yes,' he says, 'well . . . you know, maybe the sex was a mistake . . .'

'A *mistake*?'

'It was great, but I sort of felt we shouldn't have done it . . . there was something about it that didn't feel right . . .'

'Fuck it,' I say angrily, 'if that didn't feel right, what the hell do you feel when it's good?'

Jake can't answer this, so he doesn't. He tries another tack instead. 'You know,' he says, looking at me earnestly, 'I've always been worried that you weren't over Patrick yet.'

My heart leaps as I see a way through this maze. Is this the key to his inexplicable change of feeling? Does he want me to reassure him?

'I think I am,' I say slowly. 'I really think I am. If you'd asked me a couple of weeks ago, I wouldn't have known what to say. But I hardly think about Patrick at all now.'

It's a lie, but it's almost true. I do still think about Patrick; of course I do. I will probably think about Patrick for the rest of my life. But you have to tell white lies to people you love. Nobody can, or should, hear the whole truth about your feelings. So what if there's always a trace of nostalgia for a previous boyfriend? That's natural, isn't it? But the important thing is that the new boyfriend is someone you truly want to be with, not just the first spar of wood that you clutch on to to stop yourself drowning in grief. And Jake is someone I truly want to be with. I can't tell him, after what he's just said, that I am nearly in love with him. So the lie about Patrick becomes the truth, an oblique way of conveying to him what I need to.

'Really?' Jake says. 'You mean if Patrick turned up right this moment and asked you to come back to him, you wouldn't go?'

This hits me so hard I struggle for breath. Jake's right. I would. Part of my brain is asking what's wrong with me; why would I choose Patrick over Jake, when Jake is so much more compatible with me? I file that away for consideration later and manage to go on the attack (it being the best form of defence).

'I would *now*!' I say angrily. 'After what you've just been saying! I don't understand you, Jake. You knew all along that I was getting over an ex-boyfriend and it was never a problem before. And suddenly it comes up when we've been having such a lovely time, like you were keeping it in reserve to hit me over the back of the head with as soon as things got too serious . . . *Oh!*'

I stare at him. I wasn't keeping much control over my words; they just shot out of me, jet-propelled by my fury and feelings of rejection. But now I think I've hit on something very important. 'You don't really want a relationship at all, do you?' I ask.

'Yes, I do!' Jake looks at me earnestly, so handsome that I find myself thinking for a moment that I must have been mad ever to think I was attractive enough to go out with somebody who looked like that. 'I really do! I just don't feel that you and I are right for each other. I feel we were meant to be something else. That we were put in each other's paths to help each other – be a step on the way, but not the destination.'

I wonder where all this sub-Buddhist mysticism has come from. I've never heard Jake spouting rubbish like this before: in fact, he's usually all for self-determination and taking control of your own destiny.

'Then why did you bring up the Patrick thing at all?' I ask. 'If that's the way you felt anyway?'

Jake looks confused, then cross. 'We're just going round in circles,' he says. 'I don't see any point to this.'

'Right,' I say, standing up, so many emotions boiling within me that I manage to remain calm simply because they're jostling with each other so strongly that none of them is managing to get the ascendancy. I really want a drink. It's eleven in the morning and I want nothing more than a pint of red wine. That would look wonderful to a reformed alcoholic. 'I'm going to pack.'

'You're packing already?' He actually looks sad. 'But there's the whole day . . . I thought we could talk about this and then maybe get some lunch, go to the oyster bar on the wharf . . .'

It occurs to me for the first time that Jake may not be fully in touch with reality.

'I'm going home,' I say flatly. 'You can give me a lift to the station if you want to stay on longer.'

'No, of course I'll drive you back,' he says, standing up too. 'I just thought . . .'

But I don't want to hear what Jake just thought. I storm upstairs, scale the ladder and collapse on the edge of the bed staring into space. I can't marshal my thoughts at all. I keep getting jagged flashes of memory. Jake and I, making love yesterday by the fire. Jake just now, dropping the bombshell on me. Jake in Kew Gardens, being so considerate and thoughtful that he seemed to be the most understanding man I'd ever met. Patrick. Patrick, Patrick, Patrick, who turned out to be much more honest than Jake in the end, who didn't try to excuse our breakup with nonsense about destiny not meaning us to be together, but cried with me for days about his own inability to manage a proper relationship and said it was his fault. No wonder I would pick Patrick over Jake. Then the irony of this speculation hits me: here I am deciding which one I would have, while neither of them wants me. I am in total shock. My body feels almost as if Jake sneaked up behind me and hit me in the kidneys with an iron bar. I ache all over. I can barely muster the strength to stand up and get dressed, let alone start packing. And the only reason that I eventually do is because my pride is too strong to leave it long enough for Jake to get worried, come up here and find me sitting on the bed, still in my dressing gown. Thank God for my pride. It's all I've got right now, and even that will fade if I dwell in any depth upon what just happened.

'I don't *believe* it,' Daisy says.

We're curled up on her sofa, in pyjamas, drinking strawberry margaritas. They're appropriate because of the warm weather, but even if it were the depths of winter, Daisy would still have made us strawberry margaritas, pink and frothy. She's a firm believer in their curative powers. Also, the colour goes with Daisy's flat, which is Girlie Central. It looks like a magazine layout entitled 'Flower Power'. There are roses everywhere; on the sofa cushions, on the big painted screen, even on the embroidered shawls thrown over the backs of the shabby-chic pink armchairs. Nothing actually matches; they're all different prints, different shades of pink and madder and red. The oval carpet is a deep rosy-red and the walls are hung with old water-colours of bouquets. The design scheme would have been a dog's dinner in the hands of someone less skilled, but Daisy has made her flat into a gorgeous blooming girls' refuge from the cruel male world outside, and it's the best place I know to retreat to when a member of the male sex has beaten the crap out of you, metaphorically speaking. It occurs to me that any men Daisy brings home may be thoroughly daunted by the extreme femininity of her decor, but now is not the time to mention that. Besides, it's her place, she can decorate it how-ever she wants. And men like girly girls.

Actually, I don't know what men like any longer. Until this morning, I thought they liked girls who wore pretty under-wear, had similar tastes to them and loved having lots of sex, but clearly I was completely wrong. I don't know anything. I say this to Daisy. She scoffs.

'Jake was just an arsehole,' she says. 'He was playing with you. Messing with your mind. He reeled you in and as soon as you guys were getting really close, he, um, cast you off.'

'Like a fish.'

'Sort of.'

'But he seemed so *genuine*!' I drink half my margarita in one go. 'Which is the scariest thing of all! How do I know who to trust any more? He really seemed like he meant it – I mean, the whole relationship thing, not the weird "we weren't meant to be together" bit . . .'

'You were only going out for a few weeks,' Daisy points out. 'You can't start worrying about the "who can I trust" thing. It's not your fault. You did everything right. He conned you, basically.'

'But why?' I say helplessly. 'Why did he bother?'

Daisy shrugs. 'Men,' she says, managing to invest that three-letter word with a wealth of significance and worldly wisdom way beyond its surface meaning. 'They do that kind of thing. It sounds like he wanted to be in a relationship, but when he actually got it, he panicked. It happens.'

'I just wish he'd been honest with me then, instead of giving me all that mystical crap!' I complain. 'I mean, he's in AA, he's supposed to be good at talking about his feelings and being truthful about them . . .'

I make a slurping sound as my straw gathers up the last drops of margarita. Daisy promptly retrieves my glass and goes into the kitchen to refill it. 'I dunno,' she calls. 'Sounds like he loves talking about his feelings, but that doesn't mean he's actually honest with himself about them.'

'Hmm. Maybe.' I reflect on this. 'Oh, and I didn't tell you this completely weird thing he did afterwards! We got in the car, and I thought we were going straight back to London, but he was driving through Whitstable going through these narrow cobbled streets and I didn't remember going that way when we came in. Finally he stops outside this ice cream place and says: "I'll be back in a sec", and pops in, then he comes out with two tubs of ice cream and says: "I really wanted you to try this, it's the best ice cream I've ever eaten and I always used to come here when I was a kid." He hands me one and then says: "Try mine", and he spoons some of his up and fed it to me.'

'*No!*' Daisy comes back into the living room with two full pink glasses, her eyes wide with incredulity. 'He *didn't*!'

I nod smugly, reaching for my margarita.

'He *fed you ice cream*? After telling you he didn't think you were meant to be together?'

I nod again.

'That is so *outrageous*. How dare he turn you down and then start getting all sexy and suggestive with you again!'

'And he really was being sexy and suggestive,' I say, slurping down some more pink margarita. 'His eyes were gleaming and he had this little smile.'

'*God*. He's sending you *such* mixed messages. One minute it's "be my girlfriend, come away for the weekend", then it's "oh no, hang on, this isn't right", and the next it's "let me feed you some ice cream and try to seduce you all over again".'

'Exactly!' I say. Thank God for Daisy. She's restoring my sanity at the speed of light. I'm not mad. *Jake* is mad.

'And that whole "we shouldn't have had sex" bit!' she says, curling up next to me. 'What did he think you were going away for the weekend to do? He's a lunatic!'

'And it was really good,' I say. 'Not Patrick-good, but really good. He was totally into it, as well. It wasn't like I was seducing him and he was putting up a fight. He started it the second time. He was all over me.'

'Fear of commitment,' Daisy says wisely. 'He got too close and he panicked.'

'But that means I've done it again!' I wail. I reach for a pillow – pale pink satin embroidered with roses – and clutch it to my stomach. 'That's two guys in a row who are afraid of commitment! What's wrong with me?'

'Nothing's wrong with you,' Daisy says, rolling her eyes. 'Two men in a row who are afraid of commitment – that's like saying "two men in a row who like football", for God's sake! You just have to kiss a lot of frogs before you find a prince. Anyway, you're way ahead of me. You should be proud of yourself. At least yours actually go out with you. Mine just shag and leave.'

I giggle despite myself. 'It sounds like a shampoo and conditioner in one,' I say. '"No Time For A Serious Commitment? Try new Shag and Leave from L'Oréal Paris!"'

Daisy grins. 'Well, no more,' she says. 'From now on I'm going to be known as Daisy Blue Balls. They'll have to be dropping off with frustration before they get in my knickers.'

We clink glasses. Then I hear a familiar sound, but I'm a

little drunk and it takes me a few seconds to identify it. My phone is ringing. I fish it out of my bag and stare at the display in shock.

'Who is it?' Daisy asks, seeing my expression.

'It's Jake,' I say in disbelief.

'Don't answer!' she yells. She snatches the phone out of my hand as if it were a hand grenade about to go off. I half-expect her to lob it through the open window and shove my head down into the sofa cushions to protect me from the blast. We listen to the ring with bated breath. Finally it stops. Twenty seconds later come the two beeps which tell me that there's an answering machine message waiting.

'You can listen to the message, but you can't ring him back,' Daisy says, handing it to me. 'If I see you dialling his number I'll stage an intervention.'

I press 1 for the answering machine. My hand is trembling, I see in mild surprise. 'You have one new message', the recorded voice tells me. Yes, I bloody know, you moron, hurry up and give it to me! My other hand reaches out and starts fiddling obsessively with the silk fringe of the Chinese shawl Daisy has draped over the back of the sofa.

'Rebecca? It's Jake,' he says, that deep, sexy voice making me shiver, as if it's just for me. 'I miss you. I'm sorry the weekend didn't go that well. I still want to see you. I mean . . .' he pauses '. . . I meant what I said, but I do miss you. We had such a great friendship and I'd hate to lose that, I really would. Ring me when you get this. Please. I'm thinking about you.'

I can't decipher this on my own. I press the star key to replay the message and hand the phone to Daisy. I've never seen anyone having an apoplectic fit, but Daisy looks as I imagine someone in the early stages might seem: purple in the face, eyes bulging in their sockets. She slams the phone down on the table when the message is finished.

'*Bastard*,' she says. 'He's trying to fuck with your mind.'

'Well, he's doing a pretty good job,' I admit.

'Push-me, pull-you. He wants to get you so off-balance you won't know which end is up. I mean, look, if a man doesn't want to be with you any more because he doesn't think you're right for each other, and he tells you that and you get upset, what does he do then?'

'Avoids you like the plague?' I suggest.

'*Exactly*. He doesn't feed you ice cream sexily or ring you up that very evening telling you how much he misses you! This is unbelievable! I bet if you went on seeing him, you'd end up having sex every so often, and you'd think it meant you were back together, and then the next morning you'd wake up all lovey-dovey and he'd tell you it had been a terrible mistake. He wants it both ways. Bugger it, he wants it every way he can possibly have it. He's a narcissistic manipulative *bastard*!'

She jumps to her feet and starts plumping up the cushions on the armchairs, she's so annoyed. She pounds each one against the back of the faded pink chairs as if she's trying to beat the stuffing out of them.

'Daisy!' I yelp as she reaches the expensive vintage white silk one she bought last year at that insanely pricey stall at the indoor market on Church Street. 'It'll rip!'

She looks down at it in shock. 'Thanks,' she says, laying it down and stroking its silver-and-pink embroidery with a finger. 'God, you can tell how angry I am! This cost me an arm and a leg!'

'Yeah, I remember.'

'Narcissistic manipulative *bastard*,' she repeats morosely, coming back to sit down next to me.

I find it hard to completely absorb Daisy's analysis of the situation, even though my brain tells me it's spot-on. One of the reasons I can't quite believe it is that things between me and Jake were so lovely; it's difficult to turn around and, seeing them in hindsight, admit that something must always have been wrong. Also, I'm embarrassed to acknowledge to myself that I was so easily taken in. Jake played me like a . . . well, as

Daisy says, like a fish on a line. And now it's going to take some time to get the hook out of my mouth.

'You know what you were saying before?' Daisy says. 'About Patrick, and the sex with Jake not being as good?'

'Sex with Jake was great,' I say quickly. 'It's just that with Patrick, it was . . . amazing. I'm scared I'll never have sex that good again in my entire life.'

'Oh, you will,' she insists, but I can tell she's not quite sure. She's saying what she needs to, to reassure me, that's all. Daisy, like me, is old enough to know that amazing sex doesn't come along all that often. She looks at me, her blue eyes sad, and drinks some more strawberry margarita while she ponders what to say. Finally she comes up with, 'It might not be the *same*, but it'll be just as good, Rebecca. You'll find someone. And besides, you and Patrick were great, but you had lots of differences. You liked to do different things. Look at that holiday you had in Portugal.'

I stare at her. 'What do you mean?'

'Well, he wanted to go rock climbing and you just wanted to sunbathe.'

'That was fine! I didn't think we needed to be joined at the hip the entire time!'

'Yeah, but it got on your nerves a bit, didn't it?'

'Not really.'

'Oh.' Daisy looks embarrassed.

'What do you mean? Why did you say that?'

'Well, it's just . . . when I saw you and Patrick after you got back . . . you must have gone to the loo or something, but I asked him how it went, and he said it was nice but you'd got a bit sick of each other by the end of it and were glad to come home.'

I can feel the blood draining from my face. I catch my reflection in the silver-framed mirror hanging on the wall opposite – Daisy has pretty little mirrors hung all over the flat – and it confirms this sensation. I have gone as white as Daisy's precious vintage cushion.

'Rebecca, I'm so sorry . . .' she's babbling. 'I didn't think . . . I mean, he said it like it was such an obvious thing that I just assumed you felt that way too . . .' Daisy puts down her glass, horrified at what she's let slip. She pushes her hair back from her face. 'Rebecca? I'm so sorry! I would never have said it if I hadn't just assumed . . .'

'No, it's OK,' I say, but it's hard to talk because my face is frozen and it's an effort to move my lips.

'Oh God . . . I'm so sorry . . . don't hate me . . .'

'No,' I say. 'It's good. It's really good. It's like a wake-up call.'

I think about that week. I make myself think about it honestly. I remember the good times, and the difficult ones. I remember all the moments of awkwardness. Patrick was never a great one for chatting. At first, when Patrick and I were going out, we would talk all night. I could never remember what we'd talked about, afterwards; it wasn't really flirting, more getting to know each other, our lives, our work, our friends. We seemed to have so much in common. It took us a while to start having sex. I wasn't even sure how attracted to him I was; I had just broken up with someone when I met him, someone I thought could be the one, who had dumped me for another woman, and I was feeling gun-shy and insecure.

And yet once we'd started having sex, that took over everything, consumed us, and we were awkward around each other. In a way, that awkwardness never left us. The sex was so extraordinary, so powerful, that it burned up everything in its path and left us gasping; no other connection could ever be as strong as that one, certainly not mere conversation, and it scared him, I think. It became something that linked us so tightly that he pulled away from every other tie but that, whereas I wanted to throw myself into it and never come out. It held us together like a rope around our waists, and Patrick spent the rest of the relationship pulling back from me, afraid of how closely we were bound. And yes, that week in Portugal had not been perfect, as I'd described it to everyone on the postcards I'd sent.

Patrick had already known he was going to New York, and we had had several inconclusive and emotional conversations about his projected absence; what that would mean to us, what we should do. I had kept waiting for him to ask me to go with him, and of course, he never did.

I closed my eyes to the problem, the elephant in the room. I kept telling myself that he loved me and that he would never be able to do without me. That he would never be able to give up what we had between us.

I realise that I'm crying; no sobs, the muscles of my face hardly moving, just the tears welling up and flooding down my cheeks as if my body's expelling a toxin. Daisy doesn't say anything. She just goes to the bathroom, gets me a box of tissues, and puts them down in front of me. Then she turns on the TV to some idiotic game show and makes a fine pretence of being absorbed by it until I eventually muster enough energy to reach out my hand for the tissues and start mopping my cheeks. I'm as tired as if I'd run a marathon. My bones are aching. But oddly enough, I do feel better.

Chapter Twenty-five

DAISY

'I really wanted to ring Lewis and hang up last night, but I didn't. I actually find myself getting an impulse to do things I know are wrong the night before I'm coming to group. It's like I know that I can behave badly and then confess it today and sort of purge the slate. I don't know if anyone else feels like that . . . anyway, instead of ringing him, I made a list of all the reasons we ring people who've dumped us and then hang up when they answer, and I thought I'd read it out.

'Number One: Power. You feel completely powerless, because it's them who's dumped you, and the only way of reasserting a bit of power is by ringing them. You can at least make them answer the phone, and you're the one who decides to hang up. So it's kind of like you're doing a mini-dumping of them. It's pathetic, but it's all you have.

'Number Two: Connection. You miss the connection that you had with them so badly that just hearing their voice and knowing that you and they are sort of in the same place, or at least linked by the telephone line, is a way of recreating that for a few seconds, and pretending to yourself that it still exists.

'Number Three: Maintenance. Every time you ring, you know you could say something, but you don't. You just hang up. And whenever you ring, you feel for one split-second that you might say something, and you get really excited and nervous, you're sort of toying with the possibility that you're finally going to do it, but you never do. I think the reason for this is that you keep putting it off, you keep telling yourself that you might, but you don't, and it's a way of maintaining your addiction by doing the least possible damage until hopefully one day you don't pick up the phone, because you think: well, why would I even ring, because I don't have anything to say to them any more that would make any difference.

'Number Four: Control. You have control over when you ring them, even though it doesn't feel like it, because you always ring them when you break down and are really weak and miss them so much that you can't go for another second without hearing their voice and having some sort of connection to them, literally. See point number two. But even though your need is really intense, you manage not to talk to them, and that makes you feel you have the control back that you lost when you rang them in the first place, if you see what I mean. So it's like a sort of extreme. You jump off the cliff when you ring them, but when you choose not to talk and hang up instead, you realise that you actually have a parachute and you can open it to save yourself. That's not a very good metaphor – and I know, Finn, I'm a journalist, I should do better, lah de da – but that's what it feels like. When you ring them, you're throwing yourself into an abyss, but when you don't say anything, especially things like "I still love you" or "Why don't you love me? Why? Why?" or "I miss you so much, I'd do anything to get you back", you rescue yourself. So that's what it's about for me. You allow yourself to lose control, when the pressure gets too much, and then you prove to yourself that you still have control after all. It's like being about to commit suicide and then rescuing yourself just in time. God, sorry, that sounds really morbid, doesn't it?'

I hardly think about Jake at all any more, apart from screening my calls so that he has to leave messages rather than speak to me directly. He's tried almost every day now. I assume that finally he'll leave me alone, but he shows no sign of slowing down. Daisy was right. He wants to have me on a string, push me away far enough so that I don't get any ideas about a permanent relationship, but have me on call to pull me back when he wants to play at it. Every time I weaken, I remind myself of how he fed me that ice cream seductively, and I stiffen my resolve. The only thing I regret about the whole sorry mess was that I opened my mouth and let him slide that spoon in. I should have knocked his hand away and spattered ice cream all over his nice clothes and the upholstery of his car.

It may seem odd that I can dismiss Jake from my thoughts so quickly, after the intensity of our affair, but the truth is, that with Jake out of the picture, I am back in mourning for Patrick. I find it an oddly comfortable place to be: familiar territory, with nothing to let me down, no hopes that might not be fulfilled. I console myself at night with fantasies of him coming back, but they are strangely hazy now; they don't have the same satisfaction as they once did. I can't imagine Patrick changing that much. I can't imagine his demons being miraculously banished. I used to picture him waiting on my doorstep with armfuls of flowers, but now I keep seeing him with that hangdog look on his face, the one that says he's failed, he's let me down, he can't be the boyfriend I want him to be. I make myself come, and it makes me cry every time, because I remember Patrick doing it.

I tell Davey I've broken up with the guy I've been seeing. I give him the whole story – without, of course, naming Jake – and Davey says all the right things. It doesn't help. I tell Finn, and he just gives me a quick embarrassed hug, and every so often when I come in to work I find chocolate on my desk, always something different: a Cadbury's Snowflake, a praline wrapped in red paper, a chocolate-chip cookie from the coffee shop on the corner. That does help, actually. Because he's thinking about me, because he just leaves them as presents rather than making me have a conversation when he gives them to me, because it's chocolate. I'm surprised by Finn's tact.

Vanessa and Barney are still engaged, but the wedding date has been postponed while they go into couples counselling. Vanessa has stopped ringing Finn. Nobody talks about it in the office, openly, but there's plenty of gossip. The guys would give Barney huge amounts of respect for copping off with a gorgeous blonde – after all, in their eyes, he's entitled to one last fling before settling down – but there's the complication that she was, as far as they know, Finn's girlfriend. It's very messy. Meanwhile poor Vijay and Stewart have completely stopped boasting about their threesome – they're too terrified of seeming like homosexuals after Finn's comment. I am very cross with him for taking away such an innocent source of pleasure for them. But then, if they weren't latent homophobes they wouldn't have minded. Men are ridiculously complicated.

Cable TV is my undoing. On some women's channel, late at night, I find a film about an American woman who goes to Hawaii to sort out her dead mother's inheritance, and falls in love with a young local. He's tall, with dark melting eyes (check), a ponytail (check), and a beautiful body (check), and he takes her to the beach, puts tropical flowers in her hair and asks her to stay with him, but of course she can't, because she has a husband and children and she has to do the right thing. It's pure women's TV schlock, and naturally, it makes me cry. Thank God they never have sex. I cry so hard when they kiss for the first time that I have to put eye gel on afterwards (I keep it in the fridge so it will be cool in this kind of emergency). I thought I was over this by now. But I remember Jake telling me not to worry about relapses, because everyone has them and they slacken off with time, so I tell myself that this is just a momentary slip-back.

I think Jake may have been right after all: he was only a step on the way for me, and not my destination. My rebound guy, not my true love. It's odd that, despite all his bullshit and game-playing, he still managed to put his finger on the truth of the situation; and it's ironic that I resisted his analysis at first, but now seem to have accepted it, while he, with his regular, almost pleading phone calls, is contradicting everything he said. Perhaps he wanted me to plead with him instead, to try to continue the relationship, and is feeling rejected because I haven't.

I want to talk about Jake with the group. I am actually counting the days till Wednesday. For some reason I feel that talking about it will lay his ghost to rest, once and for all, and maybe the group will help me puzzle things out, confirm that it was just a rebound. But I have no idea of the crisis that's waiting for us instead.

The group's at mine this time, and I've been busy buying nibbles from the supermarket and making Pimm's: the weather's so nice it seems the perfect drink. I slice strawberries and apple, marinate them in Pimm's which I've made with lemonade and ginger ale, and set out pretty glasses and a carefully arranged cheese plate with a fresh bread selection. Charlotte's lavish hospitality has raised the bar for all of us. Last week we were at Ben's, and he ordered in pizza for everyone. It was a straight man's idea of gracious entertaining. Daisy and I giggled about it afterwards, but I have to say the pizza was very welcome.

Ben and Finn complain about the Pimm's, of course, but I tell them there's beer in the fridge and they immediately stop whinging. We're all settled on the sofas and the floor, a cosy little group dying to dish, when Ben says: 'Where's Jim?'

We look around, as if confirming his absence.

'I didn't even notice he wasn't here,' Daisy confesses.

'He didn't ring you?' Finn asks me.

I shake my head guiltily as I realise that I too didn't notice Jim's absence.

'He always turns up,' Jennifer says. 'He hasn't missed a session, ever.'

'We shouldn't start without him,' Ben says firmly.

'Should we ring him?' Finn suggests.

'He might think it was nagging,' Daisy says.

'He's a grown man,' Charlotte says shortly. 'He's got all our numbers.'

Charlotte has never had much tolerance for Jim. Like many people born to money and social status, she hasn't got time for those who wear their lack of advantages as obviously as he does. Jim probably makes her feel guilty.

'Maybe he emailed me,' I say, getting up and crossing the room to my computer. But there's no message from Jim, unless he's pretending to be someone called Sal#%880!!! who's offering me prescription Viagra online.

Ben and Finn are now worried. I'm actually pretty touched by this male solidarity; the girls aren't half so concerned. I think we found Jim an uncomfortable presence, sitting there week after week, looking depressed and never saying a word. It wasn't creepy, though – Jim is too much of a saddo to be creepy; he has no latent serial-killer-in-the-making vibe about him. It's precisely because of his sadness that the girls are awkward around him. We think we ought to be doing something – as women, we feel a socially-weighted pressure to cheer him up, which the men don't have, being free of that responsibility. And yet there seems nothing anyone can do to cheer Jim up. So we feel guilty instead, and that makes us dislike him a little. Frankly, I'm glad that Jim isn't here, even though I would never admit it.

But the boys aren't going to leave this alone.

'I'm going to ring him,' Ben says. 'Rebecca, do you have that email with all our numbers on it?'

I print it out for him, and Ben pulls out his mobile and starts dialling.

'Jim?' he says. 'Jim, mate, is that you? It's Ben. We're all here at Rebecca's and we were wondering if something was wrong . . .'

There's a long pause. We all stare at Ben, whose face is twisted up around the phone, as if he's trying hard to hear something distant and distorted.

'Jim?' he says after a while. 'Jim?' And then, urgently, 'Jim, hold on, OK? I'm coming round. Jim? What's the address?' He looks around frantically. I grab some paper and a pen and he scribbles it down. 'OK, just hang on in there – Jim, what's going on? Shit!'

He looks at us. 'I think we got cut off . . .'

He dials the number again and lets it ring. There's no answer. 'We need to get round there,' he says.

'What happened?' Daisy asks with bated breath.

'He was crying really hard – and then I heard all this crashing around . . .'

'What kind of crashing?' Jennifer asks practically.

'Like he was throwing things.'

'*Jim?*' I say incredulously, unable to imagine mild-mannered Jim throwing anything.

'You don't think he's doing anything stupid, do you?' Finn says.

'I don't know,' Ben says tersely, snapping his phone shut, 'but he sounded fucking awful. I'm going round there.'

'We should all go,' says Jennifer, standing up. 'Otherwise we won't have a good meeting anyway, because we'll all be sitting around wondering what's going on and we won't be able to concentrate.'

I stare at Jennifer, impressed. She's clearly one of those quiet people who comes over all decisive in a crisis.

'Where does he live?' Finn asks, standing up too and reaching for his jacket.

'Croydon,' Ben says.

'Ah, fuck,' Finn sighs.

'Wow,' I say, 'this is our first group excursion.'

Daisy giggles. 'To Croydon,' she says. 'How glamorous we are. I mean, couldn't we at least have done a day trip to Calais to stock up on some cheap booze?'

We all go in Charlotte's jeep. The benefits of motherhood and

310

money combined means that she drives an enormous, unnecessary Range Rover that you have to scramble up into as if you were climbing into a tank. But I must admit that it's useful to have a car that can fit four adults in the back without being too squashed – though it's lucky that Daisy and Jennifer are both so slim. The drive is still uncomfortable, however, because Finn insists on helping Ben navigate so he spends the entire time leaning forward between the front seats, squabbling with Ben and gesticulating, which means that he keeps knocking into me and Daisy, who are on each side of him. Poor Charlotte is very patient with Finn and Ben at first but finally she loses it and yells at them as if they were her own errant children. This scares them so much that they settle down and confer in hushed whispers over the *A–Z*. I'm scared of Charlotte too, so I manage not to complain too much about the fact that Finn keeps falling on top of me whenever the Range Rover takes a sharp turn.

We are all so relieved when we finally reach our destination that we spill out of the car like the Keystone Kops, and then realise that we haven't given any thought at all to how we should proceed.

'Should we all go in at once?' Ben asks.

'I think that might be a bit intimidating,' I point out. 'You know, six against one.'

We look at Jim's house. It's small and semi-detached, with a cobble wall bordering the little patch of grass that serves as a front garden, and a few scraggly bushes running along the garden path as a divider from the house next door. The other houses in the street, although identical in construction, have brightly painted doors, or incongruous neo-Georgian fan lights, or lovingly tended gardens. Jim's house stands out for its complete lack of individuality, which, sadly, sums Jim up in a nutshell.

Ben walks up to the front door and rings the bell. The rest of us hang around on the pavement, happy to let Ben be our spokesperson. Jennifer, however, takes a few steps down the path, positioning herself halfway between us and Ben. I've had the feeling for some time now that Jennifer is keen on Ben, and this adds another piece of evidence to my supposition. She's too shy to go up and stand at his side, but she wants to make it clear to him that she's supporting him. In the light from the street lamps, her red hair is like a nimbus around her head, golden-orange, seeming to light up the dusk.

The house was as silent as the grave before Ben rang the bell, but now we can all hear noises from inside. It sounds like a woman, yelling and crashing around. A door slams, and then, through the frosted glass panel in the door, we can see a body emerging into the lit hallway and charging down it towards the front door. It's thrown open so violently that Ben jumps back.

'Who the fuck are you?' the woman screams at him.

With the light behind her, it's hard to make her out clearly. She's small and wiry, like a coiled spring, and her hair straggles around her face. She's wearing tight leggings and a big baggy T-shirt which obscures the top two-thirds of her body. And she's holding something in her hand, something large . . .

'I'm a friend of Jim's,' Ben says bravely. His voice has sunk deeper than usual, probably so that he doesn't sound too nervous of this harridan.

'Oh yeah? So how come I don't know you?'

She's got her face shoved up into Ben's. Despite the fact that she's a foot smaller than him, she's scary. It's her energy. She feels like a bomb just about to detonate.

'Well—' Ben starts, but the woman interrupts.

'And that's *her*!' she screams, looking around him at Jennifer. 'Whore! I know who you are! Slut! Whore!'

She lunges for Jennifer. Ben grabs her shoulders to restrain her, but she breaks free, steps back and whacks him on the head with the object she's been holding in her hand. It's a frying pan. I have never seen someone hit over the head with a frying pan before, apart from in Saturday-morning cartoons. It makes a sound like 'boing', and it looks like it hurts a hell of a lot. Ben staggers back, trips on the front step and falls on to the lawn, while the woman makes a run for Jennifer. She'd be a great sprinter: she shoots off from the step as if it was a set of starting blocks.

She's coming at Jennifer so fast that there's no time for us to do anything. Or maybe there is, but our reflexes are terrible. I am paralysed to the spot in horror, watching this psychotic harpy bearing down on Jennifer, who looks even more tiny and fragile and child-like than usual by contrast. The woman has the frying pan raised to bring it down on Jennifer's head; it's two seconds away from making contact when Jennifer, amazingly, instead of running away, lunges into the woman, grabs her arm, and pulls her hard towards her and past her body in a kind of twisting motion. The woman goes flying into the bushes, the frying pan falling out of her hand with a dull thunk.

Finn has vaulted the wall and is running up to Jennifer. 'Are you all right?' he says.

'Yes, I'm fine,' she gasps, pushing her hair back from her face. 'Let's get into the house, quickly . . .'

She dashes over to Ben and kneels beside him. 'Ben?' she says urgently. 'Ben, are you OK?'

Ben sits up, rubbing his head. 'Ow,' he moans. 'That hurt *so much* . . .'

'Come on, mate,' Finn says, getting his hands under Ben's shoulders and levering him to his feet.

The rest of us tumble through the front gate and make for the house, skirting the fallen woman. There's another Keystone Kop moment as, jostling to be first through the door, we get stuck, but finally we all make it in and slam the front door behind us. Charlotte sensibly bolts it shut and puts the chain on.

'Jim?' Finn yells. 'Jim, where are you?'

We hear something from the back of the house, and make for the sound, bumping into each other in the narrow hallway. Tumbling into the kitchen, we see Jim, sitting at the kitchen table. His head is down, pillowed on his arms, and it sounds like he's crying.

'Jim?' Finn says uncertainly.

Jim raises his head. His face is tear-streaked, and he has the beginnings of a spectacular black eye: red contused streaks radiate out from the eye socket, already beginning to darken into a bruise.

'Oh, *shit*,' Ben says. He slumps into another chair, nursing his head. Jennifer leans over him, making soothing noises and prying his hands away so that she can see the damage.

'Jim,' Charlotte says crisply, 'who was that appalling woman?'

'My wife,' Jim mutters. 'She's not a bad person . . . she just gets really upset sometimes . . .'

'*Upset!*' Ben exclaims, sitting up straighter. 'She could have killed me! She could have killed Jennifer!'

'She came at them with a frying pan,' Finn explains to Jim.

'I thought she was going to . . .' Daisy shivers. 'If you hadn't done that . . .' she turns to Jennifer. 'How did you know to do that?'

'I did a self-defence night course,' Jennifer says proudly. 'It's the first time I've ever had to use something I've learned from it in real life.'

'You were *amazing*,' Ben says respectfully.

Jennifer blushes. 'I got top marks,' she says, ducking her head shyly.

'Jim, mate,' Finn says, drawing up the last chair and sitting next to him, 'your wife is a serious nutcase.' He puts a reassuring hand on Jim's shoulder. 'She ought to be fucking locked up.'

Jim starts crying again. Finn, violently uncomfortable, grimaces at us and then pulls Jim a bit closer, hugging him. Jim's crying so hard his words only emerge as broken fragments, but

I make out: 'Love her . . . doesn't mean it . . .' before there's a terrible banging at the back of the room and we all start like frightened hares.

Jim's wife has made it round the back of the house and is beating on the kitchen door. It seems sturdily made, which is lucky, as, from the way it's rattling, Mrs Jim has got hold of the handle with both hands and is trying to pull the door right out of the frame.

'Whore!' she's screaming. 'Slut! I knew something was going on, Jim Watts, I knew it! You and your Wednesday nights! You've been seeing that cheap whore behind my back!'

The kitchen is brightly lit; too bright for comfort, in fact. It's one of those old-fashioned kitchens with a cheap tiled floor, Formica counters and a fluorescent strip in the centre of the ceiling so that the house-proud wife can make absolutely sure that there isn't a speck of dust or dirt on any of the surfaces. And there isn't. It's scarily clean, like an 'After' picture in a magazine advertisement for New Improved Ajax Liquid. The contrast between this pristine kitchen and the howls of rage and abuse coming through the back door is so startling that I find this whole scene very hard to believe. Trapped in the kitchen with a ravening beast outside trying to break in: it's like being in a horror film. Jim's wife sounds like she's ready to slaughter us all with her bare hands. Well, maybe Jennifer, with her top marks in self-defence, will make it out alive. There's always got to be one pretty young female survivor in a horror film.

'Jim,' Daisy says helplessly, 'what's going on?'

Charlotte tuts at her. 'It's perfectly obvious what's going on,' she says impatiently. 'Jim is a battered husband. I saw a Channel 4 documentary about it last month. We need to call the police.'

'If the neighbours haven't done it already,' I add, raising my voice to be heard above the frenzied screams of 'Whore! Slut! Bastard!' and the crazed banging at the kitchen door.

'They're used to it by now,' Jim mutters. 'They used to call the police, but she'd always tell them it was just a bit of an

315

argument and send them away. They probably won't even come this time.'

Charlotte gets a martial look in her eye. Her accent becomes even crisper and more upper class. 'We'll see about *that*,' she says. 'Where's your phone?'

Jim points mutely to the front of the house; the living room, which we passed coming down the hall. Charlotte strides out of the kitchen purposefully.

'Don't,' Jim says weakly. 'She doesn't mean it – it's my fault for getting her worked up . . .'

'Jim, this isn't your fault!' I say, looking helplessly at Daisy for some back-up.

'No, it isn't,' she says. 'Your wife needs help.'

Jim starts crying yet again. 'I've tried . . .' he says. 'I tried to help . . .'

He tails off in tears, and I suddenly realise that the noise from the back door has stopped. I stare at the door in panic.

'What?' Daisy says, picking up on my nervousness.

I point at the door. 'She's gone,' I say.

Daisy immediately grasps what I mean. 'Jim, is there an open window anywhere?' she asks quickly.

'Oh, *shit*,' Ben says.

And then we hear the shatter of breaking glass very close by.

I jump out of my skin with fear and realise that I am clinging to Daisy. We clutch on to each other as Finn rushes out of the kitchen and a terrible clattering crash issues from what sounds like the room next door. Suddenly I feel a great wash of sympathy for all the pathetic victims in serial-killer films who just scream and wail while the ski-masked psycho advances on them with a meat hook. It seems almost safer to just stand here feebly, burying my head in Daisy's shoulder, than to actually do anything and risk getting slaughtered even faster.

Blood-curdling cries are coming from the next room, together with the sound of more things breaking on to a ceramic surface. I deduce they must be in the downstairs' toilet. The

316

walls are practically shaking. I can hear the unmistakable boing-ing sound that issued from the frying pan when Mrs Jim hit Ben over the head with it, and that makes me pull myself together and stop acting like a useless girlie. Detaching myself from Daisy's grip, I creep cautiously into the hallway.

I was right: it is the downstairs' toilet. Mrs Jim has made her entrance by breaking the window, presumably with the frying pan, and there's shattered glass all over the floor. Finn has got hold of her shoulders and is shaking her so hard that her teeth must be rattling. I have a brief flash of pity for the man trying to subdue a psychotic woman without actually hurting her – if Mrs Jim were male, Finn could just have punched her, but chivalry is clearly insisting that he restrain himself. Which is a mistake. Mrs Jim twists partially free, grabs the air-freshener from the shelf over the sink and sprays him in the face with it.

Finn screams like a stuck pig and grabs his face. Mrs Jim, coughing heavily from the fumes of Forest Fresh, looks around frantically for her frying pan. This is a tactical error; she should just have run straight at me and intimidated me into getting out of her way. But she bends over to pick up the frying pan, which is lying on the floor, and Finn cannons into her, knocking her over and burying her under his larger body. One of her hands shoots out, scrabbling desperately for her weapon, but I have enough courage, now that Finn is lying on top of her, to squash into the room and drag it out, away from her reach. I stand over them, ready to whack her on the head if she starts trying to scratch Finn's already-damaged eyes out of their sockets.

She's screaming like a banshee. Finn is writhing around, trying to grab her wrists while simultaneously making sure that she's pinned down. It's unfortunate that this is the moment when the police are admitted by Charlotte and come storming down the hallway. They grab Finn and pull him off her as if he were the aggressor, which means Mrs Jim is free to jump to her feet and start attacking them with the air freshener. I find myself devoutly hoping that one of them will whack her over the head with their baton. The sight of the police sends Mrs Jim into an even worse frenzy, if such a thing is possible. She's like a berserker. Her hair is wild, her eyes are popping out of their sockets with rage, her face is flushed bright red. It takes three of them to pin her against a wall and even then she's still screaming: 'Whore! Slut! Let go of me, you bastards, I'm going to rip her fucking head off!' until Charlotte appears with a vase of carnations, chucks the flowers on the floor and throws the water all over Mrs Jim's face, spattering a police-woman in the process.

Charlotte is amazing. It has exactly the right effect. Mrs Jim goes silent in shock and then starts sobbing profusely.

'Finn, are you OK?' I say, grabbing at his arm.

'It's like she fucking Maced me,' he says, barely able to open his eyes, which are painfully red and swollen.

'Oh, *Finn* . . .'

'I'll be OK,' he says. 'Jesus. This is the last time I come to the fucking suburbs.' He leans heavily on my shoulder, and I get my arm around his waist to help support him. 'Daisy was right. Next group excursion we're going to Calais to get pissed, OK?'

Chapter Twenty-six

Charlotte had the presence of mind to request an ambulance when she rang the police. I don't know what she said, but you have to be grateful for the absolute self-assurance of the English upper classes when they're on your side in any situation involving authority. She got her ambulance, which meant that there were paramedics on hand to reassure us that Ben wasn't concussed and that Finn wasn't going to lose his eyesight. They wanted to take both of them to hospital, but, being macho, the boys refused. Ben is now sporting a vastly impressive bandage, and Finn is washing out his eyes with a solution they left him. Charlotte found some uncooked pork chops in the fridge and is insisting that Jim hold them in rotation to his black eye. Mrs Jim has been placed under arrest – not before time. The police briefly wanted to arrest Finn too, but Charlotte dealt with that proposition in such blistering tones that they were practically tugging their forelocks as they backed out through the door dragging a weeping Mrs Jim with them. She went to pieces after Charlotte threw the water in her face; she kept calling plaintively for Jim and begging him to forgive her. It took the combined bossiness of all of us to insist that he press charges and not follow her to the police station.

'Top-up?' Daisy asks, but it's not really a question. She pours more cheap whisky into our mugs. We're all drinking sweet milky tea with tots of Bells, which was Charlotte's idea. Protests were made at the idea of not just drinking the whisky straight, but Charlotte insisted we needed sugar for the shock, and I have to admit that she was absolutely right.

Jim emits a sound that's almost like a laugh. We all turn to him, amazed.

'I was just thinking . . .' he says, '. . . we'd always have meetings at everybody else's houses, and I could never invite you back to mine, and, you know, return the hospitality, and I always felt bad about it . . .'

The whisky has lent a little colour to his grey cheeks.

'And now you're here after all. It's not exactly as I imagined it, though. I wanted to do something nice, you know, get some food in, make sandwiches . . . have a nice evening with all of you here . . .'

Daisy starts giggling and we all follow suit. We laugh hysterically, even though it's not that funny; we laugh as if Jim is the funniest stand-up comedian at the Edinburgh Festival and we're a bunch of drunken students. We howl and clutch our sides and roll around. It's the aftermath of the scene we've just endured; we need the release. Finn is clutching his eye sockets.

'It hurts,' he moans. 'It hurts – I'm crying and I can't stop laughing . . .' He dips his head over the bowl of eye-washing solution again and starts frantically flicking more drops into his eyes.

Gradually, we calm down. Even Jim was laughing with us, I'm happy to see.

'She hit me over the head with a *frying pan*,' Ben marvels.

'It made this amazing noise,' I say, still giggling. 'It sounded exactly like they do in cartoons . . .'

'It was *scary*,' Jennifer says, bringing us all down to earth.

Finn wipes his streaming eyes and looks at Jim. 'Yeah, it was. Seriously,' he says, 'you must have been fucking terrified all the time, mate, living with that hell bitch.'

Jim ducks his head unhappily, still holding the pork chop to his eye. 'I was,' he says so softly we can barely hear him.

'So why did you put up with it?'

'I love her,' Jim says feebly.

Please, I think, *please* don't start crying again. But actually,

320

he doesn't. He raises his head and looks at us, and for the first time I see a clarity in his gaze, a hint that Jim might have some backbone.

'I do love her,' he repeats. 'But I had to see her get this bad, hurting other people, before I realised what she was really like.'

Ben humphs.

'I'm so sorry about what she did to you,' Jim says to him quickly. 'And Finn. I'm so sorry. I never meant any of you to get hurt.'

'It's all right, mate,' Finn reassures him magnanimously. 'We came over here off our own bat, it's not like you rang and asked us to come and rescue you.'

Jim puts down the chop and stares at it as if it holds the key to all his problems. Finally he says haltingly, 'I thought I deserved it. I mean, she was always getting at me – the kitchen wasn't clean enough, I'd got back from work a bit late, I had dirt on my shoes again – I thought it was my fault. Sort of, if I could just do everything she said and get it right, there wouldn't be any problems. She could be so sweet. Honestly,' he adds, seeing that we're not convinced. 'She was so sweet when we were courting. I mean, she was a bit demanding, but I liked that. She made me pull my socks up, she took a real interest in me, it was like she was helping me make something of myself, you know? No one ever cared about me like that before.'

He glances over wistfully at the pictures of him and Mrs Jim at their wedding, which are arranged in nasty silver frames all along one of the glass shelves over the living-room sofa. Mrs Jim doesn't look remotely sweet, despite her frilly white dress and the circlet of flowers in her hair; she looks terrifyingly focused, her eyes glinting. She's Bridezilla. I can imagine her beating Jim over the head with her bouquet if he didn't say 'I do' fast enough.

'My mum was always a bit bossy with me,' Jim continues. 'I suppose that's why I liked Maureen. She was so certain of herself. I couldn't believe it when she said she'd marry me. I thought she could do much better for herself. I felt like the luckiest man in the world.'

'So when did all this start?' Jennifer asks.

'After we got married,' Jim says. 'Suddenly nothing was good enough for her. I wasn't pushy enough at work, other people were getting promoted above me . . . I'm just not that ambitious. I liked my job, all the other blokes in the warehouse are nice enough lads, I didn't *want* to be a supervisor. They all hate the supervisors. I just wanted to get on with things as they were. But Maureen kept pushing me, she said I was a bit more educated than them and that I ought to make sure I got what I deserved, she said I was weak and a failure, and then she started throwing things around a bit, and she'd push me, give me a bit of a shove or a slap now and then, and I don't know how it happened, really, it just got worse and worse . . .'

'Chop,' Charlotte says briskly.

Jim obediently raises one of the pork chops to his eye again. I must say, he's very easy to bully. Maureen found herself the perfect victim.

'You've never had a black eye or anything before,' Jennifer observes.

'She was always careful,' Jim mutters. 'Never where it would show. But today she went off her trolley. I told her I was doing a night class, you see, in computer skills, to explain where I was of a Wednesday night. But then today she bumped into someone at the supermarket whose wife's doing the course too, and he said he didn't know I was on it because she'd never mentioned it. So Maureen came home and rang her up and when I got back from work – I always come home before the group meeting, to change out of my overalls, you see, make a better impression – she was waiting. She hit me round the face with the frying pan before I could get a word out. She thought I had someone on the side.'

'Yeah, I sort of picked that up,' Ben says ironically. 'It was lucky Jennifer could handle herself.'

Jennifer beams.

'I'm so sorry . . .' Jim says again, overwhelmed by guilt.

'All's well that ends well,' Charlotte says firmly. 'And now the next thing we need to do is get Jim into a support programme. I'll ring round the local councils and see if there's anything in your area, Jim.'

Jim is panic-stricken. 'What do you mean?' he asks, dropping the chop back on to the plate.

'Well, for battered husbands, of course! There must be *some* sort of group. No point asking the feminists, of course, they think men can't be victims, but I'm sure I can find you *something*.'

God, Charlotte loves a challenge. Her eyes are gleaming with enjoyment at the prospect of rolling up her sleeves and sorting poor Jim's life out.

'But I want . . .' Jim's practically stammering '. . . does this mean I can't come back to the group?' He stares around at us piteously. 'I'm so sorry for what happened . . . *please* don't say I can't come back . . .'

'But Jim,' Daisy says gently, 'we didn't think you'd want to. I mean, your situation doesn't exactly fit in with the group . . .' Daisy tails off before she can point out that none of us can understand what Jim was doing in a group like Exes Anonymous in the first place.

'Yes, it does!' Jim insists. 'It did! Or, it will! I mean . . .' He gathers his breath. 'I came in the first place because I left Maureen. It was getting really bad, and I went back to stay with my mum.'

Finn winces and shifts in his chair. I know it's not the pain of his eye. I exchange an uncomfortable look with Daisy. Poor Jim, with nowhere to take refuge but his mother's house. That must have been out of the frying pan (a bit of a tactless simile, I know) and into the fire.

'But I really missed her, and Mum wasn't being any help. I kept thinking about her, and she was ringing me up all the time, so when I saw the ad in *Time Out*, I thought it might help me. Only after the first meeting, I went back home to Maureen, but I really liked everyone in the group, you were all so friendly, and it did help, it really did, just to have everyone being so kind and honest . . .' He looks at Ben and Finn. 'And seeing blokes being able to talk about their feelings, it was brilliant. I could never do that with the lads at work. I might as well cut my balls off in front of them. I thought that one day I might get up the courage to talk about Maureen . . . because Finn and Ben were being so brave, opening up about being unhappy . . . I really admired you . . .'

Ben and Finn are puffing up their chests and looking unbearably smug. This is the new macho, I suppose – men complimenting each other on being brave for sharing.

'And now,' Jim continues, 'I'm going to have to sort things out with Maureen properly, aren't I? I mean, we can't go on like this.'

He does a sort of mini-chest-puff-up, like the boys. Jim is finding some courage finally, bless him.

'We're going to have to be apart for a while at least . . .' he says, '. . . unless,' he adds hopefully, 'we can sort something out . . .'

'Maureen needs counselling too,' Jennifer says firmly. 'A lot of it.'

Horse tranquillisers might not be a bad idea either, I think.

'Will she go to prison?' Jim asks.

'I bloody hope so,' Finn mutters to me.

'Well, apart from everything she did to us, she assaulted the police officers,' Daisy says. 'They don't like that much.'

'We'd have to press charges, I think,' Ben says.

'Maybe we can work something out so she gets counselling instead,' Charlotte says. 'Anger management. And a suspended sentence. I'll ask Daddy.'

I remember that Daddy is a judge. Charlotte really is a very useful person to know.

'Maureen has to move out,' Jennifer says. 'You should change the locks.'

Jim looks scared, but we reassure him.

'And I can still come to meetings?' he says anxiously. 'Even if I do the other stuff as well? I mean, it'll be real this time! Because I will be apart from Maureen, and I'll need to talk about that. Please?'

'Of course you can still come to meetings,' Ben says. 'We can't afford to lose a bloke, can we, Finn? We need all the testosterone we can get!'

Finn nods. And Jim beams from ear to ear. Despite his atrocious black eye, and the drama that has just been played out, he looks the happiest I've ever seen him. It's enough to warm the cockles of your heart – whatever those are.

I don't get home till midnight. We finished Jim's whisky and started on the cooking sherry, but I don't feel that drunk, doubtless from all the excitement. I'm buoyed up by it and feeling brave, brave enough to do something I should have done a long time ago.

I dial Patrick's number. It's seven in the evening in New York, a perfect time to catch him. And I do. It's like a little miracle: God knew I needed to talk to Patrick right now, and he (or she) made it happen for me.

'Patrick?' I say, my heart pounding at his familiar voice. 'It's me – Rebecca.'

I'm so used to ringing him that I say 'It's me' automatically. But then I catch myself and add my name. For all I know, there may be another woman who rings him and just says, 'It's me' by now. I don't want a horrible misunderstanding.

'Rebecca?' He sounds shell-shocked. 'My God.' There's a long pause, and I wonder desperately if I'm the last person he wants to talk to. 'How are you?' he says at last.

'I'm good,' I say. 'Really busy.'

'That's great.'

'How are you?'

Patrick pauses. 'OK,' he says finally. 'Work's keeping me busy, I'm running seriously – I did a half-marathon two weeks ago . . .'

'Great,' I say.

There's another long pause.

'And what about you?' he asks.

'Oh, great. Work's good, I'm going out a lot . . .'

'Great.'

All we seem able to say to each other is 'Great'. I knew this wouldn't be an easy conversation, and not only because of the particular circumstances. I'm tongue-tied, and Patrick wasn't much good on the phone. He's one of those men who uses it for information exchange, not for cosiness; no little details of his life, no 'what I had for dinner', or 'this funny thing happened at work the other day'. We used to talk about films a lot. Normally, if I wanted to get Patrick relaxed and chatting on the phone, I'd ask him about the latest Jet Li or Rock vehicle and I would hear his voice become immediately more communicative, more fluent, as he went into his comfort zone and started laying out his theories on how and why the plot had been set up in a certain way. But now I don't want to have recourse to that, and nor does he: he isn't asking me about my friends, or parties I've been to, the subjects he knows will relax me as his films will do for him. We're naked with each other without our familiar topics to hide behind.

'I was wondering how you're doing,' I say eventually.

Patrick sounds a little cold, as he always does when he's surprised.

'I just said—'

'No, I mean about us,' I say, rolling my eyes; how can he not know what I mean? 'Since, you know, not being together . . .'

Patrick's voice goes so quiet I have to strain to make out the

326

words. 'Sad,' he says. 'Some days I'm just sad, some days I'm really sad.'

It helps. I take a deep breath. 'Me too,' I say. 'But I know it's over. I know you're not going to change your mind.'

Patrick doesn't say anything. I listen to the silence; I wait, but nothing happens. I wait for the miracle I know won't come. And when it doesn't come, I take a deep breath, and let the knowledge sink in.

Finally, I go on, 'That's what I was ringing to say. I've been really sad too. But I know I can't – I mean, I know it's over. I don't know why I had to ring you to say this. It should have been enough to say it to myself, but somehow I had to say it to you as well.'

A long pause.

'OK,' he says finally. It's the 'OK' Patrick uses when he doesn't know what to say, or doesn't understand but is too proud to ask for clarification.

I'm dying to ask him if he's seeing anyone, but I know I mustn't.

'So that's it,' I say.

God, I hate these long pauses when we just sit there with the phones to our ears and hear the rustle of the transatlantic line and, occasionally, the faint sound of the other person breathing.

'I'm going to go now,' I say.

'Rebecca,' he says, his voice slow and painful, as if the words are being dragged out of him with pincers, one by one. 'Be happy. Keep smiling. It's how I always think of you, happy and smiling.'

'Do my best,' I say.

I have to hang up now before I start crying.

'Bye, Patrick.'

'Bye,' he says so quietly I can hardly hear him.

I hang up.

I take long breaths, each one slow and deep, as if I'm

reminding my body how to breathe: inhale, exhale, feeling the air flood deep inside me and flow out through my nose again, warm and soft. I won't cry. I won't. I've cried enough.

I didn't really think that Patrick would break down and beg me to come back to him; I knew he wouldn't. Maybe that's why I rang him, just to confirm to myself that it wouldn't happen. And it hasn't. It's over. Patrick is the past. I close my eyes and create a little figure of him in my mind, pushing it back, making it recede down the dark corridors, like playing that scene from *Spellbound* in reverse; the doors slam shut, the clouds disappear, Ingrid Bergman and Gregory Peck step away from each other for ever. Over. Gone. Finished.

While I still have my courage up, I press the PLAY button on my answering machine and scroll back to the first message of Patrick's. I listen to him say: 'Hi, darling!' and I delete it. Then the next one, and the next. I pause for a moment over what was number five, and is now number one: the first message he left me after that last disastrous visit to New York, where we cried over each other for two weeks, when we knew that we were breaking up and weren't yet strong enough to admit it. His voice sounds like it did just now. Defeated, weary, sad. He says he's sorry. He said he was sorry in every single message, though: sorry for not ringing sooner, sorry his answering machine was on when I tried to ring him, sorry he's been working so hard and ran too late, because of the time difference, to ring me before I went to sleep. Sorry, sorry, sorry. I delete them all. No more apologies. And when I've done it, I feel free. Lonely, but free.

Before I lose my nerve, I put the Bobby Thunder tape into the video and simultaneously press the PLAY and DELETE buttons. Over, cancelled, gone. And though I feel more sad than I can express for what I've lost, I don't regret anything. Not the phone call, not the deletion of my last recordings of both Patrick's voice and his doppelgänger's image. I've cleared the decks.

And I realise why I don't miss Jake; because being with Jake wasn't enough to make me get rid of those last powerful traces of Patrick. I had to do that on my own.

Why does every piece of knowledge, every step towards wisdom and maturity, have to be so painfully hard-won? Just for once, can't I learn something without having to suffer so badly for it? I'd much rather be ignorant and blindly hopeful, still fantasising about Patrick, than have my eyes open, see the situation as it really is, and know that I'm alone – worse, that I *had* to be alone to get over Patrick. I think wistfully of my teenage years, when I ran round falling in love every twenty minutes, living in a spin of emotion without ever being aware of what was really going on in my mind. God, it's hard being grown-up. I hate it. I bloody hate it.

Chapter Twenty-seven

Davey is beaming. I haven't seen him look so happy for years. He almost bounces as he walks by my desk.

'Good morning!' he carols.

'Wow,' I say. 'Someone took extra happy pills today.'

'It's sunny! We got two new clients last week! And, um, it's sunny!' And Davey drifts off, his smile so large it seems to linger in the air behind him like the Cheshire Cat's.

Something is definitely up. I look over my computer and meet Finn's eyes. He's pantomiming wildly.

'What?' I mouth.

Finn looks over at Davey, who's safely across the office by the coffee machine, and decides that the coast is clear enough. He gestures to me and we rendezvous behind the table football.

'What *is* it?' I ask, bursting with curiosity.

'He just got a phone call,' Finn mutters. 'He's been walking on air ever since.'

'What?' I have to restrain myself from grabbing Finn's ears and twisting them to make him spill the gossip; he's clearly stretching this out, making me wait for it.

Finn grins. 'Well, it was from a lady,' he starts. 'Someone he's had his eye on for a very long time . . .'

'And?'

'She asked him out.'

'Wow! How do you know?'

Finn looks at me pityingly. 'I may be a man, but I'm not a moron, you know. They were talking about films they wanted to see, and then he said in this fake-casual voice, like it didn't matter to him one way or the other, "Shall we get a bite to eat afterwards?" and she obviously said yes, because he started wobbling his head the way he does when he gets excited. And he had this huge smile that he was trying to squash down so she wouldn't hear it in his voice and get panicked because he was too keen.'

'Wow!' I say again.

'Yup.'

There's still something Finn isn't telling me. I fix him with a piercing stare. 'You know who it was, don't you?'

Finn looks smug. 'I might have caught a name at the beginning of the conversation . . .'

'Daisy,' I say immediately.

To my delight, Finn's face crumples. 'No! How did you guess? I was saving that for last!'

'I worked out how keen he was on her that weekend at your parents' house.'

'Hah!' Finn crows, recovering somewhat. 'You're so slow! I've known that for the last six months!'

'*Really?*' I'm impressed.

'God,' Finn says, 'you girls really do think you're the only ones with any sensitivity and perception whatsoever, don't you? It's so fucking arrogant! You think men are just a bunch of grunting cavemen!'

'I wish,' I say naughtily. 'I'm sick of wimpy New Men just staring at their own navels and going on about their difficult childhoods – oh yeah, and being crap at table football.'

'Right,' Finn says, 'that's it. Best of three, and if I win I get to club you over the head and drag you back to my cave by your hair.'

He's such a dreamer. He knows I always cream him. I am so keen to ring Daisy that I don't spin it out and tantalise Finn with the hope that he might win; I beat him quickly and ruthlessly, leaving him a broken, bloody, humiliated, whimpering mess being taunted by Vijay and Stewart for losing at table football yet again to a girl. They deserve some revenge for his comments about their threesome with Baby. Then I rush to the phone.

'Hey!' I say. 'I hear you asked Davey out!'

'What? How do you know?' Daisy says crossly.

'Office grapevine, sweetie. So, is it true? Spill!'

'Bloody *hell*, can't I *ever* do *anything* without *everyone* knowing about it in two seconds flat?' she complains.

'No. Stupid question. Go on! I'm so excited!'

Daisy sighs. 'It's not a big deal. I just thought I'd like to see Davey – I haven't seen him on his own for ages.'

'Liar, liar, pants on fire . . .'

'I like him,' Daisy says coldly, 'and I'm doing this thing about only going out with nice men, so I thought I'd ring Davey. That's it.'

'So do you fancy him?'

'Tell me that he's not listening into this on some weird three-way conversation . . .'

'No, I promise, he's just popped out of the office for a meeting, he can't hear what I'm saying.'

'And no one else can hear either? I don't want Finn knowing. He'll tell Davey everything, you know what men are like.'

'Promise,' I say, deciding to keep secret the fact that Finn was the one who told me about the Daisy/Davey hook-up.

'Well, I didn't really think about Davey like that,' Daisy says. 'He's just such a good friend, you don't really think about shagging a friend, and he's so understanding and sweet, I wouldn't want to do anything unless I was sure, because it might really hurt him. But I always knew he liked me . . .'

God, I'm so stupid. Everyone knew that Davey fancied Daisy but me. Clearly I was so obsessed by Patrick that I've been wandering around in blinkers for the last year.

'. . . and then when we went down to the country for that engagement party and I saw him in his swimsuit, I had this flash: God, Davey's got a great body! It really surprised me,

332

you know? I started thinking about him as a man, not just a friend. I'd never thought about Davey like that before. But there's something about seeing someone nearly naked and going "Phwoar" to yourself – it sort of puts them in a different light . . .'

'I *know*,' I say. 'I was pretty impressed myself. He's almost got a six-pack.'

'I *know*.'

'God, we're shallow.'

'No, we're honest. Anyway, obviously I didn't do anything about it that weekend, because I was still being self-destructive and going for men who weren't available . . .'

The one downside of the group is that it does have us all talking in therapy-speak as we glibly analyse our emotions.

'. . . but afterwards, I kept thinking about Davey, and I thought, "Well, why not? We could just go out for a drink –" God, of course we can't go for a drink, what am I saying, bloody hell, how do you manage to get off with someone when you're totally sober? Wasn't it really difficult with Jake?'

'Nope,' I say, 'because I wasn't totally sober. So it was OK for me. But I did drink less when I was out with him because I didn't want him thinking I was a raving alkie.'

'Oh dear, I'm not sure I can do that – oh dear – especially because the whole thing's going to make me so nervous . . .'

'Don't start worrying about it now,' I say sensibly, 'you haven't even had a single date with him yet.'

'OK, one thing at a time. Anyway, I don't know what will happen, but Davey always makes me feel so *safe*, and if I'm going to try to go out with nice men, I couldn't get a nicer man than Davey . . . and he does have that nearly-six-pack . . . It's funny, I never really saw Davey as sexual before, you know? And now I keep thinking about him in his swimming trunks and getting all stirred up.'

'Oooh! You fancy him!'

'Of course I fancy him,' Daisy says crossly, 'otherwise I

wouldn't have asked him out. It would have been too unfair, especially because I know he likes me.'

'I just thought you might be going out with him because you were making yourself do it,' I confess. 'You know, telling yourself that you needed to find a nice bloke, looking around, thinking "Who's the nicest bloke I know?", which is obviously Davey, and deciding you were going to do it more, sort of, intellectually, not actually because you really wanted to . . .'

'Oh no,' Daisy says firmly. 'I'd never do that. I need to feel the thing.'

'And you feel the thing with Davey?'

Daisy giggles. 'I'm very curious to feel his thing, if that's what you mean.'

'That's brilliant!' I say with great relief. 'Only—'

'I *know*. I'm going to wait for *ages*. And it might not even get that far. I mean, we might not click.'

Fat chance, I think. They both fancy each other; they know they're compatible . . . I have to wrest my mind away from images of a lovely white wedding with Daisy and Davey beaming at each other all the way back down the aisle and everyone in floods of tears. Davey's a bit shorter than Daisy, but luckily he's the kind of man who won't mind having a bride who's taller than he is. Especially since she's a gorgeous skinny blonde who will look spectacular in the kind of white satin frock that would make me as squat and stubby as one of those columns they stand statues on.

'Had a good gossip?' Finn says, coming over to my desk.

'I don't know what you mean,' I say demurely. 'I would never have a gossip on office time. Boss.'

'Of course not,' Finn says, sitting on the corner of my desk. 'Accept my apologies.'

'Come to get your arse kicked again?' I say.

'No, no,' he says hurriedly. 'Once was quite enough for today. No, I was wondering something . . .' He produces a leaflet from his trouser pocket. 'They're putting on this new class at my gym, and I need a partner for it. I couldn't think of anyone else, and I know you do yoga, so I thought you might be into it . . .'

'"Urban rebound"?' I say, looking where he's pointing. 'What's that?'

'You jump up and down on mini trampolines for an hour. It's for girls.' He leers. 'We all watch through the glass. It's brilliant.'

'I can just imagine,' I say dryly. 'There's not a sports bra made that'll hold a girl in enough to stop her tits bouncing on a trampoline.'

'I know,' Finn says dreamily. 'It's like free porn. Anyway, that's not what I meant.' He puts his finger on the class next to it.

'"Balancing",' I read. '"Saturday 2pm".'

'It's this circus skills class they're starting up this weekend,' Finn explains. 'You balance on each other. A guy came to talk to us about it and I thought it sounded wicked.'

I look at Finn. Five foot ten of solid muscle. 'I'm not bloody letting you balance on me,' I say firmly. 'Are you out of your mind?'

'No, *you* balance on *me*,' Finn says. 'I asked the instructor and he said we need a partner, obviously, because you'd look a bit of a twat trying to balance on yourself, and he said that it would be better if I got someone of my own build, but if I couldn't I could bring you along. It might be fun because apparently there's lots of stuff we can do which works when one person weighs much less than the other.'

'Why can't you find someone your own build?'

'*Right*,' Finn says. 'I'll just go up to some strange bloke in the changing room and ask him if he wants to balance on my legs. Nothing strange about that, is there? Normal heterosexual men ask each other that sort of question all the time.'

'I take your point,' I admit. 'Your slightly homophobic point.'

'So, will you come?' Finn asks eagerly.

'God, you're keen on this!'

'You must be joking! I've wanted to do circus stuff ever since I saw Burt Lancaster in *Trapeze*! He used to be a catcher in a circus, you know!'

'Really?'

'Yeah, those were the real action heroes – Burt Lancaster and Robert Mitchum. Mitchum used to box, he could take out anyone in a bar fight . . .'

Finn goes all dreamy. I'm always amused by straight guys who are so scared of being gay that they won't let another man balance on them, and yet idolise macho heroes in a way that would definitely be called a girl-crush if it were me swooning over Brigitte Nielsen in *Red Sonja*. A film which, by the way, I adore.

'OK,' I say.

'Great! Saturday afternoon it is! And wear tracksuit bottoms, OK? And a long-sleeved T-shirt. The teacher said to tell you. Apparently my hands could slip if you've got bare legs and body lotion on.'

'*O-kay*,' I say. Finn is clearly taking all this very seriously. In any other circumstances he'd be telling me I need to wear a bikini and oil myself up thoroughly – preferably while he's watching.

'Finn, you've got to push me more! I'm falling over!' My voice comes out squashed, because I'm upside down, so I'm practically shouting so he can hear me.

'I'm trying . . .'

'No, you're not, you can push harder than that . . . *Ooof* . . .' I tip backwards and land on my feet, very frustrated.

'I *told* you!' I say, standing over him with my hands on my hips. 'I can't balance unless you push back!'

'I'm frightened of pushing you too hard,' Finn says, looking up at me. He's sitting in front of me with his legs stretched out, an embarrassed expression on his face.

'It doesn't *matter* if you push too hard, what matters is if you don't push me hard *enough*, because then I land on top of you and break your nose and my back . . .'

'What's happening here?' says the instructor, coming over.

'He's not pushing me hard enough . . .'

'She's whinging as usual . . .'

'Right,' the instructor says, looking a little appalled at our spat, 'let's try it again and we'll see what's going wrong, shall we?'

Shooting a malevolent glance at Finn, I bend over, put my hands on his ankles and kick up into a handstand. Yoga classes have made me very confident with being upside down; Finn was quite right to ask me to be his partner. Around the gym I can see pairs of people having trouble even getting up into a handstand, which is why Finn's incompetence is annoying me so much. If he'd just do his part of the job properly, we could be the best balancing act and show off mightily to everyone else. My favourite part of yoga is when the teacher – very occasionally – asks me to come to the front so that I can demonstrate the position for the class. I was looking forward to me and Finn being the stars of this one. I know I'm shallow and vain, but after all, everyone likes to show off, don't they?

Or maybe they don't. Maybe it's just me.

Finn's hands are in the small of my back, holding me up, or rather, giving me a solid wall to balance against. He's doing a better job now, because the instructor's watching. The instructor grabs my feet, pulling them higher.

'Stretch up a bit more – that's great – Finn, your hands need to be a little lower to give her stability and stop her back arching . . .'

Finn shifts his hands down to the top of my buttocks.

'Good. Now your job is to hold her there, give her something to press against. You're going to have to judge how hard you push, but if in doubt, push harder, because that way if she falls she goes back on to her feet again and not on top of you . . .'

'I *told* you,' I mutter.

'I *told* you,' Finn mimics my voice back crossly.

'Great!' the instructor says, letting go of my feet. 'Lovely hollow back! Everyone, have a look at this . . .'

From my upside-down position I see the class gathering round to envy us. I am filled with evil pride. I hold myself up as long as I possibly can and when I finally kick down, I feel horribly smug. Finn is grinning too.

'Are your ankles sore?' I ask, looking down at the red marks around the bone.

'Nah, I could hardly feel you,' he lies.

'Can I use you two to demonstrate the next one?' the instructor asks.

'Sure,' I say happily.

'Now, you'll probably all have done this when you were small, but with an adult,' he says. 'So you'll find it harder going now.'

He makes me stand in front of Finn and put Finn's feet against my inner thighs. I realise immediately what we're about to do, and grab Finn's feet, wedging them firmly into my groin, slightly turned out. Mercifully, for a man, his feet are fairly clean and don't smell. I'm more grateful than I can say. Weirdly enough, while I'm not embarrassed by this at all – again, I've had plenty of yoga classes doing partner work – Finn is blushing madly. He holds up his hands to me, as per instructions, and I take them, winding my fingers through his, then push up as Finn begins to straighten his legs and I lift off the ground until I'm lying above him, balanced on the soles of his feet and the palms of his hands, parallel to his body.

'You probably called this "flying" when you were little,' the instructor says, 'but we call it "the angel" . . . Do you feel stable enough to let go of his hands?'

Gingerly, Finn and I begin to untwist our fingers from each other's, until our hands are flat, mine pressing down into his.

His face below me is full of concentration, his feet wobbling slightly as he works on maintaining the balance. Then I lift my hands from his slightly, feeling for my equilibrium.

'Now stretch them out to the side . . .' the instructor says.

My arms are already opened wider than my body, but cautiously I stretch them out still further until I'm spreadeagled in the air, held up only by Finn's feet at my groin. For a few blissful seconds I hover there, my face splitting into a grin, seeing Finn, below me, grinning too in triumph. Then we start to wobble more and Finn, realising he can't hold the balance, gives me a shove backwards with his feet so that I tumble backwards and land upright rather than falling forwards on top of him.

'Nice!' the instructor says. 'Who wants to try that?'

The class bubble excitedly as they go back to their mats to copy us.

'Let's do it again!' Finn says eagerly, stretching out his feet to me. 'We fucking *rock*!'

By the end of the class I have stood on Finn's shoulders – I keep apologising for how much I weigh, but he tells me not to be silly – and, for the grand finale, we all made a line, the stronger ones linking their arms together and bracing their legs while the lighter ones clambered up on to their bent thighs to stand there and balance, touching fingertips with the people balancing on either side of them. It's probably all very basic stuff, but we love it. After class the instructor is inundated with people asking about other circus skills lessons they can take. Finn and I are beaming with success. We sign up for next Saturday straight away.

'That was so much fun!' Finn says as we walk out.

'Thanks so much for asking me,' I say.

'Are you joking? You were brilliant! We were the best pair! He got us to demonstrate twice!'

'I *know*,' I say smugly. 'I love it when that happens.'

'Me too.'

Finn high-fives me. Our palms smack satisfyingly against each other.

'Only maybe you might want to ask one of the guys if you can do it with them sometimes,' I say.

'Why?' He stares at me, running his fingers through his slightly sweaty hair.

It's such a warm day that we didn't even need to bring a tracksuit top to put on over our workout clothes; we just walked out of the gym in T-shirts and tracksuit bottoms. Finn's blue T-shirt, dampened with sweat, is clinging to his pecs, which are as round and firm as gently cupped hands. He must do a lot of weight work. I avert my eyes so he doesn't catch me staring. It's not just men gawping at women's chests nowadays. We're an equal-opportunity letch society.

Then I realise that I'm letching at Finn, and get embarrassed. I've never seen Finn this way; he's always been a sort of annoying brother-figure to me. I remember my conversation with Daisy last week, about seeing men in a different light when you take in how good their bodies are, and blush.

'Rebecca?' he says when I don't answer immediately.

'Oh, yeah,' I say, dragging my thoughts back to the subject under discussion. 'I just thought you might want, you know, to, do some of the balancing yourself for a change – not be on the bottom all the time . . .'

'Nah,' he says. 'I like being the strongman. It makes me feel all manly. Besides, it's not sex, you know.'

Now I really am blushing.

'What're you up to now?' he asks.

'I dunno,' I say. 'I was going home to shower.'

'Want to come back to mine for a sports drink first? We could sit in the garden.'

'I'm a bit sweaty . . .' I demur, plucking at my T-shirt.

'Oh, come on. You're not that bad.'

'I feel all gunky . . .'

'You're fine. Look, come on. I'm on a high after that class

340

and I don't want to come down yet.' He winks at me. 'I've got this new sports drink from the health-food shop – it's full of electrolytes . . .'

'Oh well,' I say, 'if it's got electrolytes I can't resist . . .'

'Thought you'd go for that,' Finn says cheerfully. 'All the ladies love electrolytes.'

Finn's flat is in the centre of Notting Hill, the ground floor of a terraced house, with what for London is an enormous garden. I know the firm is doing well, but this was clearly bought with an injection of family money too. When we came round before, for the group meeting, it was the evening, and though you could see some of the garden out of the living-room window, I had no idea how big and beautiful it was. I go outside and gawk at its splendour. Finn emerges a few minutes later with two large glasses brimming with a lemon drink which, despite my reservations, I have to admit is delicious.

'It replenishes all the potassium and sodium you lose when you sweat,' Finn explains.

'And, more importantly, it tastes like lemonade,' I say.

'There's more if you want it. I've got loads.'

I sip my drink and look round the garden. At a second glance, I can see that it's overgrown, but it's still amazing. 'This is gorgeous, Finn,' I say, gesturing at it.

'Vanessa was always on at me to mow the lawn and do some pruning,' he says.

'Well, she had a point.'

He pulls a face. 'Not you too . . .'

'Oh, come on, that lawn's practically two feet high.'

'All the better for falling over on!' he says, standing up, taking my glass from me and depositing it on the worn old wrought-iron table.

'What?'

He grabs my hand and pulls me to my feet. 'Come on, let's practise that handstand one again . . .'

He stands there, beaming at me, the sunlight turning his dirty-blond hair to gold, and I realise, with a slow, steady certainty, how attracted I am to Finn. Oh God. I am very glad I wore my tight pink T-shirt with 'New Orleans Hurricanes' printed on the front; it makes my tits look high and firm and it dips low enough at the hem in front to cover the slight bulge of my tummy. My bum must look huge in my tracksuit bottoms, though.

I'm overwhelmed with confusion. Now that I know how much I fancy Finn, I'm embarrassed and awkward about having so much physical contact with him. I find myself pulling my hand away, raising it instead to shade my eyes from the sun, and we stand there for a moment in a limbo state, knowing that things have changed, but not how to deal with them.

'Rebecca . . .' Finn says.

His voice has altered; he's not pretending that nothing has happened. I don't know if I'm grateful for this or not.

I can't say anything.

'Look, let's sit down.'

He goes over to the small square of lawn and plonks himself down. After a moment, I follow suit, lying down on my tummy as if to protect my vulnerable organs. He's right. It's much easier to be lying on the grass for this than sitting upright in those little iron chairs.

'I know we work together . . .' Finn starts.

'I work for you,' I correct him. My voice has gone small and pathetic. I hate it.

'. . . and we're friends, and we're in group together, and you just broke up with that bloke, and I'm still sorting out the whole Vanessa thing . . .'

I can't look at him. I stare at the blades of grass just under my face as attentively as if I were a metaphysical poet believing God was in every blade, and start picking at them convulsively. Finn's braver than me; he keeps going despite my obsessive-compulsive behaviour.

'But I must admit that I did ask you to come to the class with me because . . . uh, well it wasn't just because I knew you'd be good at it. I wanted to see you outside work and the group and I couldn't think of another way to do it. And when you held my hands in that angel balance . . .'

'I know,' I say, my voice muffled. 'I felt it too.'

'So, I mean, obviously, we could take it slow – I know we're both still getting over other people . . .'

I nod vigorously.

'But I feel really comfortable with you, I really like you . . .'

I summon the courage to lift my head and look at him. The T-shirt makes his eyes look very blue. And it's straining over his chest because of the way he's sitting, turned towards me, and suddenly I long to see what he looks like without it. I know, of course, I've seen him in his swimming trunks, but I want to see it again, now. I clasp my hands tightly so I don't grab him and start pulling it off.

'And, um, if I'm being totally honest, I really liked having your bum practically in my face when you were doing that handstand . . .'

I start giggling. It's a nervous giggle, but at least I'm laughing.

'That's why I wasn't doing such a good job of balancing you, I was terrified I was going to start feeling you up and get over-excited . . .'

I'm giggling harder now.

'And I don't want to be your rebound guy – maybe I should have waited a bit . . .'

I reach out and take his hand, awkwardly, because I'm still lying down. I turn a bit on my side, and we stay there for a while, our fingers lacing through each other's.

'I've had my rebound guy already,' I say. 'You don't have to worry about that.'

Finn clears his throat loudly to cover his relief.

'But,' I continue, 'you haven't had your rebound girl yet.'

'I don't need one!' Finn protests. 'In a way, Vanessa *was* my

343

rebound girl! Because of getting off with her that night! I'm over her, I really am!'

'You can't be over her that quickly.'

'Well, you probably still have thoughts about that guy you were seeing,' he points out, 'but that doesn't mean you're not over him.'

This is true.

'We could take things slowly,' he repeats.

'Yeah,' I say. 'That would be, um, best. I think. Particularly because of the work situation.'

There's a long pause as we think about taking things slowly.

'Can I kiss you?' Finn asks shyly. 'Just a kiss, honest, I won't push you or anything till you're ready . . .'

My heart is pounding so hard I can barely hear myself say over the noise it's making, 'OK – no, wait, wait – we have to have ground rules.'

'Bossy cow,' he says, stroking my fingers. 'What kind of ground rules?'

'First, we have to live in the moment. No talking about the future for a while.'

'Wow, I've waited all my life for a woman to say that to me . . .'

I slap him.

'Wow,' Finn says, grinning, 'I've waited all my life for a woman to do that to me . . .'

'Finn! Be serious!'

'I am, I am, honestly.' He laces his fingers through mine again and presses down tightly. 'What next?'

'Nobody is to know, in case it doesn't work out.'

'Oh, great, because I'm a bit embarrassed about getting off with you at all – you know, I usually have much higher standards . . .'

'*Finn!*' I slap him again, though why I bother I don't know, as he clearly enjoys it.

'Anything else?' he says, grinning now from ear to ear.

'We have to be honest with each other – if we don't feel it's going to work out we have to say so – and no grabbing me at work, and no hard feelings at work if it doesn't go anywhere . . .'

'Yadda yadda yadda,' Finn says, grabbing me. 'I've known you for years, I'm your boss, for God's sake, do you really think I'd be doing this if I didn't think it was going to work out?'

The next thing I know, I'm in his lap and we are kissing frantically. Finn smells of fresh sweat and tastes sweet and salty and lemony from the drink. He's a fantastic kisser. I feel a moment's incredulity for Vanessa – how could she give this up? Then I'm so grateful that she did that I can't think about anything beyond how well Finn's body fits mine. My legs are wrapped around his waist, his hands are under my damp T-shirt, the sun is beating down on our heads and though I'm scared, though this feels too fast and too soon, I'm happier than I've been in as long as I can remember. Finn isn't Jake. I realise now how nervous I felt with Jake, nervous of not living up to his high moral standards; Jake seemed to know it all, to be Mr Perfect, and even though he turned out to be very far from perfect, I still felt in a way that he was out of my league. Finn is very much in my league. I know him in a way I never knew Jake. He's annoying and stubborn, has a temper and can behave exactly like a spoilt little boy, but with him I don't feel I need to hide my own worst characteristics, my competitiveness, my vulnerability: there'd be no point anyway, he knows most of them as it is. I kiss him and kiss him until the sun and the kissing makes me dizzy and my head spins. Finally he detaches himself reluctantly, goes over to the table, gets my half-full glass and brings it back. He sits down and pulls me so that my back is resting against his chest. Then he hands me the glass and kisses the back of my neck while I finish it off.

'This is great,' he mumbles into my hair. 'This is wonderful.'

He lifts my hair so he can kiss my neck better. I put down the glass and wrap his arm around my chest as tightly as I can.

'See?' he says, and I can hear the smugness in his voice, feel how much he's smiling without even needing to look at his face. 'I told you I didn't mind it if you were all sweaty.'

'No, you didn't!' I say indignantly. 'You said I wasn't that bad!'

'I lied,' he says, 'you're disgustingly sweaty. And you weigh a ton. There's no way you're nine stone.'

'I am!' I lie.

'In your dreams, baby . . .'

I aim a slap back at his face. He counters it and grabs my hand. I slap back at him with my other hand. He falls backwards deliberately, pulling me on top of him, and we go rolling all over the lawn, laughing like two kids playing in the sunshine.